MALICE IN MAZATLÁN

Also by Kimila Kay

NOVELS

Peril in Paradise (2019)

ANTHOLOGIES

"Five Golden Rings" Crime Never Takes a Holiday (2022)

"Table Talk" Guests (2022)

"Hates Kids" A Cup of Comfort for Mothers (2010)

"Burying Bea" A Cup of Comfort for the Grieving Heart (2010)

"The Apology" A Cup of Comfort for Single Mothers (2008)

ADVANCED REVIEWS

I couldn't put this book down! **Kimila Kay** does a wonderful job of tying in pieces of her first book, **Peril in Paradise** and completely captivates you with a new set of characters using the beautiful backdrop of Mazatlán, Mexico. **Malice in Mazatlán** has it all—suspense, romance, friendship, and a twist you didn't see coming. Eagerly anticipating the 3rd book in this fabulous series! ~ *Stacy Robinson, Beta Reader*

Malice in Mazatlán grabs your attention from the start with wonderful characters and enthralling storyline that keeps the reader wanting more! I love how **Kimila Kay** set the stage for the next book by weaving in new characters at the end of **Malice in Mazatlán**, leaving the reader anxiously waiting for, **Vanished in Vallarta**. ~ *Sharon North, Beta Reader*

I had fun being a Beta reader and enjoyed reading **Malice in Mazatlán**. I love Sarita! After finishing this novel, I had the urge to go to Mazatlán, Mexico to experience the wonderful food and beautiful sunsets while sipping Patrón. ~ *Mary Eastman, Beta Reader*

Malice in Mazatlán has a splash of suspense, a touch of mystery, and a dash of romance, all of which should be enjoyed with a perfect margarita. ~ *Carolyn Adams, Beta Reader*

MALICE IN MAZATLÁN

MÉXICO MAYHEM – BOOK TWO

KIMILA KAY

www.KimilaKay.com
author@kimilakay.com

Windtree Press
http://windtreepress.com
info@windtreepress.com

Cover Art by *James McCracken*
The cover picture is of Valentino's at sunset, and I hope you enjoy the building's role in this novel.

Malice in Mazatlán - México Mayhem, Book 2
Published in the United States of America – History:
ISBN 978-1-957638-25-6
1st Release: 11/05/2022

DEDICATION

To my husband, Randy Setzer, for dragging me to Mazatlán, Mexico on our honeymoon. From the moment I stepped off the plane onto the hot, sticky tarmac of the Mazatlán airport, I instantly fell in love with … everything.

Over our thirty-one years of marriage, we've been to several cities throughout Mexico and have discovered something unique and fabulous about each place. But Mazatlán, just like my husband, will forever have my heart.

This beautiful rendering is compliments of my talented granddaughter, Sloan E. Henson. I wish you could see the vivid greens she used for the palm fronds and island, or the warm brown of the tree's trunk, and finally the bright blue hues for the ocean and message. Her simple "Thank You" encompasses how I feel about my readers whom I'm grateful to for taking the leap and reading my second novel. Enjoy!!!

MALICE IN MAZATLÁN

CHAPTER ONE

Sea foam lapped at the inert figure. A curious gull hopped closer, then screeched and flapped away when the next incoming wave pummeled the limp form, hurtling it up the beach. As the wave retreated, the body rolled back toward the sea as if tethered to the outgoing surf.

A maintenance worker methodically raked the sand in front of the Hotel Playa, preparing the beach for the Saturday crush of *turistas* who swarmed to Mazatlán to bask in the warm March sun.

Humming in rhythm to his strokes, he smiled. He loved this time of the morning. Just the ocean, the salty sea air, and him. Occasionally, a beach hawker loaded with colorful wares or a tourist with a spray tan walking a yippy dog threatened to disrupt his tranquility. Usually, though, he managed to maintain his fantasy, imagining the beach as his own private place, with a spectacular villa above belonging solely to him.

"*¡Mierda!*" he swore and marched toward the tourist lying in the sand. When would they learn? The worker had seen it before, *turistas* enjoying too many *cervezas* in the sun, followed by a night of tequila shots at Joe's. Their overindulgence often resulted in one or two vacationers a week morphing into sloppy drunks who couldn't find their hotel and slept off their boozy stupor on the beach.

He'd been at Joe's too last night, enjoying the best smoked marlin tacos in Mazatlán. But unlike the motionless *borracho* face down near the oncoming waves, he'd had a beer, then gone home to his family. A glint caught his eye, and he shook his head. Stooping down, he plucked a broken margarita glass from the wet sand, the jagged edge slicing his thumb. The worker huffed an expletive as he watched the surf wash over the man, spreading the dark stain on the back of his cream-colored shirt. The rank smell of vomit drifted on the wind and pink rivulets followed the retreating water. A pounding wave rolled the tourist face side up and the worker crossed himself.

As if the man's lifeless eyes pleaded for help, the maintenance worker reached for his walkie-talkie. Before he radioed the office, he again made the sign of the cross, and whispered, *"Vaya con Dios, señor."*

CHAPTER TWO

"¡Despierta!" A loud voice cracked Katelyn's alcohol-induced slumber and she squeezed her eyes tight against the daylight.

"¡Despierta!"

"Damn! Stop shouting, I'm awake." Katelyn eased open an eye. "What the hell?" Scrambling to a sitting position, she held up her hands. "Jesus, don't shoot!"

Two *policía* flanked the bed, guns drawn.

"¡Levántate!" The closest officer glared at her. "Get up!" He motioned for her to stand. "You are coming with us."

"What? Why? Wh–where's Christopher?" Katelyn looked from one policeman to the other, then her gaze landed on a nervous young woman cowering by the suite's bedroom door.

"Señor Fogle está muerto."

"Dead! But … but he was just here …" Friday night's hangover hammered against her skull. A mental image of Christopher holding her close as they danced at Joe's filled her mind. She could smell his cologne and almost feel the heat he'd emanated as they clung to each other on the dance floor. The thought of him now lying dead on a cold coroner's table made her want to hurl.

"I am Lieutenant Martínez." He holstered his weapon. "You are Katelyn Graham, *¿sí?*" He reached for the bed sheet. "We are bringing you in on suspicion of murder. *¡Ahora!*"

Katelyn narrowed her eyes and jerked the thin layer of cotton toward her to keep him from exposing her nakedness below the waist. "Do you mind if I get dressed?"

Martínez smirked and turned away, motioning for his partner, who'd also holstered his weapon, to do the same. "I have eyes …" Martínez patted the back of his head. "So do not try anything."

Glancing at her turquoise sundress lying on the floor, Katelyn sighed, and reached instead for a pair of jeans lying next to the small heap of clothes. Christopher's jeans would be too big, like the T-shirt she wore, but both were still a better choice than the skimpy dress. It occurred to her that she didn't recall shedding her clothes last night and blushed at the thought of Christopher helping her undress.

Katelyn slipped on the jeans and bent over to roll up the pant legs. Sour remnants of tequila bubbled up at the back of her throat. Sitting on the edge of the bed, she took a deep breath and then resumed cuffing the jeans.

Hands shaking, temples throbbing, she searched her memory. *Had she and Christopher resumed their dirty dancing under the sheets? She didn't think so. Had he told her his last name? Fogle didn't ring any bells. When did Christopher leave the room? She had no idea. She'd had too much to drink and conversation hadn't been her priority. What the hell had happened last night? She wished she knew.*

Musk, with a hint of coconut, enveloped Katelyn as she stood, tucking in the T-shirt and rolling the jean's waistband a couple of turns. Christopher's face loomed large in her mind, his ocean-blue eyes holding her gaze when they clinked shot glasses and tossed back one too many tequilas. As she scanned the floor for her sandals, Martínez wrapped her arm in a vise-like grip and propelled her in the direction of the bedroom door.

"Hey! Shoes, *por favor.*" Katelyn jerked her arm free, and when she locked eyes with Martínez, a hint of familiarity flitted through her muddled brain.

The other policeman pushed her sandals toward her with the toe of his boot and Katelyn gave him a look of gratitude before stepping into them. Martínez shoved her toward the door, and she whipped around, but her angry words died on her tongue when his cold, dark eyes met hers.

Like reaching for a lifeline, Katelyn grabbed the maid's hands as they passed her on the way to the door.

"*Señorita,* call Humberto Álvarez. Tell him Katelyn Graham is in jail," Katelyn pleaded before Martínez hauled her from the room. "He owns the *Bula,*" she added while Martínez wrenched her arms behind her back, snapped on a pair of handcuffs, and steered her toward the hotel entrance.

The early morning sun temporarily blinded her as she was dragged from the lobby. Sweat trickled between her breasts, and the T-shirt clung to her back. The jeans felt like manacles on her legs as she shuffled toward the waiting police car. Her sundress might not have been appropriate for jail, but it would've been much cooler. A small crowd gaped as Martínez shoved Katelyn into the back seat. She struggled to a sitting position, the handcuffs chafing her wrists, as the car left the Hotel Playa and headed away from the Golden Zone toward the city.

Could it really be March 16th? she asked herself. A week ago, she thought she'd be meeting Stewart at the altar of The Old Church in Portland, Oregon. Instead, she was in a cop car in Mexico on the way to jail for murder.

Tears pricked her eyes. "Damn you, Stewart!" she swore under her breath. If Katelyn hadn't caught him cheating on her with his assistant, they'd be getting married today. But could she really blame him for too many margaritas, followed by too many tequila shots, which had landed her in the arms of Mr. tall, blond, and handsome? She sniffed to clear her runny nose and told herself, *it's a mistake, Christopher can't be dead!*

The officer behind the wheel blasted the horn and slammed on the brakes, sending Katelyn careening into the wire barrier separating her from the front seat.

"Shit!" she cried and inched her way back onto the seat. The officer offered an apologetic smile via the rearview mirror while a gaggle of school kids hurried across the street. Storefronts displaying colorful Mexican blankets, funny T-shirts, beautiful hand painted pottery, and toys perfect for building sandcastles on the beach flashed by the car window. How she longed to be shopping for gifts for her friends and family, and then enjoying a bucket of beers at Joe's as she watched the waves roll onto the beach. The thought of Joe's conjured more memories of last night and launched another round of tears. She completed her mental musings with *this can't be happening*.

A couple of turns later, the police car stopped in front of a drab two-story brick building. Martínez hauled Katelyn from the back seat and steered her into the police station. He summoned a young policeman and handed her off with a look of disdain. Again, she felt a sense of déjà vu, but dismissed it, and flipped off Martínez behind her back before the next officer led her away.

"Señor," Katelyn began, searching for the right translation. "Um … *puedes llamar Humberto Álvarez?"* Katelyn hoped the young officer understood her halting Spanish. He smiled but didn't respond and removed the handcuffs.

"Can you call Mr. Álvarez?" Katelyn tried English, pantomiming a telephone to her ear. This time he ignored her. She knew the Mexican officials didn't allow a phone call after being arrested like in the States but hoped she could get a policeman to make the call for her.

Placed in a small cell, Katelyn paced back and forth, coaching herself out loud. "Okay, no need to panic. It's Saturday, right?" She chewed a fingernail. "Humberto's expecting me for dinner, so when I don't show, he'll look for me."

Humberto's warm smile flashed in her mind as she recalled their first encounter two years ago. After arriving in Mazatlán for her annual vacation, Katelyn had reached out to Jessica Sanchez, the editor of the *Periódico Mazatlán*, to see if she'd like to have dinner to discuss potential story topics. Jessica had suggested a piece highlighting Humberto Álvarez who had recently donated funds to cover the cost of opening *Casa del Ángel*, a shelter for battered women.

Katelyn had then met Humberto at Joe's Oyster Bar for lunch and an interview. They dined on fresh oysters and watched Humberto's catamaran, *Bula*, sail past the shoreline with a crowd of tourists waving from the bow. He explained he'd chosen the name *Bula*, which means "life" in Fiji, but is also used as a greeting such as "hello". Fijian's commonly say *Bula Bula*, which means "happiness and good health!"

She and Humberto became dear friends as lunch stretched into a bucket of beers and fish tacos for dinner. When they said their goodbyes, Humberto invited Katelyn to join him and his girlfriend, Lucía, for dinner at his house the following evening. From then on, she always had a place to stay while in Mazatlán.

Another round of tears hit her as she realized she'd have to tell Humberto about Stewart's infidelity and that their marriage was over before the "I Do's". Originally, she'd told Humberto she was coming to Mazatlán, since she and her now ex-fiancé had decided to postpone their wedding. Humberto had invited her to stay with him, but Katelyn had already reserved a room at Emerald Bay. She needed some space; a place to scream, cry, and hide her broken heart.

Another lap around her cell as she realized she now had even more to commiserate about than her broken heart. Katelyn's head pounded with every step and her eyeballs threatened to leap from their sockets to escape the constant throbbing. "God, I hope Humberto thinks to check the police station."

Exhausted, she swallowed a sob and plopped onto a rickety cot, which emanated a loud croak in protest of her weight. Katelyn crammed a moldy pillow into the corner of the damp brick wall and slumped against it. She pounded the thin, dirty mattress and uttered the question still circling in her mind. "What the hell happened last night?"

CHAPTER THREE

Christopher Temple couldn't stop thinking about her. Her lips, set in a soft, alluring smile. Her lips, parting to emit a throaty laugh. Her lips, salty from their tequila shots, touching his in a soft kiss.

"Shit!" The battered Chevy truck he'd been following took an abrupt left through the Saturday morning traffic and crossed the congested four-lane highway. "Damn it!" Slamming on the brakes, he whipped his rented Jeep into a U-turn and followed them. A litany of horns announced his near miss with oncoming traffic and regrettably signaled his pursuit. He didn't think he'd been made, hoping the bankers he'd been tailing were just paranoid and taking precautions.

The Chevy truck veered down a dirt road, a cloud of dirt spewing behind it. "Where the hell are they going?" Christopher's Jeep hit a deep rut and he fought the steering wheel to maintain control.

"Why the hell am I always chasing someone down an unpaved back road?" Christopher rolled up his window to keep dust from blowing into the Jeep's cab.

The FBI had placed him undercover to watch these morons six months ago after a bank manager at Pacific Community suspected three of his employees were involved in money laundering.

Christopher's team meticulously followed the half-billion-dollar paper trail and electronic clues, which eventually pointed them to Sarita

García. A Mexican National, García was using her recently purchased timeshare property in Mazatlán to launder money. Digging deeper, the FBI learned García wasn't very high up in the drug cartel chain, but she had ties to a man they'd been trying to snare for years; Agustín Castro. So, the nice clean office work ended, and the hot, dirty work began in Mazatlán.

"We could've grabbed these idiots sooner and thrown their asses in jail," Christopher muttered. But why catch three minnows, when the trio could be dangled as bait to bring in the big fish? His assignment now was to shut down García's small empire and persuade her to testify against the FBI's main target, Agustín Castro.

The Chevy slowed to a crawl, and without its rooster tail of dust, Christopher knew they'd soon see him in their rearview, so he eased off the gas. The road curved ahead, and he lost sight of the truck when it disappeared around a small hill. Maneuvering the Jeep between a couple of large cactuses, he killed the engine, and jumped out.

Proceeding on foot, he replayed the previous hours in his head. When he'd escorted Katelyn from Joe's, he'd overheard one of the bankers saying they'd be leaving in thirty minutes. Christopher had made sure Katelyn was settled into his suite, then had sat in his Jeep for the next couple of hours staking out the two bankers. After checking their phones and scanning the nearly vacant parking lot, they finally pulled onto the street. Christopher waited a couple car lengths, then fell in behind, following them away from the Golden Zone.

He'd hated leaving Katelyn in his hotel room, but in hindsight knew it was probably for the best. She'd had too much to drink and he didn't like the idea of her trying to navigate her way back to Emerald Bay in the pre-dawn darkness in such an inebriated state.

Amazed at how quickly things had escalated with Katelyn, he recalled their first encounter. They'd literally bumped into each other a few days earlier at the Purple Onion. She'd been carrying a mug of coffee and their collision caused her to spill the steaming liquid onto the bamboo floor of the popular restaurant. A waiter had hurried over to help with clean-up, while Christopher apologized for the mishap. He recalled thinking then he wouldn't mind getting to know her better and almost asked if she'd like to join him for a fresh cup of coffee. But after his quick apology, she'd rushed out before he could make the offer.

Then, when they locked eyes last night at Joe's, a flash of recognition sparked between them. The attraction he felt seemed mutual, so he intervened when he overheard the three amigos inviting her to join their table. Two birds, one stone; he could keep tabs on the troublesome bankers and spend time with Katelyn. Their innocent dancing escalated, and he became lost in the intensity of being close to her, forgetting his reason for being in the bar in the first place. The memory of her lips against his relit a flicker of desire that quickly flamed out as he rounded the corner of the small hill.

He shrank just out of view, but could see the wayward bankers, Mark and Adam, squared off with three Hispanics, their raised voices just loud enough to suggest an argument. Crouching low, Christopher moved toward the group and realized the two bankers had been waiting on Paul, who was missing from this little soirée.

The morning sun had warmed the air and a film of sweat glued his T-shirt to his back. Careful not to make any noise, he ducked behind a rock pile and could now clearly hear their conversation.

"When we get paid, we'll give her the account information," Mark said. "It's the only way we'll get the hell out of México alive."

"You do not make the rules, *señor*," a stringy haired Hispanic growled. "If you want to stay alive, give us the information now."

Adam pulled a gun from the back of his jeans and pointed it at the band of Mexicans. "No, you're going to tell that bitch you work for our terms."

Christopher eased his Glock free of his waistband and crept to the other end of the hill, which put him behind the Hispanics. To get a better look, he moved the thorny branches of a yellow blossomed scrub tree, releasing a sour, sweaty odor. Or was he smelling the fear and sweat emanating from the scene before him? All three Mexicans brandished weapons, and Adam stood next to Mark, both men now armed.

"Seriously," Christopher whispered. "The last thing I need is to be involved in a shootout."

Someone slid the slide on their weapon and Christopher's FBI training kicked in. He knew he couldn't stand by and watch the Mexican goons gun down the bankers. Stepping into view, hands raised, he said, "Let's all just calm down."

When a thug spun and fired a shot at him, Christopher dove for cover behind their vehicle as gunfire erupted around him. He popped his head up over the hood of a red Camaro in time to see Adam take a slug in the shoulder. Two of the three Hispanics bore down on Mark and Adam as Christopher scanned the area looking for the third thug. Gunfire echoed behind him, and he realized the stringy-haired Mexican had him in his sights. The gunman took aim again and Christopher hit the ground, rolling away from a bullet ricocheting off the fender of the Camaro and lodging in the cactus behind him.

Mentally cussing the situation, Christopher came to his feet, firing in the direction of the Mexican. He hit his target with the second shot, and the man's eyes grew wide as he crumpled to the ground.

"A little help here!" Mark shouted.

Christopher wheeled around, but his shot went wide, missing the squat Hispanic bearing down on Mark. Christopher fired again and brought the shooter down before he could get off another round.

Mark gestured at Christopher. "Behind you!"

Christopher turned in time to deflect the knife of the goon who came at him full force. They crashed to the ground, Christopher's gun sailing from his hand, and the knife slashing his torso. The wiry assailant sliced Christopher's left palm when he struggled to keep the blade from piercing his chest. He punched the Mexican hard a couple of times in the face and blood streamed from the man's nose as he lunged for another strike. Christopher juked to the right and the thug fell forward onto his knees. Without hesitation, he encased the Hispanic in a choke hold until he stopped struggling, then let the man's body drop to the ground.

The knife wound on Christopher's side bled profusely but didn't seem too serious. He pulled his T-shirt over his head, wrapped it around his hand, and took in the chaos. Mark had disappeared in the Chevy, Adam lay motionless on the ground, and blood oozing from the two dead Mexicans turned the sand-colored dirt dark brown.

Christopher knelt by Adam's side and checked his pulse, which seemed weak. The banker's shoulder wound bled through his shirt, soaking the ground beneath him. His face looked pale despite his tan.

The engine of the Camaro fired up and Christopher turned to see the knife wielding Mexican behind the wheel. Gravel spewed into the air as the car fishtailed and the goon hauled ass toward the highway. Christopher scrambled for Adam's gun and managed to get off a couple of shots, but the Camaro had already disappeared into a wall of dust.

"Shit!" His voice echoed across the desert. Reaching into his shorts pocket for his phone, he thumbed the familiar number and waited for the call to connect. "It's me. I'm on a dirt road off the Durango-Mazatlán Highway outside of the city just past the OXXO station. Send an ambulance and come get me."

CHAPTER FOUR

Sarita García had inherited her father's business sense and her mother's beauty; so far both had served her well. However, she hadn't inherited patience from either of them. Looking at the clock again, she grumbled an expletive. She had better things to do with her Saturday than wait on the tardy Lieutenant Hernández, who had called to say he'd been delayed with car trouble on the drive from Mazatlán to Durango.

Sarita knew her empire would not survive if she herself did not become a leader to be reckoned with. After all, she was the Boss now, the *Jefa*, and could not afford to tolerate incompetence.

Of course, her parents had had other plans for her. Her father had wanted her to go to college in the States, and then become a partner in his leasing business. Her mother had wanted what all mothers want for their daughters, a successful marriage. But a car accident had claimed the lives of Alarico and Estrella causing Sarita to choose a path far different than their dreams for her.

She glanced up from the paperwork on her desk when the tardy lieutenant entered her office, the sweet scent of jasmine drifting in with him.

"Buenas tardes, Jefa." Lieutenant Hernández spun his hat in his hands.

"Buenas tardes, Teniente." Sarita gave him her full attention. "You have news regarding the American bankers?"

"Sí, Jefa. One of them, Fogle, is *muerto."* He dropped his gaze.

"One? Correct me if I am wrong lieutenant, but were there not three Americans to be dealt with?" Anger sharpened her words.

"Sí, sí. Los otros—" Hernández began.

"English, Lieutenant," Sarita cut in. "You know you are more useful to me if you speak and understand English."

Hernández nodded and started again. "Two bankers leave Joe's with women." He hesitated. "We find Fogle alone and he stabbed in fight."

Sarita frowned and drummed her slim fingers on her desk. "Tell me Fogle gave you the bank account numbers before he died."

"No, Jefa." He shifted his weight from one foot to the other.

"¡Mierda!" Sarita pounded her desk with a fist. "I have *idiotas* working for me!"

Hernández flinched and took a step back.

Smoothing her long, dark hair, Sarita continued in a measured tone. "I want my bank account numbers." Leaning back in her chair, she decided to give Hernández another chance. "Get the information, then kill the Americans. *"¿Entiendes?"*

"Sí, sí." Hernández promised. "My men follow other bankers but no report yet."

"Bueno." Sarita needed to retrieve the remaining quarter of the half-billion dollars the American bankers were holding hostage and be done with them, sooner rather than later. Changing the subject, she asked, "And what about Jackson Brady and Clara Marsh?"

"Dejaron Mazatlán." Hernández cleared his throat. "They leave city."

Sarita arched an eyebrow and wasn't surprised the two had fled Mazatlán, but it didn't matter, she still planned to hunt them down.

"Juan Vega helped them leave," Hernández continued. "I have man working for Vega and he is looking for leads."

Sarita tapped a pen against her lips. She'd heard of Juan Vega and his vast enterprise, which dabbled in a little bit of everything, stolen goods, fake documents, and secrets. Sarita admired Vega's talents and his ability to flirt with the boundaries of the law. The rumors that he smuggled people in and out of the country on his fleet of planes suggested he had flown Clara Garza somewhere she thought she'd be safe from Sarita.

"Bueno." Sarita drilled Hernández with a dark stare. "Do not come back until you have found my money. *¿Entiendes?"*

Hernández nodded again. *"Sí, Jefa."*

Sarita waved him out of her office. Though she would rather dispense with Hernández and put someone else in charge of dealing with the Americans, she currently didn't have the manpower to replace him.

She contemplated a trip to Mazatlán to visit Juan Vega herself, which could be beneficial from a couple of perspectives. He might be a good addition to her team, and, of course, she needed him to reveal where that *puta* Clara had disappeared to. The bitch needed to pay for killing Damian. Sarita's cheeks burned at the thought of losing her younger half-brother so soon after finding him. If not for the love letters Ricardo Garza had sent her mother, Sarita would have never learned of Damian's existence.

Maybe she should return to Mazatlán and try her powers of persuasion on *Señor* Vega. Her home was here in Durango, in the villa her parents once owned, but she could always stay at her resort, Fiesta de Fuego for a few weeks. After all, she might as well stay at the property she'd bought for the purpose of laundering her drug money, which had worked well until she agreed to allow the Americans to clean her dirty cash. In the last eight months, all they had done was steal from her and place her bank accounts under suspicion.

Moving to a small wet-bar, Sarita poured herself a shot of Patrón from a heavy crystal decanter. She held the spicy liquid to her nose, inhaling the woody scent, then strolled to the large floor-to-ceiling window. Sipping the tequila, she took in the view of the garden below as late afternoon sunlight crept across the foliage, turning marigold blooms a rich, burnt orange. Sparks of light danced on the water in the fountain she'd played in as a child, and Sarita smiled at the memory of her father waving to her from this very office, and at her mother's indignation over her little princess who preferred being a tomboy.

A wave of sorrow washed over her, and she sighed. She missed them both, especially her father; particularly at a time like this. He would have brought the American bankers to Durango, tortured them for information, then killed them without delay. As *Jefe* of the family organization, he had been decisive and ruthless, respected and feared. He would not have allowed inept employees to continue working for him, let alone live.

Heat infused her cheeks as she thought about the events after her parents had died. She'd just turned twenty and found herself being controlled by two of her father's business partners. They didn't mind if she participated in the leasing business; it was a legitimate endeavor; one she could partake in even after she was married. But her father had left explicit instructions never to allow her to become involved in his shadier enterprises, which left his drug empire up for grabs.

Sarita, however, wanted to focus on the fortune to be made in the drug industry. A throaty laugh bubbled up at the idea of her massive wealth, but anger over the American bankers stealing one-hundred and twenty-five million of her ill-gotten gains boiled away the laugh.

Her throat burned as she tossed down the last of the shot. Ambling back to the bar, Sarita refilled her glass, and recalled her quest to become a drug kingpin like her father. Shortly after her parents' passing, Sarita used her feminine wiles to seduce first one partner, then the other, until she compiled enough blackmail material to force them into turning the drug operations over to her and make her president of the leasing company.

Sadly, her parents' death wasn't the only tragedy Sarita had endured at a young age. She returned to the window, the impending darkness the perfect backdrop to the romantic memory that filled her mind. How handsome the young man was and how exciting it had been to stroll the beach, kiss to the sound of the surf, make love in the quiet of his apartment. The one-night encounter had resulted in a pregnancy that shamed her parents and Sarita had acquiesced to decisions they made for her without complaint, but none of them were prepared for the devastating consequences.

The lasting impact meant Sarita could never have children, which cemented her decision not to marry. But without a husband, Sarita knew she would need the prestige of being a well-respected businesswoman to offset her immoral alter-ego.

Another sip and she decided she might have to live up to the nickname her subordinates had given her, *Belleza Mortal*. The moniker was bestowed upon her a few years ago after she'd unintentionally killed a *Federale* when he insisted Sarita run away with him. Only meaning to dissuade him with a bump on the head, she had instead caved in his skull with one blow from a champagne bottle.

"Well, he caused his own demise." Sarita frowned at her reflection in the window. "Therefore, Deadly Beauty is unwarranted." Agreeing with her declaration, she raised her shot glass in a mock toast, then finished the tequila.

Besides, she didn't have killer instincts coursing through her veins like her godfather, Agustín Castro, and was content ordering others to carry out any murderous acts necessary. Still, as much as she hated the idea, she might have to show her men how deadly she could be. If her wishes were not met, she would have to personally kill one of her own lieutenants.

CHAPTER FIVE

"Ven conmigo." A policeman unlocked the cell door. "Come, you have a visitor."

The word *visitor* invoked a glimmer of hope that whoever waited for her would bail her out of jail. Katelyn climbed off the rickety cot and followed on wobbly legs. She longed for aspirin to abate her headache. A toothbrush to remove the lingering taste of last night's liquid diet and a hot shower to wash away her tear-stained cheeks and dirty dancing workout.

The young officer led her back toward the entrance before turning into a windowless room. A small table and three chairs sat in the middle of the dingy space. Unable to see outside, Katelyn's stomach rumbled, and she guessed the time to be late afternoon. Too early for Humberto to worry why she was a no show for dinner.

The officer touched the back of the closest chair. *"Siéntate,"* he instructed with a smile.

His smile vanished and Katelyn turned to see Lieutenant Martínez enter the room. His narrowed eyes raked over her body as if he would welcome a few minutes alone with her.

"¡Teniente!" A familiar voice pierced the silence, causing Martínez to step aside, revealing Humberto Álvarez standing in the doorway.

"Oh, thank God!" Katelyn stepped toward her friend. "I'm so glad to see you."

Humberto held Martínez's stare. "I wish to speak with *Señorita* Graham alone."

"Sí, quince minutos." Martínez shot her a last look of contempt before departing.

"So, Katelyn, you have found some trouble, *¿sí?*" Humberto closed the door.

She fought off a wave of tears. "How did you know I was here?"

"The maid at the Playa knows Lucía and called her with the news of your arrest." Worry echoed in his tone.

"I didn't kill anyone!" Katelyn squeaked. "Please get me out of here."

"Katelyn, sit down." Humberto sat; his light blue eyes filled with concern. "How do you know this Paul Fogle?"

Shaking her head, she plopped down into a chair. "I don't."

Humberto frowned. "But the *policía* found you in his room at the Hotel Playa this morning."

Still shaking her head, Katelyn ran her hands through her matted hair as the memory of last night's fun morphed into dread.

"Then who were you with?" Humberto prodded.

"Christopher ..." The whisper of dread shifted to embarrassment and her cheeks warmed knowing she'd have to share her bad decisions with her dear friend.

"Bueno." Humberto waited, then asked, "Christopher who?"

Katelyn looked down to avoid Humberto's probing stare. She knew he must be asking himself about Stewart and what could have happened to send her into another man's bed.

"It wasn't a last name kind of night."

"Is this man an American?" Humberto placed his hands on his knees. "Can you describe him?"

"Yes, American. Thirty-ish, six foot plus, slender build. Curly blond hair and blue eyes." Christopher's handsome face flashed in her mind.

Humberto frowned. "The picture of the murdered man does not match that description."

"There really is a dead guy?" Her stomach flipped. "I hoped maybe this was all a mistake."

Humberto nodded, light bouncing off his coppery red hair. "*Sí.* But the dead man has dark hair, dark eyes, and I doubt he is six feet."

"Dark hair? Cut short?" Images of Christopher's friends flitted through her mind.

"*Sí.*" Humberto arched an eyebrow. "*¿Por qué?*"

"Oh, my God!" Katelyn jumped to her feet. "I did meet a guy last night who fits that description. He's really been murdered?"

"*Sí.* Katelyn, if you did not spend the night with Fogle, why were you found in his suite at the Hotel Playa?"

Throbbing resumed in her head, and she sat back down, Humberto's words bouncing around her skull. Why the hell *was* she in Fogle's suite? "I have no idea."

"Captain Torres is a friend of mine. I will explain that you do not know Fogle and tell him about this Christopher." Humberto smiled, but Katelyn cringed at his doubtful tone.

The pounding in her skull switched to lightheadedness. "Humberto, what if … Christopher is the …" Katelyn couldn't finish the horrible thought.

"Then we need to find him as soon as possible." Humberto stood. "And get you released from here."

"What if Captain Torres won't let me go?" Her brain bombarded her with questions. "Do I need an attorney? What about bail?"

"Katelyn, please do not worry." Humberto placed a reassuring hand on her shoulder. "I will take care of everything."

Once Humberto left, she let her tears flow, using the hem of the T-shirt as a tissue. *How could she have been so stupid? Why hadn't she stayed at Emerald Bay? What if her young Adonis had killed a man?*

The door opened and Humberto returned, the discouraged look on his face dissipating her hope.

"W–what did he say?" A fresh wave of tears bubbled at the corner of her eyes.

"He is not here at the moment—"

"What?" Katelyn jumped to her feet, her legs threatening to give way. "H–how long d–do I have to stay in here?"

Humberto took her hands in his. "Please believe me, I do not wish to leave you here."

Swallowing the lump in her throat, Katelyn bobbed her head. "I know you're doing everything you can."

"Captain Torres will return late this evening and I will discuss your release with him as soon as possible." Humberto's worried demeanor looked at odds with his promise.

"Okay." She attempted a brave face. "Can you go to the Hotel Playa to see if Christopher's there?"

"*Sí.*" Katelyn saw a flash of anger in Humberto's eyes. "I have already asked one of Captain Torres's men to track him down."

"Can you ask them to get my purse?" Her cheeks burned hot. "It's somewhere in the bedroom." She knew Stella Flynn, her best friend since birth, had probably called to check on her. Her besties' imagined message resonated in her mind. *Lyn, this is the third message I've left. What the eff's going on? Call me back, damn it!*

"*Sí.*" Humberto grimaced when a knock thudded on the door and swung open to reveal Lieutenant Martínez.

"*Es tiempo.*" His posture suggested impatience.

"*Sí. Un momento.*" Humberto wrapped Katelyn in a hug. "Think of how you can weave this misunderstanding into the next article you write about Mazatlán." He took her by the shoulders and offered a reassuring smile. "By this time tomorrow you will be my guest, and this will all be over."

"*¡Ahora, Señor Álvarez!*" Martínez demanded. "Now!"

"Sí, sí." Humberto kissed her on the forehead. "Try not to worry and get some rest. I will see you soon."

After Humberto left, tentacles of fear slithered through Katelyn. Martínez sneered at her and stood aside so she could exit the room. He didn't touch her but kept pace as they made their way back to her overnight accommodations. Once inside the cell, she scowled at Martínez, another flash of familiarity darting through her mind.

Bone tired, Katelyn ignored a dinner tray someone had left for her, with what smelled like refried beans and Mexican rice. Dropping onto the creaking cot, she fell asleep the minute her head hit the grimy pillow.

A nightmare filled her subconscious, complete with pounding heart and faceless bad guy.

Katelyn struggled to breathe beneath the obstruction covering her face and clawed at her attacker. Realizing she wasn't dreaming, she shifted into survivor mode, and kneed the heavy, faceless body straddling her. She made contact, eliciting a cry of agony. Her assailant fell from the cot, dragging Katelyn to the floor. Scrambling to her hands and knees, she blindly crawled away from the groaning mass. Her lungs burned and her eyes watered. Katelyn squatted in the corner of the cell gasping for air, straining to see who had assaulted her.

The dimly lit cell slowly came into focus. She could see the cot against the wall, the closed cell door, and the pillow lying on the floor.

"Okay," Katelyn croaked and stood. "Just a bad dream." Picking up the pillow, she noticed it felt damp as if someone had sucked on the casing. She licked her dry lips and pushed on the cell door, which opened.

"Shit!" she gasped. "Someone did try to kill me!"

Well, they hadn't succeeded, and Katelyn had no intention of waiting for a repeat performance. She slipped on her sandals, dropped the pillow to the floor, and stepped into freedom.

CHAPTER SIX

The setting sun kissed the horizon as Sarita finished her paperwork. Though it had been a productive Saturday, she frowned at the spreadsheet.

"*¡Maldito!* Damn those scheming American bankers," she swore eyeing the decline in profits. She had expected a slight decrease this quarter due to their interference, and because her attention had been focused on trying to obtain control over her deceased half-brother, Damian's, lucrative endeavors. Still, the numbers were down more than expected.

Sighing, Sarita recalled her attempts to reach out to Damian's father, Ricardo Garza. His silence had forced her to visit him in prison. She'd been shocked when the old man, dressed in a dirty, forest green jumpsuit, shuffled in, and took a seat across from her. He looked as if he'd aged ten years since his incarceration and the deaths of his wife and only child. But a flicker of light had shone in Ricardo's eyes when he told Sarita she looked just like her mother, Estrella. Hoping his long-ago affair with her mother would help her cause, she had lobbied hard to gain control of Damian's Los Angeles strip and gambling clubs. Unfortunately, the old man still wasn't interested in negotiating with her. Sarita knew he'd left the Garza smut empire in the hands of the family attorney, Alan Sanchez, and his head lieutenant, Pedro Gomez. She argued that shifting the businesses to her would be like keeping control in the *familia*.

The old man's eyes were soft and almost twinkled. "You are as beautiful as your mother, but sadly nothing like her." Ricardo Garza set his jaw and continued. "Estrella would be heartbroken if she saw you now. Your loveliness tarnished by ambition and greed."

He'd pushed himself up on the battered table, then turned toward the waiting guard without a backward glance at her.

Shaking her head to clear the memory, Sarita collected the various reports littering her desk and stuffed them into a filing cabinet, vowing to refocus on her little fiefdom for now. Possibly *Señor* Garza will feel differently when she reports that she personally killed Damian's murderess ex-wife. Of course, she'd have to find Clara first.

Checking the clock, she was pleased to see she had two hours before the Pérez's dinner party. Sarita had found the perfect dress for their annual spring event. She gave her office one final look, then closed and locked the door. She longed for a hot bath scented with tuberose, which would both relax her and leave a lingering hint of floral musk on her skin. Indulging herself would cause her to be late but she liked being fashionably tardy. It kept her rivals on their toes. Sarita knew what they whispered behind her back:

> *Sarita García has gone loco in trying to exceed*
> *her padre's legacy.*
> *Poor dear, she already has enough dinero.*
> *Rumor has it she mató un Federale.*
> *If she is not careful, Sarita is going to find herself*
> *growing viejo in prison.*
> *What she needs is a strong hombre to rein her in*
> *and marry her.*

A strong man indeed! How would these fine families feel if she decided to marry one of their sons? Marriage was too confining and falling in love was for fools—a mistake she would not repeat. Now, at the age of thirty-seven, she knew her circle of friends considered her an old maid. She had no intentions of settling for one man for the rest of her life. However, seducing a male from a prestigious family and dominating him for a night or two had a certain appeal. Sarita enjoyed using her beauty to captivate any man she wanted. She relished the power of a simple, inviting look that could bring a man to his knees, eager to do her bidding.

Flipping on her bedroom light, Sarita admired the royal blue satin dress she had bought for tonight; the color perfect for her complexion, and the plunging neckline ideal for attracting the attention of potential lusty partners.

Yes, it had been much too long since she, *Belleza Mortal,* had taken carnal advantage of some poor unsuspecting young gentleman.

Sarita managed to enjoy her luxurious bath and refresh with a glass of delicious *Único Cabernet*. She carefully dressed, applied a hint of makeup complete with her signature blood red lipstick. She twisted her long locks into a tumbled knot, anointing her earlobes with a touch of Scandal perfume. Finally pleased with her appearance, she checked the time on her phone and realized she'd be precisely thirty-five minutes late to the Pérez's party. "Perfect," she said, blowing a kiss to her reflection.

Sarita knocked on the Pérez's double wrought iron and glass doors. Within seconds, Juanita Pérez opened one side and greeted Sarita with an air kiss to each cheek. "What a lovely dress, Sarita. *Muy bonita.*"

"Gracias." Sarita smiled at her hostess, stunning in a sleeveless black lace mermaid gown that accentuated her small waist and showed the perfect amount of cleavage. *"Te ves deslumbrante también."*

Juanita blushed at Sarita's compliment and took her hand, the large princess cut diamond on her ring finger winking at Sarita. "Come. I want you to meet my guests."

Juanita and her husband, Raul, had always treated Sarita like a cherished member of the family. Like Sarita, Raul also owned a few commercial buildings in Durango. He had on occasion sent leasing prospects to Sarita when he couldn't accommodate the clients' needs.

Sarita noticed the appreciative glances from a few men as she trailed behind Juanita, past a buffet table laden with *caldo de camarón* and *barbacoa tacos*. A champagne fountain sat in the middle of the dessert table surrounded by *chocoflan*, chocolate Mexican wedding cookies, and *Sopaipillas*. Music drifted from the stage where a *Maríachi* band played a soulful ballad.

Juanita tapped an older man on the shoulder as she gathered Sarita closer to her.

The gray headed gentleman turned and smiled at his hostess. "Juanita, we were just complimenting you on such a *fiesta elegante*."

Color bloomed in Juanita's cheeks. *"Gracias, Federico.* You are too kind." She turned toward Sarita and continued, "I would like to introduce you to a dear friend of ours, Sarita García." Sarita smiled on cue and met Federico's eyes. "Sarita, this is Federico and Inez Díaz, and their son Dario."

Sarita shook hands with the couple, her gaze meeting Dario's when he took her hand in his.

"Mucho gusto." A hint of mischief darkened his eyes.

"Mucho gusto," Sarita parroted, slowly withdrawing her hand from his, imagining how the warmth of his touch would feel on other parts of her anatomy. "It is very nice to meet you all."

"Federico is looking for office space," Juanita said. "Raul thought you might have something available."

Sarita nodded. "Possibly, would you like to come by tomorrow?"

"The space is for Dario." Federico placed a hand on his son's shoulder. "The two of you should make arrangements."

"Ciertamente," Sarita said to Federico, before giving Dario a beguiling glance. "Dario, would you like to join me at the bar for a drink to discuss your needs?"

"My pleasure." Dario offered her his arm.

Sarita smiled and placed her hand in the crook of Dario's elbow. *After he sees to my pleasure, several times, then we can discuss his office needs.*

CHAPTER SEVEN

After a couple of wrong turns, Katelyn stumbled to the back of the police station. Cracking a door open, she saw that it led to a vacant alley. She slipped outside, making sure the door closed silently behind her. Bile burned the back of her throat as the dank smell of urine, mixed with stale alcohol and rancid vomit, greeted her. Katelyn held the back of her hand under her nose and headed for a dimly lit corner at the end of the alley.

The streets appeared to be deserted, but then she heard the rumble of a loud exhaust system and could see the lights of a *pulmonia* headed her way. She waved the driver to a stop, knowing she didn't have any money and hoping Humberto wouldn't mind paying for her ride.

"Hola, Señor." Katelyn smiled. *"Cuánto cuesta marina Mazatlán?"*

A hint of skepticism showed in his eyes. *"Novecientos pesos."*

Asking the cost was expected and she attributed his hesitancy to her chic homeless attire.

Quickly converting pesos to dollars, Katelyn calculated the driver expected fifty bucks to take her to the marina. Normally, she'd try to negotiate a lower fare, but it was the middle of the night, and she didn't remember Humberto's address, which meant they'd have to drive around in search of his house.

"Bueno." Katelyn climbed onto the backseat. *"¿Qué horas es?"*

The driver glanced at the dashboard and lurched away from the curb. He looked at her in the rearview and held up one finger.

Katelyn doubted Humberto would still be awake at one on a Sunday morning, but it was the only place she thought she'd be safe. While the driver navigated the quiet streets of Mazatlán, she tried to slow her breathing to fight breaking into sobs.

New questions dogged her. *Who had tried to kill her? Why would someone want her dead? What if the killer knew she'd escaped and was following her?* Heart pounding in her ears, she checked behind her, but the streets were deserted.

After winding through the marina's maze of streets twice, Katelyn recognized Humberto's circular driveway. The driver came to a stop under the covered breezeway. Before he could ask for his fare, she jumped out and headed for the massive double front doors. Lights appeared to be on throughout the house and the doors swung open before she could knock.

"Katelyn?" Humberto glanced from her to the *pulmonia* driver.

She stumbled into his arms, tears wetting his linen shirt. "I'm so glad you're still up."

"I could not sleep." Humberto held Katelyn from him. "What are you doing here?"

Palming tears from her cheeks, she managed, "It's a long story. Can you pay the driver?" Katelyn skirted around Humberto and stepped into the foyer.

"*Sí.*" Humberto moved toward the waiting driver. "*¿Cuánto?*"

"*Novecientos,*" the driver answered.

"Nine hundred *pesos*!" Humberto glared at the driver, who shrugged.

Katelyn heard the *pulmonia* driving away and headed for Humberto's study.

"What happened?" He asked as she reached for a tequila bottle.

Selecting a small, hand-blown, multi-colored glass, Katelyn poured a shot. "I had to get out of there." She tossed down the tequila and coughed. "Someone tried to kill me."

"*¡Mierda!*" Humberto took the *Cabrito* bottle from her before she could pour a second shot. "Come sit down and tell me what happened."

Plopping down onto the brown leather couch, Katelyn dropped her head into her hands and tried to take stock of everything that had happened in the last few hours. She raised her eyes and looked at Humberto who sat next to her in a matching armchair.

"An officer took me back to my cell after you left, and I fell asleep." She ran her fingers through her tangled hair. "The next thing I knew someone was trying to smother me with a pillow."

"Did you see who attacked you?" Humberto narrowed his eyes. "Was it the man from last night? Christopher?"

"What?" Katelyn cocked her head. "No." Giving Humberto a palms up shrug, she added, "I don't know who it was. I kneed him in the groin and suddenly I'm alone." She clasped her hands together to stop them from shaking. "Whoever it was forgot to lock the cell, so I hustled the hell out of there and came straight here."

"Why would someone want to kill you?"

Tears threatening to fall, she shook her head. "I have no effing idea."

Humberto was silent for a beat. "Possibly you are involved in something far more dangerous than we thought."

Her chest tightened. "But what? I just met these guys." Jumping to her feet, she began to pace, then stopped, her mouth agape.

"What?" Humberto stood also.

"I've been doing research for an article on the recent poisonings in Cancún." She sat back down. "But I haven't told anyone."

"Marco needs to hear this." Marching to his desk, he added, "Possibly your research is connected to the dead man and the attack in your jail cell."

Doubt flickered in Katelyn's mind, despite her head nod. This attack felt personal, like her assailant knew her. Panic crawled through her gut, but she resisted the urge to ask for a ride to the airport. Despite the possibility of being in danger, she had no desire to return to the mess waiting for her in Portland.

Humberto watched her as if he read her mind while waiting for his call to connect. "I took the liberty of having your belongings brought here from Emerald Bay. María has prepared the casita for you." He left a message for Captain Torres and returned to his chair. "Also, your things from the room at the Hotel Playa are in the casita."

"Thanks, Humberto."

"I left a message for Marco, but he probably will not be available until later this morning."

"What time is it?"

"Two-thirty."

Fear and confusion enveloped Katelyn. She squared her shoulders in an effort to keep from being overwhelmed by the terrible circumstances of the past week.

"Would you like to tell me about Stewart?" Humberto asked.

Compassion shone in his eyes, but she didn't feel up to explaining Stewart's affair or her failed nuptials. "Maybe later."

Humberto stood. "We should get a few hours of sleep."

Pushing up from the couch, Katelyn wanted a hot shower, and clean clothes first, then maybe some sleep.

"Please let me know if you need anything." Humberto headed down the long hallway.

"I'll be fine." Katelyn hurried to keep up with him.

Humberto exited the kitchen and crossed the patio to the casita. He opened the door, stepped inside, and proceeded to turn on lights. Adjusting the setting on the wall thermometer so cool air gushed into the small abode, he said, "The kitchen is stocked and there is bottled water in the refrigerator." He placed a hand on the doorknob. "You are safe here, so sleep well, and I will see you in a few hours."

Katelyn attempted a smile before closing the door. Flipping the deadbolt, she turned in a circle to take in her new surroundings. The five-hundred-square-foot dwelling felt larger, with its vaulted ceiling and picture window. A bistro table and chairs sat below a smaller window and completed the kitchenette. Lucía must be responsible for the warm earth tones, which reflected her welcoming demeanor.

Katelyn's suitcase sat open on a luggage rack inside the closet and held her toiletries, flip flops, and sandals. Her clothes had been hung on hangers or placed on shelves at the other end of the closet. Grabbing a cotton tank and sleeping shorts from a shelf, it occurred to her she hadn't seen her briefcase. Padding back to the main area, Katelyn found her purse from last night lying on the counter but didn't see her briefcase anywhere in the casita. She unzipped the small purse and dumped the contents onto the counter. A few coins bounced off the surface and onto the tile floor, followed by her lipstick. Her keycard for the Emerald Bay, her phone, and eight-hundred and fifty pesos were missing.

Her stomach flipped. "Shit!"

No phone would make it difficult to contact Stella. No briefcase meant no laptop and presented the same communication challenge. She'd locked her passport and extra cash in the room safe and prayed the hotel staff had claimed them, along with her missing items on her behalf.

"I'm not going to panic," Katelyn mumbled, peeling off her grimy borrowed clothes. A small sob squeaked out as she turned on the shower and her shoulders shook under the hot spray as she released her frustration in a burst of tears.

CHAPTER EIGHT

Sarita pushed the sheet from her naked body. Her bedroom felt suffocating despite the predawn breeze blowing the scent of jasmine through the open window. Swinging her legs over the edge of the bed, she ambled to the bathroom and placed a cold washcloth at the base of her neck.

Returning to the bedroom, she stood at the foot of the bed and admired the glorious body of Dario Díaz. Sarita liked her men tall, young, and handsome; and Dario deserved high marks for all three. He lay sprawled on his back, sleeping soundly and she congratulated herself on wearing him out to the point of exhaustion. And while Dario had proved to be the perfect distraction, Sarita knew she needed to focus her attention on the problems in Mazatlán.

When they had arrived at her villa last night, her maid greeted her with a message from Lieutenant Hernández confirming an FBI agent was investigating the *estupido* bankers. With one banker dead, she feared the agent might put the remaining two Americans in protective custody, making it more difficult for her to torture them until they returned her money. A smile came to her lips when she imagined them hanging by their wrists, naked and wide-eyed as one of her men approached with electrical cables.

Dario stirred and rolled onto his stomach when Sarita sat on the edge of the bed. She knew she needed to finalize Dario's office lease and send him home to his mother later today.

But for now, the need to release her pent-up anger lit a fire in Sarita's loins and she stroked the soft cheeks of his ass, then sunk her teeth into one luscious mound. Dario reached up and pulled her down, pinning her beneath him. He narrowed his eyes at her, and his lips curved in a lusty grin. Feathering her fingers against his torso, she found her favorite spot between his legs and gripped him in her hand. He leaned down and kissed her, his lips soothing, and a sense of calm washed over her. Sarita reminded herself she would never need this young man. Never need him to make her feel safe. Never need him to love her.

Bright sunshine cut a path of light across the foot of the bed when Sarita woke cradled in Dario's arms, his head lolling on the pillow they shared. Dario had been a different lover this time, dominating her through the early morning hours. Not that she was complaining; she'd found it exhilarating to have a man control her in her own bed. Still, Sarita knew she needed to send him away as soon as he woke. Well, as soon as he had satisfied her one more time.

Dario seemed to sense she was thinking about him and ran his hand down her torso, caressing her slowly. Sarita raised her hips and looked into his eyes.

A sardonic smile played on his lips. *"Buenos días, Belleza Mortal."*

Sarita stiffened. She knew her men called her Deadly Beauty behind her back, but she was surprised to hear her young lover use the nickname.

"Buenos días." Sarita tried to extricate herself from his embrace. Dario held her firmly in his arms, nuzzling her neck, and she fought to free herself from her lusty *lothario.*

"Cálmate, Sarita," Dario said. "I am not ready for you to leave our bed."

"Let go of me!" Sarita snapped. "Get out of *my* bed and out of *my* house!"

"Not yet, *mi amor*." He trapped her to the bed and crushed her lips with his.

Sarita struggled to free herself, but Dario kept her restrained. When her attempt to knee him in the *cojones* missed, Dario laughed as he hovered over her. Eyes closed, she pictured aiming her *pistola* at him, relishing the imagined look of fear on his face.

"¡Dime que me quieres!" Dario demanded.

"¡Nunca!" Sarita shouted. "I will not say I want you!"

"Your eyes beg me even when your words do not." He entered her slightly.

"You are wrong." She squirmed beneath him.

"And your face glows with lust for me." Dario slid into her.

Sarita gasped, and despite her anger, her body responded to him. Her hips arched to meet his and she longed to feel his mouth covering her breasts.

"Tell me you want me."

"Never!"

Their lovemaking became a frenetic war between two bodies, each seeking to achieve the pinnacle of ecstasy before the other. Finally spent, Dario lay panting on top of her, then rolled to the side, and propped himself up with pillows.

Sarita climbed from the bed and donned her robe, tying the belt tightly around her waist. Gossamer black gown billowing behind her, she marched to the bar and opened the cabinet. She glared at Dario, who smiled and stretched his naked muscular body. "I took the liberty of removing your pistol."

Sarita retrieved a jug of pineapple juice from the refrigerator. "I have no idea what you are talking about." She smiled sweetly. "Would you care for some juice?"

"*Sí*, as long as it is not laced with poison." He chuckled at his joke. "I know you are angry with me, and I know you can easily have me killed. But I am fairly certain you will not do so."

"Hmmm." Sarita poured two glasses, wishing she did have poison to add to her impertinent lover's glass. "What makes you think I will not kill you myself?"

Dario grinned at her when she set his glass on the nightstand. Gently, he grasped her arm and pulled her down next to him. Sarita sat perched on the edge of the bed and he placed her glass next to his. "Because we are very good together." He ran his fingers through her long black hair and brought her lips to his.

Sarita promptly bit his lower lip and jerked free of him. "You are mistaken, *amanté*." Standing, she walked to the window. "I will have you killed when it suits me."

"Let us make a pact," Dario said. "That you do not kill me until our raging passion has run its course."

Sarita ignored him as sunlight illuminated the beautiful garden below her. Dario joined her and traced the embroidered red roses on the back of her robe. Desire burned in her loins. When he untied her dressing gown, she did not resist. His admitting she could kill him gave her a sense of regaining some of the control she had lost.

"*Cariño, Belleza Mortal,*" Dario whispered in her ear. "*Tú y yo somos iguales.* You wish to control the world and I wish to control you." Slipping the robe from her shoulders, he let it fall to the floor, then turned her to him and covered one breast with his mouth.

Sarita held Dario tightly to her, accepting she could enjoy him, even if it proved to be for a very short time.

CHAPTER NINE

Christopher's eyes flew open as he bolted upright. The wound in his side pulled against the stitches and a jolt of pain sucked the air from his lungs. He fell back into the pillows wondering why he lay in Jade's bed. Then flashes from Saturday morning came rushing back to him.

Jade had arrived just ahead of the ambulance. While the paramedics treated Adam, she surveyed the scene—a gun battle an hour before—and barked orders at someone on the other end of a call.

After stabilizing Adam and loading him into the ambulance, a paramedic Jade had dated tended to Christopher's knife injuries. It took twelve stitches to close the wound in his side, but the cut on his hand could just be taped. The medic gave him a shot of antibiotics, bandaged both wounds, and handed him a few pain pills. Christopher knew to avoid a hospital if possible. In the states, the law required gunshots be reported to the police. Here in Mazatlán, both he and Jade knew if he landed in an emergency room, someone would report the injuries, which would draw attention to their investigation.

"*Jorge, llévalo al hospital.*" Jade pointed at Adam. "And tell them you found him on the beach."

"*Sí, amante.*" Jorge grinned. "*Me debes lo que debes.*"

"I owe you nothing." Jade glared at Jorge, who winked at her before sauntering to the driver's side of the ambulance.

Jade stood hands on hips, watching the emergency vehicle head for the hospital. A late model Ford pickup carrying her cleaning crew swerved around the ambulance, throwing up a plume of dirt and rocks.

"My guys will take care of the scene." Jade scanned the area again. "They'll report the dead Mexicans to the *policía* and deliver the Jeep to my apartment."

"I'm not sure your guys …" Glancing at her, he gingerly touched the gauze covering his hand. "Or your pal, Lisa Reyes's men …" He cocked his head and continued, "should report two dead Mexicans to the police."

"Seriously!" Jade narrowed her eyes. "Then you should've called the police instead of me."

Christopher winced at her tone and ran his bandaged hand over the laceration in his side. *God, when will the pain pills kick in?* he asked himself. He knew he should've called the police, but instinct told him the right move was to clear the scene and remove Sarita García's dead soldiers as soon as possible. Captain Torres would not be happy about the shootout, or the fact that he hadn't called in the incident, and Christopher worried Torres would ask them to leave Mazatlán.

"Coming?" Jade called over her shoulder and headed for her black Nissan Rogue.

Christopher had ambled after her, cringing with every step. Jade helped him angle into her SUV and drove to her one-bedroom apartment, located above the stores of a small shopping center, and conveniently located a few blocks from the Hotel Playa. Sitting on her sagging couch, he'd stared out at the ocean, while Jade reheated *cerdo machaca*. He washed down the spicy food and a couple of pain pills with a Pacifico. Jade then doctored his minor scrapes and left him naked in her bed. He'd been aware of her climbing in next to him at some point, but thanks to the combination of sheer exhaustion and pain pills, he recalled little else.

Christopher slowly swung his legs free of the bedding. Contemplating his nakedness, he glanced around Jade's bedroom, then saw a pile of his clothes on a chair next to the closet. After donning a white T-shirt and a pair of yellow board shorts, he emerged from the bedroom and found Jade sitting outside on her small deck. She nursed a cerveza and stared out across the aqua colored Pacific Ocean. Her beauty still took his breath away. At twenty-two, her youthful looks could let her pass for a shy teenager. Or in a designer suit and horn-rimmed glasses, she could demand the respect of a confident, mature woman. With her smoldering brown eyes, high cheekbones and strong jaw, Christopher found Jade sexy regardless of her attire.

Today, Jade wore cut-off jean shorts and a white tank, with *Joe's Oyster Bar* printed in navy blue across her chest. The late morning sun gleamed off her long, lean legs, which she'd propped on the balcony railing.

"Hey." Jade reached into a small cooler sitting on top of a rickety side table, pulled out a bottle and offered it to him. "Glad you didn't die during the night."

Christopher would have preferred coffee but took the beer and popped the top off with a bottle opener. "What's the word on Adam?"

"He's damn lucky." Jade took a sip. "Jorge called and said the bullet missed an artery but chipped some bone."

Christopher dropped into a matching aluminum lawn chair. "One of us should talk to him." The chair, missing a couple of straps of orange webbing, threatened to give under his weight. "Maybe Adam can be persuaded to give up the other two."

"Fogle's dead," Jade said. "So, Mark's the only one on the run."

"Shit! I've got to check on Katelyn." Christopher jumped to his feet. "Where's my phone?" Pain shot through him, and he grabbed the wall to steady himself.

"On the dinette table."

Stepping into her small kitchen, Christopher snatched up his phone. "Do you know the number for Emerald Bay?"

"There's a list on the fridge," Jade shouted. "Under the postcard from Ezmérelda."

Christopher dialed the resort and read the message on the back of the postcard from Jade's little sister, Ezmé, who said she was having a fabulous time in Puerto Vallarta. Jade didn't talk much about her family, but he knew she was very protective of her little sister.

Still waiting for the call to go through, he searched the refrigerator for something more substantial than beer. Jade lived on green juice, so she had a selection of spinach, kale, carrots, apples, and lemons. She also had Greek yogurt and hard-boiled eggs. His call connected as he grabbed a couple of eggs.

"Bueno, Emerald Bay. ¿Cómo puedo ayudarle?"

"Habitación de Katelyn Graham por favor." His Spanish was still a work in progress, but he managed to get by.

"Sí," the female voice responded, followed by a ringtone.

The unanswered call circled back to the front desk, and he left a message for Katelyn, asking her to call him. She was probably spending her Sunday lounging by the pool with a trashy novel. If he didn't hear from her in a couple of hours, he'd try again.

Jade strolled into the kitchen, salty sea air trailing after her, blending with the citrussy scent of her body wash. "You want an English muffin and peanut butter?" she asked as he peeled an egg.

"Sure." Christopher picked up the second egg. "You want an egg?"

"Sure." Jade fed the toaster. "Who's Katelyn?"

Christopher didn't answer right away. He and Jade hadn't been intimate for weeks and they never discussed the other people in their lives. Unless, of course, that person was needed to stitch up a knife wound.

"She was at Joe's last night." He placed the peeled eggs onto saucers, set the plates on the dinette table and took a seat. "The three amigos invited her to sit with them, so I stepped in—"

"To save her," Jade interjected as the lightly toasted muffins popped up.

Christopher raised an eyebrow at her jealous tone. "Sort of." He took a bite of egg as she set the plate of muffins and a jar of homemade peanut butter on the table.

"With Fogle dead, Adam in the hospital, and Mark on the run ..." Jade sat across from him and slathered peanut butter on her muffin. "What's our next move?"

Christopher swallowed the last of his egg. "Talk to Adam and see if he knows where Mark might be?"

"Want to visit him as a couple or go by yourself?" Jade munched her English muffin.

At the word *couple*, his mind flashed back to a prior coupling between Jade's sheets over a month ago and a rush of desire flooded his body. A long swig of beer help cast the memory aside.

"Couple, I think." He added a layer of peanut butter to his muffin. "Then if one of us has to go after Mark, the other can keep tabs on Adam."

"Maybe we should have one of our handlers question Adam." Jade over-salted her egg. "I can see if Benson will offer him a deal. Or you can ask Ferris."

Jade worked for the DEA, and, like Christopher, her current target was Sarita García. The two agents had crossed paths at Diego's when they were both following García. Their respective agencies unofficially encouraged them to work together. If they'd known, both agencies would have discouraged them from becoming lovers.

Jade had made it clear from the start she didn't want a serious relationship. At thirty, he was eight years older than Jade and knew he didn't want kids, which he felt would be unfair to someone as young as Jade. He had doubts about her interest in being a mother though.

After their last long weekend together, Jade had avoided him for weeks. When they finally had to meet to discuss the money laundering bankers, she was distant, keeping their meeting professional and on topic; an unspoken agreement to end their relationship.

Something about Jade's recent behavior bothered him. Suddenly, she had connections with some nefarious players, which had come in handy yesterday. But Jade was a strict, by-the-book agent, so her new collaborations confused him. And while ending their affair made sense, limiting her communications to the specifics of the assignment was puzzling. They'd always shared day-to-day minutia outside of their intimate liaison. Her earlier jealous tone when he explained how he knew Katelyn was also perplexing since Jade had been the one to end their relationship.

He thought he knew his former lover well, but she had changed, which made Christopher think Jade Mendoza was hiding a secret.

CHAPTER TEN

A bolt of adrenaline shot through Katelyn as she struggled to breathe. Her hands seemed to be trapped and she fought hard to free them. Violently wrenching against the obstruction suffocating her, she crashed to the floor. Disoriented, she jumped to her feet, bumping into the bedside table. Chest heaving, she gasped for air and turned on the lamp.

The casita was empty, and Katelyn could see her attacker had been the bedcovers and pillows. Laughter, blended with tears, and she couldn't decide if she was relieved, embarrassed, or both.

Katelyn tugged the sheets in place and smoothed out the light-yellow bedspread, recalling the wellness retreat she'd attended in Yelapa, México. The quaint village north of Puerto Vallarta was home to *Pura Vida Eco Retreat,* which offered several experiences ranging from personal rejuvenation; to couples' enlightenment; to healing from grief and loss. As research for an article, she was writing for *Rational Thinking Magazine*, she had attended a session designed to help people who suffered from Post-Traumatic Stress Disorder. Prior to her stay, she'd researched PTSD and learned the condition affected a broad range of people: armed forces, first responders, and survivors of violence. Based on what she'd learned, Katelyn felt she was experiencing signs of PTSD from the attempt on her life during her short stay in the Mazatlán jail.

Shrugging the idea to a corner of her mind, she plumped the pillows and placed them at the head of the bed. While what she'd been through was terrifying, it didn't compared to some of the narratives she'd heard during her stay at the retreat; horrific stories that still haunted her.

Katelyn gave the bedspread one final smoothing and headed for coffee. A bright beam of light striping the sand-colored tile told her it was morning, and the LED light on the coffee maker showed 9:30. She pushed the brew button, estimating she'd slept for about seven hours after her early Sunday morning arrival at Humberto's. The aroma of fresh coffee wafted from the glass pot and Katelyn's stomach growled in anticipation of something more substantial. Searching the cupboards, she found her favorite *orejas* and smiled at how thoughtful it was for María to remember Katelyn's fondness for the ear-shaped pastry.

She placed the cup and a saucer of *orejas* on the small bistro table, then opened the heavy blinds covering the casita windows. Katelyn sat down and tried to wrap her mind around the last week and a half. A sip of the piping hot coffee stung her upper lip. Her tongue instinctively checked for a blister as she ran her hands through her hair. The color strip felt rough against her fingers. Tears joined her pity party when the vision of her fiancé frolicking with his assistant filled her mind like a bad porn movie.

"Cilla is more me, you know," the young, blonde tart had explained on their first encounter. "I mean, seriously, *Pris*-cilla?" She laughed. "I'm so *not* prissy."

Katelyn had been at a loss for words, thinking the young woman was as ridiculous as her attire, which definitely didn't fit the dress code of the mortgage company Stewart worked for. Eventually, Katelyn managed to say, "Well, either version is lovely."

"Thanks." Cilla flashed a sultry grin at Stewart, then said, "So do you go by Katie? Katelyn seems so old lady-ish."

"Thanks, Ms. Preston," Stewart jumped into the conversation. "That will be all."

Cilla set her over plumped lips into a pout and exited Stewart's office. At the time, other than being annoyed with the young woman interrupting Katelyn's time with Stewart, she hadn't given the chance meeting much thought.

A month later, Katelyn had again stopped by to discuss last minute wedding details with Stewart. With less than a week to go, she wanted to remind her fiancé to pick up the gifts for his groomsmen from the engraver, make the last payment on their honeymoon, and complete the final fitting for his tux.

Without knocking, Katelyn had opened the door and stepped into Stewart's office, where she found Cilla sitting on the edge of the desk, her gray pencil skirt pushed up her thighs, and Stewart's face buried in her ample cleavage.

"Stewart!" Katelyn shrieked. "What the hell?"

Cilla giggled when Stewart jumped to his feet, pulling her silver silk blouse down in the process.

"Wh–What are you doing here?" Stewart asked.

Katelyn stood frozen in place as Cilla slithered off the desk and faced her. The brazen harlot flashed a triumphant smile, slowly pulling her blouse over her shoulders. She didn't bother to button the garment, leaving her breasts exposed while she tugged her skirt down over toned thighs.

Stewart rushed to Katelyn and tried to drag her from his office, but she couldn't move. Mouth agape, she stared at her beloved, taking in his loosened tie, unbuckled belt, and mussed hair. Katelyn shifted her glassy-eyed gaze to Cilla, as she sauntered toward them.

Cilla stopped next to Stewart, her hip touching his, and smirked at Katelyn. "Will that be all, Stewie?"

"Y–yes." Stewart ushered Cilla toward the door, but before he could push her from his office, she managed to call over her shoulder, "Nice to see you, Katie."

"Katelyn," Stewart began, his hands up as if he could stop her from leaving. "I can ex—"

She had slapped Stewart so hard he stumbled backwards. Unable to find her voice, she'd glared at him and marched from his office, escaping the building before tears overwhelmed her.

Katelyn swiped new tears from her cheeks. "Bastard!" A mental checklist for grief bullet-pointed in her mind as she sipped the now tepid coffee. While she knew her breakup with Stewart was nothing like the grief she'd felt when her dad had died, Katelyn recognized a similar feeling of loss. Years ago, she'd been asked to submit an essay to the *Cup of Comfort* anthology entitled *For the Grieving Heart*. She'd written her essay from the point of view of her five-year-old self, and amazingly enough, won an award for her story.

With the loss of her father, Katelyn had experienced the five stages of grief firsthand. Stewart wasn't dead, but now she was grieving the loss of a life she would never lead.

"Well since I leapfrogged over *denial*, used my *anger* to fuel my escape to Mazatlán, and ignored *bargaining* ..." She jumped to her feet. "I'm not going to waste any more time thinking about Stewie and his dumb blonde bitch." Grabbing an *orejas*, she headed for the bathroom. "*Acceptance*, welcome aboard!"

After a good cry, Katelyn showered and dressed in tan Bermuda shorts with a red T-shirt. She added a touch of makeup and contemplated her hair. The disastrous pink stripe, which she'd intended to be purple, seemed to mock her. Katelyn tilted her head, wondering what her unruly mane would look like if she chopped out the failed color block.

Stella had warned Katelyn not to attempt the dye job herself, but to go to her stylist. She didn't listen and botched the procedure, creating a neon pink swatch with un-colored bleach spots sprinkled throughout. The five shots of Hornitos she consumed during the process probably didn't help.

Pulling her auburn curls into a ponytail, Katelyn decided the stripper stripe represented the new her and would serve as a reminder not to fall in love ever again! Her stomach gurgled, obviously not happy with just coffee and a couple of *orejas*, so she left the casita in search of something to quell her hunger.

The main house was quiet and seemed empty, with no response to her greeting of, *"Hola."* Katelyn followed the enticing hazelnut scent of Humberto's dark roasted Mexican coffee into the kitchen. She found a slip of paper propped up next to a plate of fruit, sliced salami, crackers, and her favorite *manchego* cheese. Nibbling the nutty flavored cheese, she read the note.

> *Buenos días, Katelyn,*
> *I hope you slept well. I have gone to the marina to check*
> *on the Bula and María is at the market. Captain Torres*
> *will be at the house at 11:30, but I will return before*
> *he arrives. Please make yourself at home, Humberto*

Katelyn refilled her mug and grabbed a glass of hibiscus juice. She carried both to a small table tucked into an alcove where a bay window offered a spectacular view of the marina. With a heaped plate of delectable treats, she took a seat. While she enjoyed her feast, she made a mental list of what to do next. *Call Emerald Bay about her missing laptop and briefcase. Check to see if they recovered her passport and cash. Call and check in with Stella. Pray her handsome Adonis wasn't a murderer.* Christopher's smiling face flashed in her mind and she flushed at the memory of his lips on hers.

Tidying the kitchen, Katelyn added her dishes to the dishwasher, placed the food in the fridge, and warmed up her coffee. She navigated the hallway from the kitchen to Humberto's study, a masculine room with floor-to-ceiling bookcases on one wall and a large fireplace, complete with ornate mantle, on the opposite side. The two walls bookended a bank of windows that also showcased the marina. Humberto's desk sat centered in the wall across from the large windows, flanked by a wet bar and buffet.

Katelyn always found herself drawn to the massive painting above the fireplace. The artwork, *La Batalla del Cordelière*, depicted the French flagship *La Cordelière* anchored off the coastline of Mazatlán on March 28, 1864. The French military was intent on breaching the beaches and capturing the city. After a six-hour battle, the French ship was covered in smoke and fire. The crew tended to the damage done to the deck, doused the war flag, and withdrew to the nearby island of *Isla del Venado*. Despite the Mazatlán army's victory, the French gained control of Mazatlán in November 1864. Undaunted by the surrender, the Liberals' General *Ramón Corona* tried unsuccessfully to retake the city three times in 1866. Only after the French army's defection and disbanding due to lack of payment and supplies, could the liberal forces of Mazatlán regain possession of the city in November 1866.

After the collapse of the French army, many sailors came ashore and decided to make Mazatlán their home. Humberto's light blue eyes, copper hair and aquiline nose, suggested there must be a Frenchman in his family tree.

Katelyn crossed the room to Humberto's desk, picked up the handset and dialed Stella's cell number. As the line clicked and popped, she collected her thoughts, hoping her bestie hadn't been calling Katelyn's missing phone.

The call connected and she cleared her throat.

"Hello?" Stella's voice echoed over the line as someone whispered behind Katelyn.

"*Señorita* Graham."

Katelyn whipped around and came face to face with Lieutenant Martínez. "Why are you here?" she shrieked, and Stella shouted into her ear, "Katelyn, is that you?"

Martínez's lips curved in a sneer. "I have come to return you to jail."

"Katelyn!" blared from the handset.

"I'm not going anywhere with you!" Katelyn yelled at Martínez.

Stella's frantic voice blasted into the room. "What's going on?"

Martínez reached across the desk and disconnected the call. "Come with me," he growled. *"¡Ahora!"*

"Go to hell!" Katelyn gripped the back of the desk chair, using it for a shield.

Martínez licked his lips and leered at her. *"Tú y yo tenemos asuntos pendientes, chucha."* He followed Katelyn and her chair as she back peddled toward the door. "It is time you learned some respect and I have just the *polla* to teach you."

"¡Teniente!" Humberto bellowed from the study doorway.

Lieutenant Martínez narrowed his eyes at Katelyn, who abandoned her chair and stumbled through the door to hide behind Humberto.

"Señor Álvarez," Martínez said. "This woman escaped and is suspected of murder. I have come to return her to jail."

Katelyn felt someone brush past her. "Lieutenant," the man said, *"Señorita* Graham has been cleared and is no longer a suspect in the murder of Paul Fogle."

Humberto took Katelyn's hand and led her back into the study. Martínez's eyes bored into hers when she passed him, and Katelyn fought the urge to flip him off before sitting on the leather couch.

"You are needed back at the station, Lieutenant." The man motioned toward the door. "We will discuss your unprofessional behavior later."

Martínez gave Katelyn an ominous glare and made his exit. A chill swept over her and once again Katelyn sensed she knew Martínez from a previous encounter but couldn't remember when or where.

Humberto motioned to the man. "Katelyn, this is my dear friend, Captain Marco Torres."

"It's nice to meet you." Katelyn stood and offered her hand to the captain. Dressed in a white shirt with a blue *policía* badge printed on the front, along with other insignias and dark blue trousers, he looked quite dashing.

He shook her hand. *"Mucho Gusto."*

"Thanks for saving my ass." Katelyn hooked a thumb over her shoulder. "From that maniac."

"De nada," Torres said. "Lieutenant Martínez is *celoso* ..." he hesitated, "zealous when it comes to his job."

"He is *loco*," María added and set a vase of peach-colored dahlias, dotted with sprigs of plumeria, in the middle of the coffee table. The beautiful bouquet sent a sweet, tropical scent drifting through the study.

The diminutive maid asked Humberto, *"¿Puedo traerle algo?"*

"Sí, café," Humberto replied. "Katelyn, would you like anything else?"

Katelyn beamed at María. "Coffee would be great."

During previous visits, Katelyn and María had become good friends. María nodded, her colorful skirt swaying when she departed.

"Please." Humberto motioned toward the leather couches facing each other. "Have a seat."

Katelyn took a seat as Humberto claimed a matching armchair and Torres sat on the opposite couch.

"Señorita Graham," Torres began.

"Katelyn." She smiled at him.

"Sí, Katelyn, my apologies for your arrest." He continued, "When Lieutenant Martínez asked which room was *Señor* Fogle's at the Hotel Playa, he said the front desk gave him the wrong room number."

Katelyn cocked an eyebrow. "Okay."

"The room he entered is registered to *Señor* Temple and—"

Katelyn held up a finger. "Is *Señor* Temple's first name Christopher?"

Torres nodded. *"Sí."*

Dreading the answer to her next question, she swallowed and pushed on. "And do you think he killed *Señor* Fogle?"

Torres shook his head. "No, no. *Señor* Temple is an Agent with the FBI."

Katelyn hadn't realized she'd been holding her breath and, "Oh, thank God," rode out on her exhale.

María arrived with a tray bearing coffee, a plate of *pan dulce*, and a platter of cold cuts, which she placed on the buffet.

"Gracias, María," Humberto said.

"De nada," María called over her shoulder as she made her exit.

Humberto filled cups for Katelyn and Torres, which he delivered before returning to his chair, cup in hand.

Katelyn had so many questions but waited until everyone had taken a few sips before launching her barrage of queries.

"Okay," she began, "so if Christopher is an FBI agent, how is he associated with the dead guy? And if Christopher didn't kill Fogle, who did? And who the hell tried to smother me in my cell?"

Humberto and Torres exchanged a look and Katelyn's stomach knotted. Humberto set his cup on the coffee table and wiped his hands on his jeans. "Agent Temple is in Mazatlán on a case, and I am afraid we are not able to speak for him."

"Right …" Katelyn looked from Humberto to Torres. "Can you at least tell me where he's disappeared to?"

Torres shook his head. "I am sorry, but I do not know where Agent Temple is at the moment."

"Great!" Katelyn's head began to pound, and she rubbed her temples. "Any ideas on who tried to kill me?"

Humberto continued to wipe his palms on his pants, which spun a thread of fear at the base of Katelyn's skull. Torres stared into his coffee as if the answer lay at the bottom of the cup and a string of fear snaked down Katelyn's spine. Finally, both men focused on Katelyn, and her fear became a sudden urge to flee.

Torres cleared his throat, then said, "It is possible you were attacked by a serial killer poisoning tourists in Mazatlán."

CHAPTER ELEVEN

After Jade had given Christopher a sponge bath, something he knew in the past would have landed them in bed, she'd applied antiseptic cream to his scrapes and cuts before re-bandaging the knife wounds. She had been gentle; inspecting his injuries for any sign of infection, her touch reminding him of how amazing she'd been as a lover.

They drove to Hospital Balboa in Jade's SUV and decided she should pose as Adam's distraught girlfriend and Christopher would be the worried buddy. They hoped the role playing would get them past the nurses' station and into Adam's room since they weren't family.

Things didn't go as planned. Usually, Jade's perfect Spanish allowed them access to whomever or whatever their goal might be. Today, though, the head nurse, whose name tag read, *Enfermera Consuela*, wasn't buying Jade's crying girlfriend act, probably because she'd barely managed any tears.

Christopher patted Jade's shoulder, smiled at the nurse, and in deliberate Spanglish said, *"Señorita."* The nurse, long past her *señorita* days, blushed. *"Por favor, can I see mi amigo?"* Christopher managed to conjure up a couple of tears and continued, *"Estoy … so worried."*

"Sí, sí," she said. "I will show you." Completely ignoring Jade, the nurse looped her arm through Christopher's and proceeded toward Adam's room. She pushed open the door and announced, *"Tu amigo se*

alegrará de verte." The nurse patted Christopher's arm and beamed up at him.

Jade moved to the far side of the bed and took Adam's hand in hers as he looked from her to Christopher.

The nurse pointed to Christopher's wounded hand. *"Necesitas cambiar tu vendaje?"*

Christopher held up his fist, pain racing up his arm. "No, no, *esta bien.*" Christopher flashed a charming smile. *"Gracias, Enfermera Consuela.* You've been very kind."

Consuela returned the smile. *"De nada."* She backed out of the room, her warm brown eyes never leaving Christopher's.

After the nurse left, Jade dropped Adam's hand and Christopher's smile vanished. Adam looked like he wished the hospital bed would swallow him whole.

"Hey, man, glad you're okay," Christopher said.

Adam's face was pale despite his deep tan. He looked them over again. "Where the hell is Mark?"

Christopher shrugged. "In the wind." He shook his head. "I can't believe he left you behind."

Adam glanced at Jade. "Who are you?"

Christopher held Jade's dark stare and answered, "She's with me."

Adam's gaze narrowed. "She's not a cop or a fed?"

Christopher shook his head. "No, she's cool."

Grimacing, Adam shifted in the bed, creating a smelly cloud of antiseptic and bloody bandages. "She came with the ambulance."

Christopher nodded. "Dates one of the EMTs. Lucky for us."

Adam gave Jade another skeptical look before turning back to Christopher. "And Paul?"

Christopher cocked an eyebrow. "That's why I followed you guys." Waiting a beat, he then continued, "The cops came looking for you ..." Christopher ran his uninjured hand over his stubble. "Paul's dead."

Adam's eyes grew round and sweat broke out on his forehead. Christopher exchanged a look with Jade when Adam rested his head on the pillow and closed his eyes. For a few minutes, the only sound came from the din outside of Adam's room, a busy hospital going about its day.

Christopher broke the silence. "Sorry man."

Adam shook his head and opened his eyes. "That crazy bitch had him killed."

Jade held her phone in her hand and her slight nod told Christopher she'd pressed record.

"What?" Christopher leaned toward Adam. "Who do you think killed Paul?"

"I don't *think* she did." Adam glared at Christopher. "I *know* she did and probably Mark and I are next."

Christopher wanted Adam to name the *She* he spoke of but decided pressing him might cause him to shut down. "Maybe we should call the police."

Adam shook his head. "No. No police." He tried to sit up, reaching for the IV snaking from his arm. "I gotta get out of here. Out of Mazatlán."

"Hey …" Christopher placed a hand on Adam's good shoulder. "You need to chill."

Trying to shake off Christopher's hold, caused a wave of pain and Adam fell back into the pillows.

Christopher removed his hand. "Why no police?"

"It's complicated."

Christopher toggled a thumb between him and Jade. "What can we do to help?"

Adam glanced between Jade and Christopher as if sizing up their trust-ability. "Do you think you can find Mark?"

Christopher nodded. "We can try. Where do you think he went?"

Adam looked down at his hands and blew out a sigh. "If he's managed to stay alive, then he's gone after—" He shook his head. "We should've never gotten involved with the effing bitch!"

"Adam …" Christopher's FBI training echoed in his calm tone. "What are you talking about and who is *She*?"

"Sarita García." Color drained from Adam's face. "She's gonna kill all of us."

CHAPTER TWELVE

Looking from Humberto to Marco, Katelyn sensed they weren't telling her everything. Her racing pulse pounded in her ears as she stood and both men came to their feet.

Katelyn nodded. "All-righty then." She forced a smile. "Humberto, thanks so much for your hospitality, but I have to go."

"Katelyn—" Humberto began.

Holding up her palm, she said, "I've had enough of Mazatlán."

Marco took a turn. "Katelyn you—"

She wagged a finger at him. "Enough of being thrown in jail."

"Katelyn, please …" Humberto stepped closer, but she shook her head.

"Enough of almost being killed by a serial killer!"

Marco tried again. "Katelyn, you are safe here."

Hands on hips, she glared at them. "For how long?" She felt tears brewing in the corner of her eyes. "What if this maniac tracks me down?" She wiped her cheeks dry with her fingers.

Marco offered her a handkerchief and she blew her nose.

"Katelyn," Marco said. "When did you arrive in Mazatlán?"

Sniffling, she fought off more tears. "Last Tuesday …" Another nose blowing. "Why?"

Marco's brow furrowed. "And you did not meet Agent Temple until last night?"

Katelyn nodded. "Yes, wait." She held up a finger. "I sort of ran into him at the Purple Onion but didn't really talk to him until last night."

"Would you make me a list of your activities since Tuesday?" Marco asked.

"You think I encountered a serial killer sometime this week?" Katelyn offered him back his handkerchief, but Marco waved off the soiled cloth. "Oh, right." She twisted the hanky around her hand.

Marco continued, "Considering your research regarding the poisoning deaths, I would like to compare any incidents last week to your schedule."

"Okay, I'll make you a list." Katelyn held up a finger. "But I haven't done any research in Mazatlán yet. No one even—"

Humberto's desk phone rang, and he crossed the room in long strides.

María stepped into the study and Humberto looked up, receiver in his hand. *"¿María, quién llamó?"*

"Señorita Flynn …" The maid looked at Katelyn.

"Shit!" Katelyn headed for Humberto's desk phone, bumping the coffee table, a whiff of plumeria following her as the vase rocked precariously. "She's probably worried sick cause that psycho Martínez hung up on her."

María shook her head. "No, no …" Katelyn stopped mid-stride and the maid continued, "she say she on her way." María hesitated, a look of concentration on her slightly plump face, then a smile. "To pick up her ass at three."

"She must have been in LA when I called her." Katelyn looked at Humberto.

"Gracias, María." A beaming María left the study and Humberto looked at his watch. "It is almost one, so Stella lands in two hours."

"Maybe …" Marco exchanged a look with Humberto. "I should have Officer Vasquez pick her up at the airport."

"Bueno." Humberto marched from the study. "I will have María prepare dinner for the four of us."

Marco held up three fingers. "Agents Temple and Mendoza will be here soon and—"

Humberto slapped his forehead. "And Lucía is on her way." Heading for the kitchen, he called over his shoulder, *"Seis para la cena."*

The color drained from Katelyn's face, and she changed course, beelining toward for the wet bar. Hands trembling, she reached for the bottle of *Cabrito*, and flinched when Marco wrapped her hand in his.

"Allow me." He poured two shots, handed her one, and lifted his glass. *"¡Salud!"*

She clinked his glass, then tossed back the spicy agave liquid.

Katelyn felt as if she were being crushed by an invisible weight. Every decision and consequence seemed to be piling on top of her. She'd fled to Mazatlán to escape the humiliation of Stewart's cheating and now might be the target of a serial killer. Not to mention her missing belongings, her bestie racing to her rescue, and Adonis was coming to dinner.

Katelyn reached for the tequila bottle again.

CHAPTER THIRTEEN

After Christopher and Jade finished grilling Adam, they informed him they were agents for their respective agencies and convinced him to accept their protection. Jade was checking with her DEA handler to see where they could stash Adam once he was released from the hospital.

"I'll call Torre's and ask for a guard," Christopher told Jade as she waited for her call to connect, and then he headed for the elevator. He left the hospital and hired a *pulmonia* to take him to the Hotel Playa. Katelyn hadn't responded to the message he'd left for her at Emerald Bay, and when she didn't answer a call to the suite he'd left her in, he decided he'd better check the Hotel Playa himself.

The *pulmonia* driver came to a stop in front of the hotel and he handed the driver ten dollars, waving off the change. The driver tooted his horn in appreciation and headed down the cobblestone driveway in search of his next fare.

Christopher punched the elevator's up button but when the doors didn't open immediately, he headed for the staircase, taking the stairs two at a time to the third floor. He smiled at a motel maid, skirted around her cleaning cart, then stopped abruptly when he saw crime scene tape stretched across the door frame of the suite. He turned to ask the maid if she knew why, but she'd disappeared.

His pulse quickened as he removed the barrier and inserted his keycard, surprised it still worked. He entered and strode across the small living room, opening the drapes, illuminating dust mites floating in the air. Everything seemed to be as he'd left it. A half cup of coffee sat on the small dining table, a few empty beer bottles still occupied the counter next to the fridge and the handful of pesos he'd left on the coffee table for the maid remained untouched.

He crossed to the bedroom door and pushed it open. The queen bed was a tangle of sheets, and his clothes were still in a heap on an armchair in the corner. But Katelyn's turquoise sundress, sandals, and purse were all missing, and oddly so were the jeans he'd worn last night. A memory of Katelyn in his arms on the dance floor at Joe's flashed in his mind.

"What the hell?" Christopher checked the bathroom for good measure and then retraced his steps out of the suite. A buzz of panic rang in his ears, but he knew better than to jump to the conclusion something terrible had happened to Katelyn.

Christopher pulled his phone from a pocket and dialed Captain Torres, leaving a brief message about Meyers when the captain didn't answer. Hopefully, Torre's would also be able to answer questions about Katelyn and why his suite had been processed as a crime scene. He left the hotel, jogged the short distance to Jade's apartment, climbed into the Jeep, and fired up the engine.

He angled away from the curb and headed for Cameron Sabalo Avenue. The midday Sunday traffic flowed nicely, and he was soon leaving the Golden Zone on his way to Emerald Bay. Katelyn had to be at the luxurious resort, enjoying the largest pool in Mazatlán. Sampling the fine cuisine at one of the restaurants or bars. Drinking a tart margarita, or maybe a Chi Chi, and reading a smutty novel.

His phone rang as he approached the marina bridge, and he answered Jade's call on the second ring. "Hey."

"So, Benson says we're on our own finding a place to stash Adam." He heard a note of irritation in her voice.

"Because?" Christopher controlled his own annoyance.

"Benson and a crew of DEA agents are busy with a big bust in south Cali," Jade continued.

A *pulmonia* darted around Christopher and the tour bus he was following. "The pot shipment mixed with jalapeños?"

"That's the one."

"The dog who sniffed out the drugs should get a medal." Christopher braked for the large transport when it stopped at the marina's main entrance. "So, any thoughts on finding a place for Adam?"

"What about your captain friend?" Jade asked.

"Possibly." He found a gap in traffic and pulled around the bus. "What about your drinking buddy, *Rojo Mazatlán*?"

"Maybe." Christopher pictured Jade nodding. "I'll reach out to her. Where are you?"

"On my way to Emerald Bay to check on Katelyn." Silence filled his ear, so he continued, "The police were in my suite and taped it off as a crime—"

"What?" Jade interrupted. "Why?"

"No idea, but I'm wondering if it has to do with Fogle's murder."

"As in your girlfriend killed him," Jade suggested.

It was his turn to be silent.

"OMG, I'm just kidding." Jade laughed. "That's a good reason to call Captain Torres. Did you?"

"Yes, no answer, so I left a message about Adam." Christopher turned onto the street leading to Emerald Bay. "I'm still concerned about how Torres will react to yesterday's shootout."

"Right …" Jade said.

"I'm at the Emerald Bay gate." Christopher rolled to a stop. "Let me know if Mazatlán Red can help with Adam."

"Yep, keep me posted about Katelyn," Jade said, and the line went dead.

Christopher sat parked behind a long line of *aurigas* loaded with guests checking in at the guard station. The small red trucks were equipped with bench seating in the bed and could carry up to eight passengers. Usually, the guard would just take one name and match it to a room number, but for some reason, he was speaking to each individual.

While Christopher waited, he recalled his first encounter with *Rojo Mazatlán*. When he'd originally contacted Jade to meet and discuss a joint investigation of Sarita García, she suggested meeting for drinks at The Joyful Margarita. When he arrived, Jade was on her second margarita and sharing a table with Lisa Reyes, the owner of the bar. Jade introduced him to the red-headed American who ordered him a delicious concoction named Joyful Sunset.

He later learned Jade had rented her apartment from Reyes after an evening enjoying *aperitivos* and sampling almost every Joyful margarita the bar served. Jade had told him the thirty-something Reyes had been married to a Mexican who fancied himself a real estate mogul. Her husband used his influence to secure financing for himself and others; and to gather information he could sell or use against anyone who stood in his way. When he allegedly fell overboard during a fishing trip, his death took on an air of mystery. Had he drowned, or had he faked his death to avoid the endless line of creditors knocking at his door? Or was he running from someone he'd tried to blackmail?

Once he was officially ruled deceased, Lisa Reyes inherited her husband's debt problems. She sold most of the properties to settle his obligations but had kept a few buildings including the plaza which housed Jade's apartment along with two others. The lower level contained various retail shops, and Poncho's, one of Mazatlán's most popular restaurants. Jade mentioned Lisa had perfected her dead husband's knack for brokering information among some shady characters, which, combined with her fiery red hair, had earned her the name *Rojo Mazatlán*.

Finally, the last two *aurigas* pulled away from the guard station and Christopher rolled to a stop in front of the lowered gate. *"Buenas tardes."* He showed his credentials. "I'm here to see the guest services manager."

The guard examined Christopher's badge, nodded, and disappeared into the small guard house. He made a quick call, then raised the gate and motioned Christopher through.

Christopher followed a driveway lined with palm trees, bougainvillea with bright pink blooms, red flowering hibiscus plants, and close-cropped zoysia grass. He smiled when the foliage cleared allowing a spectacular view of the Pacific Ocean spanning to the north, then he came to a stop at the resort's grand entrance.

"Buenas tardes," a valet greeted him and waited for him to climb from the Jeep.

"Buenas tardes." Christopher reached for his wallet. *"Solo estaré unos minutos."* He handed a five to the valet. *"Se puede aparcar cerca?"*

"Sí, señor." The attendant pocketed the bill. "I will keep your car close."

"Gracias." Christopher headed for the lobby.

A bellman opened one side of massive glass doors and Christopher stepped into the cool lobby. He strode past a reflecting pool surrounding a large *Talavera* pot holding a floral arrangement of orange lilies, birds of paradise, and freesia, their sweet scent following him as he crossed the marble floor to the concierge desk.

"Hola," a pretty, dark haired woman greeted him with a smile.

A quick glance at her tag told him her name. *"Hola,* Aida." He held his ID for her to see. "I'd like to speak with your guest services manager."

Aida's smile morphed into a tight-lipped frown as she looked from Christopher to his badge and back. "Can I ask the reason for your visit."

Christopher nodded. *"Sí.* I'm concerned for the safety of one of your guests."

Aida didn't respond and punched a number into her desk phone. After a brief conversation, she motioned for him to follow her to a sitting area. Another smile and she said, "DeShawn will be with you in a minute."

"Gracias." Christopher looked at a text from Captain Torres.

Torres: *Can arrange guard for Adam. Need explanation about shooting. Talk soon.*

Christopher looked up as a tall, slender woman headed in his direction. He was surprised to see she was an American.

"Agent Temple." She extended her hand. "I'm DeShawn Lopez. What can I help you with?"

Shaking her hand, Christopher said, "I'm trying to locate one of your guests, Katelyn Graham, who I believe may be in danger."

A look of recognition swept over Ms. Lopez's face, which told him someone had already inquired about Katelyn.

"The police were here yesterday afternoon to search Ms. Graham's room," DeShawn said. "Have you consulted with them?"

Christopher quickly processed this information and decided on a reason why he too needed to see Katelyn's room. "Yes," he waggled his phone, "I just spoke with Captain Torres who requested I take another look at Ms. Graham's room."

DeShawn tucked a strand of honey blonde hair behind her ear. "I see." She held up a finger. "Give me a moment."

"Sure." As he watched DeShawn exit through the glass entry doors, he wondered why the police would search Katelyn's room.

DeShawn returned shortly with a tall bellman in his mid-thirties. "Agent Temple, Martíne Cervantes."

Christopher shook Martíne's hand and DeShawn continued, "Martíne supervises the bellmen and oversaw the search of Ms. Graham's room."

Christopher nodded and DeShawn added, "Since the room is currently occupied, perhaps Martíne can answer any questions you have."

He cocked an eyebrow. "Occupied?"

"Yes," DeShawn replied. "Once the police informed us Ms. Graham would not be returning, we collected the remainder of her belongings so we could clean the room."

"I see." Christopher smiled despite his disdain for the resort's need to turn the room as quickly as possible. "Did you inventory the items retrieved from the room?"

"*Sí.*" Martíne looked at DeShawn, who nodded. "I can print you a list."

"A list would be great," Christopher said, and Martíne departed with a slight bow.

"Also," DeShawn continued, "Humberto Álvarez contacted me and arranged for Ms. Graham's remaining items to be delivered to his home."

Christopher's phone vibrated and a quick glance indicated an incoming call from Torres. He recalled the connection between Torres and Álvarez, they were friends who worked together when the need arose. Christopher hadn't met Álvarez and had no idea what his relationship with Katelyn entailed. The possibility of them being romantically involved flitted through his mind.

He let Torres's call go to voice mail and returned his attention to DeShawn. "Thanks so much for your time and assistance."

"You're welcome." DeShawn smiled. "I hope things work out for Ms. Graham."

Christopher's phone chimed with an incoming text as DeShawn gave him a finger wave goodbye.

He read Jade's text: *Red has small place on beach for Adam*
Christopher: *Cost*
Jade: *Minimal*
Christopher: *Perfect*

Jade: *What's next*

Christopher: *Torres called. Stay tuned*

Jade: *K. Meet later*

Christopher: *Yes*

Martíne arrived with the list and Christopher dropped his phone into a pocket.

"Martíne, can I also get a keycard log for Ms. Graham's room?"

"*Sí.*" Martíne handed Christopher the list of Katelyn's belongings. "*Un momento.*"

Christopher scanned the list of Katelyn's belongings and noticed no mention of her passport, which he found curious because he doubted, she carried it around with her.

Martíne returned with the keycard log. "Do you need anything else?"

"Does the front desk have a copy of Ms. Graham's passport?"

"The *policía* took the copy," Martíne responded.

"Thanks, Martíne." Christopher pulled his valet ticket from a pocket. "Can you have someone bring my car?"

Martíne nodded and led the way outside. He handed the voucher to a valet, who sprinted toward a parking lot. "You will let me know if you need anything more?"

"*Sí. Gracias.*" Christopher shook Martíne's hand.

"*Bueno.*" Martíne switched his attention to an arriving airport shuttle and his army of bellmen.

The late afternoon heat engulfed Christopher and he angled his tall frame into a sliver of shade between a concrete bench and a large ornate column. He listened to Torres's voicemail with a finger in one ear to muffle the cries of a peacock fanning its brilliant feathers and strutting around a patch of grass. "*Hola*, Agent Temple. I am at Humberto Álvarez's and would like for you and Agent Mendoza to meet me there as soon as possible."

The valet who had parked his car arrived with the Jeep as Christopher mentally recorded Álvarez's address Torres had rattled off at the end of his message. He tipped the valet an additional five dollars, climbed behind the wheel, and texted Jade to meet him at the El Cid Marina.

Christopher headed south and debated how to explain the shootout on a dirt road, the dead American banker, and the disappearance of a woman he barely knew.

CHAPTER FOURTEEN

The late Sunday afternoon sun drifted toward the horizon, the Pacific Ocean waiting patiently for the dark orange orb to dip into its sparkling waters, as Sarita reviewed this quarter's Profit and Loss statement. She hadn't planned to be here in her penthouse at Fiesta de Fuego but had made the three-and-a-half-hour trip from Durango to Mazatlán at the behest of Eladio Ortiz. Sarita's cheeks burned recalling his text saying they had pressing business to discuss. God, how she despised having her presence demanded.

The heat from her cheeks flowed through her body as she remembered her morning with Dario. They were both exhausted, but Dario had been attentive, and she'd let herself relax in his hands, becoming less anxious to be rid of her *joven amante*. They'd showered together, then had breakfast at *Esquilón*, a quaint little restaurant close to Sarita's villa. When they both ordered spicy *huevos revueltos*, they giggled, and the waitress looked embarrassed when Dario leaned over the table and consumed Sarita's lips.

"So, you are serious about needing office space?" Sarita asked after the waitress departed.

"*Sí.*" Dario sipped his mimosa. "I manage my father's four office buildings, but my *pasión* is to help struggling artists."

Surprised at this reveal, Sarita arched her eyebrows. "And your father supports this endeavor?"

"No." Dario laughed. "He would rather I focus only on the leasing enterprises." He took her hand in his. "But I must fuel my *deseos* as well, *¿sí?*"

Another wave of warmth spread through Sarita as she let the memory fade wishing she'd had more time with Dario before sending him off with a promise of dinner soon. After their late brunch, she'd tended to a couple of business matters and jumped in her sleek black BMW X6. She'd considered using her driver and town car but decided the time alone on the road would give her a chance to clear her mind.

Now as she took in the view beyond a large window, the sinking sun winked at her one last time and dipped below the horizon. Sighing at the spectacular sight, she then turned her attention back to the matter at hand. Her leasing business continued to show an increase in earnings, which made the process of laundering drug money, her tax-free cash cow, more difficult; and hence, the slight decrease in profits.

Initially, she'd been able to launder cash from annual drug sales of approximately a billion dollars through her company, García Leasing Enterprises, LLC. It had been easy to create fake leases and funnel the cash through as rent payments, which still created positive earnings despite paying taxes on the revenue. But when the economy in Durango improved, Sarita's three buildings soon became ninety-five percent leased. The conduit for laundering her illegal gains was slowly shrinking.

After the new highway between Durango and Mazatlán was finished, Sarita had decided to purchase a timeshare property. The laundering process would be the same as with the phony leases, but now fake timeshare owners were purchasing endless weeks to vacation on Mazatlán's picturesque beaches. Sarita bought a rundown property for a pittance and named her new investment Fiesta de Fuego Resort. The resort sat in a private cove at the north end of *Zona Dorada* and was aptly named due to the fiery sunsets every night along Mazatlán's northern coastline.

The property had been empty for five years after a love triangle ended in a double murder and suicide. The locals claimed the ghosts of the woman, and the two men who loved her, roamed the deserted hotel. Sarita took advantage of the rumored apparitions and now honored them with a theme night fashioned after *Día de Muertos* every Wednesday. Guests booked their reservations months in advance, most likely due to the free shots of *KAH* tequila. She had selected the delicious alcohol because the bottle featured a fabulous sugar skull, a symbol Sarita had come to love.

After turning the bare bones hotel into a swanky timeshare property, Sarita decided to keep the penthouse apartment and top floor for herself. In addition to the apartment, the floor consisted of two dining rooms and a kitchen. There was also a sitting room and bathrooms, complete with showers, for her personal staff. Since Sarita liked to have her team at her beck and call, she wanted to reward them with plenty of comfort.

Staying at Fiesta de Fuego, offered the added benefit of overseeing her investment, and the staff, especially since some of them held her fate and money in their hands.

To add a layer of protection from wayward employees, Sarita had hired Eladio to train and supervise her timeshare salesmen. Her interest in *Señor* Ortiz came after observing his masterful persuasion of an American couple who insisted they didn't have an interest, or funds, to purchase vacation weeks at the newly built Serenidad de Mazatlán Resort. Gazing out across the darkening waters of the Pacific Ocean, the memory of their first encounter filled Sarita's mind.

Eladio Ortiz had been sitting a few feet from Sarita's favorite table at Pedro and Lola's. The centuries old restaurant was only half-full on this evening, allowing her to overhear the conversation between Ortiz and the American couple.

The husband shook his head. "It just seems like a lot of money for one week a year in a glorified hotel room." He rested his hands on his paunch as if to say he had nothing further to add.

Ortiz nodded. *"Sí, sí."* He took a sip from a tumbler half rimmed with salt. "But do you not feel you and your lovely *esposa* deserve a vacation every year?"

"Exactly!" His platinum blonde wife, who had diamond studs in her ear lobes and a wedding set complete with a four-carat marquise diamond, agreed. "I can always use a week relaxing in the sun." She licked salt from the rim of a margarita glass before finishing her drink with a noisy slurp.

Ortiz signaled the waiter for another round.

The husband rubbed his two-day stubble. "I guess if we owned a timeshare, it would force us to take a trip every year."

"Sí." Ortiz smiled. "And where better than the wonderful beaches of Mazatlán?"

The waiter delivered their drinks, and the husband handed him a hundred-dollar bill. *"¡Gracias, amigo!* Keep the change."

Ortiz also offered to pay, but the husband waved him off. "No, *Señor* Ortiz. We appreciate all your advice, and we'll meet with Benito first thing in the morning to seal the deal."

Eladio Ortiz smiled again and lifted his shot of tequila. *"¡Salud!"*

Sarita had waited for the Americans to finish their cocktails and make their exit, then stepped up to Ortiz's table. He looked up at her when she sat across from him. The waiter brought two shots of *Herradura*, placed them in the center of the table, gathered the empty glasses and made his exit. He knew to add the tequila shots to Sarita's ongoing tab and to remain silently at the ready.

Sarita lifted her glass. *"¡Bien hecho!"*

Eladio touched his glass to hers and they simultaneously finished the drinks.

"Gracias, Señora ..."

Sarita resisted the urge to narrow her eyes at him for his obvious slight. She was confident he knew who she was, which meant he also knew she wasn't married.

"Sarita García."

A slight smile played on his lips. "Eladio Ortiz."

"Do you sell timeshares for Serenidad de Mazatlán Resort?"

Ortiz shrugged. "I am more of a *facilitador*." A hint of mischief flashed in his dark eyes.

"I see." Sarita smiled. "I would like for you to come work for me."

"As a facilitator?" Eladio leaned against the chairback.

Sarita shook her head. "I need someone to train timeshare salesmen for my property, Fiesta de Fuego."

Sarita saw a quick flash of amusement cross his face as he said with a salacious grin, "I do not think you can afford my services."

The memory scuttled away as her phone chirped. Sarita looked at the incoming message, coincidently from Ortiz, regarding the weekly sales report.

Ortiz: *Cifras de ventas preparadas*

Sarita: *En cinco*

Sarita made her way to the elevator and toyed once again with the idea of bedding *Señor* Ortiz. He had all the attributes she required in a man: tall, toned physique, sensuous lips, dark eyes with a hint of mystery. Slightly older than her usual lover, Sarita was still drawn by his smoldering sexuality. Alas, Ortiz was her most trusted employee and Sarita knew being vulnerable to him in any way was a bad idea. Besides, she already had her hands full with Dario.

Sarita paused at the entrance, scanning the *Pulpo de Fuego* bar, enjoying the distinct accoutrements she'd once envisioned, now a reality in the handsome space. Large windows let in natural light, which complimented the subtle overhead illumination from the bronze octopus chandeliers hanging from the ceiling.

Her gaze drifted to the massive bar, positioned on the wall opposite the windows, where a few patrons enjoyed a collection of beverages. Sarita was most proud of the bar top, a creation she'd originally been told couldn't be brought to life. Jose Flores, the master woodworker she'd commissioned to craft the bar, now knew two things: To never argue with her and to trust he would be paid well for a job done to her specifications.

Señor Flores spent months carving the various sections of the enormous octopus spanning the length of the bar. The large head of the mollusk rose from the center and was flanked by various beer taps, each with a bronze tentacle for a handle. Two of the octopus's limbs spanned the underneath as if holding it in place. A clear-coated painting across the bar top showed the body of the octopus rising from the ocean at sunset with the creature's tentacles reaching over the edge where they became purse hooks on the underside of the bar.

A similar octopus occupied the top of the bar-back with the limbs dropping down to hold glass shelves of premium alcohol. A wall of mirrors reflected a stone patio beyond the large picture windows where a red brick firepit, covered by a black steel octopus screen, occupied the middle of the outdoor space.

Various sized tables with octopus bases and tentacles holding glass tops dotted the aqua colored carpet. Eladio sat at a table close to the stone fireplace at the opposite end of the room. Weather in Mazatlán is rarely cool enough to enjoy a fire indoors or out, but Sarita felt the promise of fire was an integral part of a resort with *fuego* in the name. Today with the temperatures in the mid-eighties, the fireplace sat cold behind a bronze screen adorned with a gold, bejeweled octopus.

Sarita wove her way through guests, who were laughing and sharing stories of their stay in Mazatlán. When she took her seat, Eladio raised his gaze from the paperwork in front of him and smiled. The bartender brought two tumblers of *Chamucos* neat, and a saucer of orange slices sprinkled with cinnamon.

"*Señorita* García, lovely as always," Eladio greeted her.

Sarita had gotten used to his slight dismissal of her authority by not standing when she approached. "*Señor* Ortiz." She smiled. "I only have a moment. How have sales been this week?"

"*Bien.*" Eladio handed her a report. "You can see, this week's numbers are in line with last weeks."

Sarita frowned at the, albeit slight, decline in drug sales. She looked up and met Eladio's intent gaze. "The Americans?"

He nodded and sifted through a stack of reports, while she remembered her fateful first encounter with the American bankers.

Three months ago, Eladio had been waiting for her at this same table and asked if she had a moment to meet with three enterprising *gringos* interested in becoming salesmen. Intrigued, Sarita had met with the cocky young men and decided they would be more useful in laundering her money than selling timeshare weeks.

The bankers agreed, even suggested she add a charity layer to her money laundering process. Sarita concurred and founded *Agua Limpia Internacional*, then began adding a twenty-five-dollar donation on each guest's bill to her fake water treatment foundation. Most guests declined to make the contribution and were refunded the twenty-five-dollars, but the resort's copy of the bill would still reflect the gift.

With the tightening of international money laundering laws, Fiesta de Fuego became the perfect vehicle for cleaning her ill-gotten gains with so many different channels to choose from: renovations, endless timeshare sales, advertising, charitable contributions. Perfect until she'd put the Americans in charge of the various bank accounts it took to complete the laundering cycle from dirty to clean.

Eladio handed her another file bringing her back to the moment at hand.

"As you know …" He waited for her to open the file. "Profits from drug sales are down." He picked up his copy of the report.

Sarita met his dark eyes over the top of the folder. "Can you explain the continued decline in profits when it appears sales remain strong?"

Eladio drained his shot glass. "Because we have not been able to pay our suppliers on time, we have incurred substantial penalties."

"*¡Maldito!*" She shut the file and slammed it onto the table. "Because of the *estupido* bankers?"

"*Sí.*" He reached across the small table, opened the file, and handed her a sheet of paper.

Sarita raised an eyebrow and didn't grasp the document. "What is this?" She let the report float down to the table.

"It shows what it will cost you to settle with the Americans so they will release your funds."

Sarita glanced at the information. The numbers were not outrageous, but Sarita had a different solution in mind. "And if I would rather torture and kill them?"

Eladio's full lips curved slightly. "I thought that might be your preference, so I prepared an alternative solution." He handed her another piece of paper, which she accepted.

Sarita scanned the report, stopping when she saw money being extracted from Fiesta de Fuego. "You want to take profits from the resort to pay the bankers?"

Eladio shook his head. "No." He reached over, brushing her hand, and pointed to a line halfway down the page. "I suggest you let the Americans be for now and use funds from Fiesta de Fuego to pay your suppliers." His hand almost covered hers, and a woody, sultry scent flowed over her when he pointed to the next item indicating an additional amount to be paid to the suppliers.

Sarita withdrew her hand, letting the sheet of paper land on top of the others, and leaned back in her chair.

Eladio looked up at her, his delight at her discomfort glinted in his eyes. "With a nice bonus to your suppliers for a show of good faith."

She crossed her arms. "Why should I pay them a bonus?"

He shrugged. "Because you need their drugs."

They sat quietly staring at each other and Sarita once again wondered what it would feel like to be in his arms. Eladio broke eye contact first and took a sip of water.

Sarita tossed back the rest of her shot. *"Bien!"* She popped a cinnamon dusted orange slice into her mouth. "Pay the suppliers, plus a bonus, but use funds from García Leasing instead."

Eladio pursed his lips and shook his head. "Fiesta de Fuego is the more profitable business and has the best cash flow for this purpose."

Sarita's cheeks burned, and she couldn't decide if she wanted to slap the smug smile from his face or kiss him.

"Another suggestion." Eladio grinned. "Is to forget the drug business and go *legítimo*."

Sarita ignored his comment and fired back, "What makes you think my suppliers will accept payment, plus a bonus, instead of cutting ties with me?"

Eladio shrugged. "I believe in light of the recent seizure of their products." He took another sip of water. "They will be satisfied with this proposal and anxious to funnel even more product your way."

Sarita had heard about the loss of a methamphetamine shipment hidden in the spare tires of new cars shipped from México and delivered to the wrong dealership in the States. And the unprecedented seizure of thirty plus tons of cocaine from a cargo ship in Philadelphia. Recently, two million dollars' worth of marijuana had been grabbed at a check point on the Arizona border. She tried to keep her trafficked products in to the United States to Mexican weed, despite the legalization of pot in most states, and meth. Cocaine came from Columbia and Sarita hated the idea of working with the crazy drug lords in South America. Not to mention cocaine happened to be the drug her benefactor, Agustín Castro, funneled into the States and she knew better than to cross him. Plus, *El Lobo* was probably the reason her suppliers had not cut her off entirely.

Eladio began to place the files in his briefcase. "There is another matter to discuss."

Sarita noticed a slight furrow in his brow. "Go on." She flashed two fingers over her shoulder without turning to look at the waiter ready to do her bidding.

"*Señor* Castro has expressed his displeasure concerning your decline in profits."

A warm flush enveloped Sarita as if *Señor* Castro sat across from her, instead of Ortiz, admonishing her for his waning percentage of her drug revenues. She knew her father's old friend would most likely do nothing more than scold her. Still, knowing he was disappointed in her was enough to sound alarm bells.

The waiter appeared with the tequila shots, and Sarita used the few minutes it took him to set down the new drinks and retrieve the empty tumblers, to decide on her response. Once he departed, she picked up her shot and took a small sip.

"Did you meet with him here in Mazatlán?"

Eladio shook his head. "No." He also took a sip, watching her over the rim of his glass. "He sent an errand boy."

Sarita cocked an eyebrow "And your response was?"

"You are not concerned with the temporary decline in drug profits and to tell his boss not to worry."

Sarita relaxed and grinned. "*¡Perfecta!*" She drained her shot glass, popped another cinnamon coated orange slice into her mouth, and waited for Ortiz to follow suit.

He did not and remained seated when Sarita stood and pushed in her chair. She leaned over the chairback to collect her copies of the quarterly reports, giving him a view of her ample cleavage. Eladio took in the splendid sight before meeting her eyes.

Sarita smiled at her business manager. "You will join me for dinner in my penthouse tonight." She lingered a minute longer, then smoothed her sleeveless silk, cream-colored blouse and stood upright. "I believe we need to discuss *El Lobo's* concerns further." Sarita looked at the time on her phone. 6:05. "Come at seven, we'll eat at eight."

Eladio leaned back and narrowed his eyes. Sarita knew he wasn't accustomed to being told what to do, but she decided the time had come to remind him who he worked for, and if the opportunity presented itself, teach him how to show her the respect she deserved.

CHAPTER FIFTEEN

The tequila warmed Katelyn's cheeks and she glanced longingly at the *Cabrito* bottle from her resumed seat on the couch. She picked at the salami and cheese Humberto had placed on a plate and handed to her before leaving to help María.

Marco paced the study, speaking to Officer Vasquez on his phone. Besides instructing him to pick up Stella at the Mazatlán airport, Torres mentioned something about a shootout on a deserted road.

A muffled conversation between Humberto and María drifted down the hallway from the dining room and Katelyn told herself to join them and help prepare for tonight's dinner guests. But she remained seated, paralyzed by her inability to control the actions unfolding around her.

Worst vacation ever. Then again, what did she expect?

The events after being blindsided by Stewart's face buried in Cilla's treasure chest unfolded in Katelyn's mind like a trainwreck.

Katelyn had jumped in her car and raced home. On the drive, she'd called her tattoo artist, Debra.

"Deb's Designs," her friend had answered.

"Debra, it's Katelyn." Her voiced cracked.

"Hey, everything okay?" Debra asked.

"It's a long story," Katelyn choked out.

"Okay …" Debra replied.

"Can you redraw my heart tattoo?"

"Sure, what's changing?"

"I need a broken heart with a dagger slicing through it." Another sob. "And can you see me tonight?"

"I'll come up with a couple of ideas, be here in an hour," Debra said. "Whatever Stewart did, he'd better steer clear of me."

Sobs wracked Katelyn, stealing her voice, and she ended the call.

Stewart had been staying with his best man, an arrangement the soon-to-be newlyweds hoped would make their wedding night more magical, but Katelyn knew Stewart would come home and try to explain his behavior with his brainless assistant. Thankful she kept a packed bag and her passport ready in case a big story came her way, it took Katelyn less than ten minutes to grab her things.

After Debra had worked her magic an hour later, Katelyn had called Stella on her way to the Embassy Suites hotel but hung up when her bestie didn't answer. As soon as she was settled in her hotel room, Katelyn booked a flight to Mazatlán. The rest of the night had been a blur of ignoring Stewart's calls, listening to Stella's attempts to talk her off the ledge, and way too many Hornitos shots, which no doubt resulted in her stripper pink color block.

Katelyn gingerly touched her new tattoo, fingering the dragonfly's tail Debra had substituted for a dagger, through her T-shirt as Marco ended his call.

"Officer Vasquez is on his way to meet your friend." He stepped toward her. "He also reported traffic is heavy, so they may be delayed."

"Thanks, Captain Torres."

"Please." He smiled. "Call me Marco." He tilted his head. "Are you okay?"

Katelyn nodded. "Just a tad overwhelmed."

"*Sí.*" He plucked a notepad from Humberto's desk. "Is now a good time to make a list of your activities?"

"Sure." Talking about her stupid vacation could be a great distraction.

Marco's dark eyes searched hers, pen hovering over a blank page.

"I arrived on Tuesday and checked into Emerald Bay." She watched Marco make notes, before raising his eyes to her. "On Wednesday …" Marco returned to jotting notes as she continued. "I got coffee to go at the Purple Onion, which is where I first saw Christopher. Then took a *pulmonia* to the light house and made the hike. Had lunch at *Tacos Luna*, then walked around and took some photos, ending with Valentino's. Thursday, I stayed at Emerald Bay and searched the internet for new reports about methyl alcohol poisoning." When she stopped her monologue, Marco looked at her again.

Katelyn twisted the rough color block around her finger. "You know the rest …"

He set the pad onto Humberto's desk. "Before you went to Joe's on Friday, did you take more photos?"

"Yes." Katelyn nodded. "I had lunch at Pueblo Bonito Mazatlán, walked up the beach, and took random pictures of tourists, the ocean … you know the usual stuff."

"I will have someone compare your activities with reports of crime in the areas you visited." Marco held out his hand to her. "Come, we should see what we can do to help with dinner."

Katelyn let him lead her past the dining room, down the hall to the kitchen and through the door to the back patio. Humberto and María were placing dinnerware on a round teak table decorated with margarita glasses holding floating red hibiscus blooms. Solar light strings wrapped around palm trees, which stood like sentries around the patio, the lights beginning to glow as dusk crawled toward night. A buffet table laden with serving dishes had been placed at the edge of the patio near the kitchen.

"*Hola.*" Lucía breezed through the kitchen door. "*Humberto, muy buena!*"

Humberto crossed the patio to meet her. *"Sí."* He gave Lucía a quick kiss. "Thank you for the idea."

Lucía flashed an adoring smile at Humberto, then directed her attention to Katelyn. "I am so glad to see you." She hugged Katelyn, then spoke to Marco. "Good to see you too, brother."

Marco kissed Lucía on the cheek. "And you."

At times, Katelyn felt like an ugly duckling around Lucía who, like today, always looked like an ad in *Vogue* and smelled like an exotic perfume sample tucked within the magazine's pages. Her long hair was swept up off her neck in a decorative clip, creating a beautiful cascade of dark locks down her back. She wore slate gray capris and a sleeveless, shimmering silver blouse. Already taller than Katelyn, the black wedge mules Lucía wore raised her closer to five feet six inches. Katelyn had a sudden urge to step into the casita and change her clothes, but she knew her modest wardrobe wouldn't measure up to Lucía's dazzling attire.

María had disappeared into the kitchen amidst Lucía's arrival and now returned bearing a tray with chips, salsa, and guacamole. Katelyn's stomach rumbled in anticipation of the talented housekeeper's mouth-watering dishes, which she knew María prided herself on making from scratch.

"María." Humberto met her at the buffet table and helped set the dishes down. "Would you also bring out a couple of pitchers of margaritas?"

"Sí." María opened the door and hesitated. *"La campana está sonando."*

"Gracias." Humberto followed the maid into the house.

Katelyn knew *sonando* translated to ringing and her heart began beating erratically, flooding her senses with an urge to run. What would she say to Christopher? What if he acted as if he knew her intimately? Or worse, what if he acted as if he didn't know her at all?

Humberto returned to the patio with Christopher in tow. Katelyn's urge to bolt intensified when she saw the pretty, young Hispanic woman who trailed behind the men. The *what if* she should've been worried about was, *what if he has a girlfriend*?

"Agent Temple," Humberto began as the group made a circle in the center of the patio as if gathering around a campfire. "You already know Captain Torres, and this is his sister, Lucía."

Christopher shook Lucía's hand as she said, "It is nice to meet you Agent—"

"Christopher," he interjected, "It's nice to meet you as well."

Humberto nodded at Katelyn. "And I believe you already know Katelyn Graham."

Christopher looked at Katelyn and she saw confusion in his eyes. He tilted his head slightly and offered his hand. "I'm very glad to see you're safe."

Katelyn grasped his hand, a warm flush flowing from head to toe. "Yes, safe and sound." She forced a smile and swallowed the retorts burning her tongue: *No thanks to you*! And … *You might've mentioned you were in a relationship!*

Christopher held onto her hand, and they had a mini stare down, his electric blue eyes searching hers.

Marco broke the silence. "You must be Agent Mendoza." He smiled at the young woman quietly observing everyone.

"Yes." She extended her hand to Marco. "Jade Mendoza, DEA."

"Nice to meet you." Marco shook Jade's hand, a hint of question in his eyes. "Have we met before?"

Katelyn noticed a flash of trepidation cloud Jade's face.

"No." Jade withdrew her hand and shook her head. "I've stayed in the background letting Temple run point on our joint operation."

"Humberto Álvarez." He offered his hand to Jade. "Now, I think we need to clear up a few things."

Stepping to the table, Lucía touched a chair. "Maybe we should sit."

"*Bueno.*" Marco joined his sister.

Humberto pursed his lips and hesitated, then marched to a chair and took a seat with everyone following suit.

Katelyn noticed Christopher and Jade exchange a look before they sat down. Humberto's statement about clearing up a few things had made Katelyn uncomfortable at first, but now she wanted to know what the two agents were hiding.

Christopher sat in the seat next to Katelyn, his bare knee bumping hers lightly when he adjusted his chair. Her heart betrayed her with a flutter and gooseflesh bloomed along her arms. She had to admit he was just as handsome as she remembered, maybe even more so without her tequila haze.

"*Señor* Álvarez," Christopher began, his tone professional. "Agent Mendoza and I have business to discuss with Captain Torres, which we will need to do in private."

"*Sí,*" Humberto replied. "You can use my study, but first I would like you to explain your role in *Señor* Fogle's death, which led to Katelyn being arrested for his murder."

Christopher looked at Katelyn. "Arrested?" Then he narrowed his eyes at Torres. "Why?"

Katelyn jumped in. "Just a big misunderstanding."

Christopher, attention still on Torres, asked, "Is that why you taped off my room at the Playa? You think I had something to do with Fogle's death?"

Marco held up a hand. "No, I do not think you killed Fogle." He pushed his chair back and stood. "You are right, we should speak in private."

Christopher and Jade both came to their feet followed by Humberto who said, "Come, I will show you to the study."

Before anyone could move, the kitchen door opened, and María stepped out with two pitchers of margaritas. Katelyn wanted to rush to the maid, relieve her of one of the pitchers, then guzzle down every drop of the tangy, lime concoction.

Commotion behind María caused her to hurry clear of the doorway and Stella Flynn burst onto the patio. She looked wild-eyed and her normally stylish blonde hair was a jumble of errant curls. Stella's crazed gaze finally found Katelyn. "Lyn, what the hell is going on?"

CHAPTER SIXTEEN

Standing just inside the study door, Christopher listened to Humberto instruct his housekeeper to bring beverages and snacks for his guests. Captain Torres spoke in an authoritative tone to someone on the other end of a call as he looked out a large picture window. Jade stepped close to Christopher and whispered, "What do you think is going on with Torres? Mark maybe?"

Distracted, Christopher shrugged. He wished he'd had a few minutes alone to process everything. Katelyn being arrested, Torres taping off his hotel room, and Humberto's angry demeanor. Christopher knew Torres could be upset about the shootout that put Adam in the hospital and left two Mexican thugs dead, but Christopher's actions shouldn't have led to Katelyn being arrested.

"Por favor." Humberto motioned to two brown leather couches, flanked by matching armchairs, all facing a large *parota* wood coffee table, gleaming from a fresh polish. "Have a seat." He sat down on one of the couches. "María will bring some refreshments soon."

Christopher took a seat on the opposite couch and Jade sat next to him. He met Humberto's light blue eyes. *"Señor* Álvarez, I had no idea Katelyn had been arrested."

Jade's phone pinged and she pulled it from a small purse.

Christopher continued, "I've been looking for Katelyn all day and just discovered you had her things moved here from Emerald Bay."

"Excuse me." Jade stood and left the study.

Christopher watched her leave, expecting some indication as to who had called, but she left without looking back.

"Agent Temple," Humberto said. "I believe Marco can better explain why Katelyn was arrested. But can you tell me where you were and why you left her alone in your hotel room?"

Christopher waited a beat as María entered with a tray, the aroma of *chilaquiles* filling the air. The maid placed the food on the coffee table and a bucket of Pacifico in a tall, wire stand before departing. Marco finished his call and joined the conversation.

"I believe Agent Temple was following the American bankers," Torres said.

Humberto looked at the captain and nodded before swinging his gaze back to Christopher. The two men leaned back in their seats and waited. Christopher assumed Torres knew about the gunfight and the two dead Mexicans. He had probably linked the shootings to Adam's hospital stay.

Christopher studied the frayed bandage on his wounded hand, then reached for a beer. Humberto handed him an opener and Christopher popped the top, then took a long drink from the bottle. He wished he knew how much Katelyn had shared about their night together. While nothing more than over-imbibing and intoxicated kissing had happened, he sensed Humberto disapproved of him for more than leaving Katelyn asleep in his bed.

"Captain Torres is correct." Christopher squared his shoulders. "I did follow Mark West and Adam Meyers, and at the time, was unaware of Paul Fogle's death." Christopher focused his gaze on Torres. "I assume you know about the shooting and demise of two of García's soldiers."

Torres nodded as Jade resumed her seat next to Christopher. "I called Agent Mendoza for assistance, and she arranged for Meyers' transportation to the hospital." Christopher felt Jade shift next to him and knew she had something to add. He looked at her with a questioning glance.

Jade tucked an errant lock of jet-black hair behind an ear. "I just spoke with my supervisor, Assistant Director Benson, who said arrangements have been made to fly Meyers back to the states."

"I would like to speak with Meyers before he leaves," Captain Torres said.

Christopher nodded. "I agree. We should talk to him again to make sure he isn't withholding any information about West's whereabouts or where they've stashed García's money."

"We'll have to make it quick," Jade added. "The agency plane lands tomorrow at eight AM."

Torres checked the time on his phone. "Tonight then." He stood and punched the keypad. "I will notify the deputy on guard duty to expect us at seven-thirty."

Christopher stood also, followed by Humberto and Jade. Christopher needed a few minutes alone with Katelyn to explain his disappearing act and make sure she was alright.

Humberto's phone buzzed with an incoming call. *"Bueno."* He stepped away from the group.

"Hey." Jade touched Christopher's arm. "Benson wants an update on West like yesterday."

Gritting his teeth, Christopher snapped, "Did you tell her we're not tracking dogs and we don't know where the hell he is?"

"Well, I didn't equate us to dogs." Jade tilted her head. "But I did tell her we've done everything we can to find him."

Christopher pinched the bridge of his nose and closed his eyes. Katelyn's face floated behind his eyelids, and he expected her to be standing in front of him when he opened them. Instead, Jade watched him with a narrowed stare, hands on her hips.

"Maybe," Christopher began, "we should tell Meyers he has immunity if he tells us everything he knows about this mess."

Jade shook her head. "We don't have the authority to offer Adam Meyers a deal."

"I know, but Meyers doesn't need to—"

"If there's any heat for lying …" Jade held up a hand. "It's all on you."

Christopher smiled. "Got it."

"*¡Maldito!*" Humberto swore.

"*¿Qué es?*" Marco's phone rang. He answered the call, and a red hue darkened his cheeks. "*Bueno.*" He exchanged a look with Humberto and strode from the study.

Christopher, Jade on his heels, crossed to where Humberto stood next to his desk. "What's going on?"

"Earlier this afternoon a young woman at Emerald Bay was poisoned," Humberto said.

"Oh …" Christopher nodded. "That explains why the guard at the resort spoke to everyone in each vehicle entering the property when I went there to check on Katelyn."

"*Sí,*" Humberto said as Marco rejoined them. "*¿Orto?*"

"*Sí.*" Marco glanced at Christopher and Jade, and Christopher recognized the tortured look of a police officer who hadn't been able to prevent a devastating crime. "*Y ella esta muerto.*"

"Who's been murdered?" Jade asked.

Humberto and Marco exchanged a defeated look, and then Marco said, "I believe we have a serial killer stalking tourists in Mazatlán."

A sense of alarm raised the hair at the base of Christopher's neck and his pulse rate spiked when Marco cast a worried glance at Humberto.

"Tell him," Marco said.

"Tell me what?" Christopher growled.

"My reason for being angry with you for leaving Katelyn alone, is after she was arrested …" Humberto ran his hands through his copper-colored hair, then met Christopher's stare. "Someone attacked her in her cell and tried to kill her."

Christopher heard Jade call his name as he bolted from the study.

CHAPTER SEVENTEEN

Sarita knew Eladio had waited over thirty minutes for her to join him for dinner. While she usually enjoyed running late, tonight's tardiness wasn't intentional. First, she'd received a text from Dario Díaz saying he missed her and asking if he could come to Mazatlán. Sarita didn't reply and hoped ignoring Dario sent the message she did not want him to join her. As much as she might enjoy the distraction, she needed to stay focused on the matters at hand. Then she'd received a message from Lieutenant Hernández asking her to call him as soon as possible.

In the course of an hour-long conversation with Hernández, she learned that three of her men had been in a gunfight with the two remaining bankers the morning after Paul Fogle had been killed. The shootout had left two of her soldiers dead. One of the bankers was shot and wounded, and the other had fled the scene. A third man had also been injured in a knife fight with one of her men who'd managed to get away. At first Sarita had been confused, but then it became clear that the man with the two bankers had to be the FBI Agent. Hernández didn't know the agent's name but promised to get her the information *pronto*.

Sarita checked the time on her phone, then gave herself another once over in the full-length mirror. Pleased with the little black dress that fit her like a second skin, her sparkling diamond studs and upswept hairdo, Sarita dabbed a touch of Scandal perfume deep in her cleavage and behind her ears. She colored her lips with vixen red lipstick and stepped into a pair of black, red-soled Louboutin's.

She found Eladio waiting for her in the smaller dining room, which she thought would be more intimate than the room that could seat twelve. He stood looking out a large window across the dark Pacific Ocean.

"Buenas noches." Sarita crossed the room.

"Jefa." Eladio's eyes swept over her with an admiring glance.

Sarita smiled. "Did Alba offer you something to drink?" She stepped behind a small bar.

"Sí." Eladio joined her. "I thought it better to wait for you."

Sarita pushed a button at the end of the bar. "We are having grilled rib-eyes for dinner." She reached for a bottle of *Único Cabernet* and two wine goblets. "Can I pour you a glass?"

Eladio nodded. *"Bueno."*

Alba appeared at the edge of the room and Sarita noticed Eladio smiling at the maid. A twinge of jealousy flushed Sarita's cheeks and she wondered once again why she'd hired such a pretty young woman. The answer, of course, was because no one else had applied. Sarita had grown fond of Alba, who lived up to her name with her always sunny disposition.

"Are you ready for *aperitivos*?" Alba asked.

"Sí." Sarita handed Eladio a glass of wine. "And we would like dinner served in thirty minutes."

"Bien." Alba smiled and set off to attend to their dinner.

Motioning for Eladio to join her, Sarita took a seat at a small table with place settings for two. "Please, join me."

Eladio smiled at her as he bypassed the table and began a slow stroll around the room. "Did you do the decorating yourself?" He stopped in front of a large painting of flamingos taking one-legged *siestas* on a lush green lawn, an aqua colored stream carving a path through the middle of the scene on its way to the ocean.

"Sí." Sarita crossed her legs. "I find flamingos *agraciada*."

"*Sí*, graceful." Stepping to the table, Eladio sat across from Sarita. "Why do we not have any on the property?"

"I worry the guests will not be kind to them," Sarita answered. "But I have a small flock in my private garden."

Alba returned with a tray of spicy shrimp and placed them in the middle of the table.

"Gracias, Alba."

"De nada." The maid quickly made her exit.

Sarita lifted a saucer painted with a bright pink flamingo, added three shrimp, and then handed the plate to Eladio.

He set the plate in front of him and waited for her to serve herself. As they enjoyed the appetizer, Sarita noted Eladio seemed more relaxed than he'd been this afternoon. He looked comfortable in tan chinos and a white linen shirt. Sarita had always liked the idea of bedding him, even though she knew it wouldn't be a wise decision, but now his charming dinner guest persona was melting her resolve.

Standing, Eladio retrieved the bottle of wine from the bar and refilled their glasses. "I do not mean to ruin dinner, but I believe I may have a lead on your bank accounts."

A flicker of anticipation fluttered in her gut, but she kept her face a mask of indifference. Finding her money would solve many problems, but she still wanted the *pendejo* bankers to pay with their lives.

"Continuar." Sarita took a large sip of cabernet.

"I asked the banks in Durango and Mazatlán to alert me to any new accounts opened by an American," Eladio continued. *"Banco Azteca* emailed me when an American opened three new accounts."

"And?" Sarita knew it must be the banker who'd fled the gunfight. She hoped he lived long enough for her to kill him.

"They are looking for him on the security cameras." Eladio leaned back in his chair. "Hopefully, we will have a positive ID and you can regain control over your accounts."

"¡Muy buena!" Sarita headed for the bar. "This calls for a celebration!"

As she reached for a bottle of *KAH* tequila, Alba appeared at the entrance to the dining room. She looked pale and was wringing her hands.

"¿Que?" Sarita barked at her.

"T–tienes un visitante," Alba squeaked out.

"¿Quien es?" For a second Sarita assumed the intruder was Dario. But then she heard her visitor's voice and blood drained from her face. She glanced at Eladio who'd come to his feet and looked worried as well.

"Hazte a un lado querida," Agustín Castro said to Alba, who scurried from the doorway. "Ah, Sarita, I did not mean to interrupt your dinner."

Sarita recovered her composure and smiled at *El Lobo* as she crossed to greet him. "Nonsense, you are always welcome, *Padrino*."

Castro took her hand in both of his and kissed her cheeks before nodding at Eladio. *"Señor* Ortiz, good to see you again."

"Jefe." Eladio gave the old man a slight bow. "And you as well."

"Por favor, join us." Sarita motioned toward the dining table. "We were just about to eat." Moving to the bar, she added, "I will let Alba know to grill another steak."

Castro ambled to the table and took a seat. "I do not have time for dinner." Pointing to the bottle of *KAH*, he smacked his lips. "But I do have time for a taste or two."

"Bien." Sarita selected three crystal tumblers and retrieved the bottle of tequila. The red lips of the blue and white sugar skull adorning the label seemed to reflect the tension now settling in her shoulders.

Following her lead, Eladio brought small bowls of limes and salt, which he placed in the center of the table next to the glasses.

"What brings you to Mazatlán?" Sarita poured the amber liquid into the tumblers.

"¿Qué? Your godfather needs a reason to visit?" Castro said in a pleasant tone, but Sarita knew *El Lobo* did not make social calls.

"Of course not." Sarita sat down and hoisted her shot. *"¡Salud!"*

The men chimed, *"¡Salud!"* Then the trio downed the fiery liquid.

El Lobo tapped his glass with a finger and Sarita added another splash of tequila for each of them. *"¡A la familia!"* Castro toasted, and they repeated the ritual.

Castro popped a shrimp into his mouth and the three sat in silence. Sarita's mind raced. *Why did El Lobo feel it necessary to come see her? Did he not know she had instructed Eladio to pay her suppliers, plus a generous bonus? Had one of the suppliers expressed their discontent with her late payments? Or was his visit for an entirely different reason?*

Castro washed down his food with a long sip from Sarita's wine glass. He dabbed his mouth with her napkin, then turned his steely gray eyes to her. *"Mi querida Sarita,* I am very worried about your declining revenues."

Profits ... that's why he is here, Sarita thought and relaxed slightly. *"Padrino—"*

El Lobo held up a hand, halting her reply. *"Belleza Mortal."* When he shook his head, a wisp of silver bangs drifted down his forehead. *"Lo único mortal de ti, mija, es tu coño, que escuché que devora las pollas de los hombres."*

Rage boiled up from her core, lighting a fire in Sarita's cheeks. How dare he imply she wasn't deadly. Call her a cunt. Suggest she was a whore. Sarita wanted to smash the *viejo bastardo* over the head with the white *KAH* bottle.

"Jefe, if I may," Eladio began. "I would like to explain our proposal for paying suppliers and getting business back on track."

Castro narrowed his eyes at Eladio. "I have heard your plan." He shifted his gaze to Sarita. "What I have not heard is how you intend to deal with the Americans."

"Eladio ..." Sarita smiled. "Just told me he has located my bank accounts."

Eladio raised his eyebrows.

"And the Americans?" Castro asked as his phone chimed and he looked at the screen. "I have heard there is now an FBI agent involved. *¿Verdadero?*"

"I swear, *Padrino*," Sarita said. "I will deal with—"

A large, muscular Mexican appeared in the doorway and Castro came to his feet. "I have brought you a *regalo, mija*." Castro motioned for the man to join them. When he crossed the small space Sarita felt an overwhelming urge to run. As if sensing her fear, Eladio placed a hand on her knee and met her gaze with a look that seemed to say: *do not react*.

"Allow me to introduce Hector Ramos." Castro shook the man's hand. "Hector will oversee matters such as regaining your assets and dealing with the Americans." Inviting Ramos to join them at the table, Castro said, "Come, let us toast our new alliance."

El Lobo played bartender this time, bringing another tumbler to the table and pouring a healthy shot of tequila for each of them. He held up his glass. *"¡Saludos a nuevos amigos!"*

Sarita swallowed the clear liquid and wanted to reach for the bottle. Instead, she sat taller in her chair and plastered a confident smile on her face. She knew Ramos was a *sicario*. She knew his loyalty would only be to *El Lobo*. She knew if Castro ordered him to kill her, Hector Ramos would do so without hesitation.

CHAPTER EIGHTEEN

Stella Quinn took a long sip from her margarita, then asked Katelyn, "Who the hell was attacking you when you called?"

Gulping down half of her drink, Katelyn licked salt from her lips. "Just Lieutenant Martínez. He came to take me back to jail."

Stella coughed on her next sip, a trail of margarita dripping off her chin. "Jail?" She snatched up a napkin and dabbed away the lime concoction. "Why the eff were you in jail?"

Meeting her friend's sky-blue eyes, Katelyn finished off her drink. "Wrong place, wrong time."

Lucía refilled Katelyn's glass and topped off Stella's drink. María appeared with marlin ceviche, crackers, and a plate of spicy pickled vegetables. Stella and Katelyn held each other's stare while the food was placed on the table.

"What the hell, Lyn!" Stella said, as soon as María left. "Tell me what the blazes is going on!"

"Does this have to do with the handsome FBI agent?" Lucía asked as she filled a plate.

Katelyn nodded. "We met at Joe's Friday night." Another swig of margarita. "We had too much to drink, and the next thing I know I'm being arrested Saturday morning by Mazatlán's finest."

"You're kidding!" Stella narrowed her eyes. "Arrested for what?"

Before Katelyn could answer, Christopher banged through the kitchen door and crossed the patio in long strides. She stood and he grabbed her shoulders, his face etched with concern.

"Humberto just told me someone tried to kill you in your cell." Anger mottled his cheeks.

Stella jumped to her feet. "What the frick!"

Tears welled in Katelyn's eyes. "Captain Torres thinks I was attacked by a serial killer."

Lucía gasped and reached for her glass. Humberto, Marco, and Jade stepped from the house and joined the chaos on the patio.

Marching around the table, Stella took Katelyn by the arm. "Come on." She tried to pull Katelyn free from Christopher's grasp. "We're going home."

Christopher glared at Stella. "She's not going anywhere."

"Ms. Quinn …" Humberto began as Lucía joined him. "Katelyn is safe here."

"Safe?" Stella's face was twisted with rage, and she pointed at Marco. "A serial killer tried to kill her while she was in his custody."

"Now that we have more information, I am confident Katelyn is not the target of a serial killer," Marco explained.

Shrugging away from both Christopher and Stella, Katelyn shouted, "Enough! I appreciate everyone's concern for me, but nothing serious happened." She reached for her margarita glass, took a long slurp, and continued, "Christopher didn't do anything wrong." She smiled at him. "In fact, he was a gentleman all night." Turning her attention to Marco, she added, "And Captain Torres didn't know I'd been arrested or that I'd be attacked in my cell." She drained her glass. "Now everyone knows what happened and there is no one to blame, so let's sit and enjoy the nice dinner María prepared for us."

They all stood silently in place for a few seconds, then Lucía said, "I will let María know we are ready to eat."

"And more margaritas, *por favor*!" Katelyn demanded as she took her seat.

"Temple," Jade said to Christopher before he could sit down.

Katelyn glanced over her shoulder as Christopher moved toward Jade. The two talked in whispers, but Katelyn heard the name Adam. She recalled he was one of Paul Fogle's friends.

Lucía returned with two pitchers of margaritas. María followed with a bucket of beer she sat on the buffet table before heading back to the kitchen.

"Dinner will be ready in ten minutes," Lucía said and refilled Katelyn and Stella's glasses.

Stella resumed her seat, but Marco and Humberto hovered near Christopher and Jade, who seemed to have come to an agreement about something.

"Captain Torres." Christopher said, taking a seat next to Katelyn. "Can you break down the attack on Katelyn for me?"

"Seriously!" she shot Christopher a look.

Stella touched Katelyn's arm. "It's a good question."

"I do not know what happened." Torres cleared his throat. "We do not have cameras in that section of the jail and the officers on duty did not know Katelyn was missing until the shift change at seven-thirty."

"I'd like to speak with the officers on duty." Christopher's tone held a slight edge.

"Agent Temple." Torres sat taller in his chair. "I assure you I am looking into this matter and will let you know if I discover any pertinent information."

"We ..." Christopher pointed to Jade and himself. "Can assist you in the investigation. We have resources to help identify a potential serial killer."

"If I may," Humberto interjected. "Marco and I do not believe Katelyn was attacked by the serial killer poisoning tourists." He and

Marco shared a brief look. "But your offer to assist with the matter of the recent deaths is appreciated."

"But she was attacked—" Christopher drilled Marco with a dark stare.

"C …" Jade said. "This is a conversation for another time."

Katelyn wanted to slink away and escape the tension rolling in like a dark fog. Everyone at the table sat in their chairs like rigid statues, dour looks on their faces. She found herself praying for an intervention and startled when someone's phone chimed.

Jade looked at her phone. "We should head to the hospital soon if we're going to question Meyers."

Christopher and Marco continued their stare down, then Marco nodded and said, "*Sí*. Humberto you will stay with Lucía and your guests?"

"*Sí*. What about the new victim?"

"I have Officer Vasquez on scene and will join him after speaking with Meyers."

"*Bueno,* " Humberto said. "Call when you have a chance."

Marco nodded. "*Acordado.* "

Pulling her chair back, Christopher said, "I need a few minutes alone with Katelyn."

Katelyn took his hand. Under the circumstances, she knew it was ridiculous to feel excited by his touch, but her body responded nonetheless, complete with racing pulse and tingling skin.

Christopher led her back to Humberto's study, closed the door, pulled her into his arms and kissed her. If only they were alone on a deserted island, Katelyn thought, as warm joy spread south of the border.

Releasing her lips, he led her to one of the couches. She sat down next to him, touching the bandage on his hand.

"You're hurt."

"It's nothing." Christopher wrapped his hands around Katelyn's. "I'm so sorry for leaving you. I had—"

She put a finger to his lips. "I'm fine and you had no way of knowing what would happen after you left."

His face clouded over. "Still, I should've made sure you were in a cab back to Emerald Bay before I left."

Katelyn smiled at him. "Or maybe you should have stayed with me."

"Trust me." He fingered her color block. "I wish I had."

"So, you're an FBI agent?" She looked down at their entwined hands. "And Jade is your—?" She didn't finish the question because she didn't really want to know the answer.

"Jade is a DEA agent and our agencies have us working together on a current assignment."

Despite his professional response, she still felt he and Jade were more than colleagues. Katelyn returned her gaze to him. "And Paul was involved somehow?"

Christopher nodded. "Yes." His phone buzzed and he pulled it from a pocket to read the text. "I have to go." He stood bringing her to her feet as well. "You'll be staying here, at Humberto's?"

It was Katelyn's turn to nod. "Yes, until Stella drags me home."

Touching her cheek, he said, "Please don't go until we have a chance to talk again."

"I'll try." Katelyn smiled. "I think she's a little freaked out about the whole serial killer thing."

"Understood." He cocked his head to the side. "Do you have your passport?"

Heat rose in her cheeks. "Shit! I haven't had a chance to check with Emerald Bay to see if they have it." His frown told her he already knew the resort didn't have her passport.

Pulling a sheet of paper from a pocket, he handed her the list. "I managed to get a record of what the hotel recovered for you. Your passport isn't listed."

Katelyn scanned the list, which was short and made no mention of her most important missing belongings. "Why would someone take my passport?" Tears ran down her cheeks. "And my laptop? Camera? Briefcase?"

Christopher gathered her into his arms, and she sobbed against his chest.

"There are many reasons someone would steal your passport." He wrapped his arms tighter around her. "Same for your other items."

When she pushed off his chest, a whiff of musky coconut beckoned her to lean back into him. She swiped tears from her cheeks. "How the hell do I get home without a passport?"

"Well …" Christopher grinned. "You do know someone who works for the FBI."

A sob morphed into a giggle. "And you think he'd be willing to help me?"

"For a small fee." Christopher leaned in and kissed her. "Have dinner with me?"

Dinner? He was selling himself short. She had something completely different in mind. "Dinner sounds lovely." Katelyn cocked her head toward the door. "Do you think we'll have to include the rest of the gang?"

Christopher shook his head. "I don't plan to invite your friends." He arched an eyebrow. "Unless you'd like to include them?"

Laughing, she said, "No. I need a break from my protectors."

"I'd like to apply for the job."

His kiss this time was the kind that normally would've led to something more, but he had to run off and play FBI agent.

A knock separated them, and he touched his lips to her forehead. "Coming."

The door banged against the wall and Jade shouted, "Torres just received a call. Someone tried to kill Adam Meyers in the hospital. We've got to go. Now!"

Christopher headed from the study but glanced back at Katelyn before leaving. "I'll see you in the morning."

Katelyn nodded. "Don't get yourself killed."

Christopher smiled and gave her a salute. "I'll do my best." And then he was gone.

CHAPTER NINETEEN

Christopher needed a shower, food, and sleep. He, Jade, and Marco had spent the night at the hospital sorting through the specifics of the attempt on Adam Meyers' life. The hit squad arrived at Meyers' hospital room just after Captain Torres had alerted the guard on duty that he was on his way to interview Meyers.

Rubbing the stubble on his chin, Christopher took in the scene before him. Jade stood just down the hallway talking with Agent Sandrine Mortieau, who had arrived as they finished questioning Meyers. Christopher watched as Agent Mortieau smiled at Jade and touched her shoulder. They looked like girlfriends at brunch, drinking mimosas and catching up on their lives. Slender and fit like Jade, Sandrine was two inches taller. Her dark brown, tightly curled hair seemed lighter than when he'd met her six months ago at a joint meeting with the DEA. Her ebony skin shimmered even under the harsh hospital light, and her slight French accent sounded melodic in contrast to the cacophony of chaos around them. She wore a navy-blue pantsuit with a white blouse and black loafers, and her exotic looks brought the simple ensemble to life.

Sandrine Mortieau had also caught the attention of Marco Torres, who spoke with his officers within earshot of Jade and her colleague. He met Christopher's gaze with a slight grin, then turned his attention back to Officer Rios, the guard on duty, who was pointing and gesturing, recounting the attempt on Meyers' life.

According to Rios, he noticed two men casing the corridor, so he'd radioed for backup, and then approached to inquire about their business at the hospital. Before he could ask, one turned a gun on him and the other pushed past him toward Meyers' room. As Rios fought the thug, Officer Vasquez arrived and shot the other assailant before he could shoot Meyers. Rios had managed to subdue the other Mexican, who now sat handcuffed to a gurney. Christopher recognized him as the soldier who'd sliced him during the shootout Saturday morning.

The attempt on his life had loosened Adam Meyers' tongue and he spilled everything. Mark West had recently opened three new bank accounts at *Banco Azteca*. Meyers laid out the details of how Sarita García had hired himself, Mark, and Paul to move her drug money through several banks throughout the United States. They had cleaned eight-hundred seventy-five million dollars, leaving the balance of one-hundred twenty-five million still to clean. The final step was to divide the cash into three separate accounts with *Santander* Bank, but García reneged on paying their fee for laundering her money, so Mark changed to *Banco Azteca*. Adam felt García had balked because they'd asked for double the originally agreed upon half-million each.

After a pause and a few sips of water, Adam continued, explaining the trio felt they had provided better protection for García's ill-gotten gains by adding layers to the laundering process. Their initial commitment of six months had also turned into fourteen long months, and they deserved to be paid for their efforts. When García refused to pay them double their fee, Adam and Paul wanted to take their five-hundred G's and get the hell out of México, but Mark insisted they hold out for the full one million each.

Of course, everyone knew what happened next. Paul was dead. Adam's life was in danger. And Mark was on the run with Sarita García's money.

Jade left Agent Mortieau speaking with Adam's doctor and joined Christopher.

"Sandrine thinks we should have Adam call Mark to see if he'll agree to meet." Leaning against the wall, Jade crossed her arms to mimic his posture.

"I doubt Mark's still in Mazatlán," Christopher said.

"Probably not," Jade agreed. "But if Adam gets him on the phone, we might learn something about Mark's whereabouts."

Christopher nodded as Agent Mortieau joined them.

"Agent Temple," Jade said. "You remember Agent Mortieau?"

"Yes." Christopher extended his hand. "Pleasure to see you again."

"Same." After a quick shake, Sandrine added, "Doc says Meyers is good to transport." She looked at Jade. "Did you tell Temple my idea?"

"She did." Christopher pushed off the wall. "Let's see if our new witness will make the call."

Christopher led the way to Adam's room, where nurses were finishing changing his bandages. Nurse Consuela smiled when he entered the room after Jade and Sandrine.

"Hola, Señor Christopher." Consuela met him at the foot of Adam's bed.

"Hola, Enfermera Consuela," Christopher replied as she took his injured hand in hers.

Shaking her head, she wrinkled her nose. *"Infectada."* He winced when she touched the wound in his side, and she narrowed her eyes at him. "You come." She pulled him by the wrist.

"Wait—" Christopher took her hand.

"Enfermera." Marco Torres smiled at Consuela. *"Te vera en unos minutos."*

Nurse Consuela looked at Christopher who nodded. *"Bien."* She held up a finger. *"Unos minutos."* She motioned for the other nurse to follow her and the two left the room.

"Mr. Meyers," Agent Mortieau began. "We would like for you to call Mark West and ask him to meet with you."

Adam began shaking his head at the mention of Mark's name. "No way."

Christopher stepped closer. "Look, we need you to get him on the phone—"

"I can't …" Adam crossed his arms. "I left my phone in the truck."

Fishing his phone from his shorts pocket, Christopher said, "Use this."

Glaring at Christopher, Adam countered, "I don't know Mark's burner number."

"Bullshit," Sandrine said, her accent turning the *u* sound into *oo*. "You are a numbers guy, no?" She cocked an eyebrow. "You have memorized his number."

Jade stood at the end of Adam's bed and chimed in. "Adam, this might be our only chance to protect Mark from Sarita García."

Adam was still shaking his head as he made the call. When Christopher reached over and hit the speaker icon, a ring tone echoed through the room. The call dropped unanswered, but when Adam held the phone out to him, it rang with an incoming call. Christopher touched connect, then speaker, but silence filled the room.

"Adam?" Mark asked

"Yep."

"Glad you're alive."

"Same."

"You in custody?"

Adam looked at Christopher who shook his head. "No. Hospital."

A long pause, then Mark said, "Is surfer boy with you?"

Adam glanced at Christopher who said, "I'm here. Where are you?"

"I know you're a Fed," Mark replied.

"Good." Christopher kept his tone neutral. "Then you know I can help."

"Yeah, right." Mark sounded wary and nervous.

"Let's meet and talk about your options." Christopher glanced at Jade.

"No, man," Mark said. "I'm taking the money and getting the hell out of México."

"You won't get far," Christopher warned. "Trust me, you want us to find you before García's men do."

"Adam," Mark said. "I'll keep your share safe." Another pause. "Flip the agents off for me." Then the line went dead.

CHAPTER TWENTY

Sarita peeked at the digital clock on her nightstand, the red LED numbers showing 10:15 AM. She tried to calculate how many hours she'd slept, but her befuddled brain couldn't handle the task. She sat up, immediately regretting the decision when her spiraling bedroom sent her crashing back into her pillows.

Eyes closed, Sarita ran her tongue over her dry lips, wishing she'd thought to put a glass of water on her nightstand. She tried to recall how many tequila shots she'd consumed, but her hungover mind again refused to think about anything but water. And coffee. And more sleep.

She squinted to assess the spinning bedroom, and all seemed calm. Sitting up slowly, she waited a beat to make sure nothing swirled or whirled around her, then eased her legs from the covers and placed her feet on the soft, cream-colored area rug covering the tile floor. When it appeared, she wouldn't regurgitate the liquid roiling in her stomach, Sarita took a few tentative steps toward the bathroom. A knock thudded against the penthouse door, and she thought her head would explode.

"¿Quién es?" Sarita croaked.

"Alba," the maid replied. *"Traje café."*

"Entra." Sarita sat in one of the cushioned chairs of a bistro set, which provided a view of the ocean through the floor-to-ceiling window.

Alba pushed through the door with a tray, which she delivered to the buffet counter. She filled a large cup with coffee and set it in front of Sarita. The perpetually positive maid had gained the trust of the employees at Fiesta de Fuego, who avoided Sarita, but confided in Alba if they had a need or complaint.

Alba clinked and clanked dishes as she prepared to serve coffee cake, a favorite recipe handed down from Sarita's mother, Estrella.

The pounding in Sarita's head reached a crescendo as the maid placed a platter of sliced cake on the table, along with a couple of saucers, forks, and napkins.

"*¿Esta bien?*" Alba asked.

Sarita cocked an eyebrow. "Who is joining me?"

"*Señor* Ortiz,*"* Alba answered.

Sarita rubbed her temples. The last thing she wanted was to see or talk to anyone. But since Eladio had matched her shot for shot last night, not to mention helping her polish off a few bottles of cabernet, he probably hadn't fared any better than she had.

"*Bueno,*" Sarita said. "Fifteen minutes."

Nodding, Alba made her exit while Sarita gulped down coffee. On her way to her bathroom, she grabbed a bottle of water from a small fridge. Deciding a shower would come later after more sleep, she washed her face and brushed her teeth, then swallowed a couple of ibuprofens.

Her mirror confirmed she had imbibed too much last night, and she made minimal efforts to hide her haggard appearance. Even though air-conditioning pumped cool air into the penthouse, she felt warm and opted for a turquoise cotton romper, sans under garments.

"*Entrar,*" she said as she made her way back to the bistro table.

Eladio entered bearing a tray with the ingredients for Bloody Mary's. Sarita nearly gasped at his chipper demeanor. He looked refreshed and dapper in black jeans and a short-sleeved, blue linen shirt.

"*Buenos días.*" He set the tray on the buffet. When she didn't respond, he turned, a look of confusion on his handsome face. "*¿Qué?*"

"How the hell are you not hungover?" Sarita barked.

"I did not drink as much as you." Eladio smiled.

"Bullshit!" Sarita grimaced. "Tell me!"

Chuckling, he fixed a drink. "I am larger than you." He set the glass in front of her. "It takes more alcohol."

Sarita sipped the spicy cocktail and tilted her head.

"Bloody María," Eladio said. "I think the tequila improves the taste."

Motioning to a chair, she said, "Join me."

Eladio brought his drink and sat across from her. The new drinking partners sipped in silence for a few minutes. Sarita had been furious last night after Agustín Castro left. She had thrown her crystal tumbler against the wall, sending glass shards cascading to the floor.

Her godfather's present, Hector Ramos, had stuck his head into the dining room to assess the incident. Sarita ignored him, snatched another glass, and a bottle of Patrón from the shelf behind the bar. Ramos watched her for another minute, then his head disappeared from the entryway. As Sarita poured two shots, Eladio set his iPhone to play music, put the phone in a salad bowl, and placed the makeshift sound system on a side table near the entry.

Sarita handed Eladio his shot and he smiled. "We could invite him to join us."

She had narrowed her eyes at Eladio, shook her head, and tossed down her shot. The rest of the evening had been a blur of alcohol, laughter, and scheming.

Now, Eladio looked at his watch, then met her eyes over the rim of his glass.

"Do you need to be somewhere?" Sarita asked.

"We are meeting Juan Vega for lunch at Joe's."

"*Mierda!*" Sarita said too loudly and winced when her head began to pound. The memory of calling Vega late last night jerked through her mind like a skipping record. She didn't remember most of the conversation but did recall offering to pay him well for his services.

"You meet with him." Sarita took a long drink.

Shaking his head, he said, "I am afraid you promised *Señor* Vega you would not send a *lacayo* in your place."

Sarita started to roll her eyes but feared the action would blow off the top of her head. *"Bueno."* She finished her Bloody María and had to admit she felt better. "Meet me in the lobby at twelve-thirty."

Eladio raised an eyebrow as he stood.

"I will call *Señor* Vega and apologize for our tardiness." She wanted to ask what else she might not remember but decided to wait to see if the dribs and drabs from her memory eventually painted a whole picture.

"Bueno." Eladio crossed to the counter. "Would you like another drink?"

"No. Gracias." Sarita pointed at the tray. "Alba will clean up."

He nodded, then headed for the exit.

"Eladio …" Sarita smiled. "Thank you for last night and for the Bloody María."

A broad grin graced Eladio's face and his dark eyes lightened. "It was my pleasure." He placed a hand on his heart.

He gave Sarita a slight bow before departing and once again she questioned if something more meaningful had happened last night than bonding over a bottle of Patrón.

CHAPTER TWENTY-ONE

Katelyn smiled and leaned into his kiss. The salty ocean breeze provided a perfect offset to the bright sunshine beating down from a cloudless blue sky. Christopher sat and pulled her down onto a blanket warm from the sun. The gentle surf soaked the sand just inches from their entangled feet. Christopher brushed a strand of hair from her eyes, then kissed her again.

Katelyn scowled as the image of Christopher's smiling face dissolved. Someone was pounding on the casita door.

"Lyn!" Stella shouted. "Are you up?"

Katelyn rubbed her eyes. "Hang on." According to their mothers the two girls had their own twin-like language growing up, which included *Lyn* for Katelyn and *Ella* for Stella. "I'm coming, Ella." Katelyn climbed from the bed, padded over, and opened the door, squinting at her friend. "What time is it?"

"Ten-thirty." Stella looked ready for the day in a white racerback tank top and teal shorts, and had her thick curly hair piled on top of her head. Sunlight streamed through the window, brightening the purple wings of her dragonfly tattoo as she plazed two steaming cups of coffee on the dining table and sat down. "Everyone else was up when I came downstairs."

Touching her matching tattoo, Katelyn took a seat. She didn't think she'd had more than the others, but that seemed to be the theme lately. Her pounding head certainly suggested she'd consumed one too many margaritas.

Stella sipped some coffee. "Last night was fun. I enjoyed getting to know your friends."

"They're good people." Katelyn tipped her mug to her lips.

Humberto had regaled them with stories about early Mazatlán, taking advantage of his rapt audience to brag about Lucía's artwork. Lucía had blushed at his praise before sharing her current passion for helping abused women through Angel House. Katelyn had teased, like she always did, about them getting married. Then she'd had a hysterical laughing fit, mixed with tears, over her own failed nuptials.

As if Katelyn's memory from last night were her cue, Stella said, "Our moms texted. They're having a blast on your honeymoon in the Caymans."

Katelyn rolled her eyes. "Well, I'm glad we had travel insurance so they could go on the trip."

"And your mom wanted to know why you weren't answering your phone. Stewart keeps texting her about wedding expenses and refunds." Stella watched Katelyn over the top of her cup. "I told her to tell Stewart to eff off."

A plethora of nasty retorts for Stewart bloomed on Katelyn's tongue, but Stella's reply would suffice for now.

Grinning at Katelyn, Stella continued, "Instead of telling your mom about your recent adventures, I said you dropped your phone in the pool."

Katelyn blew on her coffee. "Great."

"Also, I overheard Humberto on the phone with Captain Torres." Stella took a drink. "Humberto is meeting with a Juan Vega because he has information about your missing things."

Katelyn, mid-sip, sloshed coffee onto her palm tree print pajama top when she straightened from her slouch. "That's fantastic!"

Stella nodded. "So, why would someone take your phone?"

Katelyn shrugged. "No idea." She dabbed the spill with a napkin. "Christopher said there's lots of reason for someone to steal my stuff." The acidic coffee began to churn in her stomach.

"Sucks about your passport. That means you're stuck here." Stella emptied her cup. "Do you think someone is trying to keep you from leaving Mazatlán?"

"Ever the conspiracy theorist." Katelyn stood and went to the kitchenette to make more coffee.

A burst of memory from being attacked in jail made her hands shake as she filled the glass carafe with water. In the recollection, Martínez became her attacker, and her hands shook as she tried to fill the back of the coffee maker. She took a minute to collect herself, then flipped the brew switch and returned to her seat.

"I know that look." Stella's eyes twinkled. "What?"

Shaking her head, she mumbled, "Nothing."

"Come on, Lyn." Stella leaned forward. "You're a journalist and your specialty *is* detail. What tidbit just came to mind?"

Katelyn met Stella's inquiring stare. "I can't shake the feeling I know Martínez from somewhere other than him arresting me at the Hotel Playa."

Stella sat back. "Okay … where do you think you met him?"

Katelyn coaxed an errant strand of hair behind her ear. "That's the problem. I don't remember meeting him before the Playa. But he seems so familiar and …"

"And?" Stella prompted.

"Well, I just had a burst of memory from the night I was attacked in my jail cell, and my mind thinks Martínez tried to kill me." Katelyn stood and headed for the coffee pot.

"What the hell?" Stella called after her. "You need to tell Captain Torres."

Katelyn plopped a hot pad onto the table for the glass carafe and refilled their cups, the aroma of the rich Mexican roast wafting through the casita.

"Tell him what?" Resuming her seat, she shook her head. "My crazed mind has solved my mysterious assault?"

"For starters." Stella crossed her arms. "Torres would want to know he has a killer on his force."

"Okay, okay." Katelyn held up a hand. "I'll think about it and try to remember where I originally met Martínez."

"Any chance the attack has something to do with the article you're writing about the poisonings throughout Mexico?"

"I doubt it since no one knows I'm working on the piece."

"I thought you reached out to the editor at the *Periódico Mazatlán*?" Stella rippled the coffee in her cup with a breath, then took a drink.

"I did, but she hasn't responded to my email." Katelyn made a mental note to reach out to Jessica Sanchez again. "So other than doing a lot of online research, I haven't talked to anyone yet. Besides, the deaths I'm researching took place in Cancún."

"But didn't you tell Torres you're working on this story?" Stella asked.

"Sort of." Katelyn sat her cup on the table. "We didn't get into specifics yet."

"Okay …" Stella grinned. "Spill the beans about Special Agent Hottie."

"There's nothing to tell." A blush colored her cheeks. "We met at Joe's and had fun dancing."

"And?" Stella pressed.

"And nothing."

Stella narrowed her eyes. "You were arrested in *his* hotel room."

Holding Stella's skeptical stare, Katelyn tried to suppress a smile.

"Oh, come on, Lyn." Stella begged. "No one would fault you for enjoying Agent Sexy after what Stewart did."

"Trust me, Ella, I wish I had a better story." Katelyn drank more coffee.

Unpersuaded, Stella crossed her arms. "The way the two of you look at each other doesn't say *nothing* happened."

An impish grin curved Katelyn's lips and made her feel like a schoolgirl. "I can't explain it, there just seems to be this *thing* between us."

"I'll say." Stella smiled.

"But seriously, nothing happened …" Katelyn knew her blushing cheeks betrayed her.

"Except?"

"Well, there was some dirty dancing and a little kissing …" an all-over flush spread through her body, "but I had too much to drink, and the fun ended."

"So, you're hoping Humberto can't retrieve your passport from this Vega guy right away …" Stella flashed a knowing smile.

"Maybe …" Katelyn nodded. She knew she couldn't leave until she and Christopher had their dinner date. She hated the idea he could simply be her rebound guy. But since he seemed to feel the same magic as she did, possibly, Christopher could be her new beginning instead.

Stella snapped her fingers. "Hey, Lyn?"

Katelyn blinked at her friend. "What?"

"I was saying let's go to Joe's for lunch." Stella stood. "You've talked about the place for years and I'd like to visit the infamous Joe's for myself."

"Sounds good." Katelyn jumped up. "I need a quick shower."

Stella thumbed her phone alive. "I'll arrange for an Uber to pick us up in fifteen minutes."

"We don't need an Uber; we can take Humberto's old VW bug." Katelyn headed to the bathroom. "I'll meet you in the kitchen in fifteen."

"Got it." Stella replied. "And cut that ugly stripe out of your hair."

Katelyn turned on the shower, then selected tan shorts and a bright pink tank top from the small closet. She plucked underthings from the shelves and picked up a pair of white flip flops. As she placed her clothes on the counter next to the sink, she noticed her hair swatch almost matched her top.

"I'm keeping it!" she told her reflection. She peeled off her pajamas, realizing that for the first time since she'd fled the chaos at home, she felt the urge to look pretty.

CHAPTER TWENTY-TWO

Christopher tucked into a plate of *huevos rancheros*, but barely tasted the delicious combination of fried eggs, salsa, and tortillas. Jade sat across from him picking mango from a bowl of fresh fruit mixed with yogurt. After arriving at The Joyful Margarita, they'd slugged down cups of coffee in hopes of clearing the cobwebs from their all-nighter.

Once things were under control at the hospital and they handed Adam Meyers off to Agent Sandrine Mortieau, the starving partners agreed food topped the list of what to do next.

Lisa Reyes placed three Tequila Sunrises in the middle of the table and sat in the chair next to Jade. Selecting a glass, she pointed to the other two. "I thought you both could use something a little stronger than coffee after your wild night."

Jade picked up her drink and guzzled down half of the orange juice concoction. She met Christopher's questioning gaze. "What?"

"Cheers." He took a sip. "Thanks, Lisa."

"My pleasure." Lisa slid a set of keys across the table. "Jade tells me you need a place to stay. I had the beach bungalow prepared for your witness, so it's stocked with the basics, including beer in the fridge."

Christopher picked up the keys. "How much for a month?"

Lisa waved off the question. "No charge." Flashing a smile, she added, "I use the term bungalow loosely. You'll see what I mean when you get there."

Jade's phone vibrated and she looked at the screen. "Since we had to cancel the agency jet, Sandrine says she now can't get a flight out until six." Another glance at the text. "So, Torres is escorting her and Adam to the police station for safekeeping."

Pushing his empty plate aside, Christopher nodded. "Good plan."

"I'm surprised Captain Torres has time to babysit them," Lisa said. "You'd think he'd be at the El Cid hotel investigating the newest death of a young female tourist."

Christopher shared a concerned look with Jade. "When did this happen?"

"Sometime last night," Lisa said. "She and a group of girlfriends were here yesterday afternoon." Flashing three fingers at a waiter, she continued, "One of Torres's officers called me in the middle of the night and told me to meet him here at the bar." She finished off her drink. "He confiscated all of my rum because the dead girl had been drinking Lava Flows."

"Did they all have the same drink?" Jade asked.

"Yep …" Lisa nodded. "A couple of cocktails each. Plus, they had a bunch of appetizers."

Dragging a hand across his chin stubble, Christopher said, "As much as I hate the idea, maybe we should check out the crime scene."

"No!" Jade cried. "I need sleep, not to mention a shower for chrissake." She wrinkled her nose as if she emanated a malodorous odor.

"Same." Christopher smiled at her flash of anger. "I'll text Torres saying we can help later."

Jade looked at her phone again. "Sandrine texted that Torres sent Vasquez to the crime scene so he could stay with her and Meyers."

"Captain Torres could probably use the help. This is the fourth tourist death in the last three weeks." A touch of worry echoed in Lisa's tone.

Christopher tapped out his text: *Can help Vasquez with latest victim after a shower.*

Torres: *Gracias, but he almost has scene wrapped up. We can talk specifics later.*

Christopher: *Copy*

When the waiter arrived with a second round of drinks, Christopher noticed Jade was still frowning at her phone.

"Anything else, Red?" The waiter loaded a tray with the empty glasses and dirty dishes.

"No, thanks, Julio." Lisa smiled, and the waiter headed for the kitchen. "Wait." Julio returned to the table. "Were the other deaths at hotels too?"

He shook his head. "No, a man at a hotel along the *malecón*, a woman at a bar near Machado Plaza and another woman was found in the rocks near Valentino's."

"Gracias, Julio."

Julio did a two fingered salute and departed.

While Jade and Lisa slurped their drinks, Christopher mulled over the need to arrest Mark West. If he was in custody, they could wrap up their case against Sarita García, which would free them to help Torres. And, maybe, he could spend more time with Katelyn. He rubbed his eyes with his thumb and forefinger. He really needed some sleep.

"C …?" Jade gave him an arched eyebrow stare.

"What?" Christopher took a drink.

"Lisa was saying she has a friend who works at the medical examiner's office who told her these deaths are all from poisonings."

Christopher looked at Lisa. "Were they all killed with the same poison?"

"She thinks so," Lisa said. "Something called methanol."

"Wood alcohol," Jade added. "You can't see, smell or taste it, but drink even a small amount and it can kill you."

"Damn …" Lisa said. "My staff also thinks the killer might be one of them."

"A waiter?" Christopher asked.

"That's their theory, someone who works in a restaurant or bar." Lisa stirred her drink. "Because they would have access to alcohol and food."

"And probably know how to make methanol." Jade narrowed her eyes at her cocktail.

"I'd read about a cell of suspicious deaths in the Dominican Republic which seem to be linked to tainted alcohol." Christopher pushed his glass away. "And a few weeks ago, a young woman was found floating in a resort pool in the Mayan Riviera, but her death was ruled an accident."

"I remember you talking about that." Jade leaned forward in her chair. "Her fiancé went to the men's room and returned to find her face down in the shallow end."

Lisa glanced around the table. "So, do you think the same guy is poisoning people here in Mazatlán?"

Shrugging his shoulders, Christopher said, "Could be."

Jade's phone buzzed and she frowned at the screen.

Christopher's phone chimed too, and he read the incoming text from Humberto: *Can you meet me at Joe's at 2 to talk to Juan Vega?* Christopher checked the time on his phone. 9:30. If he left now, he could shower and sleep for a few hours before the meeting. He typed his reply: *Yes.*

"I've got to go." He tapped the table so Jade would look at him. "I'm meeting Humberto at Joe's at two to talk to Vega."

Jade nodded. "I'll check in with Torres after I get some sleep."

Reaching for his wallet, Christopher asked, "Lisa, what do we owe you for breakfast and drinks?"

"On the house," Lisa said. "Just promise to keep me in the loop about the crazy person killing tourists."

Christopher smiled, since he doubted Lisa was ever out of the loop. "Will do."

Jade's phone buzzed again. This time she gave it a quick look and her cheeks glowed as if sunburned. "Ladies' room before we leave." Jade laid her phone face down and walked toward the bathrooms located at the back of the bar.

"See you later, Temple." Lisa headed for the kitchen. "Say goodbye to Jade for me."

"Thanks for everything, Lisa," Christopher said to her retreating back and she gave him a thumbs up before pushing through the kitchen's swinging doors.

Curious about what had brought on Jade's sour demeanor, Christopher picked up her phone before the screen locked. He read a text from Sandrine about being trapped at the Mazatlán police station. He had to read the last line twice: *Are you sure you're not related to Torres?*

CHAPTER TWENTY-THREE

When she stepped from the elevator, Sarita smiled and took in the busy Fiesta de Fuego lobby. Arriving guests received a Paloma served in colorful handblown tumblers and were wooed by the resort's event director. They were promised comped activities if they spent ninety minutes listening to a timeshare presentation. Most guests said yes to the offer, assuming all they had to do was enjoy a complimentary breakfast with a charming salesperson, and then they'd be off on their adventure. The guests who declined knew all too well the ninety-minute spiel could last for hours.

Eladio had his head bent over his phone and looked up when she approached. His slight smile told her he approved of her attire—a skintight, floral print sundress that emphasized her breasts and small waist.

"Vega texted saying he has a table at Joe's." Pocketing his phone, Eladio pushed open one side of the glass entry doors.

Sarita stepped outside and stopped abruptly at the sight of Hector Ramos. Eladio bumped into her, causing him to place his hands on her hips. A warm flush flooded her cheeks, and she was glad she faced away from him.

Ramos, dressed in his usual uniform of black cargo pants, black combat boots, and a black T-shirt, waited next to a Kia Sportage, his face void of emotion. The last thing Sarita wanted was for this brute to tag along to her meeting.

"Buenas tardes, Señor Ramos." Sarita forced a smile. "I will not need you for a few hours." She continued around the SUV to the passenger door, a bellman close on her heels. "Please enjoy a nice lunch, and we can talk later."

Ignoring Sarita's instructions, Ramos crossed the stone portico in long, quick strides. The bellmen scurried out of the way of the large Mexican and Sarita turned to face the *sicario*.

She glared at Ramos and swallowed the urge to ask him what the hell he thought he was doing. Instead, she arched an eyebrow. *"¿Qué es?"*

Ramos glanced across the top of the SUV at Eladio, then looked at Sarita. "Hernández and his men failed to kill Meyers last night."

Sarita met Eladio's gaze, then asked, "What happened?"

"There were more police in the hospital than planned." Ramos's phone buzzed and he looked at the screen. "Hernández reported one soldier dead, one in custody."

As she processed the *sicario's* information, Sarita focused on suppressing her rising anger. "Tell Hernández to eliminate the man in custody." She opened the car door. "And tell him I want him to kill Meyers, or his family will attend *his* funeral in the near future." When Sarita slid into the passenger seat, Ramos placed his hand on the door. She narrowed her eyes at him.

He bent down to face her. "I will take care of it." Then he closed the door.

Sarita had no doubt Ramos would do her bidding and eliminate the soldier being held by the *policía* himself, and maybe even kill Lieutenant Hernández for good measure.

Eladio climbed behind the wheel and cranked the engine. Sarita watched Ramos in the side mirror. The *sicario* stood glaring at them as they made their exit down the resort's long driveway.

As he pulled into traffic, Eladio said, "I do not think Ramos is happy being left behind."

"What the hell am I going to do with him?" Sarita slapped the dashboard.

"I think you handled him well."

"He is going to be trouble."

Smiling at her, Eladio shrugged. "We will think of something." He swung wide of a work crew trimming coconut trees along the side of the road. "So, Hernández's men came up short last night?"

Sarita nodded. "*Sí*, and I believe I just gave Ramos his first assignment." Her hangover resumed beating a drum in her head. "Why are we meeting *Señor* Vega at Joe's?"

"You suggested the restaurant last night." Eladio accelerated around a tour bus. "You insisted Joe's has the best *ostras* in Mazatlán."

Sarita vaguely remembered her oyster declaration, and while it was true, she would've preferred something a little more upscale than Joe's. Eladio silently navigated traffic as her mind dredged up a memory from long ago.

Sarita had traveled to Mazatlán with her parents for vacation, which meant her father would work and her mother would shop, leaving Sarita to while away her days by the hotel pool. She'd just celebrated turning fifteen with her *quinceañera*, so her parents trusted her to stay out of trouble. And, for the most part, she did. Except for one late afternoon, when she wandered into an enticing open-air restaurant, and, eventually, into the arms of a handsome, young Mexican intent on stealing her heart.

"¿Señorita García?" Eladio glanced her way.

"Lo siento," Sarita said, the memory scuttling back to its hiding place. "You were saying?"

Braking for traffic, he continued, "I asked if you had an agenda in mind."

Sarita stared out the window at the dull wilderness giving way to the outskirts of the city and collected her thoughts. The priority, of course, was to see if Juan Vega knew where to find her missing money. If not, then she would see what it would take for him to find the bank accounts. She wanted to solicit him to come to work for her but given his reputation of working both sides of the law, she would see how this meeting went first. The matter of Clara Marsh's whereabouts was also extremely important to Sarita, but again, she would weigh whether to press the issue now.

Switching her gaze from the passing scenery to Eladio, she said, "The priority is to see what Vega knows, or can find out, about my bank accounts."

"*Sí.*" Eladio focused on the road. "Agreed."

Sarita knew Eladio would follow her lead and only interject his opinion if he felt the need. A snippet of last night's boozy bonding flitted through her mind. She was pretty sure nothing untoward had happened between her and her handsome business manager, but she had to admit she liked Eladio's more relaxed demeanor. How he could not be hungover was still a mystery to her. He wore the same attire from this morning, and Sarita noted a musky citrus scent.

Warm sunshine beat through the passenger window as Sarita took in sidewalks full of tourists mixed with street hawkers and Mazatlán citizens going about their day.

After Eladio swung the Kia into Joe's lot and parked, Sarita exited the car, heat slamming into her as if she'd stepped into a furnace. She smoothed wrinkles from her dress and Eladio came to her side. They crossed the parking lot to a long sidewalk separating an outdoor eating area from Joe's open-air bar.

The memory of dancing at Joe's with her attractive mystery man on a hot summer night flitted through Sarita's mind. She cast the image aside and searched the tables for Juan Vega. Eladio stood slightly behind her, and they both spotted Vega at the same time. From the few pictures she'd seen of him, Sarita knew he always dressed casually and usually looked a little disheveled. Today, he wore tan dress slacks and a short-sleeved, tropical print button down. He was handsome in a rugged way, with leathery brown skin and hooded dark eyes.

Vega looked up from the papers littering the four top he occupied and waved them over.

Standing, he extended his hand. *"Señorita García."*

"Por favor." Embracing the handshake, she continued, *"Llámame Sarita."* She turned to Eladio. "And you know my business manager, Eladio Ortiz."

Vega nodded, motioning to the chairs across from him. *"Siéntate."* He signaled a waiter. "What you like to drink?" In stilted speech, he continued, "I like to practice English. Okay?"

"Of course." Sarita flashed a smile, then spoke to the waiter. "Do you have *Chamucos Blanco*?"

"Sí."

"Fine tequila." Juan agreed, adding, "And a large bucket of *Pacifico*."

The waiter gave a small nod and departed.

Offering Sarita, a menu, Juan asked, "And, you like to order lunch?"

The idea of food, combined with the aroma from a passing tray of *carne asada fajitas*, made Sarita's stomach flip. "Maybe we eat after business."

"Sounds good." Juan said.

"I think you speak English well." As she crossed her legs, she noticed Juan took in the sight. "It is good to master both languages."

"Yes." Juan leaned back in his chair. "I pretend I do not understand English so I can hear things I should not know," he said, dropping his dis-jointed Spanglish.

"¡Brillante!" Sarita clapped her hands together.

The waiter arrived with their drinks. He set the tequila, shot glasses, and a plate of cinnamon-sprinkled orange slices in the middle of the table. Another server placed the bucket of beers in a tall wire stand and added bowls of limes and salt next to the oranges.

Wondering if a touch of tequila might lessen her hangover, Sarita poured three shots, then handed one to each gentleman. "To new friends and fruitful collaborations."

"¡Salud!" Vega tossed down his drink.

Sarita and Eladio followed suit, each popping a slice of orange into their mouth. Eyebrows raised; Juan looked from one to the other.

"The orange and cinnamon are a wonderful compliment to the tequila." Sarita offered him the plate.

Juan selected a slice, took a nibble, then popped the remainder into his mouth. Smiling in appreciation, he reached for three beers and set them on the table. He dipped a lime wedge into the salt, then rubbed the salted lime around the mouth of the bottle, taking a long pull from the Pacifico before setting it in front of him.

"So, Sarita," Juan said. "How can I help you?"

Sarita took a dainty sip of beer. "I believe Eladio explained to you the matter of my missing money."

Juan nodded and glanced at Eladio. "Something about American bankers hiding your bank accounts."

"Sí. Yes. The bankers were hired to …" she hesitated.

"To invest profits from Fiesta de Fuego," Eladio interjected. "In order to achieve a reasonable return."

Juan looked around the restaurant, which had a few patrons scattered about chatting over drinks and enjoying a cloudless sky reflected in the azure ocean. He leaned forward, closer to Sarita, looked at Eladio and smiled. *"En otras palabras, lavaron el dinero."* After a booming laugh, he slugged down some beer.

Sarita assumed he had switched back to Spanish in case anyone was listening to their conversation. Knowing Eladio had already explained their laundering process to Vega, she checked the packed restaurant to see if anyone had overheard his comment.

"Do you think you can locate my money?" Preferring tequila to beer, she poured another shot and took a sip.

Juan nodded. "I have already looked into this matter and think your accounts are now with *Banco Azteca*."

"*Sí,*" Eladio agreed. "The bank emailed me when three new accounts were opened recently."

"How do I regain control of my accounts?" Focusing on managing her rising anger, she added. "Preferably before the *bastardos* move my money again."

After Juan drained his beer, he reached for another bottle. "How much do you want to spend to get your money back?"

Resisting the urge to shout, Sarita smoothed her hair from her face. "Whatever it takes."

"Within reason." Eladio leaned forward. "The Americans have already cost us money and time."

"Within reason," Juan repeated. "You will not ask for *El Lobo's* help?"

Sarita narrowed her eyes. "No."

"*Bien.*" Juan drank some beer. "I will contact the bank manager to see what he needs, and how much it will cost, to change the name on the accounts."

"*Bueno,*" Sarita said. "How long do you think this will take?"

"As long as it takes." He signaled the waiter. "We eat now."

Since she had little interest in eating, Sarita wanted to ask more questions, but she could press on after they ordered.

"Juan." She lightly touched his arm. "You should order for us." She looked at Eladio, who nodded in agreement.

"I know you like *ostras*." Juan grinned.

Sarita's stomach rebelled at the idea of raw food while the waiter took Juan's order for a dozen oysters, a platter of fish tacos, and marlin ceviche with chips and salsa.

"I have another meeting soon." Juan looked at his phone. "Anything else on your mind?"

She decided now wasn't a good time to discuss Vega coming to work for her. And, as badly as she wanted to know where Clara Marsh had disappeared to, she didn't think she should pursue that topic either.

"Retrieving my bank accounts is a priority, so nothing else for now." Sarita sipped some tequila, welcoming the warmth spreading in her core.

"Nothing else means we drink!" Juan poured himself and Eladio shots, then topped off Sarita's. "Oh, I hear you have new addition to your staff."

Sarita exchanged a look with Eladio before returning her gaze to Vega. She knew her anger reflected on her face and didn't try to mask the edge in her voice. *"¿Perdona?*

Juan Vega lifted his shot glass, looking from Sarita to Eladio, then back to Sarita. *"¡Salud a tu sicario!"* He tossed down his shot and slammed the small glass onto the table. "What? You are not happy to have your own assassin?"

CHAPTER TWENTY-FOUR

Katelyn guided the old Volkswagen along the highway leading from the Mazatlán Marina toward the Golden Zone. The sky was a perfect shade of blue. The early afternoon air, while hot, was void of humidity. She had asked herself more than once why she hadn't relocated to this perfect paradise. Now that she was minus a fiancé, making a move would be less complicated.

Co-pilot Stella had her right arm through the open window, hand porpoising through the wind, eyes closed behind her sunglasses. Maybe both she and Stella should move to Mazatlán, two besties living the dream.

"We should have brought our swimsuits and hung out on the beach for a while," Stella said, eyes still closed.

"What a fabulous idea." Katelyn braked for a *pulmonia* stopping curbside for passengers to disembark. "Maybe tomorrow. Or we can hang out at the Emerald Bay pool."

Stella shook her head. "My soul needs the soothing sea." She pulled her arm in, swept golden strands of hair from her face, and looked at Katelyn. "As much as I think we need to get you the hell out of town, I could get used to this," she threw her arms wide, "this beautiful paradise."

Katelyn laughed. "Right?"

Traffic started to slow in front of them, so Katelyn down shifted, grinding the VW's gears. She turned right at *Pastelerías Panamá,* following the familiar route to Joe's. She whipped into the parking lot and found a spot near the small gift shop.

After she hopped out of the car, Stella looked through the shop windows. "Maybe I should buy that cute tank top?" She grinned at Katelyn. "Not quite as good as *your* souvenir from Joe's, but who can compete with tall, blond, and dreamy?"

"Funny." When Katelyn stepped closer to the store, the massive plate glass window reflected their images. A slight movement behind them caught Katelyn's eye and she studied the smudged window.

"Are we going in?" Stella reached for the door handle.

"Wait," Katelyn whispered.

"What?" Stella looked at Katelyn, then behind them. "Did you see something?"

The person who had caught Katelyn's attention moved quickly toward the Emporio Hotel. When she turned to get a better look, the man disappeared into a throng of guests leaving the hotel lobby.

"Lyn." Stella tapped her shoulder. "Did you see Martínez?"

Shaking her head, she headed for Joe's entrance. "I thought someone was following us, but it's just my overactive imagination."

"It's the heat." Stella hurried and caught up to Katelyn. "What you need is an ice-cold beer."

Quieting a twinge of fear, Katelyn led the way down the sidewalk and into the open-air bar.

"Hey." Stella pointed at a raised platform. "Is this the stage where you danced with the dog a few years ago?"

Ignoring her, Katelyn shoved her sunglasses on top of her head and blinked to adjust her eyesight. Stella pushed past her, making a beeline for the sea wall.

A waiter greeted Katelyn with, "Would you like a table?"

Katelyn nodded. *"Sí."* She followed the waiter to where Stella stood, taking in the stunning view.

"What are you drinking?" he asked.

"A bucket of Coronas."

The waiter gave her a thumbs up and hustled back to the bar.

Straddling the sea wall, Stella looked down, then at Katelyn. "How far down is it?"

"I don't know." Katelyn peeked over the edge. "Maybe ten feet, but no need to jump."

Stella laughed and Katelyn pointed past her. "There are stairs down to the beach."

The waiter delivered the bucket of beers, complete with lime and salt. "Something to eat?" He added a basket of chips and salsa to the table.

"In a bit." Katelyn pulled a beer from the bucket. *"Gracias."*

He gave a quick nod before he headed for a table in the center of the bar and Katelyn found herself staring at a trio enjoying lunch. There was something familiar about one of the men. Katelyn didn't know many Mexicans other than Humberto, Marco, and Lucía, but she couldn't shake the sense she knew the big guy at the table.

When she pulled a bottle from the bucket, Stella rattled the ice, and drops of water dotted her teal shorts.

Katelyn dipped a lime wedge in the salt, then squeezed the salty concoction into her Corona. "Lime and salt?" she asked Stella.

"Yes." She held her hand out for the garnish. "Why are you looking at that table?"

"Not sure." Katelyn took a drink. "The larger guy looks familiar."

Stella raised her eyebrows. "As in you danced the night away with him, too?"

Katelyn smirked at her friend, then drained half her Corona. "We can take our beers down to the beach and go for a walk if you want."

"Let's eat first." Stella slid from the wall down onto the bench. "I'm starving."

"I love the Marlin tacos here." Katelyn signaled the waiter.

"What about the oysters?" Stella dipped a chip in the salsa.

"Well, Joe's *is* famous for their oysters," Katelyn agreed as the waiter arrived.

Munching her chip, Stella pointed at Katelyn. "You order."

"We'll have two orders of the marlin tacos and two Joe's Special Shooters."

He noted the order on his pad and departed.

Stella chugged some beer. "Special shooters?"

As Katelyn plucked her second Corona from the bucket, she grinned. "You'll see."

A group of young women stumbled into the bar, all laughing and talking at the same time. They headed for a large table at the end of the sea wall where it joined the building's supporting wall. A couple of them started chanting, "Shots! Shots!" and another waiter hurried to their table.

"Oh, to be young again." Stella lifted her empty bottle in toast, then slipped the last Corona free of the melting ice, added salted lime juice, and took a long swig.

"And stupid." Katelyn laughed and cast a glance at the group of women clinking their glasses together.

The bartender placed two oyster shooters on the table and winked at them. "Tacos coming soon."

Stella eyeballed the shot glass in front of her. "What the hell?"

"This." Katelyn lifted the concoction. "Is the best oyster shooter you'll ever have."

Stella held the Joe's Special under her nose. "Hot sauce?"

Katelyn grinned. "Yes, *Tapatío.*"

"And?"

Katelyn pointed to the bottom. "A fine fresh oyster." Moved her finger up a smidge. "Lime juice." She took a sip. "Hornitos Silver." She motioned for Stella to raise her glass, then clinked it. "The hot sauce brings the flavors all together. *¡Salud!*"

"Here goes." After Stella swallowed the mixture, her eyes watered, and she coughed. "Not bad," she rasped.

The waiter delivered their tacos. *"¿Mas cerveza?"*

"Sí, y agua, por favor," Katelyn said.

Stella added, "Pacifico this time."

"Sí." He raced off.

The two friends dug into the tacos, moans of ecstasy escaping between bites.

Stella blew out a breath. "Oh my God, these are so good." She emptied her second Corona. "I'm thinking we may need an Uber back to Humberto's."

Katelyn giggled. "Right?" She mopped taco juice from her chin. "We'll drink some water before our next beer."

As if on cue, the bartender set two glasses of water on the table, placed the bucket of Pacificos in a wire stand, and returned to the bar.

Katelyn drank half of her water, then looked out at the ocean. If she and Stella lived here, they wouldn't have to worry about being responsible. They could while away the rest of the afternoon, watching the tourists below on the beach and the ever-changing sea.

As if reading her mind, Stella said, "We're too young to retire." She hoisted her water glass, then took a drink.

"I know …" Katelyn took a Pacifico from the bucket. "But a girl's gotta have dreams."

"Maybe we should have two more Joe's Special Shooters and take an Uber," Stella picked up her second taco.

Katelyn raised her hand to signal the waiter. "What are you doing here?"

"Duh." Stella laughed. "Drink—"

"Not you." Katelyn pointed. "Humberto."

"Buenas tardes," Humberto called, approaching their table. "I thought I recognized my Volkswagen in the parking lot."

Stella shot Katelyn a look and said, "Katelyn borrowed the car so she could show me the infamous Joe's."

Humberto frowned, and Katelyn's cheeks warmed at his disapproval. She hoped Stella wouldn't mention Katelyn's paranoid delusion about the man in the parking lot following them.

"I–I … thought it would be safe to come to Joe's." She shrugged. "You know, during the day."

A smile replaced Humberto's scowl. "*Sí*, but next time let me know your plans."

"Okay." She offered Humberto an apologetic smile. "Join us."

"Actually, I am here to meet with Juan Vega." Humberto cast a glance at the trio Katelyn had noticed earlier. "But he is still in a meeting."

"Oh …" Katelyn took a quick look at Vega. "I thought I recognized him. But I don't remember meeting him before."

"He has been to my house in the past," Humberto said. "Perhaps during one of your previous stays."

Katelyn noticed his frown had returned. "What's wrong?"

"Nothing." Humberto shifted to a smile. "I would like for you to join us since Vega might have information about your missing belongings."

Stella selected a Pacifico. "Can we bring our bucket?"

"*Sí.*" Humberto chuckled. "Give me a minute."

Katelyn watched as Humberto headed for the other table and noticed the woman stiffen as he approached. The other male stood when Humberto got close and extended his hand. Humberto completed the handshake, then said something to Vega.

"Does that seem a little weird to you?" Stella asked.

"Yes." Katelyn tried to get a better look. "Wonder who the woman is?"

"And I wonder what Agent Hottie is doing here?" Stella asked.

Whipping her head around, Katelyn found Christopher standing at the table, smiling down at her.

"You started without me?" Christopher said to Katelyn.

"Late lunch," Stella answered.

Christopher flashed a skeptical look at Stella as she tipped her bottle toward her lips.

"What?" She took a sip. "We just finished tacos and Joe's Special Shooters."

"Glad you could make it," Humberto said to Christopher. "I thought maybe you would be at the El Cid."

"Jade is covering for us," Christopher said. "Would it help to discuss this latest poisoning with you and Captain Torres later?"

Humberto nodded. "We can all meet at my house again tonight."

"Since Agent Mortieau won't have Meyers on a plane to LA until this evening, Jade plans to keep her company at the station," Christopher explained.

"I see," Humberto said.

"If it's okay, I'd like Katelyn to join me for dinner." Christopher grinned at Katelyn.

Stella choked on a swig of beer and grabbed a napkin to wipe up the mess.

His frown was back, but Humberto said, *"Bueno."*

"Maybe we can meet tomorrow?" Christopher suggested.

Pulling his phone from his back pocket, Humberto said, "I will text Marco and have him inform Jade."

"Would you guys like to sit?" Katelyn asked. "Have a beer?"

Christopher's smile vanished and his face clouded. He was staring beyond Katelyn at Juan Vega's table. His eyes trained on the woman and her companion now making their exit. Katelyn saw Christopher's jaw muscle twitch as he turned to watch the pair leave Joe's.

In a barely audible voice, Katelyn heard Christopher ask Humberto, "Sarita García?"

Humberto responded, *"Sí."*

CHAPTER TWENTY-FIVE

Christopher wanted to yell, "Stop, FBI!" He wanted to slap handcuffs on Sarita García and haul her to the Mazatlán jail. But all he could do was watch her walk out of Joe's. The man escorting her glanced over his shoulder at Christopher, then they were out of view.

"It is too bad you cannot arrest her," Humberto said.

Christopher nodded. "I'd like nothing better, but we don't have enough evidence."

"Perhaps the man Marco has in custody will provide what you need." Humberto turned his attention to Katelyn and Stella.

Christopher hoped the thug Marco was holding would help tie up the García investigation. He was anxious to hear what, if anything, Sarita's goon had told Sandrine.

He heard a loud, *"Mucho Gusto,"* behind him and turned to see Juan Vega take the chair next to Katelyn. She smiled at Christopher, but quickly returned her attention to Vega as he leaned in to tell her something. Katelyn's cheeks colored, and Vega released a thunderous laugh.

Christopher caught Stella's eye. She smiled and patted the space next to her and Katelyn, then scooted to make room for him.

Humberto sat in the last available chair and Christopher slid onto the bench, taking Katelyn's hand in his.

A waiter arrived with a partial bucket of Pacificos, a half bottle of *Chamucos*, and all the accoutrements. He looked at Vega. *"¿Algo más?"*

Holding his hands palms up, Juan scanned his guests. "Anything else?"

There was a collective shaking of heads and a chorus of, "No, *gracias*." Juan waved the waiter away.

"I just told my new *amiga*"—he patted Katelyn's shoulder with a beefy hand—"that I know the *pendejos* who have her property."

"Bueno," Humberto said. "Have you been able to retrieve the items?"

After a swig of beer, Juan said, "As much as I would like to simply steal them back, it will cost money for their return."

"How much?" Katelyn and Christopher chimed in unison.

"Five thousand US," Juan replied.

"¡Mierda!" Humberto slammed a fist onto the table. "That is absurd."

"Sí, sí." Juan nodded. "And that is only for the iPhone, laptop, and camera."

"Do you know who robbed Katelyn?" Humberto asked as Katelyn blurted, "What about my passport?"

Juan held up a finger and everyone waited. "No," he said to Humberto. "I do not know who committed the theft." He finished the tequila. "But I do have my suspicions."

"Comparta, por favor." Impatience echoed in Humberto's tone.

Juan leaned forward, scrolled through his cell, and tapped the screen. "Do you recognize this *hombre*?"

Humberto studied the picture, shook his head, and handed the phone to Christopher. "Who is he?"

"The leader of a bump and run crew." Juan folded his hands and set them on his paunch. "He either pays or threatens maids to leave doors ajar after they clean a room."

Christopher snapped a photo of the man, then handed Juan back his phone. "Someone must scout the rooms first for valuables."

"*Sí*. I think maybe a bellman," Juan agreed. "Someone with an all-access key."

"Or a maid," Stella suggested.

"Possibly," Humberto said. "Maybe a maid is connected to this man."

"Do you have a name?" Christopher asked.

Juan shook his head. "No. One of my guys just happened to overhear negotiations between this *cabrón* and another *imbécil* about the purchase of phones." He drained the beer bottle. "There is a strong market in Mazatlán for electronics from other countries, especially iPhones."

"What about my passport?" Katelyn asked again. Christopher heard panic in her voice and squeezed her hand.

"I do not know." Juan poured another shot of tequila and placed the bottle in the middle of the table. "But there is an even bigger demand for passports." He took a sip. "Usually, my crew is the first contact for stolen passports." He cut his eyes to Christopher. "We do try to return the passport to the owner, but by the time we receive them the person has already applied for a replacement from the Consular office and left Mexico."

"Where's the Consular office?" Katelyn asked Humberto. "Do you think they're still open?"

Before Humberto could respond, Christopher said, "You have to have proof of citizenship or a copy of your passport to file for a replacement."

Katelyn narrowed her eyes at him. "Well then maybe you should use your FBI resources to get me a new one."

"Did you leave a copy at home?" Stella asked. "Maybe with Stewart?"

Katelyn shook her head, reached for the *Chamucos* bottle, and poured a shot.

Christopher arched an eyebrow. "Stewart?"

"Long story." Katelyn lifted the small glass in toast and slugged down the citrusy tequila.

Christopher grinned at her comment, then said, "If you file for a lost passport, the number becomes invalid." He shifted his gaze from Katelyn to encompass everyone. "It would be better to wait and see if we can recover her passport before she reports it stolen."

"So how long do we wait?" Stella asked, drilling Christopher with her eyes.

"Juan, I can arrange the five Gs," Christopher continued without answering, "if you can set a meet to recover Katelyn's items."

Juan nodded. "You want to be there, *¿sí?*"

"Yes." Christopher looked at Humberto. "Want to join us?"

Humberto did a head shake. "I think I would raise a red flag given my known association with Captain Torres."

Christopher nodded but was thinking these bandits would only be the front men. He wanted the leader, and, he guessed, so would Captain Torres.

CHAPTER TWENTY-SIX

Upon their return to Fiesta de Fuego, Eladio had been summoned to speak with a couple who were having regrets about purchasing their timeshare weeks, so Sarita waited alone for the elevator to her penthouse.

Tapping her foot on the gleaming tile floor, she glanced at the time on her phone, 3:06 PM. While she waited for the car to arrive, Sarita processed her meeting with Juan Vega. It bothered her that Vega knew about Hector Ramos to begin with but taunting her about having her own *sicario* was seriously annoying.

The elevator arrived with a ping and the doors whooshed open. Sarita stepped into her private lift and pressed the penthouse button. The meeting with Vega wasn't the only thing on her mind. She assumed the tall American with Humberto Álvarez was the FBI agent competing with her to capture the bankers. She doubted, though, his goal was the same as hers: to kill the last two after obtaining the information she needed to find her freshly laundered cash. A niggling sense of worry gave her pause. She contemplated whether the pesky FBI agent could also be interested in her—and shutting down her empire.

Another ping announced her arrival and the doors slid open. Sarita expected to find Ramos waiting for her but found the hallway empty when she stepped from the elevator. Exhaustion from her late night with

Eladio, not to mention her lingering hangover, swept over her and she decided to sequester herself in her bedroom and enjoy a nap.

Sarita headed down the hallway and noticed the door to her suite ajar. She stopped and pulled her phone from her purse, wishing she had a gun instead. Where was Ramos when she needed him? Or was Ramos waiting for her? Did he have orders from *El Lobo* to kill her?

She pulled Eladio's name up in her contacts, thumb hovering over the green call button. She didn't want to sound the alarm just yet. Maybe Alba or one of the other staff was the intruder. She had a strict policy, though, of allowing no one in her suite when she was gone. Sarita toed the door, inching it open, and entered slowly.

Her intruder, who stood with his back to her while he poured a shot of tequila, had left a trail of his smoky, sexy cologne lingering in the air. "Jesus!" Sarita slammed the door closed. *"¿Qué demonios estás haciendo aquí?"*

Dario Díaz turned and flashed a dazzling smile. "This is how you greet your *¿amante?"* He closed the distance between them in long strides, embraced Sarita, and covered her lips in a hungry kiss, a mix of salt and Herradura on his lips.

Sarita wanted to push him away. Slap his face. Demand he leave. But lust consumed her, and she leaned into Dario, dropping her phone, forgetting her anger. Dario's hands burned through her clothing as they roamed her body. He lowered the zipper, slipped the straps from her shoulders, and sent her dress floating to the floor.

Sarita gasped as Dario covered an exposed nipple with his warm mouth. She held him to her breast as he ripped off her thong, leaving her naked in front of him. He captured her other nipple and dropped his chinos. She tugged at his tan linen shirt, and he slipped out of the garment. He kissed her and lifted her in his arms, then carried her to the bedroom.

Dario placed her on the bed and stood staring down at her, desire burning in his eyes. Sarita reached out and cupped him in one hand while pulling him to her with the other. He lay next to her, returning his mouth to her breasts, first one, then the other, while his hand caressed her flat stomach.

She arched her hips in anticipation, a soft moan escaping her dry lips. When he stroked her lush mound, she shouted, *"¡Dios!"*

Dario abandoned her breasts and met her dark stare. "Tell me you want me," he rasped.

Sarita narrowed her eyes at her young lover. She hated to admit she wanted him, but when he laid on top of her and lowered his hips to meet hers, she could barely contain herself. He teased her, slowly entering, then withdrawing, and Sarita clawed his butt cheeks to draw him to her.

He kissed her and slid inside her, their hips finding the perfect rhythm. Then, once again, he withdrew. "Tell me you want me," he whispered in her ear.

Sarita sunk her nails deeper into his ass and cried, *"¡Sí, maldita sea, te quiero!"*

Dario plunged into her. Sarita whimpered but matched his intense rhythm. He pulled her arms forward, pinned her hands above her head, and sucked her nipples. Sarita found the tinge of pain, mixed with her burning passion, exhilarating. He released her hands and lifted her up, continuing to bury himself deep within her. As he kissed her, crushing her breasts against his taut chest, she could feel his heartbeat. Sarita's passion increased with each thrust, but when Dario laid her back down and returned his mouth to her breasts, her crescendo stole her breath and left her gasping for air.

A loud thudding resonated through the penthouse rousing Sarita from a deep slumber.

"Stop pounding," Sarita growled. "I am trying to sleep."

"Nena ..." Dario nuzzled her neck. "Someone is at the door."

Sarita sat up and glared at Dario. The incessant knocking on the door to her penthouse continued. She looked at the bedside clock to check the time, which read 6:08 in glaring red letters.

Dario wrapped an arm around her waist. "Tell them to leave so we can return to our fun."

Sarita shoved him away, climbed from the bed, and donned a blue dressing gown embroidered with pink flamingos. She glanced at Dario lying on his stomach, his tight ass taunting her, beckoning her to stay. Sarita sighed and left the bedroom, pulling the door closed. She found her now dead phone still lying on the floor, along with their clothes, and her cheeks warmed with the memory of Dario's greeting.

"Sarita!" Eladio called through the door, along with another round of knocking. "I need to speak with you."

Sarita smoothed her hair, checked to make sure her dressing gown covered her nakedness, and, hoping she didn't look like she'd just been ravished, opened the door.

"Señor Ortiz." She swallowed to clear the huskiness from her voice. "What is so urgent you need to beat down my door?"

Eladio pursed his lips and stared at his boss. Sarita knew she'd offended him but thought it best to remind him both of his place and that he needed an invitation to visit her penthouse.

"Well?" She crossed her arms.

"My apologies, *Jefa.*" Eladio's tone echoed with insolence. "There has been a shooting involving the American banker in custody and I thought the incident urgent enough to disturb you."

Sarita narrowed her eyes at Eladio's impertinence but bit back her own apology. He was right to bring her this news immediately.

"Cariño," Dario said as he came to her side, a towel wrapped around his waist. "What is going on?"

Sarita didn't answer and ignored Eladio's raised eyebrows. "I will meet you in the small dining room in ten minutes," she said to Eladio.

"Would you ask Alba to prepare a light dinner and make sure the refrigerator is stalked with water?"

Eladio cast a glance at Dario, then back at Sarita, as if waiting for an introduction. A few seconds passed, then Eladio said, *"Sí."* He held her gaze for a moment, then departed.

"You should have stayed in the damn bedroom," Sarita barked at Dario as she pushed past him.

Dario laughed and trailed after her. "I do not understand your desire to hide me out of sight, *Caro*." Dario wrapped his arms around Sarita, his hands enveloping her breasts.

She squirmed and fought to free herself. "Let go of me!"

He brushed her ear with his lips. "Surely, you are not ashamed of your young lover?"

"Dario …" She struggled to mask her hunger for him. "I have an urgent matter to attend to."

He continued to massage her breasts and press his engorged package into her backside.

"You should …" She sighed. "Um, freshen up and …"

He released his hold on Sarita and peeled off her silk robe. He dropped his towel and pressed his cock hard against her ass, his hands back on her breasts. She turned in his arms and kissed him deeply.

Dario lifted Sarita and she wrapped her legs around his torso as he carried her back to the bed. There was no teasing this time when he entered her, and he set an urgent tempo as if he knew she was needed elsewhere. Sarita matched his frenzy and embraced her explosion of ecstasy.

CHAPTER TWENTY-SEVEN

Katelyn took in the stunning ocean view from Christopher's bungalow. The sun hung low in the sky, slowly making its exit from another day in paradise, and a cool breeze blew through the open windows of the cozy cabin. Four walls boxed in the living area and were topped with a tall, pitched ceiling. Katelyn thought this made the small abode seem a tad bigger than the casita at Humberto's. A beige comforter embellished with dark green palm trees covered the double bed that sat at an angle where two of the walls met, making it the centerpiece of the living area.

Blushing at the sight of the bed and the possibilities it might hold, Katelyn swung her gaze to the right side of the space, where a door leading to a bathroom stood slightly ajar. Beyond the white wrought iron headboard, she could see a closet of sorts, where empty hangers hung from metal rods suspended from the ceiling. On her left an antique desk held a pad, pencils in a chipped coffee cup, and an old landline phone.

Christopher worked behind her in a tidy kitchenette, tossing a salad as he spoke to Jade on his phone. Mostly, he seemed to be agreeing with everything she said, with an occasional comment about Adam and how to proceed with finding Mark. He ended the call with, "I'll tell her."

Katelyn met his eyes, which seemed a darker blue tonight, over the rim of her wine glass.

"Jade says hello."

"Is she still with Captain Torres?" Katelyn followed him through the open door onto the wide wraparound porch.

He gave a slight nod and set the salad bowl onto a bistro table. A lit hurricane lamp, a hint of coconut drifting from the chimney, provided the perfect ambiance.

"She's helping Agent Mortieau get Adam to the airport." He pulled his phone from his shorts pocket and checked the time. "In an hour."

"So exactly what crime are Adam and his cohorts accused of committing?" Katelyn sipped some wine. When Christopher didn't answer, she laughed. "Oh, is this like on TV, where you can't talk about an ongoing investigation?"

Christopher's grin crinkled small laugh lines at the corner of his eyes. "Something like that." He stepped closer to her and touched her lips with his. Pulling a chair out for her, he said, "Have a seat and I'll check the grill."

As she sat, Katelyn turned her attention back to the darkening ocean. White twinkle lights were wrapped around the support poles of the porch, giving the quaint cabin a festive feel. The aroma of sizzling beef flowed over her, and her stomach rumbled in anticipation. It had been a few hours since her fish tacos at Joe's.

Christopher joined her, wine bottle in hand, and poured a splash of cabernet into her glass. The red wine was a nice change from her usual margaritas or tequila shots.

"Thanks." Katelyn lifted her glass. "And thanks for inviting me to dinner."

"I thought a proper date might give us a chance to get to know each other." With a clink, he said, "Cheers."

Katelyn took a larger sip than she intended, forgetting one doesn't guzzle vino. "Yes …" She coughed a little, then drank some water. "I'd like that."

Flashing a mischievous smile, he headed back to the grill. "I don't want to burn the steaks since you said you like yours still mooing."

She laughed and watched as he flipped the steaks with an exaggerated flair. Once he returned to his seat, she blurted, "So you and Jade are more than partners?"

Glass halfway to his lips, he paused. "And Stewart is your …?" He sipped some wine.

Their questions hung in the air like strings from pretend soup-can phones.

"Point taken." She picked up her wine, reminding herself to sip. "Where is home, Agent Temple?"

"San Diego," Christopher said. "And you're from Portland?"

"Yes, born and raised Oregonian."

Ignoring his buzzing phone, he asked, "Family?"

"Just me and my mom." She decided not to mention that her mother, along with Stella's mom were enjoying the honeymoon in the Caymans Katelyn couldn't cancel. She definitely didn't want the conversation to circle back around to Stewart. "Were you named after Saint Christopher?"

He fingered the medallion hanging around his neck. "No." He smiled. "My mom gave me the medal for my tenth birthday with a note: *For my traveler son, may the grass never grow long under your feet.*"

Katelyn giggled. "Where did you travel at ten?"

"Just the neighborhood. My dad used to tease, saying he was going to put a bell around my neck so they could find me, like the family cat."

They both laughed, then Christopher said. "And you're an award-winning journalist."

Katelyn's cheeks colored. "I've enjoyed some success as a writer."

"What are you working on now?" He ignored his buzzing phone again.

She hesitated. Would telling him about her interest in the recent deaths in Mazatlán, and how she felt the poisonings were related to previous events in the Mayan Riviera, ruin their evening?

"Well …" she began.

Christopher tipped his glass and waited.

"I've been following various poisoning deaths, which came to my attention last year while I was on vacation at a resort just north of Cancún."

"And you think they're related?" His tone sounded all business.

"Possibly." Katelyn leaned forward and touched his hand. "But I'd rather talk about you." She smiled when he turned his hand palms up, grasping hers, and asked, "Is it just you and your parents?"

Cocking his head slightly, he said. "Okay, we can revisit your article another time." Christopher's phone signaled another incoming text, but he continued, "I have a baby sister who takes care of our parents in Palm Springs. I split my time between the family home in San Diego and an apartment in LA"

"Did you always want to be an FBI agent?"

"I was considered a detective in high school. Tracking down a group of girls who vandalized my buddy's car and uncovering an angry student who kept lighting garbage cans on fire, just to name a few crimes." He ran his thumb across the tops of her fingers. "My senior year of college a recruiter for the bureau convinced me the FBI would be a good fit because I like solving puzzles."

Three rapid pings from his phone suggested someone needed a response. Releasing her hand and holding up a finger, he stood and looked at his phone as he headed for the barbeque.

Katelyn glanced over her shoulder to see him texting before he loaded the steaks onto a platter. Disappearing into the cabin, he returned with another bottle of wine. He one-handed the platter onto the table and then re-filled their wine glasses almost to the top.

"Medium rare." He forked a ribeye onto her plate. "As requested."

Katelyn's mouth salivated, but she refrained from slicing into the perfect cut. Christopher passed her the salad bowl and she served herself, then filled his bowl with the garlicky Caesar. He plucked a *bolillo* roll from the breadbasket, then offered her one.

"How's your steak?" he asked, cutting into his.

Katelyn sliced through the tender meat and its savory juices flowed onto her plate. She forked in a bite and answered with a slight moan, then swallowed. "Delicious."

Christopher raised his glass in toast and then touched hers. "A good start to what I hope will be a perfect evening."

After they sipped some wine, they ate in silence for a few minutes, the rhythmic sound of the ocean serenading them. An earlier breeze had stilled, but the air was still pleasantly cool. Diamonds of light danced on the water as the sun inched its way toward the horizon.

"How long have you and Stella been friends?" Christopher pushed his plate forward.

"Practically since birth." Katelyn tucked the last piece of ribeye into her mouth and washed the bite down with a sip of wine. "My compliments to the chef."

"Thank you." Christopher emptied the bottle into their glasses. "Stella's very protective of you."

"She is." Katelyn folded her napkin. "We both lost our dads as toddlers and neither of us have siblings." A memory fluttered through her mind. They were eight and Stella was slicing their palms with a knife, then the two blood sisters melded their wounded hands together in a death grip. "We made a pact to be sisters and always be there for each other."

He tapped his chest with his finger. "And your new tattoo?"

A rush of heat colored her cheeks. "I had too much to drink at Joe's, so I wondered how I ended up in your T-shirt." She reached for her wine.

"I tossed it to you just in time." A hint of mischief twinkled in his blue eyes. "I saw the tattoo when I covered you with the sheet and the T-shirt dipped down, revealing a dragonfly slicing through a broken heart." His brow furrowed, drawing his eyebrows together. "Something to do with Stewart?"

"Let's just say …" Katelyn sipped some wine. "The tattoo represents closure."

"And …" He pointed to her stripper stripe.

Katelyn fingered the block of hair and giggled. "Stella warned me not to try it myself, but I wanted to announce I'm starting over in a big way."

Christopher touched her glass with his. "To new beginnings."

Sipping some wine, the ocean filled their silence with a soothing melody. Katelyn felt as if she were in a romantic scene from an old school love story set in a tropical paradise complete with a handsome suitor.

"Sorry I left you alone the other night." Christopher said.

Katelyn waved off his apology. "It's not your fault work called you away."

"Still, leaving you alone set you up to be arrested," Christopher continued, "which I still don't understand."

"Captain Torres explained his men were given the wrong room number when they inquired about Paul Fogle." Katelyn shook her head. "What still bothers me is Martínez's overzealousness in arresting me."

"I agree," Christopher said. "And I find it curious you were attacked, because it makes no sense for someone to break into a jail to commit a murder."

She shivered at the memory of the assault and sipped some wine.

"Are you cold?" Christopher asked and stood.

"No … let's change the subject."

"Would you like to take a walk in the surf?" He offered her his hand.

"Is that what's for dessert?" She stood.

He drew her into his arms and murmured, "Hardly." His lips covered hers in a deep kiss.

Katelyn ran her fingers through his curly hair, conveying her own urgency. Christopher picked her up and carried her inside, kicking the door closed with his foot. He laid her on the bed, his kiss growing more intense, and stretched out next to her.

Finally, he released her lips and propped his head with an elbow. "I do have chocolate torte for dessert." He traced her jawline with a finger. "If you're interested."

Katelyn raised up and kissed him, then pulled her tank top over her head. She bussed his lips again. "I'm guessing you can think of something better."

Christopher stood, pulled his T-shirt off, and shed his board shorts, then helped her remove the rest of her clothing. Katelyn ignored her little voice questioning the wisdom of what she was doing—being naked with a man a few years her junior who had a physique Adonis would envy.

"You're so beautiful," he whispered, kissing her neck, then gently tracing her new tattoo with the tip of his finger.

"Does your hand still hurt?"

A husky *no* crossed his lips, but he sucked in air when she tenderly touched his side near the bandaged knife wound. She searched his eyes for a hint of pain, but all she saw was the same longing she felt reflected back at her.

Fighting the urge to pull him on top of her, she touched the tattoo on his upper arm. "Saint Michael?"

He nodded, then placed a soft kiss next to her broken heart artwork before leaving a trail of fire as his lips moved to her breasts.

Katelyn sucked in air when his mouth covered a nipple and dug her nails into his back. Christopher kissed her lips again, then returned his attention to her torso. She glanced at him, then closed her eyes and reveled in the delicious pleasure of his mazattlán.

His exploration stopped just shy of her bikini waxed border and she let out a moan. He chuckled. "Anxious, are we?"

"A tad" She stroked him. "Besides, we have all night for seconds."

"And thirds." He leaned across her, his taut chest brushing her nipples, further igniting her desire.

Christopher fumbled in a nightstand drawer and produced a condom. Katelyn kissed his neck and nuzzled his ear as he tore the small package open with his teeth. He dropped the condom to the bed and kissed her. He held her face in his hands and searched her eyes with a longing stare. She found the condom, pulled it free from the wrapper and dressed him in protection as his lips found hers again.

He hovered above her, pausing at the sound of his buzzing phone. He waited until the noise stopped. Katelyn was in awe of his ability to hold himself up as if he were executing the perfect plank. He gently parted her legs with his knee and lowered to meet her arching hips.

His phone emitted a string of pings.

Christopher held himself in place with one arm and snatched his phone from the bedside table. "Shit!" he said, then climbed from the bed and stood with his back to Katelyn.

He thumbed a number as he gathered his clothes from the floor. He shouldered his phone and headed for the bathroom. "Tell me," he demanded before closing the door.

Worry churned Katelyn's stomach. She jumped from the bed, donning her thong and shorts. Unable to find her bra, she pulled on her tank top, opened the door, and stepped onto the wide porch. Dusk had turned the water a slate blue and stars announced the coming night with faint flashes of light. Katelyn turned to enter the cabin as Christopher stepped outside.

"What is it?" she asked.

"There's been a shooting." He placed his hands on her arms. "I have to go."

"Is anyone hurt?" Katelyn regretted the question as soon as she asked.

"Yes." He kissed her forehead. "I'd really like for you to stay."

She nodded, but said, "Maybe we should have Humberto come get me."

Christopher's jaw muscle jumped. "I'll come back as soon as I can." He kissed her. "Please stay."

"All right."

"I've gotta go." Christopher leaped from the porch. "The torte's in the refrigerator."

Katelyn watched as he climbed into his Jeep and drove away. Sighing, she headed back inside. She would probably need the whole torte and a bottle of wine to cool the fire Christopher had ignited below her bikini line.

CHAPTER TWENTY-EIGHT

Sarita had left Dario in the shower. She told him to wait for her text saying when he could join her for dinner. For her meeting with Eladio, she'd dressed in tan capris, black blouse, and black flats. She hadn't bothered with makeup and had pulled her hair into a loose ponytail. Despite feeling relaxed after her hours with Dario, she still felt exhausted. She looked at the time on her phone and headed for the penthouse door. She'd kept Eladio waiting for fifteen minutes, which had probably done nothing to lessen his annoyance with her for not being available earlier.

When she opened the penthouse door, Eladio leaned against the opposite wall. Without speaking, he grabbed her by the elbow and proceeded to herd her toward the small dining room.

Sarita jerked her arm free. "What the hell are you doing?"

Anger flashed in Eladio's eyes. "Ramos is waiting for you in the lobby." Eladio headed down the hall. "I turned off your elevator to keep him downstairs."

Fuming at being manhandled, Sarita squared her shoulders and followed him.

Eladio marched straight for the bar, grabbed a bottle of Hornitos, and poured a shot. Sarita noticed Alba standing to the side, wringing her hands.

"Alba?" she barked at the maid. *"¿Qué es?"*

"*Señor* Ramos is asking the elevator be turned on," Alba choked out.

Sarita cursed *El Lobo* for bringing the *sicario* into her life. "Is dinner ready?"

"Sí." Alba turned to leave.

"Alba," Sarita said, stopping the maids retreat. *"Por favor*, tell Ramos I have company and I will talk to him *mañana.*"

Alba glanced at Eladio. *"¿Cuántos para la cena?"*

"You always have the cook prepare more than enough." She smiled at Alba. "So, what she's made will be fine."

Relief washed over Alba's face. "Would you like served now?"

"No." Sarita joined Eladio at the bar. *"En quince minutos."*

Alba gave a slight bow and made her exit.

Eladio plucked another tumbler from the shelf, set it next to his, and poured two shots.

"Maybe you have already had enough," Sarita said.

"Maybe I will have had enough after the bottle is empty." Eladio tossed back his second tequila.

Sarita picked up her glass and sat down at the dining table. *"Sentarse,"* she instructed.

Eladio grabbed the bottle and his glass, then took a seat.

Sarita downed her shot and ran a finger over her lips. "Tell me about the shooting."

Eladio added another splash to his tumbler, but before he could drink it Sarita reached across the table and moved the glass toward her. He met her dark stare, the contempt in his eyes making her uncomfortable. She coached herself not to react to his insolence.

"Your *sicario* took it upon himself to take some men and launch an attack at the airport where Meyers was boarding a plane for the States."

"And the outcome?" She willed herself to remain calm.

"Meyers is dead." Eladio reached for his absconded shot glass. "An agent was shot, and you lost three men, including Lieutenant Hernández." He sipped some tequila.

Sarita poured herself another shot. Why hadn't Hernández apprised her of this plan? A sliver of fear snaked through her stomach. What if Ramos had orders to take control of her men? It would be the first step in undermining her and taking away her power.

"The male FBI agent following the American bankers?"

"A female DEA agent." Eladio shook his head. "I do not know her condition."

Sarita thought she saw a flash of worry in Eladio's eyes before he finished his tequila. Why would the DEA be involved in the FBI's quest to arrest the American bankers for laundering her money? A whisper of fear rang an alarm bell in her brain, jumpstarting the muted drumbeat of her hangover.

"How many agencies do you think are involved?" Sarita quelled her anxiety with another sip of tequila.

Eladio shrugged. "I know of the FBI agent. I have seen him with a younger female agent." He held her gaze. "And now the wounded DEA agent."

Alba appeared at the dining room door bearing a tray of food. *"¿Ahora es bueno?"* She asked.

"Sí." Sarita motioned her in. "Please set the tray on the bar."

The aroma of chicken tortilla soup filled the air as Alba walked by. She placed a bowl of fresh guacamole, salsa, and a basket of chips on the dining table, along with two small plates.

"Need something more?" Alba asked, a tinge of nervousness still in her voice.

"No, gracias," Sarita said. "That will be all for the evening."

Alba smiled and quickly left.

Eladio drug a chip through the chunky avocado dip, popped it into his mouth, and poured more tequila. He munched the chip, then said, "Your man in police custody was also dispensed with."

Sarita drained half her shot glass and processed Eladio's news. The loss of her men was unfortunate, but inevitable. She hoped Meyers had died before he shared what little he knew about her and her business. The loss of Lieutenant Hernández would make it easier for Ramos to step into the role, but Sarita still didn't feel like she could trust him.

As if measuring her response, Eladio studied her, and Sarita sensed he hadn't told her everything.

"Do you know where Mark West is?" Sarita asked.

"I know he is no longer in Durango." Eladio selected another chip, dipped it into salsa and took a bite. "The manager at *Banco Azteca* said the three accounts were consolidated into one. He also said several small transfers, each under ten thousand dollars, have been sent to a bank in the States."

"*¡Maldita sea!*" Sarita swore, jumped to her feet, and began to pace. Her money was slipping away! It was only a matter of time before *El Lobo* came to deal with her. Sarita knew the time had come to set her escape plan in motion. She stopped at the plate glass window and stared out at the Pacific. She would miss this view, but it was better to be alive to enjoy another place than to be dead and buried next to the sea.

"*Jefa.*" Eladio stood behind her. "I believe the money has only recently begun to transfer."

Sarita turned to face him, and this time, thought she saw conflict in his eyes.

Eladio took a step back. "I have paid the manager to delay any more transfers for as long as possible."

"And West?" Sarita didn't try to hide her concern. Maybe if she killed the last American banker, she could make peace with *El Lobo*.

Eladio shook his head. "I truly do not know where he is."

"Do you think he will come here?" Sarita made her way back to her chair at the table and poured more Hornito's. "Now that his transfers are being delayed?"

Eladio followed her and resumed his seat. "I would not think so." He pushed his glass toward her for a refill. "But the Americans have not made the best choices."

"And what of the *policía* or the FBI? Will they link the airport attack to me?"

Sarita noticed another flicker of concern in Eladio's eyes.

He nodded. "*Sí*, I believe they will."

Sarita picked up her tequila, but before she could take a drink, Dario strode into the dining room. It annoyed Sarita that her young lover looked refreshed and handsome, dressed in chinos and a salmon-colored cotton shirt.

"*Cariño,*" he said. "What smells so *¿delicioso?*"

Eladio tossed his shot and came to his feet. "I will leave you to your dinner."

Dario extended his hand to Eladio. "Dario Díaz." He smiled at Sarita. "Sarita's ... *amigo cercano.*"

Eladio shook Dario's hand. "It is nice to meet you." He gave Sarita a nod. "I will be available if you should need anything."

Dario blocked Eladio's exit, tilted his head slightly, looked at Sarita, and then back at Eladio. "I feel as if we have met before."

Sarita watched Eladio and wondered at the look of caution clouding his face.

Eladio flashed a smile. "I do not believe so, *Señor Díaz.*" He gave a slight bow. "Enjoy your evening, *Jefa.*"

Warning bells began to chime in Sarita's head as she watched Dario watching Eladio march from the dining room.

When Dario turned his attention back to her, she asked. "Where do you think you know him from?"

Dario leaned down and kissed her, then poured tequila into her glass. "I believe he is a *Federale*." He tossed back his shot.

Sarita didn't miss the flash of anger on Dario's face. And if Eladio Ortiz was indeed a *Federale*, she intended to release her pent-up frustration and rage over not capturing the American bankers on the man she'd thought had her back.

CHAPTER TWENTY-NINE

Punching the Jeep's accelerator, Christopher raced toward the Mazatlán Airport. Jade had been hysterical when he'd finally answered his phone. After a litany of swear words, she'd told him about the shooting. Adam Meyers was dead, along with one of Torres's men. They had managed to take down three of the shooters, but Agent Mortieau had been shot as well.

Jade told him she'd ridden with Sandrine in the ambulance. He was not to come to the hospital, because Torres needed him at the airport. Christopher had agreed with her, but knew he'd be on his way to the hospital as soon as he finished with Torres.

Even though Mortieau had to book herself and Adam onto a commercial flight to Los Angeles, Christopher knew they would board before the other passengers from a secure gate. The downside was they had to cross the tarmac to the plane, which put them out in the open. No one had said it yet, but Christopher assumed Sarita García was behind the shooting.

He could see emergency lights through the gate Jade had told him to take and navigated toward the cluster of police cars. He parked, stepped out, and headed for Captain Torres, who barked orders at a group of policemen. There was no breeze, so smoke from the gunfight hung like a cloud under the harsh lights of the airfield, a lingering metallic blending with the haze.

"Captain Torres," Christopher said. "I just got Jade's call."

"She is very upset about Agent Mortieau," Torres replied. "Gunshot wound to the upper torso, just to the side of her vest."

Surveying the scene, he asked, "Were the shooters García's men?"

"*Sí.*" Torres pointed at the closest body. "I recognize this one. Hernández, one of her lieutenants." He walked toward the next victim. "I do not know this man, but …" he waved toward a covered body, "that is the thug we captured at the hospital."

Christopher followed Torres's line of sight. "Why was he here and not in jail?"

"Sandrine was instructed to bring him with Meyers." Torres shook his head and Christopher knew they were both thinking the same thing: now they had no witnesses against García in custody.

Torres indicated a hanger not far from the plane. "There is another body on the roof." He motioned across the carnage to where a body was being loaded into an ambulance crew. "That is one of my men." He ran a hand through his dark hair.

Christopher flinched at the anguish in Torres's voice. Losing someone under your command, or a partner, or anyone fighting the same fight as you was never easy. Telling their family members, they were gone was almost unbearable.

"What can I do to help?" Christopher asked.

"Come." Torres signaled him to follow. "One of my men took a photo of the assailant who seemed to be in charge. Maybe you can identify him."

Doubtful, but he wanted to help as much as possible. They crossed the tarmac to a second ambulance. A paramedic tended to the head abrasion of a policeman Christopher remembered from the attempt on Adam's life in the hospital.

"Officer Vasquez," Torres said. "Agent Temple."

Vasquez attempted a smile but only managed a scowl. "From the hospital."

Christopher nodded. "Right. Captain Torres said you got a picture of one of the shooters."

Vasquez thumbed his phone alive and handed it to Christopher.

He enlarged the photo. The thug wore a bandana over his nose and mouth. He had narrowed, dark eyes, hair to his chin, and a massive build.

Vasquez reached over and pointed a finger at the man's forearm. Christopher expanded the angle, and a tattoo filled the phone's screen, a black snake in the shape of an *S* with a skull for a head and a devil's tale. Christopher recognized the artwork but looked at Vasquez for confirmation.

Vasquez nodded. *"Sicario."*

Christopher's mind raced with questions. *Had Sarita García hired an assassin? Were they all on the sicario's hit list? Or had someone else with an interest in protecting García's drug empire decided to join the party?*

Christopher picked up his cell to call Katelyn, swearing under his breath when he remembered she didn't have a phone. He hoped she'd fallen asleep. The image of her laying naked in his arms brought him to attention, but his arousal was quickly replaced by his buzzing phone. Jade's name flashed on the screen. He answered with, "I'm on my way to the hospital."

She didn't respond.

"Jade?" He waited. "I'm ten minutes out."

The call ended and he panicked for a beat, thinking Sandrine might have died. What had Torres said? A shot to the side of her vest in the upper left torso. Not necessarily a deadly wound depending on the angle. He shoved the gas pedal to the floor.

When he skidded to a stop at the emergency entrance of Balboa Hospital, a security guard waved him forward. Christopher ignored him and jumped out. "FBI."

He flashed his badge. "My partner's been shot." *Close enough*, he told himself.

The guard held out his hand and Christopher gave him the Jeep keys, then bolted for the ER's double doors.

He found Jade pacing the waiting area. When she saw him, she started to crumple to the floor. He instinctively wrapped his arms around her. "It's going to be okay," he whispered.

Jade sobbed for a few minutes, then pulled away and swiped tears from her cheeks.

Christopher knew to go slow, ask a question, and wait. "You were at the airport?"

She nodded. "Torres and I came to offer additional security."

"Where were you when the shooting started?" He'd already drummed up a mental image of the shootout but wanted her to confirm his theory.

"Inside." She gave him a tortured stare. "Watching from the area where we'd waited for the plane."

"First shot from the sniper on the roof?" Christopher asked.

Another nod. Then a sob. Then quiet. Finally, Jade said, "By the time we joined the fight, Meyers and the goon we also had in custody were dead and there was a lot of chaos."

Christopher's turn to nod. "Understandable." He waited.

Jade wiped her nose with the hem of her T-shirt. "Vasquez fired at the sniper, who retreated." Jade looked puzzled for a moment, then continued. "I'm pretty sure Vasquez was hurt."

"Just scrapes and bruises," Christopher reported. "Tell me about Sandrine."

Jade's shoulders heaved with a fresh wave of tears, and he drew her into his arms again.

A last sob and she pushed off his chest. "I saw a huge thug bearing down on her." Jade looked past him as if she saw the whole thing unfolding again. "I shouted at Sandrine, who had her back to him. She turned as he fired. Bullet entered …" She pointed to her left side, just below her breast. "Here." Anger flashed in her eyes. "I fired on him, but his men closed ranks and he got away."

"Vasquez got a picture of him. His face is covered too much for FRT," Christopher said. "But he has a snake tattoo, complete with skull and devil's tail, on his right forearm."

"*¿Sicario?* You think Sarita—"

A doctor stepped through double doors marked NO ENTRY. He scanned the waiting area, then made a beeline for Jade and Christopher. "I am looking for Agent Mortieau's people."

"That's me." Jade stepped toward the doctor. "Us." She indicated herself and Christopher.

"We have removed the bullet, which nicked a rib and was stopped by muscle before any further damage."

Jade let out a breath. "Thank, God."

"*En efecto,*" the surgeon said. "She is very lucky. You can see her once she's out of recovery. Check with the nurses' station." He gave a small nod before turning his attention to a waiting nurse.

Jade ran her fingers through her hair and slumped into a seat. Christopher sat next to her and waited.

"You don't have to stay," Jade said.

"I'm good," Christopher replied. "I can hang if you want to go get some sleep."

"I'm good." Jade gave him a slight smile.

"You and Sandrine are close?" Christopher probed.

Jade pulled her phone from her back pocket and checked an incoming text. "Torres checking in."

He could tell she didn't want to answer his question, but he planned to wait until she explained her relationship with Sandrine, which seemed more involved than a couple of colleagues.

"Álvarez came to the station." She changed the subject. "Updated Torres on your meeting with Vega."

Jade glanced at him when he didn't respond.

"Fine!" She jumped to her feet. "Sandrine and I worked a case together a little over a years ago." She began pacing. "We were undercover building a case against a drug kingpin in Miami."

Jade stopped. He cringed at the pain he saw in her eyes, but he stayed seated and waited.

"We were always supposed to be undercover at the same time, but one night we got separated and …" Tears resumed streaming down her cheeks. "And …"

Christopher stood and she stumbled into his arms. "It's okay," he whispered into her hair. "You don't have to tell me."

Jade took a deep breath and exhaled into his chest. "I was raped by one of the …" He held her tighter, and she continued, "Only Sandrine knew." Jade stepped from his arms but didn't look at him. "We didn't alert our supervisors because we didn't want our case against the head of the organization to fall apart."

"Thank you for sharing." He kissed her on the forehead. "I know it wasn't easy."

Jade sat back down. "It's in the past."

Christopher's phone pinged and he looked at the text from Captain Torres, then at Jade. "Torres wants to know about Sandrine."

Jade thumbed her phone awake and began texting Torres. "I overheard Torres tell Álvarez one of his officers has been MIA for a couple of days." She looked up from her phone, her brow scrunched with concern.

"And?" Christopher said.

"Torres said it's the officer who arrested Katelyn for Paul's murder." Jade stood. "And then tried to arrest her at Álvarez's. Torres is concerned this Martínez might still be stalking Katelyn."

Christopher headed for the exit doors. "Call me when you've talked to Sandrine."

Outside, he waved at the officer who had parked his Jeep, then swore again remembering he couldn't call and check on Katelyn. *She's fine*, he told himself. Probably enjoyed a slice of torte, had another glass of wine, and went to sleep. *Probably*, echoed in his mind.

He'd be back at the cabin in thirty minutes, but he'd left her alone again and wouldn't blame her for being angry with him. He hoped she'd let him apologize with a hug and a kiss … and … Christopher pushed down hard on the gas.

CHAPTER THIRTY

Sarita stepped to a wall phone, punched *0*, and waited.

"Bueno," a cheery voice answered.

"Necesito hablar con el Señor Ramos," Sarita instructed. "He should be in the lobby."

"Un momento," the voice said, followed by silence.

"Sí." Ramos's baritone filled Sarita's ear.

"Detain Ortiz in his office," Sarita ordered. "I will be there shortly."

"Bien." The line went dead.

Sarita imagined the fear in Ortiz's eyes as the menacing *sicario* approached him. She turned her attention to Dario, who filled a bowl with soup. She could barely contain her irritation as she watched him adding baked tortilla chips and cheese.

"Why do you think *Señor* Ortiz is a *Federale*?" Sarita barked.

He set his bowl down, sat in a chair, and took an exaggerated slurp, holding her gaze as he dabbed his mouth with a napkin.

"A few years ago …" He circled the spoon through the soup. "A friend of mine invited me to a party at a warehouse in the old marina." Another bite. "We had only been there an hour or so before the *Federales* raided the place." Reaching for the Hornitos bottle, he poured a shot into her glass.

Dario looked at the amber liquid, then tossed back the tequila. "They handcuffed us and hauled us to some site deep in the country."

Sarita waited, despite her anxiousness to confront Eladio. She took her tumbler back, filled it, and took a sip as Dario continued.

"The *pendejo* throwing the party didn't know his dad was running drugs and girls out of the warehouse." Dario took another taste of soup, then pushed the bowl away. "Of course, we had our own contraband, so the *Federales* charged all of us with trafficking." Dario leaned back in his chair. "Ortiz interrogated my friend, then I saw him speaking with my dad."

Dario reached again for her glass and finished the shot. "The next thing I know I am being released with all charges dropped. It took two weeks for my friend to be cleared."

When Sarita stood, Dario also came to his feet.

"Cariño ... " Dario stepped close to her. "Let us walk away from the nefarious side of your business."

He searched her eyes. For a moment she wanted to tell him her plan and ask him to run away with her. When she didn't respond, Dario continued unveiling his version of their possible new life.

"Between us, we make enough money to live comfortably." He brushed her cheek with a finger. "Imagine not having to worry about *Federales* or being arrested."

Or being killed, Sarita added mentally.

"Por favor, mi amor ... " Dario kissed her, then said, "Let your *sicario* deal with Ortiz until we finalize our plans for you to retire your crown."

A river of conflicting emotions flowed through Sarita. God how she wished she could just walk away and enjoy a simpler life. She knew it was an impossible dream. She also knew she couldn't tell Dario all her secrets, especially that if she just tried to walk away instead of disappearing, *El Lobo* would see her beheaded—with her crown securely in place.

Sarita bussed Dario's lips, then said, "No, I will speak with Ortiz first." She turned and headed for the elevators.

Dario matched her stride. "At least let me come with you."

She didn't dissuade him and exited the Penthouse. As they waited for the elevator to arrive, her mind raced with questions. *Was Eladio investigating her? Or was he planning to use her to get to El Lobo? Had he been faking having her back all this time?*

The doors whooshed open, and they stepped inside, riding to the lobby in silence. Sarita's heels tapped a staccato on the polished floor tile as she headed for the hallway behind reception. She smiled at a few employees who said hello as she passed by. Normally, the cacophony of many guests checking in would bring her pleasure, but nothing could dislodge the anger building within her—not even the sweet smell of honeysuckle permeating the air from the large *justicia* bouquets scattered about the foyer.

Dario followed closely but remained quiet.

Sarita spotted Ramos standing at Ortiz's office door. He wore his usual monochrome uniform, and the black T-shirt accentuated his muscular build.

"*Jefa,*" he greeted her.

"Any problems?" Sarita's questioning gaze met his cold, dark eyes.

Ramos shook his head.

Sarita glanced at Dario. "Wait here." She entered the office and closed the door.

"*Señorita García.*" Ortiz gave her a wry smile. "My apologies for not standing." He waggled his hands, which were handcuffed to the arm of the chair he occupied.

Sarita noticed Eladio's phone and a Glock on the desk, a .45 caliber bullet and magazine lying next to the weapon.

"Lucky for you, your gun is disabled." Sarita glared at Eladio. "Otherwise, I would gladly shoot you with it."

His smile faded; his brown eyes darker as he held her stare. She wanted him to beg for his life but knew he would be too proud to do so.

"Did you hire the bankers to steal my money?" Despite her resolve to remain calm, anger colored her tone.

Eladio shook his head.

"Are you investigating me? Or *El Lobo*?" she asked.

He nodded. "You as a means to build a case against Castro."

"How much have you told your bosses?"

Uncertainty flashed in his eyes, but he kept his voice void of emotion. "Everything."

"*¡Bastardo!*" Sarita growled despite the skepticism she saw on his face.

"Once I had enough evidence on Castro, I suggested you give up your drug dealings and go legit." Eladio nodded toward an envelope placed in the center of the desk, her name penned in his bold handwriting.

Sarita didn't reach for the packet but turned her gaze back to Ortiz. Another hint of doubt clouded his eyes.

"My resignation letter." He held her stare. "My superiors disagreed with my recommendation to make you a deal." A slight smile curved his lips and for a moment her fury lessened. The memory of their camaraderie fueled by a night of tequila shots flashed in her mind. Her anger flared again, but mostly at herself for thinking she could trust a man. *Any man.*

"I have been pulled from this assignment and had planned to leave tonight." He now offered her a sardonic grin. "It would have been a perfect time to slip away since you have—company."

Sarita swallowed the scathing retort on her tongue. "Why are you still here?"

"Ramos's attack at the airport." Eladio no longer smiled, and deep furrows creased his brow. "I actually considered whisking you away to safety." He shrugged. "Alas your young *lothario* recognized me and ..." He rattled the cuffs. "I am not even able to save myself."

A moment of weakness fluttered her heart and Sarita wished Eladio *had* rescued her. But she knew she could only rely on herself and would need to set her escape plan in motion.

"How much time before the *Federales* come?"

"I do not know," Eladio answered. "I was given a week to extricate myself."

A week, she repeated in her mind. Sarita needed twenty-four hours to prepare to leave. Sadness swept over her unexpectedly and she knew from the softness of Eladio's eyes her face betrayed her. She didn't have time for melancholy or regrets.

Sarita squared her shoulders and Eladio sat as tall as possible in his chair. "I will make arrangements for you to be moved so you do not have to spend the night shackled to a chair."

"As you wish." Eladio nodded, an edge to his tone.

Sarita lifted his phone and knew by the preset factory screen he'd wiped the cell clean before Ramos secured him. She slipped it into her pocket, gave Eladio Ortiz a last look of contempt, and left him wondering his fate.

CHAPTER THIRTY-ONE

Reaching out, Katelyn patted the empty space next to her. She opened an eye, confirming she was alone in Christopher's bed.

"What the …? Why do I keep waking up in a man's bed without the man?" she mumbled into her pillow. She flipped onto her back and stared into the darkness. "I need water," she said past her dry tongue.

After Christopher left, Katelyn had done their dishes and tidied the small kitchen, then rewarded herself with a slice of torte and a glass of cabernet. She took them outside, enjoying the soulful sound of the ocean from the cabin's porch. A second glass of wine led to another sliver of torte. As she savored the slice, she explored the inside of the bungalow. Coming across a dusty copy of James Michener's *Mexico,* she settled into bed with the last of the wine and a bigger piece of torte.

But now, without a phone or clock, Katelyn had no idea what time it was. She yawned, planted her bare feet on the floor, and shuffled to the small kitchen.

Plucking a bottle from the fridge, she noticed the water wasn't very cold, and the fridge light hadn't come on. She flicked the switch above the sink, but nothing happened. She remembered there were lamps on the nightstands flanking the bed, so she crossed to the closest light and twisted the knob. It didn't work either.

Hair stood up on the back of her neck and she sat on the edge of the bed. *Probably just a power outage*, she told herself. Gooseflesh erupted on her skin when the sound of creaking porch boards whispered through the cabin. Katelyn could hardly breathe but knew she couldn't stay where she was. She crept to the area behind the bed that served as a closet and hid next to a four-drawer dresser.

"Sé que estás aquí, puta," a menacing voice echoed through the dark. "Show yourself and we can talk."

Katelyn immediately knew the voice belonged to Officer Martínez. Something about hearing Martínez without seeing him snapped the pieces into place. A flash of memory played like a film clip in her head as she recalled her first sighting of him. He'd been talking to a young woman on the *Malecon*. She'd found him in her lens when she was taking pictures of Valentino's, the building now a ghost of the once fabulous complex that had held several bars and a clear dance floor providing a view of the ocean below. Katelyn snapped a few photos, thinking she could crop the couple from the pictures. To make sure she had a good shot of Valentino's for her travel article, Katelyn walked past Martínez to get a different angle. As she passed by, she heard him tell the woman she needed to do her part or there would be consequences.

"Señorita Graham." Martínez said, evaporating her musings. "I am willing to exchange your passport for the memory card."

Memory card. Katelyn did a mental head slap. She'd taken the full card from her camera and zipped it into the little pocket of the purse she'd had at Joe's the night she met Christopher.

Katelyn heard the crash of the bedside lamp on the opposite side of the room and decided it was now or never to flee. She inched around the dresser using the wall as a guide and bolted for the open cabin door.

Martínez pulled her feet out from under her.

Her forehead bounced off the porch boards. "Shit!" Katelyn freed a leg and flipped onto her back. She kicked out as hard as she could and connected with Martínez's chin.

"You bitch," he growled.

Katelyn rolled onto her knees and tried to crawl away, but Martínez grabbed her by the waist, lifted her off the floor and turned her toward him. She couldn't see him clearly in the dark, but his foul breath made her eyes water. The odor conjured up a memory of the assault in her jail cell. Martínez had been her attacker. Katelyn raised a knee hard toward his jewels but missed the mark.

He pinned her arms behind her back and forced his leg between hers. "I am going to enjoy teaching you how to please a man."

Martínez turned to drag her to the bed and Katelyn managed to free a hand. Blindly reaching out for a weapon, she found the landline telephone on the desk. She gripped the old phone and swung it with all the strength she could muster, aiming for Martínez's head.

A sickening crack was accompanied by a howl, and then a loud thump as he hit the floor.

Katelyn wanted to turn and run, but where? She strained her eyesight bringing Martínez into focus. He lay crumpled at her feet, unconscious. A trickle of blood flowed from the back of his head.

Wiping sweat from her brow, she studied his duty belt, hoping to find his car keys or handcuffs. She finally saw the cuffs and pulled them from the belt, snapped one side around a wrist and looked around for something to secure him to.

The white, wrought iron bedframe gleamed in the darkness. Holding onto the empty cuff, she inched toward the frame, but couldn't quite reach the footboard. Martínez moaned, and Katelyn felt a rush of adrenaline. She pulled him close enough to loop the cuff through the frame before securing his other hand, raising both above his head.

Trying to catch her breath, Katelyn stood and assessed her work. She felt confident Martínez couldn't get free of the bedframe. When Martínez opened his eyes, she jumped, and her heart slammed against her chest.

"¡Te voy a matar, maldita perra!" Martínez yelled, his speech slightly slurred.

Katelyn flipped him off and turned to leave but froze when she heard the bedframe lift off the floor. She whipped around to see Martínez coming to his feet, his hands now low enough for him to reach his shirt pocket. A wave of dread washed over her as she realized what he hoped to retrieve.

"Damn it!" She rushed him. This time her knee connected, and Martínez yowled as he and the bedframe crashed to the floor. Standing as far away as she could, Katelyn reached into his pocket and grabbed the handcuff keys. Martínez regained some composure and kicked out at her, sending her stumbling backwards.

She hovered in the open doorway and matched Martínez's glower with her own scowl. Their stare-down ended when a faint light flickered from his pants pocket.

"Ven, Chica," Martínez taunted. "I will not hurt you."

If she got close enough to retrieve his phone, Katelyn knew he'd be able to hurt her. She remembered seeing a cast iron skillet in a stack of pans on the stove. She marched to the kitchen, grabbed the heavy frying pan, and faced Martínez.

"We can do this the easy way or the hard way," Katelyn said.

Martínez narrowed his eyes at her.

"The hard way then." As she raised her arm, she stepped close enough to nail him with the skillet.

"¡Para!" Martínez yelled.

Katelyn lowered the pan, her arm aching from the weight. "Get on your knees and turn your head toward the bed."

Martínez knelt, sneered at Katelyn, then turned away.

Still lugging her cast iron weapon, Katelyn moved in and quickly snatched the cell from Martínez's pants pocket. She jumped back as he kicked out again, trying to sweep her off her feet.

"This is not over!" Martínez screamed at her. *"Te mataré pero sólo después de que disfrute de tu dulce coño."*

Ignoring his filthy rant, Katelyn thumbed the phone alive. "Seriously!" she yelled, realizing she held a burner. She'd counted on being able to find Captain Torres's number. There was nothing stored in the cheap phone except a few incoming calls. She doubted the calls were from anyone that could help her. Martínez began laughing, a demented sound that emphasized the crazed look in his eyes.

Katelyn skirted around him and grabbed the comforter from the bed, then backed out of the cabin, closed the door, and stared into the darkness. She checked the time on the burner, 10:15. The screen also showed the battery was down to twenty-five percent. Behind her she could hear Martínez cursing and banging the bedframe. He probably couldn't free himself. But if he did, she didn't want to be standing on the porch.

She hurried down the stairs and headed in the direction of the ocean, which continued its never-ending job of pounding the beach. The crashing waves sounded louder in the dark and Katelyn stopped just short of the wet, hard-packed sand. Brine swirled around her as she used the phone's light to search the beach. Lots of sand leading back to palm trees but no houses. And no sight of whatever vehicle Martínez had arrived in, not that he give her the keys willing, nor could she hotwire a car.

Katelyn hadn't paid attention to the drive from Humberto's to Christopher's rented cabin. She recalled driving in from the highway about five miles on a narrow, winding road, but didn't like the idea of trekking down the dark road to the highway. She started to dial 911, then remembered that wasn't the number for emergency services in Mexico. And she didn't know her location.

Katelyn continued to shine the cell's fading light around her and caught something in her second sweep. She crept closer to the large shape, finally illuminating an overturned boat. She huffed a sigh and sat behind the wooden craft. Exhaustion swept over her, and she felt an overwhelming need to close her eyes. Wrapping the comforter around her and sat down next to the boat. She checked the phone and 10:30

winked back at her in dimming red numerals. It was going to be a long night.

"Where the hell is Christopher this time?" Katelyn asked the ocean, which responded with a booming round of waves. Then the tears came, complimented by shivers, punctuated with a round of sobs.

CHAPTER THIRTY-TWO

Racing around a *pulmonia,* Christopher almost hit a gang of drunk tourists in the middle of the road. "Damn it!" He swerved and rode part of the median for a few feet, their shrieks of laughter echoing through the night.

Torres still hadn't answered his phone. Since Christopher didn't have Humberto's number, he felt the only option was to drive back to the cabin. He checked the time on the dash, 10:15. Maybe Katelyn had fallen asleep.

His phone buzzed and he touched the screen to connect Jade's call.

"Hey," he said. "How's Sandrine?"

"I just saw her for a few minutes." Jade sounded as tired as he felt. "She looks terrible, but she's still feisty as hell."

"Let me guess …" Christopher chuckled. "She's demanding to be released."

"Yes, but her doctor said he'd like to keep her for at least a week." Hospital noise reverberated in the background.

"Are you staying with her tonight?" Christopher hit his high beams as the lights of the city faded behind him.

"Sandrine said for me to go home, but …" Her voice trailed off.

"You need some sleep, Jade," he urged. "They'll call you if anything changes with Sandrine." He pictured Jade nodding, chewing a fingernail.

"I'm sure Katelyn's fine. She's probably asleep." Jade yawned. "We should *all* be asleep."

"Do you have a number for Humberto?" Christopher swallowed his own yawn.

"No, sorry," Jade said.

"Have you heard from Torres?"

A sigh, then, "No. Did you call him?"

"Yes. No answer." An oncoming car flashed its lights at him, so he dimmed his.

"If I hear from him," Jade said. "I'll have him call you, or I'll get Humberto's number."

"Okay, I'm headed back to the cabin." Christopher stifled another yawn. "Go home and get some sleep."

"Back at'cha," Jade mumbled. "Talk to you in the morning."

God he was tired. He rubbed his eyes and concentrated on the road. The lights of a gas station shone brightly against the night sky. Christopher pulled into the parking lot. Maybe a Red Bull would help him stay awake. He whipped into a slot, grabbed his phone, and stepped from the Jeep.

At first, he thought he was seeing things when Mark West walked out of the OXXO market. Christopher reached for his badge, which of course he didn't have because he'd left in a hurry. No gun either. He swore under his breath and decided following Mark would be the next best plan, so he climbed back into the Jeep. Feigning interest in his phone, he clicked a couple of pictures of Mark as he got behind the wheel of a silver, two-door sedan.

Mark backed out and exited onto the highway, going in the opposite direction of the cabin. Christopher waited a few seconds, then followed at a safe distance as they made their way back toward the city.

Christopher found Jade's last call and pushed redial.

She answered with, "What's up?"

"I just found West at the OXXO market near the marina." Christopher slowed to keep distance between him and the sedan. "I'm tailing him now."

"Tailing him where?" Jade asked. "I just left the hospital and can head your way."

"We're on a side road off of Cameron Sabalo Avenue, but don't come." Christopher lagged back as Mark slowed down. "I'll call you if I need you."

"Why didn't you just arrest him?" Jade's tone echoed with annoyance.

"No gun or badge." Christopher could picture Jade's eye roll.

"Jesus, C!" Jade said, followed by, "don't do anything without back up."

"Not planning to." Christopher cringed at the edge in his voice. They were both tired and nothing would be gained with an argument over the phone.

"Text me when he lands, and I'll call Torres." Jade continued to bark orders.

"Copy that. And can you make sure Torres asks Humberto to go pickup Katelyn?"

"Yep," Jade replied. "Be careful."

Dead air-filled Christopher's ear, negating a need for any further comment. He concentrated on Mark's car as it made a right hand turn onto a side road which Christopher knew led to the Golden Zone. He must be staying at one of the hotels somewhere along the three mile stretch of beach. But instead of following the road to the left, he stayed right. Christopher knew Mark was headed to Sarita García's resort, Fiesta de Fuego.

"What the hell is he thinking?" He continued following the sedan. "Damn it, I should've made a move at the OXXO station."

Christopher had never been to Fiesta de Fuego but had seen before and after pictures of the transformation from dilapidated compound to extravagant resort. Mark West obviously now had the funds to stay at the high-end hotel, so Christopher was surprised when he continued down the road past the entrance.

After a couple of miles, Mark pulled into the parking lot for Hacienda del Sol, an old but quaint inn. Christopher drove on, then made a U-turn and circled back, stopping on the side of the road across from the parking lot. He watched Mark climb from the driver's seat and head for the hotel lobby. Mark paused to look around, so Christopher leaned over the Jeep's passenger seat. He stayed down for a count of ten, then eased back up just as Mark pushed through the glass entrance door.

Christopher had no idea what Mark's plan might be, but feared the errant banker intended to see Sarita. He checked the battery on his phone, which showed ninety percent. He doubted he'd be able to stay awake all night, so he needed to disable the sedan in case he fell asleep. Christopher dragged a ballcap from underneath the seat and placed it on his head.

The most efficient way to ensure Mark couldn't drive away without help would be to let the air out of a couple of tires. He popped open the glovebox, grabbed a pair of needle-nose pliers, and climbed from the Jeep. Crouching by the back passenger side tire, he removed the valve cap and twisted the metal pin counterclockwise with the pliers. The tire would slowly lose air without him having to hold down the pin. He repeated the process with the front tire, satisfied that Mark would need assistance to before he could drive away.

Back in the Jeep, Christopher rolled down his window and breathed in the cool night air, which carried the scent of grilled fish. He wasn't hungry, but a bag of tortilla chips sitting on the dash would keep him company. Popping one in his mouth, the oily stale taste immediately made him wish he had a Red Bull to wash down his snack. He set the alarm on his phone for midnight, guessing he could stay awake until then. He felt he needed an additional safety net, so he set an alarm for every half hour to help him stay alert.

Christopher settled back against the seat; thankful the temperature wouldn't drop below sixty-two. He trained his eyes on the lobby entrance and contemplated how angry Katelyn might be after being left alone, again, stranded at the cabin. Maybe he should've had Jade stakeout West since the fugitive banker probably wasn't going anywhere tonight. Jade could've cat-napped in her car as he planned to do and waited for West to make his next move. But he knew she was worried about Sandrine and would want to be available if her friend needed anything.

With nothing else to entertain him, Christopher let his mind rehash his questions about Jade. *Was her secret being raped by the drug kingpin? Or was she hiding something else? And what about the text from Sandrine asking if Jade was related to Torres?* Picturing Jade in his mind, he tried to see any resemblance to Torres, but all he could see was Jade, tormented by her past, worried about Sandrine, and striving to be strong despite her inner turmoil.

CHAPTER THIRTY-THREE

Katelyn's chin bobbed off her chest, a thread of drool suspended between the two points like a cobweb. It took a few seconds to remember why she sat on the wet sand, chilled from the cool ocean air. The twilight of dawn scattered light across the tops of palm fronds and shards of daylight pricked the earth below.

Unable to relax, the last thing Katelyn recalled before finally falling asleep had been the moon drifting toward the eastern horizon and the lightening skies snuffing out the stars.

"Well at least I didn't sleep long." She jumped to her feet and fled from the encroaching tide. Foaming waves swallowed the capsized boat and washed away her ass print in the sand. She took a minute to enjoy the ocean's changing color—from steel gray to light blue as daylight smiled on the undulating water.

Inhaling sea brine, Katelyn looked toward the cabin, and patted her grumbling stomach. "Well, you can forget going in search of breakfast." She looked around for a suitable place to hide and wait … for what? Maybe now she should navigate the road from the cabin back to the highway and flag down a passerby for help? As much as she hated the idea, she should probably check on Martínez to make sure he was still secured to the bedframe. She brushed sand from her hands and fingered her hair away from her face.

The rank smell of decaying seaweed blended with the ocean breeze as Katelyn trudged through the sand toward the cabin, the crashing waves making it hard to hear any other sounds. Carefully climbing the wooden stairs, she prayed the weathered wood would not groan under her weight and announce her arrival. Katelyn paused at the edge of the porch, draped the damp comforter over the railing, and cursed herself for closing the cabin door.

She inched forward to avoid any creaking boards and flattened herself against the rough wall. Breathing deeply to calm her nerves, she mentally coached herself. *If Martínez had freed himself, he would have come after her. Right? Obviously, he still sat cuffed to the bedframe. Probably.*

Katelyn turned the knob and toed open the door, but still stood to the side so Martínez wouldn't see her. Heart beating against her ribs, she waited for the explosion of swear words she expected him to hurl at her.

Silence.

Panic sent her pulse racing. Maybe the whack on the head with the old phone had killed him. More deep breathing and Katelyn poked her head around the jamb. "What the hell?" She stumbled inside toward the bed, careful not to step in the small pool of blood on the floor where Martínez had been sitting. Following dried red droplets, she eventually saw where a white swirl had been bent and separated from the wrought iron frame.

"Seriously!" Katelyn kicked the bed frame and pain shot up her leg. "Shit!" She hopped on one foot, turning a circle, scanning the small abode for any signs of the crazy lieutenant. The only thing she saw was his parting gift—he'd left her bra hanging from the bedframe.

Her stomach rumbled, her headache demanded coffee, and her bladder threatened to burst. But first things first. Katelyn grabbed the cast iron skillet and proceeded to check every nook and cranny where Martínez might be hiding. Satisfied the corrupt cop wasn't lying in wait for her, Katelyn grabbed her bra and tucked into the small bathroom to silence her bladder.

Hands washed, she gripped her weapon and headed for the kitchen, stopping abruptly by the queen bed. What if Martínez had slunk his way underneath? The sheets were still askew and there was no bed skirt, not to mention it was a very narrow space. Katelyn gathered her courage and leapt into the middle of the bed, her weight compressing the mattress and box springs toward the floor, the heavy skillet slamming into her knee. "Ouch!"

She sighed. "Damn! I think the asshole escaped." She pushed off the bed and headed for the fridge. Unless Martínez had helped himself, there should be one last piece of torte. "Yes!" She set the frypan onto the stove, lifted the cardboard plate from the box and set the torte onto the sliver of counter next to the sink. "Now, coffee." Katelyn licked chocolate from her thumb. She opened a cupboard and froze at the sound of creaking boards. Her eyes on the open door, she groped for her weapon.

Another squeaking plank, then, "Katelyn?"

"Humberto!" rode out on the breath she'd been holding. She set her pan down and rushed toward him.

"Sí." He glanced at the cast iron skillet, then searched her eyes. "You are, okay?"

Katelyn nodded. "Yes, fine." Tears threatened her composure, and she stepped back from Humberto. "How did you know to come?"

"Agent Temple," Humberto answered, "he told Jade something urgent came up and he had left you here alone, but she did not reach Marco until early this morning. I came as—"

"What the hell!" Stella shouted from the porch, then stepped into the cabin. "Is she—" She rushed to Katelyn and wrapped her in a hug. "Jesus, Lyn, I can't believe Agent Hottie left you here all alone!"

"I'm okay." Katelyn gave Stella a tight hug, then held her at arm's length.

Humberto had moved to the end of the bed and stooped down to the floor. "Blood?" he asked.

"Martínez was here." Katelyn shook her head. "But he escaped."

"For chrissake!" Stella grabbed Katelyn by the arm. "That's it! We're going home!"

"Ella …" Katelyn covered her friend's hand with hers. "I'm alright." Then she said to Humberto, "I want to tell you, and Torres, everything. But I could really use some coffee." She returned to the kitchen, put the torte back in its box, and then headed for the door. "And a shower."

Katelyn stomped down the steps and marched to Humberto's car. Stella was right, Agent Hottie shouldn't have left her at the cabin alone. If she could, Katelyn would pack her things and leave Mazatlán. But when Christopher's blue eyes flashed in her mind and the memory of his lips on hers sparked the fire still simmering below, Katelyn's resolve to leave melted. Clearly, the lack of a passport wasn't the only reason she had to stay in paradise … for a little longer.

CHAPTER THIRTY-FOUR

The loud air compressor jolted Christopher awake. He sat up and strained to see around a repair truck parked behind the passenger side of West's car. Someone was holding an air hose against the flat tire. No sign of Mark West.

Christopher checked the time on his phone. 7:12 AM. He knew the tire wouldn't inflate until the stem was realigned. That would give him time to devise a plan to talk to, and hopefully, capture West.

While he waited, he checked his text messages. Two from Jade, the first saying she'd given Torres a message about Katelyn being alone at the cabin. The second saying she would be at Humberto's later this morning.

He replied: *Staked out West. Waiting for him to appear. Hoping to talk to him without incident.*

Relief relaxed his tired, stiff muscles. Katelyn was safe at Humberto's. He mentally ran through ideas of how to apologize for leaving her alone … again. *Flowers? Dinner? Tequila?*

Christopher's thoughts scuttled away when he spotted Mark heading for the sedan. He sat up, hand on the Jeep's doorhandle, and waited for Mark to be caught up in a conversation with the repairman.

Mark tossed a duffle bag into the back seat and looked toward the Jeep. Christopher looked down hoping the bill of his cap would hide his face. He waited, then took a quick peek. Mark was leaving the parking lot, ignoring the man calling after him, and heading for the beach.

Christopher jumped from the Jeep and jogged after Mark. "Damn it!" Christopher shifted to a run as Mark turned the corner at a small shopping mall. Following, Christopher plowed into early workers sweeping out their shops and displaying their wares. He offered apologies in response to their startled squeals and lengthened his stride. He could see Mark crashing through an outdoor cafe, picking up speed, and widening the distance between them.

Christopher shouted, "Sorry," as he danced through guests holding their breakfast plates, the aroma of *chorizo* following him as he pressed on. His lungs burned as he increased his pace, and he was thankful for the cool morning air. But he cringed when he saw Mark turn down a sideroad that dead ended onto a bluff.

"Where the hell does he think he's going?" Christopher closed the distance between them in time to see the dumbass jump down onto the sand.

Christopher stopped at the edge of the hill and saw Mark headed south down the beach. "Shit!" Running in sand would really test his endurance, but he leapt anyway. His hand burned when the knife wound split opened, and he sucked in air as the stitches in his side pulled at his skin. He jumped to his feet, wiped sweat from his brow, and continued his pursuit.

The deep sand had slowed Mark's progress and Christopher wondered why he hadn't made his way to the wet, hard-packed surface. The answer came when Mark cut to his left, thrashing through weeds and underbrush on his way to the Pueblo Bonito Mazatlán resort. He was headed for the streets.

Christopher gathered what strength he had left and sped up, his body screaming in pain with every step. Instead of following Mark's path, he continued onto the steps leading up from the beach to the hotel.

He knew the property had been fenced in recently to keep out non-guests and other riffraff. He took the stairs two at a time, skirted the swimming pool, and pushed through glass doors to the lobby.

Christopher scanned the guests and staff milling about but saw no sign of Mark. A maid came toward him and pointed to the floor. He looked down and saw drops of blood, which meant Mark was hurt. He must've injured himself scaling the fence. Christopher strode toward the lobby's main doors and stepped outside, the warm air a precursor to the day's impending heat.

Cars clogged the hotel's wide driveway and Christopher had to dance around arriving guests and hordes of luggage. He arrived at the street to find Mark trying to board a city bus as it chugged away from the curb. Mark spotted Christopher and banged harder on the side.

Christopher reached the bus's rear bumper as the doors opened and Mark climbed aboard. Mark held his head through the open door, smiled, and gave Christopher a one finger salute.

Christopher paid the Uber driver double his fare since the man was kind enough to give him a towel to wrap around his bleeding hand. The man flashed a *hang loose* sign in appreciation and sped off. Christopher made his way through the Hacienda del Sol parking lot to West's abandoned sedan. Officer Vasquez pushed off a fender and held the duffle bag out to Christopher.

Christopher grabbed the straps. "Did you look inside?"

Vasquez shook his head and pointed to one end. A padlock held the zipper tabs together.

Christopher smiled. "I hope there's incriminating evidence inside." He squished the duffle with his good hand, checking for anything hard, like a gun. "How did West register?"

"Adam Fogle," Vasquez answered.

Christopher squinted at Vasquez and ran the fictitious name through his brain. By using Adam's first name and Paul's last, it was clear West wasn't trying to hide. "And what about Martínez?"

Vasquez shrugged. "We have not located him." Vasquez pointed at Christopher's hand. "You, okay?"

Christopher nodded. "Yes."

Vasquez continued, "And I am to tell you *Señorita* Graham is safe and at *Señor* Álvarez's."

"Gracias." Christopher gestured at the car, which still had two flat tires. "And the sedan?"

"The rental company is sending a tow truck." Vasquez looked at his phone. "I am needed at Costa de Oro."

"Something I can help with?" Christopher asked.

"Following up on another poisoning last night." Vasquez headed toward his patrol car. "Captain Torres plans to update you."

"Understood." Christopher handed the duffle to Vasquez. "Ask Torres to hold this for me."

Vasquez tossed the bag onto the passenger seat, gave Christopher a mock salute, then jumped into his car and drove away.

Christopher strode to his Jeep, climbed behind the wheel, and headed for Cameron Sabalo Avenue. He doubted Mark West was stupid enough to leave any information regarding Sarita García's absconded funds in the duffle, but the bag indicated West was traveling light and probably had somewhere else to stay. Finding him could be challenging—unless he really was stupid enough to use his dead cohorts' names as aliases again.

Christopher mentally thanked Humberto for bringing Katelyn back to his place as he navigated the morning traffic. Heat infused his cheeks as he imagined Katelyn's anger. Once again, he shifted his thoughts to an apology gift, but what said, *"I'm so sorry for leaving you alone—again?"*

CHAPTER THIRTY-FIVE

Eladio's blank phone mocked Sarita from the center of the small dining table. Ignoring her now cold breakfast, she picked up her cup and sipped lukewarm coffee. Her night had been spent pacing her bedroom, ignoring Dario's persistent sexual overtures, and she'd been thankful when dawn arrived.

The rising sun sparked aqua diamonds across the ocean's surface. Sarita suddenly longed to be splashing in the surf as if she hadn't a care in the world. But she had more than one worry to deal with. The sooner she had an exit strategy, the sooner she might be able to stroll in the ocean's frothy water, trouble free.

Her escape plan might afford her such luxury if she executed her exit without error. Sarita had checked the safe in her office before dawn, double checking her new passport, and verifying bank statements showing the current value of the funds she'd tucked away for years. She'd touched the keys for the Audi she'd stashed at the rental house where her new life would begin. Lastly, she'd contemplated the gun she hoped she wouldn't need to use.

An underling coughed behind her, and she motioned him into the small dining room without turning.

"*J–jefa,*" he stammered. "*He terminado de revisar la computadora de Ortiz.*"

"And?" Sarita finally looked at the young man and offered a smile. She needed to put him at ease so he could share what he had learned from Ortiz's computer. "Did you find anything of interest?"

"*Sí ...* " Nodding, he cleared his throat. "He has reports on several people I think may be of importance." He set the laptop onto the bistro table and refreshed the screen.

A four-by-four picture of a smiling man with striking blue eyes and curly blond hair stared back at her. To the right of the photo, she read his specifications. Name: Temple, Christopher R., Age: 32, Agency: FBI Special Agent, Current Assignment: Mazatlán/Sarita García.

Sarita stared at the photograph, memorizing the face of the agent sent to take her down. *Well, he hasn't succeeded ... yet*, she said to herself.

The underling coughed again, and Sarita shot him an angry look, instantly regretting the mistake. "And there are more files like this?"

"*Sí.* " He nervously pointed to the Word document symbol. "If you click the icon, you can view the other documents."

Sarita clicked on the blue logo and the screen filled with other files to choose from. She gave the underling a warm smile. "*Gracias*. I can manage from here."

The young man gave a slight bow and made a hasty exit.

Sarita selected the next document and the face of Marco Torres appeared. Though she had never met Torres, Sarita already knew his background and status as captain of the *Policía de la Ciudad de Mazatlán*. She studied his image, sensing something familiar about the dark eyes, jet black hair, and sensuous lips. Maybe he seemed familiar because she followed news clips of him at various crime scenes once she'd decided to purchase Fiesta de Fuego.

She opened the next file and recognized the face of Humberto Álvarez. Álvarez was well-known throughout Mazatlán for his various enterprises, all legal, and his generosity in funding things like the new animal shelter and an art gallery for local artists. Álvarez had also financed the opening of *Casa del Ángel*, a shelter for battered women. Sarita had originally become aware of Álvarez when he helped Clara Marsh escape after she killed Damian.

After I disappear, I will have time to search for Clara and make her pay, Sarita told herself.

A whisp of anger flitted through her mind, but she dismissed it with a click and opened the next document, revealing the photo of a young female. Sarita's breath caught in her throat when her mother's eyes stared out at her from the picture. Her hand shook as she fingered the cursor to the zoom function and enlarged the photo. The woman appeared to be in her twenties and had long, jet black hair to compliment her dark, brown eyes. She hadn't smiled for the photo, her full lips set in a hard line as if having her picture taken annoyed her.

Sarita scanned the girl's specifics. Name: Mendoza, Jade, Age: 24, Agency: DEA, Current Assignment: Mazatlán/Sarita García. *Eladio did not say Jade is a DEA*, Sarita thought, curiosity brewing in her mind.

"Nena," Dario said, placing his hands on her shoulders. "What is so interesting you did not hear me call your name?"

Sarita lowered the laptop screen before Dario could see what held her attention. "Nothing." She stood and stepped into his embrace. He smelled of her herbal shampoo and she allowed him a longer-than-necessary kiss but pushed away when his hands slipped under her cotton blouse.

"You are so tense, *cariño*." Dario tried to pull her to him. "Come, let me help you relax."

Sarita ignored him. "I will have Alba bring you some breakfast." She lifted the wall phone receiver.

"Sí but have her deliver a tray to the bedroom." Dario flashed a lusty grin.

Sarita shook her head. "I have work to do." She held up a finger. *"Alba,* please bring breakfast for *Señor* Díaz."

She replaced the receiver, crossed back to the table, and scooped up the laptop. "You will need to entertain yourself for a few hours." Sarita headed for the elevator.

"Sarita, I am worried about you confronting the *Federale*." Dario grasped her hand. "Would it not be better to have your *sicario* kill him and be done with the matter?"

Sarita spun around. "How I handle Ortiz is no concern of yours. *¿Entender?*"

Dario narrowed his eyes at her curt tone. "*Entendido, Jefa.*" He held her stare before she exited the dining room.

Sarita crossed to the elevator and punched the down arrow several times. She hadn't decided what to do about Eladio Ortiz. She intended to glean whatever information he had regarding the FBI and DEA's investigation concerning her. She hoped extracting what he knew didn't require torturing him. Or … killing him.

CHAPTER THIRTY-SIX

On the car ride back to his house, Humberto insisted Katelyn share the details of her encounter with Martínez. As she outlined the corrupt police officer's attack, Stella punctuated Katelyn's story with an occasional expletive.

Katelyn offered her theory of Martínez's involvement in the Bump and Run theft ring and that he'd most likely tried to kill her in jail. Captain Torres had his hands full with another poisoning at Costa de Oro, so Humberto texted her theory to Marco suggesting he dispatch other officers to hunt down Martínez.

Back in the casita, Katelyn stripped off her clothes and stepped under the steaming hot water. She started with her hair, hoping the shower head's cascading jets would dislodge sand hiding in every crevice. The fogged mirror reflected her face as a ghostly mirage before she toweled away the moisture. Christopher's compliment from last night, *You're so beautiful*, echoed in her mind. She studied her image and struggled to see what he saw.

"Obviously, he's blind," Katelyn told the mirror, then stepped in front of the small closet. She selected a blue knit skirt with a white tank top and dressed. She found Stella seated at the nook in Humberto's kitchen; waiting for her with arms folded across her chest, foot bouncing from a leg crossed over a knee.

Katelyn grabbed a cup of coffee, cut the last piece of torte in half, and served them each a slice. She washed down a bite of torte with a sip and met Stella's questioning gaze. Her BFF, staring at Katelyn as if she'd lost her mind, hadn't said a word.

"What?" Katelyn forked in another bite.

Stella gestured at the torte. "Is this what you had for dessert last night?"

Katelyn's cheeks burned as she licked chocolate from her thumb. "We didn't have time to … um … have dessert."

"I knew it!" Stella reached for her coffee cup. "I get that Agent Hottie is hard to resist, but we need to find a way to leave Mazatlán before psycho cop kills you."

Katelyn set her fork down and held Stella's angry stare. "I agree, Ella." She kept her tone neutral. "Martínez is a problem."

"A prob—"

Katelyn held up a finger. "But you know I can't leave without a passport. Maybe Christopher can help me replace mine now that Martínez has admitted stealing it."

"Which Agent Hottie should do ASAP."

"He's been kind of busy."

Stella snorted. "I'll say."

"Look …" Katelyn stabbed another bite. "I'm on vacation."

"Yes, but—"

"No!" Katelyn waggled the empty fork at her friend. "There's *no* but! I'm tired of being angry. I'm tired of being sad. And …" Katelyn swallowed a sob. "I'm tired of feeling …" She swiped at tears pooling in her eyes.

"Oh, Lyn …" Stella reached out and grasped Katelyn's hand. "I'm going to fricking kill Stewart!"

Katelyn laughed. "Get in line." She sipped some coffee. "Stewart robbed me of my happy ending, so I guess I'm looking for a little—"

Stella grinned. "Passionate sex with Agent Hottie?"

Color warmed Katelyn's cheeks as she nodded. "Exactly!"

"Maybe you should chain the sexy agent to the bed in the casita?" Stella swallowed a bite of torte. "That way he can't leave you in the middle of the night."

Katelyn's blush deepened and she giggled. "Then *I'd* never leave the casita."

The two friends stifled their laughter when Humberto joined them, phone to his ear. He continued his call and poured a cup of coffee. "*Sí*, Jade." Humberto sat in a chair at the nook dining table. "We will be here. See you soon." He placed his phone on the table and sipped some coffee.

"Humberto," Stella began. "We were just wondering, since you know Martínez has Katelyn's passport, can't you arrange for her to get a replacement?"

Humberto set his cup down. "Marco has contacted Juan Vega to see if he knows where Martínez might be hiding." He shrugged. "No luck so far. Also, I believe a replacement passport would be better handled by Agent Temple."

"Any idea of where the elusive Agent Hottie is?" Stella smiled at Katelyn and forked in her last bite of torte.

"*Sí*. He is on his way here to meet with Marco." Humberto nodded. "There has been a development regarding the last remaining banker." His phone buzzed and Humberto checked the screen, then took another sip of coffee. "Katelyn," he said. "I am sure you have no plans to go sightseeing, but I would like you to promise you will not leave here unless Marco or I go with you."

"Funny you should mention not leaving the premises." Stella grinned at Katelyn. "We were just discussing ideas for how to entertain ourselves here at *Casa Álvarez*."

Humberto cocked an eyebrow, then asked, "Katelyn, do you have the camera memory card?"

Katelyn nodded and slid the small chip across the table to Humberto. "I don't know how you'll view the contents without my camera."

Stella leaned close and peeked at the memory card. "It should fit any camera."

"¡*Bueno!*" Humberto stood. *"Un momento."* He hurried from the kitchen with the memory card.

Katelyn gathered her dirty dishes from the table and carried them to the sink. María had gone to the market for groceries, so Katelyn rinsed the dishes and placed them in the dishwasher. Stella brought her cup and plate to the counter.

"I'm glad Humberto suggested you stay put." Stella handed Katelyn a fork.

Katelyn kept rinsing and loading, finally looking at her friend. "Ella, I know you're worried, but Christopher didn't expect to be gone long when he left me alone in the cabin."

Stella shrugged. "Maybe." She grabbed the almost empty coffee carafe, poured the remnants down the drain, and handed the glass pot to Katelyn. "But he's left you alone twice, and both times put you in harm's way."

Katelyn handed the now clean carafe back to Stella, who grabbed a dishtowel and dried the water drops. "But neither time was intentional, and you should blame me for the first time. If I hadn't had too much to drink, I would have made it back to Emerald Bay and been fine."

"I guess Martínez might've found you at the resort anyway," Stella speculated. "Since he wanted the memory card so bad."

Katelyn dried her hands. "Let's sit outside in the sun for a while," she said and headed for the door. Grabbing two bottles of water from the fridge, Stella followed Katelyn onto the patio. They each stretched out on a lounge chair, closed their eyes, and basked in the warm, mid-morning sun.

Katelyn soon became lost in her thoughts. The memory of Christopher's lips on her breasts erupted gooseflesh along her arms. She could still feel his hands on her skin and knew she wanted to finish what they'd started last night. Her reverie was interrupted by Humberto as he burst onto the patio.

"The memory card does fit my camera!" He continued to stare at the digital screen. "I found the photos of Martínez, and I think I know the woman he is talking to." Frowning he showed them the photos. "I need to ask Marco to be sure, but I think this woman was the supervisor for El Cid's housekeeping department."

"Was?" Stella asked.

Humberto's frown lines deepened. "I believe her body was found in the rocks below Valentino's."

"Shit!" Katelyn jumped to her feet. "Do you think Martínez killed her?"

"Possibly." He checked the time on his phone. "We'll need to ask Marco, who should be here any minute."

The kitchen door opened and María appeared. *"Señorita Jade está aquí,"* she announced.

"Bueno." Humberto headed toward the house. "We will have lunch in an hour," he called over his shoulder before the kitchen door closed.

"Lyn …" Fear shown in Stella's blue eyes and Katelyn braced herself. "We seriously need to find a way to get you out of Mazatlán."

"What I seriously *need* is a drink!" Katelyn jumped to her feet. She knew Stella was right, as long as Martínez was on the loose, Katelyn wouldn't be safe. She crossed the patio and reached for the knob as the door swung open.

"I'm so glad you're here." Christopher gathered her in his arms. "I know it's lame, but I *am* very sorry for leaving you alone—"

Katelyn clung to him and wished Christopher would whisk her away some place safe.

"Hey." He held her from him. "What's wron—"

Standing, Stella said, "We just found out that Martínez probably killed a woman who worked for the El Cid."

"Ella …" Katelyn began.

Stella glared at Christopher. "I'll give you two a moment." She stalked across the patio and into the house.

"She's right to be mad." He wrapped his arms around Katelyn. "I shouldn't have left you alone, *again*, last night."

"I'm fine." Katelyn hugged him and he flinched. "You're hurt." She touched his blood-stained shirt.

"It's nothing," Christopher said as she reached for his wounded hand.

"It's more than nothing." She pointed to a chair. "Sit."

"Katelyn," he began.

"No arguing," she said over her shoulder.

She found María in the kitchen preparing chicken tostadas for lunch. *"Hola, María,"* Katelyn greeted the maid.

"Hola." María continued chopping tomatoes.

"Do you have a first aid kit?" Katelyn asked.

María nodded. *"Sí, sí."* She motioned for Katelyn to follow her to the laundry room. The petite maid grabbed a stepstool, climbed two steps, and stretched to reach the top shelf. She grabbed the kit and handed it down to Katelyn.

"Gracias." Katelyn offered her hand to assist the maid's descent.

María went back to her lunch prep and Katelyn headed for the patio. She stopped short when she saw Jade down on her knees inspecting the wound in Christopher's side. Flushing from head to toe, she cursed herself for being jealous of his beautiful young partner.

Stella opened the kitchen door into Katelyn's back. "Shit, Lyn!"

Katelyn turned to find her friend laden with a bucket of iced beer and a bowl of limes. Stella looked past Katelyn, then they exchanged a knowing look.

"I'll take those." Katelyn took the bowl of limes and headed for the patio table. She paused and offered the first aid kit to Jade. "This might help."

Jade smiled at Katelyn. "Thanks." She placed the kit on the concrete and popped it open.

Katelyn met Christopher's eyes for a moment before Jade held up a brown bottle and exclaimed, "This should do the trick!"

"Get that shit away from me, Jade!" Christopher stood and backed away from his partner.

"Sit your ass down, C!" Jade ordered. "The wound in your side is infected and your hand smells like dead fish."

Katelyn read the label of the bottle, *Peróxido Hidrógeno*, and guessed Jade planned to douse Christopher's injuries with hydrogen peroxide.

Christopher shook his head and glared at Jade. "There's got to be something else. That stuff burns like—"

Humberto joined them, bottle of tequila and shot glass in hand. He took in the scene and nodded. "Ah, María suggested I bring this to you." He poured a shot and handed the glass to Christopher. "It will help take the sting out of the *peróxido*."

Christopher glared at Jade, tossed the shot, and blew out a ragged breath. He angled his long frame back into the lounge chair.

"Maybe you should go hold his hand," Stella whispered in Katelyn's ear.

Katelyn shot Stella a look, but her attention shifted to Jade lifting Christopher's T-shirt over his head.

"Damn," Stella whispered, and Katelyn worried she might actually whistle.

Jade pushed Christopher's shoulders back onto the lounge chair and peeled the blood-soaked gauze from his wound. "Katelyn," she said without looking up, "can you bring a bowl of hot water and some washcloths from the casita?"

Katelyn startled at the request but recovered with a nod. As she stepped inside the casita, she heard Christopher say, "Humberto, can I have the bottle of tequila?"

Stella had followed her and rummaged through bathroom cupboards in search of washcloths. Arms full of clean rags, she met Katelyn back at the kitchen sink. "Do you think these will work?"

Katelyn turned off the hot water. "Yep." She lifted the large bowl from the sink and followed Stella back to the patio.

Christopher had the tequila bottled tipped to his lips and took a long pull as Jade prodded the slice on his left hand. Katelyn winced at the pain in his eyes despite his attempt to smile at her.

Stella added the rags and said, "Jesus …" She wrinkled her nose. "Maybe he should have a doctor check his injuries?"

"Probably." Jade dunked a rag into the water, wrung it out, and wiped grime from Christopher's hand. "But he doesn't have a fever yet and we're supposed to avoid doctors and hospitals."

Christopher sucked in air and closed his eyes. "Humberto, tell me about Martínez," he said.

"Thanks to Katelyn," Humberto smiled at her, "we believe Martínez is behind the Bump and Run theft ring."

Christopher opened his eyes and looked at Katelyn. "And?"

"This is going to hurt." Jade applied peroxide to the cut in Christopher's hand.

"Damn it, Jade!" He tried to pull his hand away.

"Stop squirming!" Jade shouted back. "I'm almost done."

Christopher took another pull from the tequila bottle, then said, "What aren't you two telling me?"

Katelyn glanced at Humberto, then back at Christopher. "Martínez found me at the cabin after you left—"

"What?" Christopher jerked his hand free. "Jade, enough!"

"C …" Jade sat back on her heels. "I need to finish this, or you *will* need to go to a doctor."

"Agent Temple," Humberto said. "Katelyn actually captured Martínez, but he managed to escape."

"Katelyn …" Christopher's eyes met hers with a concerned gaze as Jade resumed treating his hand. "I'm so sorry for putting you in danger—again." He shifted his attention to Humberto. "I'm assuming Torres's men are looking for Martínez."

Humberto nodded. *"Sí."*

María stepped through the kitchen door and motioned for Humberto to come inside. *"Perdona,"* Humberto said to Christopher, then headed for the house.

Jade tied off the gauze she'd wrapped around Christopher's hand. "I'm not sure how long the medical tape will hold." She tied a final knot. "But at least the wound's clean now."

"It'll be fine." Christopher took another hit from the tequila bottle. He looked down at the oozing wound on his torso, then at Jade. "Let's get this over with."

"Sorry, C …" Jade attempted a smile as she picked up the peroxide bottle. "This one's really going to hurt."

Katelyn moved closer to the makeshift triage center. "What can I do to help?"

Christopher set the tequila bottle down and took her hand. "Maybe now is a good time for you to regale us with the story of how you managed to apprehend Martínez."

"I'm going to see if I can help María with lunch." Stella pointed to the house. As she passed by Katelyn, she scooted a lounge chair closer to her friend.

Jade pushed on Christopher's wound, expressing a foul-smelling gob of puss. Christopher gasped and crushed Katelyn's hand in his. His eyes held her worried stare. Leaning in and touching her lips to his, she said, "Just breathe."

CHAPTER THIRTY-SEVEN

Christopher wiped steam from the casita's bathroom mirror. He'd ignored Jade's order not to take a shower and rinsed off anyway, careful to keep water off his wounds. Difficult, but doable. He checked his injured hand and wrapped a length of clean gauze around his palm. The wound in his side looked angry but felt better. Pain shot through him again when he applied a new bandage.

He looked at his haggard face and lifted his razor from his duffle, which also contained clothes, deodorant, and a toothbrush. He'd learned after too many overnight stakeouts to always have the bag stocked and stowed in whatever vehicle he was driving.

As he removed his stubble, Christopher's stomach growled. Clearly, his few bites of chicken tostada after Jade's medieval torture hadn't been enough to stave off hunger. His last memories before passing out in the lounge chair were Katelyn holding his hand and Jade saying she'd bring him the duffle.

Obviously, he'd needed the two hour nap, but now he wanted to hear more about Martínez and hoped Torres had a plan to arrest the rogue cop.

He dressed and headed into the house to find the others. As soon as he stepped into the kitchen, he heard Lucía explaining brushstroke techniques to someone. When he came even with the dining room, he found Lucía and Stella examining a painting of a catamaran cutting through azure waters.

Stella gave him a wry grin. "He lives."

"Ladies," Christopher said.

"Agent Temple …" Lucía began.

"Please, call me Christopher."

"*Sí*, Christopher." She smiled. "The others are in Humberto's study."

"*Gracias.*" Christopher's stomach rumbled.

"Would you like something to eat?" Lucía asked.

Christopher shook his head. "I don't want to be any trouble."

"No trouble." Lucía pushed past him. "I will have María bring you a plate."

"Thanks, Lucía." Christopher continued toward the study.

"Wait!" Stella commanded.

Christopher rolled his eyes, then mustered a dazzling smile and faced Stella.

She offered him a sardonic look. "I don't usually meddle in Katelyn's business …"

Christopher did a slight head shake. "Of course, you don't."

Stella narrowed her eyes. "But she's in a fragile place—"

Christopher nodded. "Stewart."

"She told you?"

"Not really." Christopher shrugged. "We decided discussing our exes would ruin our evening."

"Right." Stella held up a finger. "So, here's the Cliff Notes version. They were together for five years, engaged for two. Stewart cheats with a co-worker the week before their wedding day. Katelyn flees to Mazatlán."

"Copy that," Christopher replied. "I have no intentions of hurting Katelyn."

"Copy that," Stella parroted. "I just thought you should know."

"Thanks for telling me," Christopher said. "I'm sure it's hard for her to share what happened."

Stella nodded. "She's a tad embarrassed." She stepped past him. "I'll see if Lucía needs a hand."

Christopher processed the new information about Katelyn. He truly didn't want to hurt her. Given the job he still had to do, he should probably distance himself from her—let her finish her vacation and go home to Portland.

He stopped in the doorway to Humberto's study, his gaze meeting Katelyn's. He flashed a goofy grin when she smiled at him. He couldn't quite understand why the sight of her sent his heart racing, caused his palms to sweat and made him wish they were alone together on a deserted island.

"Good?" Jade asked.

Christopher shifted his attention to her, and she pointed to his side. "Good."

"I'm on my way to see Sandrine, then home." Jade checked her phone and turned the screen toward him. He read an all-caps text from Sandrine: *GET ME THE FRICK OUT OF HERE!*

"Did the doc release her?" Christopher asked.

"Not that I know of." Jade stepped past him into the hallway. She tilted her head, inviting him to follow her.

Christopher looked at Katelyn, who was listening to something Captain Torres was saying, then followed Jade to the massive front doors.

Jade fished her keys from a small purse. "Are you staying here?"

Christopher shook his head. "No. I need some sleep."

"Same," Jade said. "Think maybe we should bring West in before he ends up dead?"

"Agreed," Christopher replied. "I'll see if Torres can have his men help locate him."

"Sounds good." Jade laughed at another text from Sandrine. "I've been ordered to bring her some *effing* clothes too." She pulled one door open. "Let me know if you get a line on West." She gave him a goodbye wave over her shoulder and closed the doors.

Back in the study, Christopher found María and Lucía fussing over a charcuterie platter. Stella and Katelyn shared the couch, still engaged in conversation with Captain Torres. Humberto finished a call and greeted Christopher.

"Agent Temple, you are just in time to answer questions about replacing Katelyn's passport." Humberto sat on the couch facing Katelyn and Stella and motioned to an armchair. "I just spoke with Juan Vega, who believes Martínez still has Katelyn's passport. Would it be a good idea for her to file for a new one now?"

"Or …" Stella joined the conversation. "Can you wave your magic FBI wand and, voilà, new passport?"

Christopher smiled at Katelyn. "I'm afraid it's not quite that easy, but—"

"I underst—" Katelyn began.

"Seriously?" Stella cut in. "You can't call someone?"

Christopher cut his eyes to Stella. "Sure, I'll make some calls."

"Thanks," Katelyn said. "I guess I have to go home at some point." She smiled at him. "But I'm in no hurry."

Christopher wanted to take Katelyn by the hand and lead her away from the others. Suggest they take a trip together as soon as he finished the Sarita García case. Instead, he refocused on Martínez and the danger he still posed to Katelyn. "Have you located Martínez?" Christopher asked Torres.

Humberto answered instead of Torres. "Juan heard Martínez is hiding in La Noria, twenty plus miles from here, where he has family."

Marco added, "I have men looking for him there, but no luck so far."

Christopher nodded. "Understood."

Humberto pulled a phone from a pocket and handed it to Katelyn. "We still need you to not leave the house." Katelyn nodded and Humberto continued, "I have added our numbers. Should you find yourself in danger again, you can call one of us."

"Thanks, Humberto." Katelyn set her new phone on the coffee table.

Lucía brought Christopher a plate of prosciutto, *manchego* cheese, and butter crackers. "You should eat." She handed him a napkin and María offered him a cold Pacifico.

Christopher smiled at them and took the plate. He loaded a cracker with meat and cheese, then popped the snack into his mouth. After a swig of beer to wash down the savory treat, he asked, "Captain Torres, would it be possible to have a few of your men look for Mark West? Jade and I need to bring him in before García's soldiers find him."

Torres nodded. *"Sí."* He started texting. "I will instruct Vasquez to issue a locate and detain order for West."

"Gracias." Christopher sipped some beer.

Humberto stood. "We should all enjoy the delicious *aperitivos* Lucía and María prepared for us."

Stella popped up from the couch. "I could use a *cerveza*!"

Christopher held Katelyn's gaze as everyone moved to the buffet.

"How are you feeling?" Katelyn asked him.

"Better." Christopher smiled. "Sorry I passed out after Jade's *tender* care."

Katelyn laughed. "She meant well."

Christopher laughed too. "Good thing she's an agent, because she'd make a terrible doctor."

Katelyn nodded. "Right?"

Stella returned to her seat and handed Katelyn a Pacifico. "What's so funny?"

"We were just commenting on Jade's bedside manner," Christopher replied.

"Or lack of." Stella raised her beer in toast. "To Jade and her gentle touch." She clinked her bottle against Christopher and Katelyn's. *"¡Salud!"* As Stella held her beer to her lips, she paused and added, "It's bad luck if you don't drink after a toast."

"¡Salud!" Katelyn and Christopher chimed and tipped up their bottles.

Humberto joined them. "Agent Temple …"

Christopher held up a hand. "Please call me Christopher."

Humberto nodded. "Would you like to join us for dinner?"

"Gracias, Humberto. But I need to take care of a few things and get some sleep." Christopher shifted his gaze to Katelyn.

Stella finished her beer, then added, "And replacing Katelyn's passport is at the top of your list, right?"

Christopher gritted his teeth and swallowed a "mind your own business" retort. "Yes, at the top of my list."

"Humberto," Lucía said, "would you be available to accompany us tomorrow so I can show Katelyn and Stella my paintings at Michael's Gallery?"

"Por supuesto," Humberto replied. "It would be my pleasure."

Lucía smiled at Christopher. "You are welcome to join us."

"Thanks for the invite," Christopher said. "But Sandrine might be released today or tomorrow, and Jade will need my help getting her settled."

"You should bring Agent Mortieau here," Humberto offered. "I can have María prepare the sitting room for her. It makes sense if you and Jade will be busy with West."

"Sí," Lucía added. "Sandrine would be in good hands with both María and I tending to her."

"I'll suggest the idea to Jade and Sandrine." Christopher held out his hand to Katelyn. "Walk me out?"

Katelyn took his hand and Stella jumped up beside her. Christopher tried to suppress a frown, but felt his eyebrows draw together.

Katelyn turned to Stella. "I'll be just outside and back in a sec."

"A few seconds," Christopher added. "I promise to make sure she's safely back inside before I leave."

"Oh, I'm not worried." Stella hooked a thumb over her shoulder. "I've gotta pee." She headed for the bathroom. "Toodles, Agent Hottie."

Christopher's cheeks warmed. Katelyn squeezed his hand and led him from the study.

"Adiós," Humberto said. "Please keep me updated on Agent Mortieau."

"Will do," Christopher replied. He pulled Katelyn to his side and looped his arm around her shoulder. "Finally," he whispered in her ear. "Alone."

Katelyn giggled and Christopher opened one of the massive entry doors. He followed her outside, pulling the door closed behind them. He took her hand and led her to a side garden blooming with bright pink bougainvillea and fragrant freesia. Christopher bent down and kissed her, welcoming the feel of her arms wrapping around his neck. As he devoured her lips, he marveled at how good Katelyn felt in his arms. It was as if she'd been the missing puzzle piece in his life. He released her lips, and she smiled up at him.

"Quite the goodbye kiss."

"I'm hoping to convince you to accept a date night redo." He smoothed her quirky swatch of pinkish hair.

"It sounds like you're going to be busy for a few days." Katelyn took a slight step back, but he kept his arms around her waist. "But I'm thinking about changing my return flight."

"You might extend your stay another week or two?"

Katelyn tilted her head. "Is that how long it will take to replace my passport?"

"I won't know until I make a few calls."

"Maybe I should just cancel my return flight, then rebook later."

Christopher nodded. "I agree. I should have my case wrapped up in a couple of days." He drew her close again. "I'd really like a do-over date night." He searched her eyes, and she stood on tiptoes to kiss him.

"Maybe next time we can finish dessert."

Christopher held her face in his hands. "I think we should *start* with dessert."

CHAPTER THIRTY-EIGHT

The coffee mug in front of her now held cold remnants of her first cup of the day. Katelyn scanned her friends' faces and could tell by their somber looks that news about recent poisonings was cause for concern.

A frown clouded María's face, echoing the mood in the kitchen, as she cleared the table. "I brew fresh pot."

"Bien." Humberto ran a hand over his face, then looked at Marco. "You are sure this is the same poison used on the previous victims?"

Shrugging, Marco said, "Not sure until I see the coroner's report, but witnesses reported the same types of reactions as with the others who died."

"But how can you be certain, since these deaths occurred in Manzanillo?" Katelyn asked.

"We will not be positive until lab tests are complete," Marco continued. "But I feel confident it is the same individual—using methyl alcohol as a weapon."

"Will you need to travel to Manzanillo?" Humberto asked as he took a plate of *empanada de manzana* from María.

The baked apple tarts' aroma caused Katelyn's stomach to flip, and she thought about the poor victims who had ingested their sweet tropical drinks unaware they had been poisoned. Despite her hunger, she didn't think she could keep an *empanada* down.

Stella followed María with fresh cups of coffee, placing them in front of Marco and Katelyn.

"Is Lucía joining us?" Katelyn asked.

"She is finishing a call in my study," Humberto answered, then said to Marco, "So, you will be leaving?"

"I am waiting to see what Lucía learns from the young lady who arrived at *Casa del Ángel* this morning." Marco checked his phone. "Apparently, the woman believes she was poisoned at the Gaviana Resort."

Humberto nodded. "Possibly she will have useful information."

María returned with small plates and the coffee carafe. *"¡Por favor coman todos ustedes!"* she instructed, placing the dishes next to the platter of *empanadas* and refilling Humberto and Stella's cups.

"Gracias, María." Humberto selected a tart.

"De nada," María replied. *"Voy al mercado."* Not waiting for a response, she headed from the kitchen.

"Sí, sí ..." Lucía said into her phone, passing María and making eye contact with Marco. "If she is sure she does not need to go to the hospital, bring her here." She listened for a few seconds, then said, *"Bien."*

Humberto stood. "We should meet with her in my study."

"Agreed." Marco, too, was on his feet and followed Humberto from the kitchen.

"These are delicious," Stella said, covering her mouth as she chewed a bit of *empanada*.

"We should probably be in the study when they question this woman …" Katelyn began.

"For your article?" Lucía claimed the chair vacated by Humberto.

"That …" Katelyn sipped some coffee. "And if she actually saw who served her the drink, you might be able to sketch their face."

"Oh, what a fabulous idea." Lucía was back on her feet. "I will check my supplies in the study." She turned at the hallway. "You are coming too, *¿sí?*"

Katelyn gave Lucía a thumbs up. "Yes."

"You go," Stella said. "I'll clean up."

"We've got time to finish our coffee."

"Good, because I'm starving." Stella snapped off a hunk of *empanada* and made moaning sounds as she chewed. "I think I've gained ten pounds since I've been here."

"Right?" Katelyn laughed. "And my liver probably needs a break too."

Stella eyed Katelyn across the top of her mug. "Talk to Agent Hottie this morning?"

A blush colored Katelyn's cheeks. "Texted."

"Making plans to give him another opportunity to leave you stranded?" Stella prodded.

Katelyn narrowed her eyes at her bestie.

"Okay, okay …" Hands palms up in surrender, Stella grinned. "Sorry for the dig at Agent Hottie."

Drilling Stella with her eyes, Katelyn finished her coffee. "He's with Jade at the hospital trying to reason with Sandrine."

"She's still insisting on being released?"

"Evidently. But the doctor wants to keep her one more day."

"How effing bizarre this has all been."

"Bizarre is an understatement." As if to emphasize Katelyn's comment, the doorbell chimed.

"Go …" Stella began to clear their dishes. "I've got this."

"Thanks, Ella." Katelyn, anxious to escape the lingering fragrance of the apple tart, hurried toward the study.

A young woman, with shoulder-length dark hair perched on the edge of one couch, flanked by what Katelyn guessed were her parents. She looked pale despite a slight tan and twisted a tissue in her shaking hands.

Marco sat on the opposite couch, Lucía beside him with a pad and pencils at the ready. Humberto motioned for Katelyn to join him at his desk, and she tip-toed across the study.

"I know this is difficult, Lyndie …" Marco began. "But can you take us through the few hours before you became ill?"

Lyndie's lip quivered. "I was drinking mimosas and reading a book …"

"Her younger sister, Lanie, played in the pool nearby," the mother interjected.

Marco smiled at Lyndie's mom, then asked, "Were you drinking mimosas when you began to feel sick?"

Lyndie's face scrunched into a frown, and she shook her head. "No, a different waiter came and said it was happy hour with a two-for-one drink special."

Marco tilted his head. "Sweet drinks?"

"Piña Coladas," Mom answered. "Laney kicked over one of the drinks." She placed a hand over her heart. "Thank God! And Lyndie only drank half of hers—because it tasted funny."

Looking up from his note pad, Marco fixed his gaze on Lyndie. "You are very lucky."

A wave of tears flowed down Lyndie's cheeks, and her dad placed his arm around her shoulders. Marco waited for the young woman to recover, looking up as Stella entered the study and moved to Humberto's desk. Handing Stella a pad, Katelyn tapped her notes with the tip of her pen.

"Lyndie, this is my sister." Marco placed a hand on Lucía's knee. "Do you think you can describe the waiter who brought you the drink so she can draw a sketch?"

Lyndie cast a nervous glance at Lucía, then looked back at Marco. "I–I think so."

"Bueno," Marco continued, "Lucía will ask you questions now to help with her drawing." He leaned back so Lyndie's focus would be on Lucía.

A warm smile graced Lucía's face as she laid her pencils on top of her pad. "Lyndie, it seems like a funny place to start …" Lucía touched her nose. "But can you remember the waiter's nose?"

Touching hers, Lyndie said, "Squished. Like it's been smashed."

Still not using her pencils, Lucía asked, "Do you remember any scars or distinguishing marks on his face?"

Lyndie closed her eyes for a second. "He … he had a red mark here …" Using her fingertip, she drew a curving line from between her eyes to the top of her scalp.

Pencil in hand, Lucía said, "We are ready to begin." She moved the pencil across the blank paper. "Lyndie, while I capture these details, close your eyes and see what else you can remember."

Marco's phone pinged and he eased off the couch, leaving Lyndie in Lucía's capable hands.

"¿Quién fue?" Humberto asked when Marco rejoined them.

"Vasquez." Marco continued to read the incoming text. "He received an alert that a *Federale* has been reported missing."

An unexpected chill washed over Katelyn. She contained the shiver running down her spine but controlling the fear spinning through her mind wasn't as easy. *Did the missing Federale have anything to do with the case Christopher was working? And if so, could he and Jade be in danger? Or had the Federale been investigating Martínez, who dispensed with the agent before fleeing to La Noria?*

CHAPTER THIRTY-NINE

Sarita hadn't slept well. Stress over leaving the life she'd built mingled with fear of what, if anything, Eladio had reported to his bosses. And her mind raced with regret at not being able to tell Dario everything, but instead needing to vanish without a goodbye.

Her young lover had slept soundly, oblivious to Sarita's tossing and turning next to him. She doubted a *Maríachi* band could wake him, since he'd played cards with some guests in the *Pulpo de Fuego* bar until 2:00 AM. Dario had tried to engage Sarita in drunken sex, but she'd rebuffed him, telling him if he didn't leave her alone, she'd have her *sicario* remove him from her bed.

Finally giving into her insomnia at 5:00 AM, she'd slipped from her bedroom, closed the door, and brewed a pot of strong coffee. Now, sitting at the table in the sitting area of her penthouse, she lifted the lid on Eladio's laptop, and the screen came to life. Sarita stared at the photo of Jade Mendoza, willing the picture to reveal who she was. The young woman had the same eye's as Sarita's mother, Estrella. The rest of her features were carbon copies of Sarita and Damian when they were younger. Could Damian have fathered a child? Had the baby been given up for adoption? Or maybe Damian had been unaware of the child's existence.

A more troubling question was this: why did Eladio Ortiz have photos of Jade Mendoza, Christopher Temple, and Marco Torres on his laptop? Was he working with the trio to bring down Sarita's small fiefdom? Did he suspect the young woman was Damian's daughter?

She'd spent the last two hours trying to wrap her head around the latest events unfolding around her when her phone pinged with an incoming text from her *sicario*.

Ramos: *Ortiz pregunta por ti*

A whisper of anger added to Sarita's dark mood. She didn't care if Eladio was asking for her. She hoped he'd spent a horrible night like she had, worrying about his fate.

Sarita replied to Ramos: *I'll be down in half an hour*

Ramos: *Bueno*

She stood in front of her closet, hoping a shower would refresh her and help clear her mind. As she selected black Bermuda shorts and a blood red, sleeveless blouse with a plunging neckline, her mind circled back to the issues that had kept her awake. She knew before she made her exit from her existing life, she'd have to deal with Eladio. Another wave of anger at the *Federale* washed over her, and she contemplated adding his bleached, white skull to the skull of Rubén Soto. Rubén had tried to take her down also, but his downfall had been thinking he was smarter than Sarita and that she'd fallen in love with him. Neither belief was true and when he told her she either had to run or he would arrest her, she'd clubbed him on the head with a full champagne bottle. Lieutenant Hernández had disposed of his corpse and later delivered Rubén's clean, bleached skull back to her. Sarita had painted the skull in bright colors, and most people never looked closely enough to see the concave dent hidden by a yellow rose.

She'd learned her lesson though and had formulated her escape plan, perfecting it over the past two years. Dario stirred and rolled onto his stomach. The bedding tangled around his legs, revealing his spectacular ass. Sarita knew she couldn't take Dario with her, nor tell him she was leaving.

She'd already had her lawyer draft the necessary documents to transfer Fiesta de Fuego and her leasing company to Dario. She'd included a bank account with enough funds to run the resort until he decided whether to keep or sell the property. Sarita had also written him a personal letter, thanking him for the past few weeks. She didn't explain why she was leaving or where she was going, just that she needed to disappear.

"Sarita …" Dario mumbled; his eyes still closed. She glanced at him and wondered how her new name, Lupita Vargas, would sound on his lips. Sarita blinked to stem tears collecting in her eyes and checked the time. Since she'd planned a romantic dinner with Dario at her private pool, she needed to start her day. The thought of skinny dipping, followed by erotic, passionate sex, sent tendrils of anticipation snaking through her loins and eased some of her current stress.

Sarita had taken extra time with her makeup, partly to hide the exhaustion reflected in her eyes and partly because she wanted the last time Eladio Ortiz laid eyes on her to be seared in his memory.

She found Ramos waiting for her when she stepped from the elevator.

"*Jefa,*" he greeted her in his deep baritone.

"Is everything okay?" She continued past him, her red sandals clicking on the polished tile floor.

"*Sí.*" Ramos fell in step with her. "Alba said you were on the way down."

Sarita had spoken briefly with Alba before heading down, asking her to see to anything Dario might need. She'd left him a note by the coffee pot explaining she had a busy day, and she would see him at dinner.

She crossed the lobby with Ramos in tow. They turned left, following a hallway that led to an unrenovated section of the resort. Ramos had posted a guard at the door of the suite, who came to attention when he saw her.

"*Jefa,*" the young man greeted her.

"*Buenos días,*" she replied. "*Estás excusado.*"

The guard glanced at Ramos, then gave her a quick nod and departed. Ramos wouldn't like her dismissing the guard, which put him back on duty, but he needed to be reminded she was still in charge. For now.

Sarita placed her hand on the doorknob and said to Ramos, "*Espera aquí.*" She ignored the flash of anger in the *sicario's* eyes at being left outside, then stepped into the suite and closed the door.

Eladio sat at a small table, cup of coffee between his hands, his breakfast untouched. Sarita saw her own exhaustion in his haggard eyes.

"You are not hungry?"

"It is not what I would order for my last meal." His sardonic smile did nothing to improve his disheveled appearance.

"How do you know Jade Mendoza?" Sarita asked.

"I have not met her." Eladio shrugged. "So, you see the resemblance also?"

Sarita nodded. "I did not know my brother had a daughter."

Eladio tilted his head and his lips parted as if he had something to say, but he stayed silent.

Sarita changed the subject. "Is there anyone we should notify?"

Eladio's eyes narrowed, and he shook his head. "I do have one request."

Sarita expected him to beg for his life. "*Sí?*"

"When Ramos brings you my skull …" He forced a grin. "I would like you to paint a red hibiscus bloom to hide the bullet hole."

Sarita held the *Federale's* dark stare. The story of Rubén Soto's painted skull had circulated since his death and most people considered the tale to be a myth.

"*Adiós*, Agent Ortiz." Sarita turned to go.

"You have not read my letter of resignation." Eladio's words halted her exit.

Sarita spun around; her cheeks hot with anger. "I do not need to read how you pretended to be a loyal employee who had my best interest in mind!" A swell of tears surprised Sarita, and she blinked to keep them at bay. "Pretended to be my friend."

"The envelope contains information about your missing money." Eladio pushed the slim packet across the table. "Juan Vega helped me persuade the Azteca bank manager to place what was left of the funds into an account in your name."

Sarita snatched the envelope from the table and tore it open. She slid two sheets of paper free, a bank statement in her name and a handwritten letter, signed by Eladio. The bank statement showed the total of $124,395,000 printed below a bold line. A note had been penned at the bottom.

> *Jefa, please let me know if you need any help recovering your funds.*

Juan Vega had signed his name and added his phone number. Sarita would not have time to withdraw the money, so Dario would be the one reaching out to Vega. Still, she took pleasure in knowing most of her funds had been returned to her. And now that she was leaving everything behind, she hoped the handsome FBI agent and Damian's daughter arrested, or killed, West before he had time to enjoy his stolen money.

Sarita folded the statement and glanced at Eladio's note, which simply said:

Forgive me. Always, Eladio Ortiz

Sarita shifted her gaze to Eladio. "This changes nothing. *¿Entender?*"

He nodded. "Understood."

Sarita locked eyes with the *Federale* for a few seconds, then turned and reached for the doorknob.

"Sarita." Eladio's husky tone made her turn around. He stood in the middle of the room, his eyes filled with regret. "I am truly sorry."

Sarita went to him and held his face in her hands. She brushed his lips, intending a brief goodbye kiss, but Eladio wrapped her in his arms and pulled her close. He returned her kiss passionately as she ran her hands through his hair. Sarita wanted to let the kiss lead to something more but enjoying the sexy *Federale* was not part of her exit plan.

She placed her hands on his chest, his heart beating wildly beneath her palms, and searched his eyes. Eladio returned her gaze, his eyes filled with longing and sorrow.

He kissed her on the forehead. *"Adiós, Jefa."*

"Adiós." Sarita kissed him one last time and made her exit.

CHAPTER FORTY

God, Christopher wished they'd stop arguing. Jade and Sandrine had been at it for over twenty minutes, fueling a headache brewing at the base of his skull since he'd arrived. The hospital's bouquet of antiseptic and cleaning solutions grated on his nerves, exacerbating the pounding in his head.

"I am fine and if you won't help me leave …" Sandrine spat at Jade.

"You are not fine—" Jade began.

"Bloody hell!" Sandrine one-handed her belongings into a plastic bag supplied by the hospital. "I'm leaving and staying at a hotel until I can get a flight out of here!"

Jade grabbed items from the bag and tossed them onto the bed. "You're staying in the hos—"

Stepping between the two women, Christopher extended his arms, keeping them apart. "That's enough!" Jade slapped at his hand. "Jade!" He glared at her. "Why don't you go get us some coffee."

"I'll go get her effing doctor!" Jade called over her shoulder as she marched toward the door.

"Brilliant!" Sandrine returned her clothes to her makeshift suitcase. "Thanks for sending her off."

"Sandrine …" Christopher kept his tone calm. "If your doctor says you're good to leave, I can take you to Humberto's."

Tears slipped down her cheeks and she looked up at him. "I'm not used to needing help." She pointed at her wounded side. "Or being injured."

Christopher held his bandaged hand in the air. "Same."

Carrying a cardboard tray housing three coffees, Jade appeared in the doorway. When her phone pinged simultaneously with Christopher's, she quickly crossed to the bedside table and set down the coffee.

"It's from Ferris and Benson." Christopher didn't look up from his phone. "They've received intel that Agustín Castro has sent a rival cartel to eliminate Sarita García."

"Shit!" Jade dragged her hands through her hair. "We've got to find West and bring him in!"

"Agreed." After a quick glance at Jade, Christopher checked his phone again. "Ferris has sent Captain Torres a formal request for assistance in arresting West."

Reading the same text, Jade nodded. "But no mention of apprehending García."

"You'd think both agencies would want to at least offer her protective custody," Sandrine added.

"It's probably in the works, but not finalized," Christopher replied. "Sandrine …"

Eyes closed, Sandrine heaved a sigh, then she looked at Jade. "Sorry for being such a sodding bitch." She angled into an armchair in the corner of the room. "Go … do your jobs."

"If the doc releases you, text me and I'll come back as soon as I can," Jade said.

Texting Torres, Christopher headed for the elevators.

"Sure!" Sandrine called as Jade darted from the room, hustling into the car before the doors whooshed closed.

"How do you want to play this?" Jade asked Christopher.

He had no idea. With West and García in danger, he and Jade would probably be tasked with rescuing them both. "I texted Torres that we need to meet to discuss our new orders."

The elevator dinged when they arrived in the lobby of the hospital. The doors slid open, and Jade popped out first. Christopher lengthened his stride to catch up as she aimed her key fob at the Nissan and the locks released. They climbed in, Jade cranked the engine and pulled out of the parking lot.

"Torres asked us to come to Humberto's," Christopher reported. "Said they are following up on a new lead regarding another poisoning."

Jade guided her car toward Humberto's house but didn't respond. Christopher assumed she was mulling over her argument with Sandrine, so he mentally contemplated their next moves. By the time they arrived, he'd decided to ask Torres for help with García— regardless of whether they had orders from Ferris. He was more than ready for this assignment to end. *Better to ask for forgiveness than permission*, he told himself.

Already at the big double doors, Jade pushed into Humberto's without knocking or waiting for Christopher. Obviously, she felt the same way he did, ready to be on to some new adventure.

Humberto appeared in the hallway and motioned them into his study. "Can I get you something to drink?" he asked.

As if they had built in radar for each other, Katelyn's eyes met Christopher's as soon as he entered the room. The tension in his neck eased a bit when she grinned at him before Stella dragged her from the study.

"We'll grab some drinks," Stella said.

Christopher smiled as they passed by, then turned his attention back to the room. Humberto stood at his desk and looked over Lucía's shoulder as she focused on her task. A young woman and two people who appeared to be her parents' occupied chairs in front of the desk.

Lucía asked, "And his hair? Long or short? Color?"

"Please," Marco motioned toward the couches. "I have requested an arrest warrant for Mark West."

Their hips bumped when Christopher and Jade sat down at the same time. Jade scooched over a tad and asked, "Can your men help us look for him?"

"Si," Marco replied. "Vasquez will change the "locate and detain" notice to "apprehend" as soon as we have authorization."

"Captain Torres," Christopher began, "can you also help us secure García?"

Marco's phone rang and he looked at the screen. "I have to take this."

Christopher and Jade waited as Marco listened, offering the occasional, *sí,* before ending the call. "One of my men spotted Martínez in La Noria."

Standing, Marco turned to Humberto as he joined them. "Are you leaving tonight?"

Marco nodded. *"Sí."* The two men exchanged a glance. "You should stay here."

"Bueno," Humberto agreed.

"I will update you when I arrive," Marco said to Humberto, then turned to Christopher. "Agent Temple, I will have Vasquez keep you informed regarding the warrant for West and I will ask him to assist if you are able to contain Sarita García."

"Gracias." Christopher stood.

"Agent Temple …" Glancing at Christopher and Jade who'd also stood, Marco continued. "You should get permission from your agencies to apprehend García so I can request the authority to arrest her."

"Understood." Christopher offered his hand. "Good luck with Martínez."

Marco shook hands with Christopher and Jade, and Christopher noticed the look Torres gave Humberto. He wondered whether the two friends had decided if Martínez resisted arrest, he'd die in the process?

"Hasta luego." Marco exchanged a slight wave with Lucía, then exited the study as Katelyn and Stella returned with a coffee carafe and the platter of *empanadas.*

"Adios," Stella called after Marco.

On her way to the buffet, Katelyn glanced at Christopher. He started to follow her, but Jade touched his shoulder. Eyebrows raised, he turned to his partner.

"Benson wants us to do a conference call with her, Ferris and Sandrine," Jade said.

"Does the offer still stand to bring Sandrine here?" Christopher asked Humberto.

"Sí. Is she being released?"

Jade shrugged. "Not sure, but thanks for offering to let her stay here when she gets out of the hospital." Another incoming text pinged her phone and she thumbed keys as she headed from the study.

"Keep me posted," Humberto called after Jade.

Christopher crossed the room to Katelyn. "Hey," he said, taking her hands in his. "Duty calls."

Winking at him, Katelyn said, "Well you *are* here for work."

"I'll text when I'm done and maybe we can grab a drink."

"A drink sounds fun," Stella agreed.

He cut his eyes to Stella, a retort of "you're not invited" on his tongue. Before he could reply, Jade called from the door. "C!" She waggled her phone. "We've got to go!"

Christopher touched Katelyn's lips in a quick kiss. He turned to leave and bit his lip when Stella called after him, "We might have to start drinking without you, Agent Hottie."

"Stella! Seriously!"

Christopher's grin at Katelyn chastising her BFF elicited an exaggerated eyeroll from Jade before she turned and headed for her car.

CHAPTER FORTY-ONE

Sarita closed the lockbox she'd filled with information for Dario and checked the time on her phone. 5:00 pm. Plenty of time to dress for their dinner date. She stared out her office window at the undulating Pacific Ocean and thought about her first year on the run. She planned to move from town to town, along Mexico's vast coastline. Maybe she would even encounter Damian's ex-wife, Clara and ask her about Jade Mendoza before she finally killed the woman who had murdered her brother.

Her thoughts shifted to her morning encounter with Eladio. Sarita believed he was truly sorry for being the *Federale* sent to investigate her in hopes of building a case against *El Lobo*. She was grateful he'd managed to obtain most of the money the American bankers had stolen from her and hated to have him executed. She wished she could just allow him to leave, but she needed him detained until she was far away from Mazatlán. *His fate is in Ramos's hands now*, she told herself.

When she'd left the suite, she ordered Ramos to watch Eladio until she sent further instructions. The *sicario* frowned at her, creating a unibrow across his forehead, and took a step toward her. Sarita glared at him and stood her ground, departing for her office once he gave her an affirmative nod. She knew it would be only a matter of time before the menacing hulk called *El Lobo* and reported Sarita's inability to resolve the matter of the *Federale*. She was counting on her godfather's proclaimed love for her to keep him from eliminating her along with Eladio Ortiz.

Sarita scanned her To-Do list again. She assumed by now Eladio had taken a shower and donned the clean clothes she'd had Alba deliver from the stash of men's clothing she'd acquired over the years. Her lips tingled with the memory of his kiss and a warm flush flooded her groin.

She stood and crossed her office to the small wet bar she kept well stocked. Sarita poured a shot of Hornitos Silver and tossed down the citrusy liquid. Coughing, she poured another shot, took a sip and stared at the magenta dress she'd selected for her date with Dario. She'd texted him after her meeting with Eladio telling him she'd meet him at seven by her private pool for a champagne toast at sunset.

She stripped off her clothes and slipped into the skintight, sleeveless dress, sans under garments. She tugged the hem down over her taut ass and checked her reflection in the mirror above the credenza to make sure the low-cut back was just above the curve of her butt cheeks. She adjusted her breasts, so they appeared in the teardrop cutout in the neckline of the dress. Sarita did a couple of slow turns, admiring herself in the mirror. She stepped into silver Badgley Mischka heels and smiled at the sparkling crystals adorning the strap across her toes. Replacing her signature red, she added dark pink lipstick to her lips. When she dabbed her favorite Clive Christian behind her ears and between her breasts, the sensual jasmine fragrance filled her nostrils. She took one last look in the mirror before leaving her office and heading to meet her lover.

Sarita navigated the hallway to her private elevator and stepped inside. After Dario was properly sated and asleep, she would return to her office to retrieve the small suitcase she'd already prepared for her departure. Her heartbeat accelerated as she descended to the lobby. "Am I really going to flee?" she asked her reflection in the elevator's brass paneling. "Yes. Yes, I am."

The doors whooshed opened, and Sarita strode into the lobby of Fiesta de Fuego, staccato from her heels announcing her arrival. She could feel people staring at her and reveled at the thought of the stories they would tell after she disappeared.

She looked exquisite
Like royalty
Exotically beautiful
Ran away with a Federale

Sarita smiled at a desk clerk before turning down a narrow passage. When she reached the end, she punched in a code and pushed open the glass door. Dario stood at the edge of a large grassy area, admiring her Flamingos as the large male watched over his flock from across a small pond. The drifting sun, bathed the majestic bird in dark orange light, turning his feathers a deep magenta. The birds started clucking when they noticed Sarita, and Dario turned toward her, a lascivious grin on his handsome face.

"Cariño." Dario took her hand, turning her in a pirouette. "You look ravishing!" He pulled her to him and devoured her lips. Sarita leaned into him and pressed against his hardness. Dario slipped a strap from her shoulder, but before he could expose her breast, she pushed off his chest and headed for the bistro table Alba had set for dinner. Dario let loose an appreciative whistle and followed her.

The sun flirted with the horizon before heading to the other side of the world and the ocean embraced the coming night with a steely blue shimmer.

"Would you open the champagne?" Sarita asked.

"Sí." Dario plucked the bottle from the ice bucket and worked the cork. "Your Flamingos are very entertaining." The cork exploded from the bottle and Sarita placed a flute under the flowing bubbles.

"They fascinate me," Sarita said as Dario filled the second flute.

"They are beautiful, but not as beautiful as you," Dario crooned.

Sarita smiled and handed him a glass, then led the way to a large, cushioned bench at the edge of the bluff.

"What a spectacular view." Dario sipped from his glass. "Thank you for sharing this with me."

Soon it will all be yours, amante, Sarita thought to herself. She sat down and Dario followed suit. "The ocean calms me." She took a sip. "I find it odd that something so powerful can be soothing."

"Interesting point." Dario stretched his arm across the back of the bench, his thumb caressing her shoulder. "I know I am no match for the ocean, but I hope I bring you a sense of calm too."

Sarita laughed. "Oh, *mi amor.*" She kissed him. "You bring me so much more."

Sunlight painted them in a flaming red glow as the bright orb dipped into the ocean. They sat silently watching the end of another day, then held their flutes aloft and chimed, *"Salud!"*

Dario clinked her glass and then they both took healthy sips.

"Cariño ..." Dario nuzzled her ear. "Any chance you are the appetizer before dinner?"

Sarita laughed again, something she rarely did, and actually felt giddy. Dario kissed her neck, and she allowed his hands to roam her body. Could she be so happy because she was disappearing from a life that had become too demanding? Escaping persecution from the law? From Eladio Ortiz? From herself?

"Come." Sarita took Dario's hand. "I had the kitchen make your favorite dishes."

"But I am not hungry for food." Dario pulled her into his arms and kissed her deeply.

Maybe dinner can wait, Sarita thought. After all, the dishes were housed in warming trays inside the pool house.

Sarita freed her lips from her young *lothario's* hungry mouth and held up a finger. Dario's breathing came in short pants. Sarita lowered the straps of her dress off her shoulders and let the dress fall to her waist.

"Dios mío, eres tan hermosa," Dario exclaimed, his voice thick with lust.

Sarita smiled and turned her back to him. She inched the dress slowly down over her ass and stepped free of the garment. Naked except for her diamond studs and dazzling, silver heels, she looked over her shoulder. "Care to join me for a swim?"

She walked slowly toward the pool and Dario followed leaving a trail of clothes behind him. Sarita kicked her sandals aside, descended the steps into the sun-warmed pool and shrieked when Dario dove in beside her. He came up in a wall of water and wrapped her in a wet hug. First, he kissed her passionately, then his mouth covered a nipple. Slowly, he moved from one breast to the other, until she cried out.

Dario lifted Sarita out of the water, and she wrapped her legs around his waist as he continued his assault on her breasts. Desire flooded Sarita and she wondered how she could possibly leave Dario behind. She brought his lips back to hers and he carried her from the water to a padded lounge chair built into the side of the pool for sunbathing.

He laid her down gently and caressed her body as if memorizing every curve and erogenous zone. He left a trail of kisses as he moved down her torso. When he arrived at her perfectly manicured V, Dario slipped under the water and came up between her legs.

He kissed the inside of her thighs, flirting with the edge of her hot zone until she begged, "Dario, please!" Then he satisfied his hunger as Sarita dug her nails into his ass and screamed, *"Oh, Dios, no te detengas!"*

They sat naked at the candlelit bistro table, drank champagne, munched on bacon wrapped shrimp and Caesar salad. Dario fed her bites of lobster dripping with drawn butter and Sarita cut slices of tri-tip for him. Sarita brought the raspberry drizzled cheesecake to a cabana and Dario enjoyed his slice off her belly.

Their second round of love making was slower, more intimate, and Sarita savored every moment with her young *amante*. Finally spent, they lay in each other's arms on the cabana bed looking up at the stars.

"Te amo, Sarita," Dario whispered.

"I love you too," Sarita whispered back, and she meant it. She knew Alba would come to wake her at midnight, but for now she wanted to pretend this night with Dario would last forever.

CHAPTER FORTY-TWO

Christopher steered the catamaran into the ocean breeze, the sails catching the wind and pushing the dual hulls through the waves. Katelyn, stunning in a coral-colored bikini, smiled from the bow as she rubbed coconut scented suntan lotion onto her glistening skin. She stood and headed his way, swaying with the pitch of the boat.

"Hola, Capitán," she greeted him, and he kissed her in response. "What a beautiful day."

Christopher drew her to him with his free arm. "You're what's beautiful about the day."

Katelyn leaned against him, another salty kiss offering the promise of more to come.

Christopher looked at the helm. "Why is the wheel ringing?" he asked Katelyn, but she'd vanished. The ringing grew louder, and the catamaran seemed to be spinning in a circle. Christopher grabbed the side rail to hold on but landed in the ocean. Then his eyes flew open.

He snatched his ringing phone from the bedside table. "What?" he barked.

"Agent Temple …" Vasquez said.

"Y–yes." Christopher cleared his throat. "What's up?"

"One of my men reported seeing West at Fiesta de Fuego," Vasquez continued. "He said West is drunk and demanding to see Sarita García."

"*Gracias*, Vasquez." Christopher rubbed sleep from his eyes. "Is your man still there?"

"No," Vasquez answered. "He was there at the bar with his wife and called in the report as they were leaving."

"Got it." Christopher climbed out of bed. "I'm on my way."

"Do you need backup?" Vasquez asked.

Christopher cradled the phone between his shoulder and chin. "No, *gracias*." He pulled on a pair of blue board shorts and slid handcuffs into a pocket. "If West's drunk, it should be an easy arrest. Thanks again for the call."

"*De nada.*" Vasquez disconnected.

Christopher checked the Glock's magazine. He really did think West would come willingly, but he didn't want to be unprepared like last time. He donned a white T-shirt, cinched up his running shoes and headed for the Jeep. Plugging the charger into his phone, he noted the time: 12:03 AM.

As he drove toward Fiesta de Fuego, he contemplated calling Jade, but ditched the idea. After their conference call with their bosses and Sandrine at the hospital, he'd headed back to the cabin. When he'd talked to Jade before falling asleep, she'd reported Sandrine's doctor agreed to release her tomorrow, which was now today. He knew moving Sandrine to Humberto's would be a challenge so he'd rather she was rested for the task.

The beach bungalow was fifteen miles from the resort, and he should make good time since there was no traffic at this hour. The dark night slipped past him, and his mind returned to his dream of the catamaran cruise with Katelyn. It had seemed so real, and he wondered if a cruise would be a good apology gift before he had to leave for LA. He'd checked on a replacement passport for Katelyn and was advised to take her to Mazatlán's Consular Office. Maybe he could get her to agree to stay in Mazatlán until he could return. And with any luck, Stella would go home without Katelyn.

Fiesta de Fuego's huge sign loomed large in the distance and Christopher shifted his attention back to the matter at hand. If West was smart, he'd welcome his arrest and surrender without a fight. Then again, the errant banker was drunk and demanding to see García, suggesting he wasn't thinking rationally.

At least now, Christopher had approval to bring West in. Ferris was still waiting for an official warrant for Sarita García. All parties agreed the sooner they could arrest the drug queen, the better for her safety, and theirs.

Christopher turned into the resort's driveway and swung into a parking spot. He angled out of the Jeep, dropped his phone into a pocket and stowed his Glock in his waistband at the small of his back. Tugging the T-shirt hem down and over the weapon, he strode toward the entrance of Fiesta de Fuego with a silent prayer for a smooth arrest on his lips.

He could see West stumbling and waving a gun. "Great, he has a weapon." Christopher made a split-second decision to act drunk, hoping West would find camaraderie in a fellow drunkard.

Christopher pulled open one side of the glass entry doors and tripped into the lobby, making a production of not falling down.

"I'm okay," he slurred and lurched toward West. "Hey!" He tapped him on the shoulder. "I know you." Christopher grabbed West's arm. "Ca'mon, I'm buying."

West jerked his arm away. "Get away from me, asshole!" West pointed at Christopher with his gun, the Sig Sauer wobbling in his hand.

Christopher instinctively reached for his gun.

"Everything's gone to shit because of you!" West shouted.

Christopher kept one hand on his Glock and pointed to himself with the other. "Me?" He took a few steps forward. "What'd I do?" he mumbled. It was hard to pretend drunkenness with a gun pointed at you, while focusing on how to diffuse the situation.

"Big FBI Agent ..." West lost his balance and staggered sideways. "You got Paul and Adam killed."

Before Christopher could respond with a denial, he saw one of García's men approaching West from behind. Christopher reached for West's arm again, but froze when a cold voice behind him growled, "Do not move, *cabrón*."

Christopher held his hands up. "It's okay. I'm just here to take my friend home."

He was relieved of his gun and a menacing hulk circled in front of him. The other man had forced West to his knees and secured his weapon.

West looked around wildly. "I need to see Sarita García, *pronto*!" West's captor bashed him on the side of the head with his gun.

Christopher recognized the hulk that now stood in front of him as García's *sicario* and instantly regretted his decision not to call Jade for backup. Christopher's arms were wrenched behind him, and his hands were zip-tied together. He was searched, and his phone and handcuffs were removed from his pockets, while West suffered the same treatment.

The *sicario* led the way and two soldiers hauled Christopher and West after him. No one spoke as they trudged down a long hallway. He stopped at a door, unlocked it, and motioned Christopher inside.

Before he could move, West lunged forward and head butted Christopher in the mouth, splitting his bottom lip.

"You bastard!" West shouted. "I hope they cut off your head and hang your corpse from a bridge."

Christopher narrowed his eyes at West but didn't try to retaliate since one of the soldiers had stepped between them.

"*Llédalo a la misma habitación que el otro preso,*" the *sicario* instructed his men.

"*Sí, Ramos,*" the soldier holding West said and proceeded to drag him down the hallway.

Christopher's ears perked up at the word *preso*, which he knew meant prisoner. For a beat, he panicked that Vasquez had called Jade and she'd been captured. But of course, he knew better, Jade would have called him for backup.

"Wait!" West struggled against his captor. "He's the one you want to kill." West cast a crazed stare back at Christopher. "He's an effing Fed."

Ramos glared at Christopher as he stepped inside, then pulled the door closed.

Christopher looked around the empty office. A standard desk faced a window framing an outdoor garden. Two paintings hung on the walls, one of *vaqueros* on horses rounding up cattle, the other a colorful depiction of a bull fight. No phone on the desktop and the window was a solid pane of glass. He pulled open drawers looking for a pair of scissors to cut the plastic zip-ties but found only a couple of pens. He managed to tuck a pen into his back pocket, which could possibly be used as a weapon if he had the chance. He toed open a door, revealing a small bathroom, also void of anything useful.

Christopher returned to the desk and sat down. Sarita García must have converted some of the rundown hotel's guestrooms into offices. His mind flipped back to the other prisoner. *Who could it be? A rival drug dealer? Or whoever had previously occupied this office?*

CHAPTER FORTY-THREE

Sarita placed a hand on Dario's hip.

"Jefa."

She frowned at the intrusion.

"Jefa."

Sarita snuggled closer to Dario.

"Sarita," a voice growled.

Her eyes flew open, and she sat up, the sheet falling away exposing her nakedness. Ramos stood over her.

"What the hell are you doing here?" Sarita glared at the *sicario*, who's gaze was focused on her breasts. "Ramos!" Sarita barked.

"I have the American banker, West, locked in the suite with Ortiz," Ramos reported.

Sarita sprang from the cabana as Dario reached for her. *"Cariño,"* he mumbled, his eyes still closed.

"Baño," Sarita whispered. "Go back to sleep."

She marched naked past Ramos, grabbing a plush bathrobe from a hook on the way to the door. She donned the robe and said, "Tell me what happened."

"West appeared in the lobby, drunk and demanding to see you," Ramos replied. "Security asked him to leave and when he refused, they texted me."

"Bueno," Sarita said.

They reached the empty lobby and Sarita noted the time. 11:48 PM. She stopped at the front desk where a clerk came to attention.

"Bueno noches, Señorita García," the clerk said.

"Call Alba and tell her there has been a change of plans and she will not be needed tonight," Sarita instructed.

The clerk nodded. *"Sí,* I will call now."

"Gracias," Sarita called over her shoulder and headed for the older section of the hotel.

"Jefa," Ramos said behind her.

"Sí," Sarita replied.

"There is more," Ramos added.

She kept moving. "Tell me."

"An FBI agent is in Ortiz's office," Ramos said.

She stopped and turned to face him. *"¿Qué?"*

"He claimed to be West's buddy and tried to take him from the resort, so I put him in Ortiz's office."

"And he told you he is an FBI agent?"

"No." Ramos shook his head. "West did."

Sarita's muddled brain tried to process Ramos's news. A shiver ran through her, and she pulled the robe tighter around her. She needed clothes and time to think. Facing West in a robe was one thing, but the FBI agent changed matters.

"I need to go to my office," Sarita said. "I will meet you at Ortiz's office in thirty minutes.

"Bueno." Ramos continued down the hallway.

Sarita changed course and headed for her private elevator. What the hell was she going to do now? It was one thing to kill a *Federale* or an idiot banker, but an FBI agent?

The elevator doors opened, and Sarita stepped inside. She punched the button for her office and then screamed, *"¿Qué demonios hago ahora?"*

CHAPTER FORTY-FOUR

Christopher jumped to his feet at the sound of a hand on the doorknob. Despite his efforts to control his emotions, his pulse rate accelerated and sweat erupted along his hairline. The door swung open, and Ramos stepped into the room followed by Sarita García. Ramos moved aside and leaned against the wall.

"*Por favor*, Agent Temple." Sarita motioned to the chair he'd just vacated. "Sit." Settling in a chair facing the desk, she crossed her toned legs. Dark smudges under her eyes suggested fatigue, but she still looked stunning in a blood-red blouse and black capris.

Christopher awkwardly resumed his seat, his arms throbbing from being trapped behind him.

"Cut his hands free and leave us," Sarita ordered Ramos.

Ramos hesitated, then produced a switchblade. Christopher stood and presented his hands to the *sicario* who cut the zip-ties with one swipe. Christopher rubbed his chaffed wrists, turned, and held Ramos's dark stare.

Ramos headed for the door. "I will be in the hall." Sarita didn't acknowledge the assassin who shot Christopher a menacing look before closing the door.

"I don't think he likes me." Christopher sat back down.

Sarita smiled. "He likes no one."

Noting she spoke almost perfect English, albeit with a slight accent, Christopher returned her smile. He had to admit, Sarita García was an exotic beauty. Then it hit him like a bolt of lightning. She had Jade's smile. Small dimples at the corners of her lips like Jade's. Sarita also tilted her head slightly to the right like his partner. And when she tucked a long strand of raven black hair behind her ear, Christopher felt as if he were meeting an older version of Jade Mendoza.

"Agent Temple?" Sarita said, jolting him back to attention.

Blinking to clear the image of Jade's face superimposed with Sarita's, he held his hands palms up. "I don't suppose you'd consider letting me leave with West?"

"And you would consider dropping your investigation?" Sarita countered.

Christopher leaned back in his chair. "If you will testify against Agustín Castro, I can make you a deal."

"If I testify against *El Lobo*," Sarita replied. "I will not need a deal from the FBI because I will be dead."

Christopher contemplated telling her that her godfather had sent a small army intent on executing her but decided the information would make a better trump card if he had to negotiate for his own life.

He shrugged. "All right, say you have your men drop me and West somewhere on the highway." Lacing his fingers together, he continued, "It would be hours before we caught a ride or could call for help." He grinned. "You'd have time to make your escape."

Sarita shifted in her chair and a whisper of panic showed in her eyes, telling Christopher she already had a plan to disappear.

His phone vibrated, inching toward the handcuffs and his car keys lying in the center of the desk. Christopher could see Katelyn's name on the screen and struggled to read her upside-down text that said: *Goodnight.*

Sarita also stared at his phone, then raised her eyes to his. "How do you know Jade Mendoza?"

Searching her dark gaze for a hint behind the question, he decided a simple answer was best. "We're partners."

"She is also investigating me?" She asked.

Christopher hesitated. Sarita clearly knew who he was, so she must have seen him and Jade together. "We are part of a task force building a case against Castro." He shrugged. "Unfortunately, you are a means to an end."

Sarita raised her eyebrows. "Surely, you do not need me and my small enterprise to arrest *El Lobo*?"

"The task force is intent on making the strongest case possible." He turned his palms up again. "Maybe you have something you could share with me before you vanish."

This time Sarita didn't respond to his assumption. "What good would this information be if I plan to kill you before you can report anything?"

Christopher feigned a wince. "Kill is such an ugly, permanent word."

A knock echoed on the door before Ramos entered the office. *"Jefa."* He glanced at Christopher. "West is sick and vomiting. Should I call a doctor?"

Christopher noticed a flash of anger in Sarita's eyes as she shook her head. "No. Wake Alba and have her tend to him." Sarita gave him a dismissive wave. "Leave us."

Ramos's eyes narrowed to dark slits, but he did as instructed and departed. Sarita turned her attention back to Christopher, which told him she didn't care if West died.

"Since you've recovered your money," Christopher guessed. "Why not let us leave?"

Sarita leaned forward, her cleavage begging for a glance. "Agent Temple …" Her smile didn't reach her eyes, which had gone cold, and a chill ran down Christopher's spine. "It is not my practice to allow men who make my life difficult to live."

Another knock sounded against the office door, but it didn't open.

"¡Maldita!" She stood and opened the door.

"Cariño," a tall young man murmured as he pushed through the doorway. He wore pants with no shoes and an unbuttoned white linen shirt, exposing a muscular chest. He pulled Sarita to him before she could protest and before he noticed Christopher.

Sarita placed a hand on his bare chest. "Dario, I have some business to finish, then I will join you."

Glowering at Christopher, Dario asked, "Who is this?"

Christopher wanted to stand, offer his hand, and say, "Special Agent Temple, FBI. Man, your lover is about to kill." but kept his seat instead.

"He is a business partner." Sarita guided Dario back to the hallway.

Pulling her to him, Dario glanced at Christopher over Sarita's shoulder. "Why not let Ramos handle him?"

"Dario!" Sarita barked, and the young *lothario* looked like a scolded child. "I am almost done with this matter and will join you shortly."

Dario kissed Sarita, consuming her lips, then smirked at Christopher before strutting off.

Standing in the doorway, Sarita met Christopher's inquisitive gaze. Without a word, she closed the door leaving him alone. He jumped up, grabbed his phone, and punched 28@333 in reply to Katelyn's text. Then he dropped the phone into a pocket and stared at the closed door. Should he open it and hope Ramos didn't wait on the other side? Should he wait for Katelyn to share his coded text with Jade and sit tight until she came to his rescue? Should he take a chance that Sarita García would come to her senses and let him, and West, leave?

Before he could make a move, the door swung open, and Ramos motioned Christopher from the office. Christopher stepped toward the *sicario*, who squared his shoulders as if he expected Christopher to attack him. Probably not a good idea since Ramos outweighed him and was a trained killer. Turning and heading in the diréction they'd taken West. Christopher knew all he had to do was keep himself and the sick banker alive until Jade could rally a rescue. *God, I hope she gets my message,* Christopher silently prayed.

Opening a door Christopher had passed by, Ramos said, *"Aquí."* Backtracking, Christopher entered and found himself in an older hotel suite. He recognized the man sitting on a couch as Sarita's acquaintance at Joe's. The man cast a glance at Christopher, then returned his gaze to a muted television program.

Christopher took in the rest of the suite, noting an armed man standing near the still open door. Ramos nodded at the guard and closed the door as he left. A loud moan emanated from the bedroom and Christopher crossed to the doorway where he could see West writhing on a bed. A young Hispanic woman sat on the edge of the bed mopping West's forehead with a cloth. Christopher inched forward and she jumped to her feet.

"Está bien." Christopher put a hand to his chest. *"Soy su amigo."*

"Está muy enfermo." Alba looked at West.

Mark's eyes fluttered and he muttered, "Doctor," before passing out.

Christopher started toward the bed, but Ramos had returned and grabbed his shoulder. *"¡Teléfono!"* He extended his hand.

Christopher thought about denying he had his phone but decided handing it over was more appealing than being searched. He fished his phone from a pocket and glanced at the screen before handing it to Ramos. No messages.

Ramos's voice softened when he spoke to the young woman. "Alba, you need anything?" He even offered her a slight smile.

Alba jammed her hands onto her hips and demanded, "Doctor!"

Ramos shook his head. "What else?"

Glaring at Ramos, Alba stomped her foot. *"Bactiver.* Thermometer. Ice-chips. Red wine."

Ramos cocked an eyebrow as Alba continued, "And bring the others some food and drink."

Christopher was surprised to see Ramos give Alba a slight bow before narrowing his eyes at Christopher and leaving the bedroom.

Alba put the back of her hand to West's forehead. "You are his friend?"

Christopher nodded. *"Sí."*

Alba studied Christopher as if measuring his trust worthiness. "You know why he's so sick? What he eat or drink?"

Shaking his head, Christopher said, "No, except he was very drunk."

He recalled the information he'd learned about someone poisoning people in Mazatlán with methyl alcohol. The best way to treat methyl poisoning was to get to a hospital, but that didn't seem to be an option for West. The only thing Christopher could think to try was lots of water and something like Gatorade.

"¿Señor?" Alba prompted Christopher.

"Alba …" Stepping closer to the bed, his stomach lurched when the stench of vomit and urine slammed into him. "He needs water and Gatorade, or something with electrolytes."

Alba pursed her lips, then clapped her hands. *"¡Agua de coco!"*

"Great!" Christopher smiled. "Is there coconut water here at the resort?"

"Sí." Alba marched from the bedroom and Christopher followed, listening while she instructed the guard to tell Ramos she needed coconut or vitamin water from the bar. The guard gave her a skeptical look until Alba shrieked, *"¡Pronto!"*

The tiny dynamo watched the guard until he had completed his call to Ramos. He smiled at Alba and reported, *"Ramos, está trayendo el agua."*

"Bien." Stepping back into the bedroom, Alba blushed and asked Christopher, "You will help me undress him?"

Christopher tilted his head and hesitated. If Jade did come to their rescue, she'd be less than thrilled to be saving a naked Mark West. Alba ignored Christopher's hesitancy and strode past him into the bathroom. She returned with a pair of pants and a white polo shirt with the Fiesta de Fuego logo embroidered in purple on the left side.

"The clothes are for me," the man said behind Christopher. He extended his hand. "Eladio Ortiz. I am sorry to see you here Agent Temple."

Christopher shook his hand. "Care to explain why Sarita García has her business manager under guard?"

Eladio smirked. "*Federale*. I believe we have the same assignment."

Nodding, Christopher saw in Ortiz's eyes the same question running through Christopher's mind, *Is the cavalry coming?*

Alba snapped her fingers. *"¡Ahora, por favor!"*

Christopher grinned at Eladio. "Heads or tails?"

Eladio shook his head. "He is your target, you get tails."

"All right." Christopher reached for West's shoes. "Let's get this over with."

After sponging down West's body, Alba rebandaged a scrape on his upper arm, which was probably from climbing the Pueblo Bonito Mazatlán fence. Then the two agents helped her redress West. His offensive smelly clothes had been bagged and handed to the guard who looked like he might vomit.

Having limited medical training, Christopher knew how to check for a pulse and dilated pupils and could perform CPR. He hoped Mark wouldn't need any life saving measures because he doubted, they could save him.

"He is cooler." Alba gave them a wane smile.

"You are doing a great job, Alba," Eladio said.

She cast a nervous glance at the *Federale*, and Christopher wondered if she already knew their fate.

Ramos entered the bedroom and deposited the items Alba had requested onto a dresser. "Food is coming," Ramos told her. "And ice."

Alba smiled at him, then began to organize the bottles of water. She plucked the thermometer from the bottom of a bag and shook it at Ramos. *"¿Bactiver?"*

"I sent a man to pharmacy," Ramos replied.

"Gracias." Alba grabbed a bottle of coconut water and tried to coax her sleeping patient into taking a few sips.

Ready to help if needed, Eladio and Christopher stood to the side. Christopher flirted with the idea of he and Eladio trying to take on Ramos and the other guard but worried it could be a futile attempt and could possibly get one, or both of them, killed.

Hovering at the end of the bed, Ramos watched Alba tend to West and glowered at Christopher when he stepped too close to Alba.

"Is he taking some water?" Christopher asked.

"Sí." Alba raised the bottle to West's lips again. "A little."

A knock sounded on the door, followed by the smell of chicken and pork. Ramos stepped back into the main area and instructed someone to place bags on the table.

Eladio led the way and Christopher trailed him into the kitchenette in time to see Ramos following the guard from the suite, leaving a new guard in his place. Grabbing plates and silverware, Eladio placed them on the table.

"You should eat something." Eladio filled a plate and grabbed a bottle of water.

Christopher selected a few tacos, some chips and guacamole, and headed for a chair in the sitting area. They ate silently for a few minutes with a muted soccer game playing on the TV. Christopher looked over at the guard who was filling a plate as well.

"Do you think he speaks English?" Christopher asked about the guard.

Eladio shook his head. "No. But I would be vague."

"I managed to send a text from my phone." Christopher filled his mouth with half a taco.

"To Torres?" Eladio popped a chip into his mouth.

Christopher raised an eyebrow, but then if Ortiz knew who he was, he would be well informed of the others. "No, a friend."

Nodding, Eladio added, "I think our target is going to run."

"Same." Christopher dipped a chip into guacamole. "Tonight?"

"Yes." Eladio sipped some water.

"Do you think there are more men on guard?" Christopher whispered.

"Probably." Glancing at the bedroom, Eladio continued, "West will be a problem."

"Possibly." Christopher drank some water. "Also have intel indicating a small army is enroute."

Eladio gave a small nod. They ate and watched the silent soccer game for a few minutes.

Christopher had no doubt he and Ortiz could take the lone guard watching them, but not knowing what waited on the other side of the door was a problem. And, Ortiz was right, in his condition, West would be impossible to move without one of them practically carrying him.

The soccer game ended, and the programming switched to news. Christopher noted the time, 1:12 AM. Jade usually woke early to get in a run, and he hoped Katelyn had asked Jade about his bizarre message. Or maybe Jade would be concerned when he didn't check in. All he had to do was keep himself, Ortiz, and West alive for four more hours.

CHAPTER FORTY-FIVE

Katelyn exchanged a smile with María, who asked, *"¿Bueno?"*

"Muy bueno." Turning in a slow circle, Katelyn took in the revamped sitting room. The overstuffed floral couch had been covered in a clean, yellow sheet. A lightweight, cream-colored blanket and plump pillows occupied one end. The coffee table had been relocated to the same end as the pillows and now contained magazines and puzzle books. María had added a vase of fresh-cut flowers, complete with sprigs of verbena, perfuming the room with a zesty lemon scent. All the room needed now was the patient.

After a whirlwind morning of coffee, cheese Danish, and fruit; Humberto had left with Lucía and Stella for their excursion to Michael's Gallery to view Lucía's paintings. Katelyn had decided to stay at Humberto's to help María prepare for Sandrine's arrival. Jade would arrive any minute with the patient, and Katelyn took a deep breath to calm her nerves.

Heading back to the kitchen, María said, "I see to food and drink for *Señorita* Sandrine."

"Good idea," Katelyn called after her, then sat in one of the cushy chairs they'd placed near a window looking onto the circular drive. As a substitution for her missing laptop, she picked up the pad and pen she'd borrowed from Humberto's study. Tapping the pen on her lips, she thought about her missing stuff. Before he'd left for La Noria, had Martínez pawned her laptop and camera, given away her briefcase, and sold her passport? She prayed Torres and his men had captured or … otherwise dispatched with Lieutenant Martínez.

Katelyn focused on the blank page of the large note pad. All her notes for her article about the methyl alcohol deaths were tucked safely in her briefcase, but luckily for her, she still had a good memory. What the article needed now was an ending wrapping up the mysterious deaths. There hadn't been a new death for a few days, nor had there been any arrests. Frowning at the wordless page, Katelyn thought about how writing an ending without a resolution would be hard, and less than satisfying for readers. But Jessica Sanchez, editor of the *Periódico Mazatlán*, wanted an article warning citizens and tourists alike about a killer whose weapon was methyl alcohol.

The sound of an approaching car had Katelyn looking out the window. Jade stopped in the driveway and Katelyn headed for the double front doors. She opened one side of the large portico as Jade helped Sandrine climb from the passenger seat. Katelyn hadn't met Agent Mortieau, who seemed frail, but determined.

"I can walk on my own," Sandrine snapped at Jade who tried to put an arm around her friend's waist.

"I know …" Jade followed closely. "Just here in case you need help up the stairs."

The two ambled slowly toward the terracotta steps. Sandrine smiled at Katelyn and placed a foot onto the first stair. Her face morphed into a grimace as she tried to navigate the second step. Hurrying down the steps, Katelyn gently grasped Sandrine's arm.

"Oh, fantastic!" Sandrine said. "The bloody cavalry."

Jade and Katelyn helped Sandrine to the couch and guided her slowly down onto the cushions.

Pushing a lock of damp hair off her forehead, Sandrine said, "Someone get me a bloody drink."

"María is preparing some refreshments," Katelyn said. "I'll check to see if she's finished."

"Not lemonade, *chica*," Sandrine ordered.

Katelyn gave her a thumbs up, turned, and almost ran into María, who handed Katelyn a tray and dashed off.

Placing the tray, laden with chips, salsa, guacamole, and three large shrimp cocktails, onto the coffee table, Katelyn said, "Um … drinks are coming."

"Thanks, Katelyn." Jade plopped into one of the chairs.

"No problem." Katelyn looked from Jade to Sandrine, who'd closed her eyes, then back to Jade. "Is there anything else you need right now?"

Jade shook her head and looked at Sandrine, who said with eyes closed, "Still waiting on that drink."

"*Sí, sí.*" María appeared with another tray complete with a pitcher of margaritas and glasses filled with ice.

Dashing to help the housekeeper place the tray on the coffee table, Katelyn smiled and said, "*Gracias*, María."

"*De nada.*" María made her exit.

Jade had already poured and handed a margarita to Sandrine, who was taking a noisy slurp. "Only one," Jade said, receiving a glare from Sandrine. "You still have to take your next round of meds."

"Yes, *Mum*." Sandrine took another sip.

Jade offered Katelyn the next glass. "Have you heard from Christopher?"

Katelyn took the drink. "No, not yet."

Jade's forehead scrunched into a frown as she poured herself a margarita.

Katelyn's stomach flipped and her sip of margarita gurgled back up her throat. "Is something wrong?"

"I'm not sure. He usually checks in with me every morning, but not today." Concern darkened Jade's eyes. "Thought maybe he'd called you instead."

After another noisy slurp, Sandrine offered, "He's probably sleeping in."

Shrugging, Jade countered, "Maybe, we're supposed to bring West in today, so I expected to hear from him by now."

"Shit!" Katelyn's cheeks burned as she ran toward the casita. Exiting the kitchen, she dashed across the patio and yanked opened the door. She scooped up her new phone and tapped the screen alive. Christopher hadn't called, but he'd replied to her 'Goodnight' text.

His text read: 28@333

Katelyn's hands shook as she contemplated a reply. "What the hell?" she yelled at the screen, then rushed back to the sitting room.

Jade stood and Katelyn handed over the phone.

"He–he texted." She pointed at the message. "I don't know what it means."

"Damn it, C!" Jade shouted and handed the phone to Sandrine.

"Not good." Sandrine passed the phone back to Katelyn. "Where the hell is he?"

Pulling her phone from a pocket, Jade said, "Fiesta de Fuego, I think. I'm checking the numbered code."

"Wh–why—" Katelyn jumped when her phone rang.

"Is it Christopher?" Jade asked.

"It's not the same number." Katelyn showed Jade the screen.

"Answer it on speaker," Jade instructed.

Katelyn nodded. "He–Hello."

"*Hola, perra,*" a voice growled into the room.

Katelyn's knees weakened at the sound of Martínez's voice.

"I am enjoying your friends," Martínez snarled. "But they do not like my company."

"Don't touch me, you bastard!" Stella's voice echoed through the phone.

"Stella!" Katelyn shrieked.

"Escuchar, puta," Martínez said. "You bring me camera card; I give you your amigas."

"Where?" Katelyn asked.

"I will call with time and place," Martínez said as another scream echoed in the background, then the line went dead.

Her flipping stomach had become a full-on acid storm. "Oh, God," Katelyn mumbled.

Jade took her by the shoulders. "Where's Humberto?"

The doors crashed opened, and Humberto stormed into the house shouting, "Katelyn!"

"We're in here!" Jade shouted.

Marching into the room, Humberto looked around wildly. "Lucía and Stella are not here?"

Katelyn shook her head and Jade answered, "Martínez has them."

"¡Mierda!" Humberto rubbed his temples. "Where?"

Shrugging her shoulders, Jade said, "He's calling with a time and place. He wants some camera card."

Stepping toward the door, Katelyn said, "I'll get it."

"No." Humberto caught her elbow. "I will handle this."

"Humberto," Jade said. "Where is Torres?"

"On his way back from La Noria." Humberto replied.

"Do you think I can use some of his men?" Jade asked. Humberto cocked his head and she continued, "I think Sarita García is holding Agent Temple at Fiesta de Fuego."

"His men here are stretched very thin." Humberto ran his hands through his copper hair and his disheveled appearance worried Katelyn.

Struggling to her feet, Sandrine said, "We just need a couple."

Jade shot a look at Sandrine. "You are not coming with me!"

"Bullshit," Sandrine fired back. "I'm all you've got. Now get me a damn gun and let's go get your boy."

"Do you have Officer Vasquez's number?" Humberto asked Jade.

Thumbing her phone alive, Jade nodded. "I'll text him to meet me at the resort."

"Bueno," Humberto said over his shoulder. "I will be right back."

Typing into her phone, Jade said to Sandrine, "Look … I know you want to help, but you just had surgery."

"I'm coming, so stop worrying about me and come up with a bloody plan!" Sandrine commanded.

Humberto returned and handed a gun to Sandrine, who weighed it in the palm of her hand. "Nice, a Glock 43."

"Vazquez says he can meet us in thirty minutes." Jade checked the magazine in her gun. "How long before Torres returns?"

Shaking his head, Humberto answered, "I cannot wait for him."

"I'm going to need a gun too," Katelyn said.

Jade stared at her, then exchanged a headshake with Humberto. "That's not a good idea."

"Jade is right," Humberto said. "You cannot go with her."

"I'm not going with Jade …" Squaring her shoulders, Katelyn looked from Jade to Humberto. "Martínez wants me, well, and the camera card, so I'm coming with you. It's time to end the bastard's reign of terror."

Katelyn jumped when her phone rang. The same number Martínez had called from before flashed on the screen. "It's him," she whispered.

Stepping to Katelyn's side, Jade instructed, "Answer on speaker again."

Katelyn connected the call. "Yes."

"Katelyn …" Stella said.

"Stella! Are you okay? Where are you?"

"We're okay," Stella replied. "He wants you to bring the camera card and meet him at Valentino's at one."

"I'll be there."

"Lyn, everything is fine," Stella continued. "It's just like that time you and I hid from those mean girls." She laughed, but Katelyn could hear fear in her voice. "Remember how we had to hug the wall to avoid the rotten fl—" The line went dead.

"She's telling you something isn't she?" Jade asked.

Katelyn swiped at a tear rolling down her cheek. "I think they're being held in a room with a damaged floor."

"Clever," Sandrine said.

"Valentino's is being renovated." Humberto disappeared down the hall.

"Stella and Lucía are strong." Jade touched Katelyn's arm. "They'll be okay."

Humberto reappeared with an old newspaper in hand. "About a month ago the *Periódico Mazatlán* ran an article outlining the timeline for the repairs." He flipped through the pages, folded the paper in half, and tapped a photo of Sheik Night Club. "The glass floor has large cracks and is being restored."

Jade took a closer look, then said. "Be careful." She helped Sandrine to her feet. "We have to go."

"I'm fine, damn-it!" Sandrine scolded and headed for the main doors.

Following them, Humberto said to Jade, "You also be careful and good luck."

Jade's smile didn't erase the worry lines creasing her brow. "Will do." She looked at Katelyn. "Don't get yourself killed."

Katelyn managed a slight nod before Jade and Sandrine left. Katelyn had an overwhelming urge to run after the two agents and jump into Jade's car. Christopher was in danger, and she wanted to help rescue him, but Lucía and Stella were being held in exchange for an image of a psycho and a woman he probably killed imprinted on her camera card.

Striding from the sitting room, Humberto motioned for Katelyn to follow. "I will get you a gun and then we must go."

Fear stole Katelyn's voice. Snaked through her gut. Brought sweat to her brow. She had no idea how she would help Humberto save their friends. But thanks to her BFF, they might have one advantage …

knowing the floor where they were being held was damaged, could serve as an equalizer against the maniac holding them hostage.

CHAPTER FORTY-SIX

Fresh from a hot, soothing shower, Sarita sipped coffee and watched Dario sleep, his chest gently rising and falling. She would miss watching him. Miss his company. Miss their lovemaking.

Sarita had sent Dario back to her suite after he interrupted her meeting with Agent Temple. She'd found him pacing the bedroom, furious she'd left in the middle of the night. But Sarita kept her own temper in check, explaining the agent and his friend had caused a drunken scene in the lobby, and she'd been called to assess whether they should be turned over to the *policía*.

The doubtful look Dario gave her told Sarita he knew she was lying. She guessed he chose to ignore the lie as he had ignored all the rumors about her nefarious activities.

He'd wanted them to return to bed, but she'd convinced him she needed a glass of champagne to settle her nerves. Sarita pulled a new bottle of sparkling wine from the fridge in the sitting area of her penthouse, popped the top and selected two crystal flutes from a cupboard. Taking advantage of Dario's need to use the bathroom, she dropped a two-milligram tablet of valium into his flute and added champagne. The pill fizzed as Sarita swirled the glass, then dissolved just in time for Dario's return.

Sarita handed him the flute and clinked hers against his. *"¡Salud!"*

"*¡Salud!*" Dario gulped some bubbly, but Sarita only held her glass against her lips.

She took him by the hand. "Come, let's sit on the balcony and watch the ocean lighten with a new day."

Flashing a lecherous grin, he declared, "And then we return to bed."

Kissing him deeply, Sarita hoped to placate him, so he'd quickly finish his champagne. She needed him sound asleep so she could complete the finishing touches for her departure.

Dario stirred, bringing Sarita back to the current moment. He mumbled what sounded like, *"No, nena ..."* turned onto his side and reached for her.

For a split second, she wanted to strip naked and climb in beside him. Forget she needed to flee. Forget she had the last annoying banker, a *Federale,* and FBI agent, locked in a suite. Forget that by leaving, they would be at the mercy of Hector Ramos and whatever orders *El Lobo* would give.

Satisfied Dario would not wake anytime soon, Sarita bid adieu to her fabulous penthouse and exited one last time. She breathed a sigh of relief when she saw that no one waited for her at her private elevator. Stepping inside, she caught a glimpse of herself in the mirror. Since her plans to leave in the middle of the night had gone awry, she now wished her earlier stroll through the lobby on the way to her private garden and romantic dinner with Dario hadn't been noticed. Smiling in the mirror at her subdued attire of tan capris, white scoop neck T-shirt, and white ballet flats, she pulled her long, dark hair into a ponytail. To compliment her plain outfit, she wore no makeup and small diamond studs in her earlobes. A whiff of her new fragrance, Escape, enveloped her. For a nanosecond, Sarita mourned the glamorous woman she was leaving behind. Then the elevator doors whooshed open.

Barely noticing the early guests lining up for the breakfast buffet at the Aqua Bar, Sarita crossed the lobby. She didn't look around, intent on not attracting any attention, and turned down the hallway leading to her office. Again, a flicker of relief washed over her when she saw the empty hallway and her unguarded door. She keyed the lock and stepped inside.

She'd already cleared her office, removing anything that might incriminate her or place someone on her trail. Sarita sat behind her desk, opened the middle drawer, and stared at her new official identification, iPhone, and Sig P365. She collected the items and tucked them into a black clutch embroidered with a white sugar skull.

She needed to send one more text from her old number, then she would remove the sim card and battery before stashing the disabled phone in a desk drawer.

Sarita: *Alba, por favor, encuéntrame en mi oficina*

Alba: *Sí, en mi camino*

After she'd tucked Dario into bed, Sarita had texted Ramos to see how the captives were behaving.

He'd responded: *Alba tended to West. Improving. Agents stare out window.*

Sarita doubted either Ortiz or Temple was accepting their fate. Fear that the two agents would try to escape fueled her need to leave sooner rather than later. She told Ramos if he felt the situation was under control, to get some sleep and they would meet this morning to decide what to do with the trio.

But I will be long gone by then, Sarita told herself.

A light knock sounded against her office door and Sarita said, *"Entra."*

Alba entered and greeted her boss with her usual sunny smile. Dark smudges under Alba's eyes told Sarita the young maid hadn't slept much either.

"Buenos días, Jefa," Alba said.

"Buenos días," Sarita replied. *"Por favor, tenga un asiento."*

Taking a seat in a chair across from Sarita, Alba smoothed the purple skirt of her uniform.

"Thank you," Sarita began, "for attending to *Señor* West last night. I trust he is well this morning?"

Alba nodded and stifled a yawn with the back of her hand. "*Sí.* He ate, or drank, something bad, but is better now."

"*Bueno.*" Sarita pulled a file folder from a desk drawer. "I need you to deliver ..." Sarita slid an envelope across the desk, "this to *Señor* Díaz when he wakes."

Tilting her head, Alba gave Sarita a questioning glance.

Sarita handed a second envelope to Alba. "This is for you to open after you give Dario his envelope. *¿Entiendes?*"

Alba touched the envelope with her name scrawled across the front, then a knowing look flashed across her young face.

"Now, I would like for you to bring food to the men Ramos is detaining."

"*Sí.*" Alba nodded. "I already bring coffee, rolls, and fruit."

"*Bueno.*" Sarita smiled at her efficient aide. "Thank you, you can go."

Standing, Alba searched Sarita's face. "Can I bring you something?"

Sarita shook her head. *"No, gracias."*

Alba picked up the two envelopes and turned to leave.

"Alba," Sarita said. "You have been a *maravillosa* assistant."

Beaming at Sarita, Alba bowed slightly, then exited the office.

Sarita slipped the sim card from her phone and dropped the card into her purse. She placed the disabled phone in the bottom of a desk drawer and set files filled with miscellaneous paperwork regarding Fiesta de Fuego on top.

Running her plan through her mind one last time, she leaned back in her chair and stared out at the Pacific Ocean. She expected Dario to sleep until noon or later, which would mean no goodbye in person. *I have already said goodbye,* Sarita thought to herself.

She had given Alba her instructions and hoped the young woman would appreciate her generous bonus. And love driving Sarita's BMW.

Sarita hoped Ramos was still asleep but doubted it. She assumed he'd been in touch with *El Lobo*, making her escape even more urgent.

Crossing to the credenza, she poured herself a shot of Patrón. She toasted her past in the large mirror above the cabinet, tossed down the citrusy alcohol, and hung her purse from her shoulder. All she had to do now was leave her office, navigate the lobby, and step from Fiesta de Fuego into her new life.

"Estoy lista," Sarita said. "Ready as I will ever be."

CHAPTER FORTY-SEVEN

Christopher stared at a muted baseball game on TV and tried to come up with another escape scenario. It appeared Mark West wasn't going to die, which would make fleeing easier since he'd be able to walk out of Fiesta de Fuego on his own.

Once Alba stabilized West, Christopher and Eladio had quietly discussed their limited options. Ramos had added a guard to the bedroom to watch over West, and one remained guarding the door. They agreed a guard was probably stationed outside the suite. Without weapons, Christopher knew overpowering the guards would be difficult. It would require a surprise attack.

Christopher glanced at Ortiz, who slept sitting upright in a chair. They'd taken turns dozing through the early morning hours but were still exhausted. The door swung open, and Alba entered with a tray of sandwiches, bags of chips, and a pitcher of pink juice. She placed the tray onto the dining table.

Motioning to the guard who stood by the door and the guard who'd followed her into the suite, Alba said, *"Por favor, disfrute."* She pointed to the table, lifted the pitcher, and poured the pink liquid into a glass. *"Jugo de hibisco."* Alba also handed a glass to the bedroom guard when he joined them. *"Gracias,"* he said.

Approaching Christopher, Alba leaned over the back of the couch and whispered, "Do not drink the juice."

Christopher did a slight head bob as Alba turned and headed for the bedroom, where West still slept. Poking Ortiz on the shoulder as he passed by, Christopher motioned for the *Federale* to follow Alba. Christopher stepped inside and watched Alba place the back of her hand on West's forehead.

"Alba, why shouldn't we drink the juice?" Christopher asked.

"I brewed it with passion and hibiscus flowers," Alba whispered. "It will put them to sleep."

Christopher exchanged a glance with Eladio, who asked, "And why would you do that?"

"I think *Señorita* García is going away." Alba looked at each of them. "And you are in danger, *¿sí?*"

Eladio nodded. *"Sí."*

Mark sat up and glared at them, then dropped his head into his hands. "Ugh! Why does my effing head hurt so bad?" Moaning, he fell back into the pillows.

Rushing to his side, Alba said, "You were very sick, *señor*." West cracked an eyelid and Alba smiled at him. "You feel better, *¿sí?*"

"Water," Mark rasped.

"I will grab him a bottle." Eladio crossed to the dresser where Alba had her supplies.

"Alba," Christopher met the maid's brown eyes with a concerned stare. "You will need to come with us."

She shook her head. "No. I leave on my own."

Eladio returned with the opened water bottle and handed it to Alba, who offered it to Mark.

"Gracias." After guzzling half the bottle, Mark looked down at his clothes, then at Alba. "Nice duds, but where are my clothes?"

"Trust me." Christopher wrinkled his nose. "You don't want them back."

Glaring at Christopher, Mark muttered, "What the hell is going on?" He switched his gaze to Eladio. "Who are you? Why am I here?" He started to climb from the bed but sat down suddenly. "Whoa."

"You go slow." Alba propped pillows behind Mark, then moved closer to Christopher and Eladio.

Pointing to the door, Alba whispered, "As soon as they sleep, you need to leave."

The two agents nodded, and Eladio asked, "Alba, where is Ramos?"

"I help him sleep too." Her blush told Christopher he didn't need to ask how. "But you need to hurry," she added.

"Has Sarita left yet?" Eladio asked.

Shrugging, Alba said, "Not sure. She was just in her office."

Loud thuds came from the kitchenette. The trio inched toward the door, and Christopher poked his head around the jamb. "They're asleep."

"We need their guns." Eladio began stripping the guards of their weapons.

"Alba," Christopher said, "is there a back way out of this wing?"

"No." Frowning, she continued, "you go toward lobby. Take *alcoba* door to garden. Find the side road."

Eladio handed Christopher a gun and tucked one into his waist band. "*Por favor,* Alba, come with us."

"Ortiz is right." Christopher touched her shoulder. "You'll be safe with us."

"*Está bien.*" Alba held up a set of car keys. "Sarita gave me her BMW." Grinning, she added, "It drives fast, *¿sí?*"

CHAPTER FORTY-EIGHT

To quell her fear, Katelyn clasped her hands together and tried to appear calm. During the fifteen-minute drive to Mazatlán, they hadn't spoken. She assumed, Humberto, too, was running different scenarios of what awaited them at the abandoned Valentino's building.

Guiding his Land Rover to a stop on a side road lined with vendors selling a myriad of dishes from food carts, Humberto cut the engine and climbed from the SUV. When Katelyn stepped onto the sidewalk, the scent of spicy food assailed her. The uneasiness she'd felt in the car morphed into a queasy stomach. Ignoring the bile that bubbled up at the back of her throat, she joined Humberto behind the Land Rover.

"So that I'm not seen, I will enter through a service entrance on the other side of the building." The SUV's gate whooshed up and Humberto checked a semi-automatic rifle, then zipped the case closed. "Martínez is probably watching to see if you are alone. But we are early, so we might catch him by surprise."

Handing Katelyn, a small gun, he pointed to the side of the weapon. "The safety is on." He touched the lock. "To turn it off, you swipe down with your thumb."

"Got it." Katelyn looked at her friend.

Reaching around her, he touched a spot above the waistband of her shorts. "Tuck the gun here." He searched her face. "Do not use the gun unless you have to."

Katelyn squared her shoulders to reassure herself and Humberto that she was ready to do whatever it took to rescue Lucía and Stella.

Humberto's phone pinged and he checked the screen. "Marco is still an hour away."

Katelyn's pulse rate spiked, and she saw her dashed hope reflected in Humberto's eyes. He, too, had hoped Marco would arrive in time to help them.

Swallowing her fear, she said, "Tell me about the building."

Humberto looked up at the stark white stucco structure that looked like an old Arabic Castle. He moved to the front of the SUV. "There are several businesses within Valentino's besides the Sheik Restaurant." He drew a crude drawing on the dusty hood. "I will go up the stairs from the service level." He placed an X in the middle of his drawing. "You enter here, up the stairs and through the main entrance." Humberto cast a glance at the building, then continued, "It may look as if the doors are locked, but I am guessing Martínez has removed any restraints."

Katelyn looked at the building. "Will you be able to hear me once we're inside?"

"*Sí.*" Humberto slung the rifle case strap over his shoulder. "Katelyn, this is very important. No matter what Martínez does or says, do not walk on the glass floor."

A picture Katelyn had discovered when doing her research on the famous structure flashed in her mind. Her heart stuttered at the memory of the rocky beach and churning surf below the restaurant's glass floor.

"Katelyn?" Humberto touched her hand. "Ready?"

"No." Katelyn blew out a breath. "But let's do this."

"*Bueno.*" Humberto stepped off the curb and Katelyn followed.

They crossed the street and Humberto tapped her shoulder when they reached the building. He showed her five fingers, then pointed to the wide staircase that led to Valentino's main entrance.

Katelyn understood she was to wait five minutes to give Humberto a head start. A mental countdown began in her mind as she watched him hug the stucco walls and slip around the corner of the building. She looked at her phone and tried to slow her breathing. Finally, it was time. She left the shade of a palm tree and crossed the busy street.

Sweat instantly bloomed on her skin and the afternoon sun temporarily blinded her until she reached the top of the stairs. Humberto had been right—the glass doors were unlocked. When she pulled one side open, a length of yellow "Do Not Enter" tape tugged against a stack of empty paint cans, sending them rattling across the tile floor.

"You are early, *chica*," Martínez hissed somewhere ahead of her. "Come and join the party."

Blood pounded in her ears as she crept toward the restaurant. She pictured Humberto waiting on the other side of the wall. Scuffs against the floor echoed through the empty building, and Katelyn strained to hear the exact location of the noise. She reached another set of glass doors, said a quick prayer, then stepped into a large dining room. Massive floor-to-ceiling windows showcased the ocean and provided a picturesque backdrop. In contrast, a dilapidated table and several broken chairs rimmed the large dance floor.

Lucía sat in the only remaining good chair. She had a gag tied over her mouth, and a trickle of blood running from her forehead down her cheek. Katelyn met Lucía's stare and was relieved to see a flash of anger in her eyes. Scanning the room, Katelyn didn't see Stella. She looked back at Lucía, who tilted her head toward a closed door behind the bar.

Katelyn knew she had to draw Martínez into the open so Humberto would have a target and could take a shot. "Show yourself, Martínez, and I'll give you the camera card."

Silence.

"Stella?" Katelyn called into the cavernous room and moved closer to the closed door. She reached for the handle and the door flew open.

Martínez lunged at her. *"¡Te voy a matar, perra!"*

"Humberto!" Katelyn fought the crazed cop, but she was no match for him. "Let go of me you, bastard!"

He dragged her toward the cracked restaurant floor. "You need to pay for ruining my life!"

"Humberto!"

Martínez looked around, then sneered at her. "No one is coming to your rescue, *¡perra!*"

The report of the rifle boomed through the room, and she saw Martínez's eyes grow wide. He clung to her as they toppled backward. The next thing Katelyn heard was cracking glass. Blood poured from Martínez's shoulder, but he still managed to wrap her in a bear hug. His dark eyes probed Katelyn's and his lips curled into an evil grin.

"Can you fly, *¿puta?*" Martínez asked, the floor rumbling beneath them.

Humberto shouted, "Katelyn, get free of him!"

Katelyn jammed her thumb into Martínez's shoulder wound, and he yowled, loosening his grip enough for her to roll away from him. Reaching behind her, she brought the gun forward and took aim.

Martínez emitted a crazed keening sound and grabbed at the gun. She lost her grip and the weapon skidded along the floor. Another shot from the rifle struck Martínez in the side. The echo from the rifle mingled with the boom of the floor giving way. Katelyn scrambled to avoid being sucked into the vortex as Martínez fell through the hole.

"Humberto!" She braced herself with one foot on a large metal I-beam as Martínez grabbed her other ankle.

"Hold on!" Humberto called from behind her.

Martínez had his arm hooked over the same joist and jerked hard, trying to pull her from her precarious perch.

Humberto crawled to the widening hole and grabbed her under the armpits.

Katelyn tugged against Martínez's grip, wiggling her foot free of her canvas shoe, then kicked him square in the face.

Martínez lost his hold and screamed, *"¡Puta!"* A booming round of waves punctuated the sickening sound of his body landing on the jagged rocks below.

Humberto hauled Katelyn up onto the floor, and the two scrambled to safety. He jumped to his feet and raced to Lucía. Katelyn dashed into the room Martínez had come from and crept toward a heap on the floor.

Squinting into the darkness, she whispered, "Stella …"

"Wait!" Humberto said from the door. Pulling his phone from his pocket, he thumbed open the flashlight app, illuminating the darkness. "Lucía thinks Martínez set a trap."

"Stella is not in there," Lucía said behind Humberto. "That is just a broken chair covered by a drop cloth."

Katelyn spun around. "Then where the hell is she?"

Holding up a hand, Humberto said, "Quiet."

A tapping noise floated up from somewhere below them. Humberto gingerly moved closer to the opening. "Martínez is still there."

"Stella must be downstairs." Katelyn bolted from the restaurant and flew down the staircase, Humberto and Lucía close on her heels.

Once she made the sidewalk, she dashed around the outside of Valentino's, stopping abruptly on the *malecón* and stared down at a cliff of jagged rocks. Katelyn pulled off her other shoe, then turned and began to climb down backwards.

"Katelyn!" Humberto reached for her, but she'd already moved down too far.

"I'm fine!" Katelyn continued her descent.

"¡Mierda!" Humberto followed Katelyn down the rocks, almost catching her before she leaped down to the sand.

"Stella!" Katelyn shouted; her words swallowed by a round of thundering waves.

"Katelyn …" Humberto came to her side. "The tide is coming in."

"We have to find her!" Katelyn turned in a circle. It was barely audible, but she could swear she heard her BFF say, "Lyn."

Humberto had waded to the other side, then waved at her. "I found her."

Katelyn raced to join him and gasped when she saw Stella. She sat chained to a chair, with the surf now up to her breasts. She had a swollen black eye and a cut on her cheek. Dried blood matted her blonde hair. Katelyn rushed to her friend and tugged at the chain.

"What took you so long?" Stella croaked.

"Oh, Ella …" Katelyn choked back a sob. "I'm so sorry."

Jangling the cuffs on her wrists, Stella pleaded, "Get these the eff off of me."

Humberto stepped closer and found the padlock holding the chain together. "I will search Martínez for the key."

"Don't bother." Stella shook her head. "The bastard swallowed it."

"Marco is on his way, and he'll have a key." Katelyn brushed Stella's hair from her eyes.

"We don't have time to wait." Humberto looked around, then waded deeper into the water to the edge of the rock wall. He scanned the rough surface, then picked up a boulder and headed back. "Stella, you are going to need to hold your breath."

"What? Why?" Katelyn didn't get an answer. Humberto tipped the chair onto its side, putting Stella under water. "Humberto!"

Without hesitating, he lifted the boulder over his head then brought it crashing down onto the chair. Two of the legs broke free and floated away on an outgoing wave. Humberto repeated the process, and the chair broke into pieces.

Stella stood, coughing and spewing sea water. "Th–thanks."

A large wave sent them all stumbling backward, and Stella swayed on her feet.

"We need to get away from these rocks." Humberto looked back the way they'd come, but the water was now almost to the top of the rock formation. He slogged back to where he'd found the boulder and disappeared from sight.

Katelyn wanted to scream, "Don't leave us here!", but she knew her dear friend would not abandon them.

Humberto returned, the water now up to Katelyn and Stella's armpits.

"The water will be deep, but I think we can reach a narrow strip of sand that will lead us up the beach. He wrapped his arm around Stella's waist and motioned for Katelyn to follow.

Katelyn stared at Martínez, who floated in the waves like a marionette doll cut free from its handle. "Hope you enjoy hell," Katelyn said to his corpse, then followed Humberto and Stella.

The waves seemed to have doubled in size. With each step, the trio was pushed precariously close to the rock wall. A few men emerged from the crowd at the edge of the surf and came to their aid.

"Help the women," Humberto gasped.

A couple of tourists slathered in suntan lotion grabbed Stella's arms and helped her up the beach. A hawker who'd been carrying colorful sombreros on his head assisted Humberto as he guided Katelyn onto the hard-packed sand.

Lucía raced toward them. "Thank God you are all safe!" She hugged Humberto. "Marco is meeting us at Hospital Balboa."

Katelyn checked Stella's head wound.

Stella winced. "Ouch."

"It's not bleeding anymore," Katelyn reported.

"Well, it still hurts like hell," Stella replied. "Lucía are you okay?"

"*Sí,*" Lucía said.

Handing the car keys to Katelyn, Humberto said, "You drive." Then he put Stella's arm around his neck and guided her toward the street.

Katelyn looked up at Valentino's, then cast a glance toward the rock formation at the bottom of the building. Though she couldn't see Martínez, she relished the idea of him in his watery grave—eventually becoming fish food.

CHAPTER FORTY-NINE

Eladio Ortiz backed into the alcove.

Stop!" Jade shouted. "DEA!"

Dragging Mark West with him, Christopher stepped into the entry way. "He's with me," Christopher said to Jade, who lowered her weapon.

West stumbled to a shabby couch and passed out.

Securing her gun, Jade motioned past Christopher. "Who's waiting for us?"

"Her soldiers." Eladio extended his hand. "Eladio Ortiz, *Federale*.

Sandrine and Jade shook Eladio's hand.

"Where are Torres and Álvarez?" Christopher tucked his gun away.

Jade exchanged a look with Sandrine. "Torres is on his way back from La Noria."

Christopher braced himself for what else Jade had to say. "Tell me."

She met his concerned gaze. "Martínez grabbed Lucía and Stella from Panama's while Humberto was on the phone …"

"Damn it!" Christopher read Jade's concerned face and knew there was more. "And?"

"Temple …" She narrowed her eyes. "We need to focus on arresting García."

He knew Jade was right, but he also needed to know if Katelyn was at risk. "Tell me," he growled.

"Bloody hell." Sandrine stepped between them. "Katelyn's gone with Humberto to rescue their friends."

"What?" Christopher looked at the ceiling, then back at Jade.

"C … Torres is on his way to help them." Jade moved closer to him. "You know Humberto won't let anything happen to Katelyn."

Christopher agreed, Humberto would protect Katelyn. Fighting the urge to rush to her rescue, he refocused on the task at hand. They needed to arrest Sarita García and get the hell out of Fiesta de Fuego alive.

"All right then. Where might we find García?" Sandrine asked Eladio.

"Her office is on the fifth floor, on the other side of the resort." Eladio looked at Christopher. "Her men are probably patrolling the lobby. And if Ramos is not already awake, I doubt he will sleep much longer."

Wiping sweat from her brow, Sandrine said, "Well, we can't stand around and debate this any longer."

Pointing at Sandrine, Jade added, "She's right. No one knows who we are, so we'll take a stroll to see how many soldiers are in the lobby." She checked her phone. "It will also give us a chance to see if Vasquez made it."

"Vasquez?" Christopher asked.

"I texted him before we left Humberto's." She waggled her phone. "But no response."

Christopher ran a hand over his stubble. "Maybe he's with Humberto."

"Maybe." Jade agreed, but Christopher saw doubt in her eyes.

"Checking the lobby is a good idea." Eladio looked at Christopher for confirmation.

Christopher observed the sweat glistening on Sandrine's dark skin and wondered if she was up to the task.

"Want to act like tourists?" Sandrine asked Jade.

"Sure, girls gone wild …" Jade suggested. "Or honeymooners?"

Sandrine swayed on her feet. Christopher and Eladio each grabbed an arm. "I'm fine," she insisted, but her weak tone suggested otherwise.

"You're bleeding!" Jade lifted Sandrine's shirt and inspected the bandage under her arm. "Shit!" Jade cut her eyes to Christopher, and he could tell she was worried.

"Do you still think you can manage the drunken friend ruse and make it outside?" Christopher asked Jade. "See if Vasquez is waiting?"

"We're fine." Draping an arm across Jade's shoulders, Sandrine added, "We'll be right back."

Christopher glanced at Sandrine, then met Jade's gaze. "You're sure?"

"She's bloody sure," Sandrine groaned. "Let's get this over with."

Turning her butt to Christopher, Jade said, "Take my phone." He plucked her phone from a back pocket as she continued, "If it's clear, we'll text you."

Christopher nodded, and Jade guided Sandrine from the alcove. He watched them stagger down the hallway toward the lobby.

"West is still alive," Eladio said behind Christopher. "But he is not well."

Crossing the small space, Christopher looked out through the glass door. "Where does this lead?" He pointed to the well-worn path cut across an overgrown patch of grass.

"To a side road." Eladio stepped to the door. "Which is probably where your friends left their car."

"Do you think any of García's soldiers are patrolling the area?"

Eladio shrugged. "I would think—"

Gun shots punctuated by shouting echoed down the hallway from the lobby. Christopher pulled his gun from the small of his back. "Stay with West."

"He is not going anywhere." Eladio checked the magazine in his gun and stepped into the hallway.

Casting a glance at West, Christopher joined Eladio. Another barrage of gunfire rang out and the two agents each hugged a wall. They picked up their pace and hurried toward the lobby. Jade backed down the hallway thick with gun smoke, sheltering Sandrine behind her and firing at approaching soldiers. Christopher stopped and held up his hand, bringing Eladio to a halt. A bullet ricocheted off the wall above Christopher's head, and he turned to see a female bearing down on them.

"Mierda!" Eladio aimed and fired at the woman. She quickly ducked through an open door.

"Temple!" Jade shouted. "A little help!"

"Hold her off," Christopher barked at Eladio. "Go!" he shouted at Jade, then stepped in front of Jade and Sandrine. He returned fire at the soldiers hunkered down in the lobby. Guests were screaming and fleeing through the entry doors.

The acrid smell of gunfire burned the back of Christopher's throat and shots boomed behind him. He turned to see Eladio fall into the wall and slide to the floor. Sarita García stepped into the hallway and fired several shots toward Christopher. Sandrine stumbled and Christopher stooped to help her up as García ducked into the alcove, Jade hot on her heels.

Half carrying, half dragging Sandrine, Christopher entered the nook behind Jade.

"Stop, DEA!" Jade yelled.

Sarita stood looking out the glass door, gun at her side, then turned and glared at Jade. Christopher wanted to shove Jade aside and shoot García, but he still held Sandrine.

"Shoot the bitch …" Sandrine growled.

Sarita brought her gun up and took aim.

Stepping closer, Jade said, "I wouldn't if I were you."

Sarita glared at Jade. "Your father would be disappointed to know you work for the other side."

Christopher saw a look of confusion cloud Jade's face, but she stayed on script. "Drop your weapon and raise your hands."

"No, hermosa sobrina," Sarita said. "Unfortunately, I am going to leave before I get to know you better. You, *mija,* are not going to stop me."

Jade inched toward Sarita. "Try to leave and I will shoot you."

Sarita squared her shoulders, and this time didn't try to hide her anger. "Your father is turning in his grave knowing his daughter is a DEA agent."

Jade shook her head. "You know nothing about me."

"I know you made a mistake thinking you and your FBI friend could bring me down," Sarita said. "You do not have the authority to arrest me."

"She does not …" Eladio said behind Christopher. "But I do." Blood darkening his tan shirt, Eladio moved in front of Jade. "Sarita García, you are under arrest."

Christopher guided Sandrine to the couch and she sank down next to West, who was now wide awake and taking in the dramatic scene unfolding in the alcove.

Jade moved forward; her gun aimed at Sarita's head. "Drop your weapon, *Mother.*"

Sarita cocked her head slightly as Christopher joined Jade. Even though he'd recognized the similarities between Jade and Sarita, he wasn't sure he'd heard Jade correctly. Glancing at her, he could see she meant what she said. He turned his attention back to García.

"Everyone …" Jade said. "I'd like for you to meet my mother. Sarita García: Drug Queen, Murderer, Bitch."

CHAPTER FIFTY

The alcove walls seemed to close in on Sarita. Sweat ran in rivulets from her temples, down her back, and between her breasts. Jade couldn't be her daughter. She'd been told the baby had died. Surely her parents wouldn't have lied to her. Now that she looked more closely at Jade, she could see the young woman looked just like her at that age. *I have a daughter*, she thought, but her overtaxed brain doubted Jade's proclamation.

She squared her shoulders. Jade's announcement changed nothing. She had a plan, and she had no intention of going to jail. Surrendering was not an option, since being caged would only make her easier prey for *El Lobo*.

Backing into the glass door, Sarita said, "I am not going to surrender." She cracked the door open with her butt and a whisp of hot air slithered into the small room.

A bullet ripped through the wall next to the couch. "I've been hit!" West shouted, gripping his arm.

Christopher turned toward the nook entry, while Eladio and Jade kept their weapons trained on Sarita. Rapid gunfire rang out and men rushed past the entry as Christopher returned their fire.

"Sarita …" Eladio moved closer. "I promise to get you the best deal."

Leveling her gun at him, she shook her head. "You know I cannot be locked up. *El Lobo* will terminate me before I can testify against him." Sarita swallowed to clear bile burning the back of her throat. She wasn't used to begging … for anything. "You know you have to let me go."

Sarita saw Eladio's eyes shift to a spot behind her and prayed it was one of her soldiers coming to her rescue. Leaning into the glass, she almost fell on her ass when the door flew open.

"I have them, *Jefa*," Ramos said. "Step outside."

Eladio steadied his aim on Sarita until she was clear of the building, then he met the cold dark eyes of the *sicario* who had a gun in each hand. Ramos kicked the door closed, and Christopher shattered the glass with a shot that went wide, missing Ramos. The *sicario* fired back, a bullet finding the wall on the other side of the hallway.

"*¡Adiós, querida hija!*" Sarita shouted without looking back and headed down the path she knew would take her to a side road.

She heard Jade yell after her. "Sarita, this isn't over!"

Rustling behind Sarita and Ramos suggested the agents were still in pursuit. When they came to the edge of the dense foliage, a black Nissan Rogue sat waiting for them. Sarita stopped and looked back, past a struggling plumeria tree dotted with a few fragrant, white blooms. She couldn't see Jade or the others, but she knew they were there, waiting for a chance to kill Ramos and capture her.

Jumping into the driver's seat, Ramos called to her, *"Jefa."*

The *sicario* cranked the engine as Sarita fired a couple of shots into the air above the shrubbery and then climbed into the passenger seat. *"¡Conducir!"*

Ramos whipped the SUV around, punched the gas, and headed toward the main highway.

"How did you know?" Sarita asked.

"Alba," he replied.

"¿Qué?" Why would Alba betray Sarita after she gave her a generous bonus and the BMW?

"She drugged me," Ramos said, and Sarita was surprised to see a smile on his face. "I guessed she also drugged the guards, helping the agents and West escape."

"*¡Perra!*" Sarita pounded her fist against the dashboard.

Laughing, Ramos careened onto the highway. "When I find her, I will tell her you are glad she left."

A whisper of panic flitted over Sarita, but she strived for a stern tone. "You will not hurt her?"

Ramos glanced at Sarita, and she saw confusion in his eyes. "No. I care for her …"

She filled in the blank left by Ramos's hesitation: he was in love. Nonetheless, he was a *sicario* and now had her trapped in a car. "Where are you taking me?"

Turning toward her, Ramos grinned. "You are not the only one who wants to escape."

Sarita held her breath. "You are not taking me to *El Lobo*?"

Glancing at her, he shook his head. *"No, Jefa.* We both want to be free, *¿sí?"*

Questions jumped into Sarita's mind, and she took a minute to sort through them, deciding what she really needed to know.

"Did you know Ortiz was a *Federale*?"

"I did not trust him." Ramos looked at her. "But no, I did not know."

Focusing back on the road, Ramos swung wide of a landscaping truck, narrowly missing a worker exiting the vehicle. The man waved his arms and hurled profanities after them as they raced down the boulevard.

Palming the dashboard for support until Ramos had the car under control, Sarita selected her next question. "Why did you participate in the airport attack?"

"It is my job, *¿sí?"* He honked at a slow-moving car, then cut around the dilapidated vehicle. "The bankers needed to be stopped."

They rode in silence for a few miles and her cheeks warmed as she mulled over Ramos's revelations. She had been convinced the *sicario* was put in place to spy on her for *El Lobo*, and eventually, see to her demise. Ramos was the main reason she'd stepped up her plans to disappear and here he was helping her execute her escape.

"You did not tell Castro about Ortiz and the FBI agent?" Sarita tilted her head.

Switching lanes, Ramos answered, *"No, Jefa."*

She gazed out the window at the blurring buildings and sidewalks teaming with people, but she could only see Eladio aiming a gun at her, tarnishing the memory of his kiss. Despite her anger over his betrayal, Sarita hoped his bosses were furious with him and sent him far away from Mazatlán, safely out of *El Lobo's* reach.

"I think, Castro …" Ramos cut into her thoughts, "will have trouble now with both *Federales* and Americans investigating him." He grinned. "He will be too busy to look for us or Ortiz."

Pointing at Ramos, she asked, "You hate Castro?"

"Sí." Ramos's grin became a scowl. "He had my fiancée murdered, tortured me, and kept me in a hole until I agreed to become *sicario*." He blasted the horn at a slow-moving taxi. The driver hugged the curb and flipped them off when they raced by.

Sarita took in Ramos's profile. Had she been so angry and afraid that she hadn't noticed how handsome he was? She'd heard similar stories about how young men were forced into becoming *sicarios*. Despite seeing him in a new light, she still couldn't imagine this hulk of a man being tender and loving with Alba.

"You have planned to leave for a while, *¿sí?*" Ramos asked Sarita.

Smiling at him, Sarita said, *"Sí.* I no longer have the stomach for the drug business and the ever-changing demand, especially for fentanyl." She sighed. "And I am tired of worrying about being arrested or … killed. *¿Entiendes?*"

"*Sí.* I had *Señor* Díaz held in your penthouse with orders not to allow him to leave until the shooting was over."

Sarita knew a shocked look accompanied her tilted head.

"You are in love too, *¿sí?*" Ramos grinned at her.

Sarita laughed at his directness. Good question! Was she in love with Dario or did he simply assuage a primal need? Could she have fallen in love with Eladio if their circumstances were different? Another good question. She shrugged. "I am not sure."

"*Jefa,*" Ramos said, his tone serious. "You will be careful looking for Jade, *¿sí?*"

She nodded. "And you will need to be careful finding Alba."

"*Sí.*" He swerved around a cab cutting too close in front of them.

They drove in silence for a few minutes, the afternoon traffic clogged with workers making their way out of the city.

"Alba will be *enojado* …" Ramos interrupted the quiet. "When she has to ditch your BMW."

"*Sí.* But neither of you will be safe driving a flashy car if *El Lobo* is looking for you."

Pulling a small box from his pants pocket, he handed it to Sarita. "Peace offering," he said.

When she lifted the lid, a trio of diamonds set in a gold band winked back at her. Sarita touched Ramos's arm. "She will love it." She removed the diamond studs from her ears, slipped them into the box, then handed the package back to Ramos.

His eyebrows pulled together, creating a unibrow. He looked from her to the box, to the road, and back to Sarita.

"No, *Jefa.*" He shook his head. "It is too much."

"*Bien.*" Sarita retrieved her earrings and handed him the box. "Instead of the earrings then, repay me by sending the BMW off *Puente Baluarte.*"

She knew the highest cable-stayed bridge in the world, one of fifteen bridges on the highway from Mazatlán to Durango, hovered

1,322 feet above the valley below. A look of understanding crossed Ramos's face. It would be a fair assumption that Sarita had headed back to her villa in Durango, putting her on the treacherous bridge. Of course, Ramos would have to sell the idea of the BMW careening over the edge, a task she knew he could handle. Also, it was doubtful anyone would brave the valley below to look for Sarita. *Besides*, she thought, *cartels kill people all the time.*

Laughing, Ramos tucked the box into his pocket. "How you say, *dos pájaros …*"

"Exactly," Sarita giggled. "Two birds, one stone." Waving toward a bus stop just ahead of them, she said, "Pull over there."

"I can drive you to the airport." He flipped the blinker anyway.

"No." Gathering her purse from the floorboard, she looked up and met his eyes. "This is better for both of us." She exited the car. "Good luck with Alba and your new life."

"Same, Boss." Ramos grinned, gave her a two-finger salute, and drove away in the stolen Nissan.

Sarita watched until she lost the car's taillights in the crush of traffic, then turned away. She left the bus station and headed for her rented house five blocks away.

As she wove in and out of tourists and locals clogging the sidewalks, recent events competed for attention in her mind. She had a beautiful daughter. And despite Jade working for the DEA, Sarita couldn't help but be proud. Sadness stepped in front of her moment of pride when she realized she'd never get to know Jade—the woman who had once been the baby she thought lost forever. New questions demanded attention, but she knew she had to focus on finalizing her escape.

Soon she'd have time to contemplate Ramos being in love—and his desire to disappear with Alba. The reality she had left her old life behind, including Dario. The mind-boggling news she had a daughter. Smiling to herself, Sarita knew she would find a way to be part of Jade's life, even if it meant doing so from afar.

CHAPTER FIFTY-ONE

Christopher pulled the shattered glass door open and stormed into the alcove where Sandrine and Mark shared the couch.

"All quiet." Eladio took a step back to make room for Jade who followed closely on Christopher's heels.

"Damn it!" Jade screamed at no one in particular. "We almost had her."

"We'll find her." Christopher faced his partner.

"How?" Jade fired back, her face crimson. "We can't even get the hell out of here!"

"Bloody hell," Sandrine mumbled. "Stop shouting."

"It is possible Ramos called off Sarita's soldiers after they escaped." Peeking into the hallway, Eladio reported, "It seems quiet."

"C!" Jade punched Christopher in the arm. "What the hell were you thinking coming here without backup?"

Christopher didn't respond. He knew he couldn't answer to Jade's satisfaction, given her current state of mind.

"And ... and ..." Jade pointed a finger at him. "You texted your girlfriend the rescue code, not me!" Shoving a sweaty lock of hair off her forehead, she glared at him.

"I had to act fast, so I responded to the last text on my phone," Christopher growled.

Jade shook her head. "And you thought your new, untrained lover would know what the numbers meant?" Jade threw her hands in the air. "Unbelievable!"

"Hey …" Mark said. "Does anyone care that I've been shot and need a doctor?"

"No!" Christopher and Jade yelled simultaneously.

Waggling his bandaged hand at Mark, Christopher yelled, "You're not the only one effing wounded!"

"He is fine." Eladio tilted his head at West. "Like mine, it is just a flesh wound." Looking from Jade to Christopher, Eladio continued, "Calm now?"

"Hardly." Christopher checked the ammo clip in his gun. "Three rounds."

Following Christopher's lead, Eladio checked his weapon. "Six." He frowned. "Guess we should have grabbed the guards' extra clips."

Jade checked her Glock, then took Sandrine's borrowed gun from her shaking hand. "I'm half empty." Pulling another clip from her back pocket, she held it out to them. "Plus, this and Sandrine's weapon is almost full."

Trying to come to her feet, Sandrine added, "But no extra clip." Winded by the effort, she sunk back down onto the couch.

"My Jeep's in a side lot, but they took my keys." Christopher said.

"And I'm guessing García and her *sicario* took my car, since we came from the direction they used for their escape," Jade added.

Christopher pointed through the shattered glass door. "How far to the side road?"

"Quarter mile," Jade answered.

Eladio cut his eyes to Sandrine and Mark. "But it will be difficult."

"Is the spare key still in the Jeep's wheel well?" Jade asked Christopher.

He shrugged. "If it hasn't fallen off."

"All right," Jade said. "What's the fastest way to the lot?"

Hauling West to his feet, Eladio replied, "Outside the door to the right."

Sandrine stood, bumping into West, who moaned pathetically and mumbled, "I need water."

"We all need water." Sandrine glared at West. "Stop your bloody whining."

"I think Ramos knew Sarita was running," Eladio said to Christopher. "And directed his men away from this area."

Looking at Jade, Christopher asked, "Do you think she'll have any trouble?"

"I'll be fine." Jade shrugged. "They're not looking for me."

Eladio glanced at Christopher, then said to Jade, "You cannot see it at first, but once you get close to the bougainvillea hedge, you will find a small opening the staff created."

"Copy that," Jade said. "C … take my gun since I have Sandrine's." She handed her weapon to Christopher. "And I'll need my phone back."

"Jade." Christopher handed her the phone and tucked the gun away. He placed his hands on her shoulders. "Thanks for coming to our rescue." Bowing his head until their foreheads touched, he inhaled the scent of her lavender shampoo. "Good?"

She gave him a wan smile. "Good."

Raising his head, he searched her eyes. "You're sure?"

"She's bloody sure," Sandrine groaned. "Let's get this over with."

Jade looked at her phone, then showed Vasquez's text to Christopher: *The front is covered by García's soldiers. Looks like they are fighting new arrivals.*

"*El Lobo's* men?" Eladio suggested.

"Probably," Christopher said. "Their timing's good …"

"Yep," Jade added. "García's men will be too distracted to worry about us."

"Ready?" Christopher asked.

Jade nodded. "I'll find the Jeep and pick you guys up at the end of the path." She held the frame of the exit door open. "Once I'm in the Jeep, I'll text Vasquez to meet us too."

"Bueno." Eladio said, dragging West into the overgrown garden.

Following Eladio, Jade held the door and Christopher helped Sandrine through the opening.

"See you in a few." Jade headed for the hedge.

"Jade …" Christopher called after her.

She turned and smiled at him, and for a second, he doubted he could let her go alone. Jade gave him a salute and faded into the shadow of the building.

"Come on, Temple." Sandrine tugged his arm. "She'll be fine, but this heat is killing me, not to mention I'm bleeding and …"

Christopher tightened his grip around her waist, stealing the rest of her words, and trudged after Eladio.

CHAPTER FIFTY-TWO

Katelyn touched her swollen, bloody lip, wishing she had a glass of water, or a shot of tequila, to wash the metallic taste from her mouth. Hospital staff were working on Stella's injuries; and of course, she was insisting she was fine.

Katelyn juggled her emotions as she watched. One minute, she felt grateful she and the others were now safe. Then anger would swoop in and steal her relief, causing her to want to kill Martínez all over again. Of course, tears found their way to her eyes once reality finally settled in. She'd survived. They'd all survived.

"Señorita," the ER doctor said to Stella. "You are not fine." Swabbing blood from the cut on her cheek, he added, "This wound can be taped, but the gash on your scalp will need stitches."

"Thanks, Doc." Trying to sit up, Stella winced from the effort and laid back on the pillow. "Lyn? Where's Lyn?"

"I'm here, Ella." Katelyn stepped closer to the bed and held Stella's hand. "Be a good patient so we can take you home."

As the nurse cleaned blood from Stella's hair, she asked. "Lucía's okay?"

"Yes." Katelyn took Stella's hand, resisting the urge to wrinkle her nose as the stench of dried blood and antiseptic assailed her senses.

Cringing as the nurse cleaned her matted hair, Stella asked, "And Martínez is still dead?"

"Yes." Katelyn squeezed Stella's hand. "I'm going to let Humberto know you're almost ready to go."

Stella closed her good eye. Katelyn waited a few seconds before going in search of Humberto. He and Lucía waited in a triage room two doors down from Stella's. The same ER doctor checked Lucía's pupils with a penlight, while Humberto held her hand and watched from the side of the bed.

"You seem to be fine, *Señorita* Torres," the doctor said. "I believe it is safe for you to go home as long as you will not be alone."

"She will be staying at my house, Dr. Morales," Humberto said.

"Bueno," Dr. Morales replied.

"When will *Señorita* Quinn be released?" Humberto asked.

Pulling a prescription pad from his shirt pocket, the doctor said, "She will be staying with you as well?"

Humberto nodded. *"Sí."*

"I will write prescriptions for them both." Scribbling on the pad, the doctor added, "One to aid with sleep and one for pain."

Turning to Katelyn, Humberto said, "I will get the prescriptions filled if you could stay close by."

Dr. Morales handed the slips to Humberto and smiled at Katelyn as he exited Lucía's room. "I will see to your *amiga's* head wound, then you can go."

"Katelyn …" Lucía waved her closer. "How are you?"

Katelyn shrugged. She swallowed to clear the lump forming in her throat.

"You were very brave." Lucía held her hand out to Katelyn. "I am grateful Humberto had you to help rescue us."

Katelyn took Lucía's hand in both of hers. "And Stella was lucky to have you with her, otherwise we might not have been able to res—" Katelyn swallowed a sob.

Lucía nodded. "*Sí* … We are all very lucky."

A nurse looked at the monitors behind the hospital bed and made notes in Lucía's chart. "*¿Necesitas algo más?*" the nurse asked.

"*No, gracias.*" Lucía smiled and shook her head.

"*Bueno.*" The nurse headed from the room just as Humberto returned.

"I have the medication." He showed them a small white bag. "We can leave as soon as Stella is ready."

Katelyn hooked a thumb over her shoulder. "I'll go check on her." Stepping through the doorway, she bumped into Christopher. "Oh, thank God you're safe!" Wrapping her arms around his waist, she noticed his grimace and tried to pull away.

He held her close. "Same to you."

"Christopher …" Concern flashed in Humberto's eyes. "Where are Jade and Sandrine?"

"They are down the hall." Christopher motioned behind him. "The doctor is checking Sandrine's wound."

"*¡Gracias a Dios!*" Humberto shook Christopher's hand. "And Sarita García?"

Sighing, Christopher said, "Long story."

"As is ours," Humberto said. "Will Sandrine need to stay in the hospital?"

"Not if she has anything to say about it," Stella said. "She's giving the doc more trouble than I did."

"Are you okay to walk?" Katelyn rushed to her friend. "Do you need a wheelchair?"

"I'm good, Lyn." Stella grinned at Christopher. "Glad to see you're still alive, Agent Hottie."

"Likewise." Christopher pointed to her left eye. "Nice shiner."

"You should see the other guy." Stella laughed, then winced.

"Shall we go check on Sandrine?" Lucía took Humberto's arm. "Then maybe we can go home."

"You should all go," Christopher said. "I'll bring Jade and Sandrine once Sandrine's released."

Pointing first to Christopher's hand, then to his side, where a hint of blood showed on his grimy T-shirt, Katelyn said, "You need medical attention too."

"I'll have a nurse do some rebandaging." Christopher kissed the top of her head. "Go with the others."

"But …" Katelyn touched his cheek.

"I have to check on Mark West." Shifting his gaze to Humberto, Christopher added, "He's here, too. Torres is with him, along with a *Federale*, Eladio Ortiz."

"A long story indeed," Humberto said.

"I asked Vasquez to have two officers guard West." Marco joined the conversation. "He is evidently very dehydrated."

"Yes," Christopher agreed. "We think he drank tainted alcohol and was very sick, but Sarita García's maid managed to get him stable enough for us to escape."

Katelyn sucked in air, then said, "If he drank methyl alcohol, he's lucky to be alive."

"Also …" Marco continued. "Agent Ortiz has been summoned to his headquarters."

Katelyn observed the varied glances the three men shared and suspected being summoned to headquarters didn't bode well for Agent Ortiz.

"For debriefing?" Humberto asked Marco.

Marco gave a slight head bob, and Christopher added, "I'm guessing Jade and I will need to be debriefed as well."

"*Sí,*" Marco answered. "But it can wait until we have returned to Humberto's."

"*Bueno,*" Humberto said. "Marco, we should bring the women to my house." Pulling his phone from his shirt pocket, Humberto continued, "María is preparing dinner. I will let her know we are on our way."

Katelyn felt like she was watching a tennis match with three players as her attention bounced from Christopher to Humberto to Marco. Finally, her gaze settled on Christopher.

He smiled at her and said, "I'll update Jade and Sandrine and we'll come to Humberto's as soon as we can."

Katelyn sensed something more than the news about Ortiz was bothering Christopher and she knew he'd explain everything when and if he could. Or maybe it was none of her business. In the meantime, it had been a hell of a day for all of them. Regrouping at Humberto's would give them a chance to finally breathe.

CHAPTER FIFTY-THREE

Christopher watched Katelyn help Stella settle onto the couch in Humberto's study. Frown lines creased Katelyn's forehead as she tucked a blanket around her friend. The pained expression on Stella's face belied her claims of being fine.

When Jade carried a plate of chicken burritos and Mexican rice past him, the aroma of spices made his mouth water. Sandrine sat on the leather cushions of the other couch with a pillow propped under her arm to keep pressure off her rebandaged wound.

"Thanks …" Sandrine took the plate. "But what I really need is a bloody drink!"

"Same …" Stella said. "Lyn, how about a couple of shots for me and my injured *amiga*?"

Katelyn shook her head and looked at Jade. "You're both on painkillers! Drinking can wait!"

"Agent Temple …" Marco stood next to Christopher. "Once you have eaten—"

"You'd like a debriefing." Christopher glanced at Marco.

Meeting Christopher's gaze, Marco replied, *"Sí."*

Christopher broke eye contact. "Do you want to wait until Agent Ortiz can be present?"

"I spoke with his superiors and will be meeting with them tomorrow," Marco said. "Ortiz has already been reassigned and will be heading for Puerto Vallarta in the morning."

Christopher held Marco's dark stare, but the captain's eyes reflected nothing in the way of answers. Ortiz was most likely being sent on a menial assignment as punishment for letting Sarita García avoid capture.

Looking down, then raising his gaze back to Christopher, Marco added, "Also, Special Agent Ferris reached out to me. I am to make sure you, Jade and West are on a plane as soon as possible."

Christopher gritted his teeth and his jaw muscles tightened. Torres was just doing as asked, so Christopher reigned in his anger. "When?"

"Tonight, as soon as we complete the debriefing." Marco shifted his stance. "I tried to buy you more time, but Ferris has already sent a plane."

"Thanks, Captain Torres." Christopher attempted a smile. "It's time to wrap things up."

Joining them, Humberto asked, "You told him?"

Marco nodded.

"Christopher, Marco's officers found Katelyn's passport in a safe in Martínez's house," Humberto said. "Since he is no longer a problem, she will be safe here."

"Thanks, Humberto," Christopher said. "If you'll excuse me, I'd like to make my goodbyes."

"Certainly," Humberto said as Christopher walked away.

He'd known he'd have to say goodbye to Katelyn at some point but didn't expect the time to be now. His mind raced with scenarios of how he could spend more time with her. Maybe she could stay in Mazatlán, and he could return shortly. Or maybe he'd fly her to LA for a few days before she returned to Oregon. Maybe, he should just take her hand, and, like Sarita García and Hector Ramos, they could disappear too.

"Hey, Agent Hottie." Curling her finger, Stella summoned him over. "Did you hear the good news?" Smiling at Katelyn, she continued.

"We've decided to stay another week and finally have an effing vacation."

"That's great." Taking Katelyn's hand, he said, "Okay if I borrow Katelyn for a minute?"

"Of course." Stella forked up a bite of burrito.

Christopher led Katelyn from the study toward the front doors. Pulling her into the sitting room, he covered her lips with his. They both pulled back, touching their wounds, and laughed. He gently kissed her again, then guided her down next to him onto the floral couch. He ran her stripper stripe through his fingers.

"What's up?" Katelyn asked.

"I'm leaving for LA tonight …" Taking her hands in his, he continued, "My bosses want us to return with West. They've already sent a plane for Jade and me."

"It's okay …" Katelyn smiled. "I knew you were here for work and that this … whatever this is … would have to stay in Mexico."

"What if you stop in LA for a few days on your way to Portland?" Christopher searched her eyes. "I'm sure I can take some time off …"

"And …" Katelyn bussed his lips. "We can finally finish our desser—"

"TEMPLE!" Jade screamed.

Both Christopher and Katelyn jumped to their feet.

"What the hell?" Christopher crossed to the door and yanked it open. "Jade!" he called after her as she stumbled back toward Humberto's study.

"C!" Jade rushed toward him and Katelyn. "It's my sister! Ezmé … she–she's missing!" Jade handed him her phone and covered her mouth with her hands.

Humberto and Marco stood behind Jade, and Marco caught her as she began to crumble to the floor.

"Come," Humberto said. "Bring her back to the study."

Wrapping his arm around Jade's waist, Christopher helped Marco guide her down the hallway. Sandrine took Jade's hands in hers as they eased Jade into a chair.

Christopher knelt next to the chair and read the message on her phone: *Jade, it's Joy. Ezmé is missing! I think she's been abducted! How fast can you get to PV? Call me!*

"Jade, look at me." Touching her chin, he raised her eyes to meet his and her terrified gaze caused his heart to skip a beat. "Let's break it down." Christopher kept his tone calm. "Did you call Joy?"

Jade shook her head as Marco reached for her cell phone. "I will call to see what I can find out."

"Thanks. Joy is Ezmé's chaperone." Christopher stayed focused on Jade. "When was the last time you and your sister talked or texted?"

Jade gave him a haunted look. "Two days ago."

"When I was in the hospital?" Sandrine asked.

Jade rubbed her temples. "Texted while in the waiting room."

Handing a shot glass to Jade, Humberto said, "Drink this."

Looking up from Jade, Christopher noticed Katelyn and Stella standing next to Humberto. He shifted his attention back to Jade. "Do you know any of Ezmé's friends we could contact?"

Clutching the shot glass, Jade shook her head.

Marco returned, small notebook in hand. "I spoke with Joy, and she said Ezmé was with her most of yesterday on a modeling assignment. But she did not return home after meeting friends for dinner." Consulting his notes, he added, "Joy spoke with the friends, but none of them had any idea where Ezmé might be."

Nodding at Marco, Christopher then said to Jade, "Ezmé hasn't been missing that long. We'll find her."

Jade jumped to her feet. "I need to go!"

Christopher stood, exchanging a look with Sandrine. Sandrine said, "I'll go with Jade to Puerto Vallarta, and you return to LA with West. Yes?"

Placing his hands on Jade's shoulders, Christopher asked, "Jade, do you want me to come to PV too?" In his mind, he could hear the tongue-lashing their handlers would give them for not following orders.

Jade took a deep breath and blew it out with a head shake. "Take West to LA." Turning to Sandrine, Jade asked, "Can you get a plane to take us to Puerto Vallarta?"

"I called Juan Vega," Humberto said. "He has a plane that can be ready in a half hour."

"Thanks, Humberto," Christopher said, then turned to Sandrine. "You'll keep me posted."

Sandrine frowned. "You're going to need a bloody phone."

"Text us when you get a new phone, C," Jade instructed, and Christopher could tell she'd shifted from worried sister to focused agent. "Humberto, can we bring guns on Vega's plane?" Jade asked.

"You could have a problem with customs when you arrive." Punching the keys on his phone, Humberto asked, "Do you have your credentials with you?"

Sandrine nodded and Jade said, "I have mine."

"*Un momento*," Humberto said into his phone, then spoke to Jade, "I will have Vega tell his pilot to be prepared to cover for you." He continued his phone conversation.

"I can drive you to the airport," Marco said to Jade. "Christopher, I am afraid our debriefing will have to be in the car. I will meet you all outside."

"C …" Jade met his concerned gaze, and despite her stoic demeanor, Christopher saw worry in her dark eyes. "I need my gun back."

Extracting the Glock 27 from his waistband at the small of his back, he handed the gun to her.

She tucked the weapon away. "Say your good-byes. I'll meet you at the car."

Christopher closed the space between himself and Katelyn in quick, long strides as the others left the study. "I have to go."

Katelyn brushed stray strands of hair from his forehead. "Go and be—"

Christopher quieted her with a kiss.

"I'm gonna join the others …" Stella made her exit too.

Katelyn wrapped her arms around his neck and leaned into his kiss, then, she palmed his chest.

"Go …" She stepped back and attempted a smile.

Christopher fingered her botched color panel. "Don't fix it. It suits you." He winked at her, then strode from the study.

CHAPTER FIFTY-FOUR

Sarita sipped champagne, the tiny bubbles tingling her nose, and read the article in the *Periódico Mazatlán* a second time.

SARITA GARCÍA DISAPPEARS IN A HAIL OF BULLETS
Jessica Sanchez, Editor
While our motto is "No Bad News", we would be
negligent if we did not bring you the most
recent report regarding Sarita García.
For the record, this reporter predicted *Señorita* García
would flee when the walls of justice closed in on her. The
Mazatlán *policía*, led by Captain Marco Torres, scoured
Fiesta de Fuego and the surrounding grounds for the
elusive drug queen after a shootout between a menagerie
of law enforcement officers and García's soldiers.
According to sources, Sarita García knew the *Federales*,
as well as the FBI and DEA Agencies from the United States,
were closing in on her. Guests and employees from Fiesta
de Fuego reported seeing *Señorita* García the night before
her disappearance dressed as if she were attending a black
tie gala. Others noted seeing her later wearing a non-

descript outfit before vanishing into thin air.

Evidence that Queen Sarita planned her escape in advance lies in the details. She left the Fiesta de Fuego property, and millions in ill-gotten cash to her paramour, Dario Díaz. When asked if he knew of his lover's whereabouts, *Señor* Díaz said, "*Señorita* García is on holiday and will return soon." That is doubtful, since there have been several Sarita sightings throughout Mexico. Sarita García, I suggest you keep moving and never return to Mazatlán.

From the balcony of her Puerto Peñasco hotel suite, Sarita looked across the vast Sea of Cortez, imagining she could see the shoreline of San Felipe.

She folded the paper, sending her musings back to the corners of her mind, and poured another glass of champagne. The sea breeze fluttered her hair, and she brushed dark strands from her face. Popping the last bite of a chocolate *concha* into her mouth, she contemplated where she should go next. A hint of sadness brought tears to her eyes. Even though she knew she should move again in a few days, she was tired of being unsettled. Images of her penthouse swirled in her mind like a kaleidoscope, each new view a blend of luxury, beauty, and … Dario.

Swiping a stray tear from her cheeks, Sarita mentally ticked off potential destinations in her mind. Maybe she needed a location without a spectacular view. Then she could focus on her original plan to read all the classics, learn to paint, and plant a garden. But as satisfying as Sarita had thought those activities might be, she now doubted her patience to accomplish one, let alone all of them.

One thing Sarita knew for certain: nothing would satiate her longing for Dario. A seagull called across the beautiful view spanning to the west, winging its way to an unknown destination. Sarita wondered if the bird was looking for its mate. Or possibly a new partner.

Maybe, like the seagull, Sarita should find a replacement for Dario. Maybe she should send for Dario once she was settled. Maybe she should stop speculating and take a cold shower.

CHAPTER FIFTY-FIVE

Thankful to have her laptop back, Katelyn re-read the draft of her article for the *Periódico Mazatlán*. It recounted her investigation into a depraved individual who poisoned people with wood alcohol. Her article suggested the murderer hated tourists and might work as a waiter rotating through the various Mazatlán resorts. The killer added his concoction of methanol to guests' drinks, and in most cases, the consumption of their favorite tropical beverage resulted in the tourist's death. A couple of victims had survived their poisoning. Also, thanks to one young woman, Captain Torres now had a sketch of a possible suspect. But despite his men's efforts to locate the killer, there had been no arrests.

She'd begun following the random deaths last year while on vacation in the Mayan Riviera and Katelyn suspected the serial murderer had, once again, simply moved on. Perhaps he was looking for his next vacation spot full of unsuspecting prey.

Memories of the Riviera vacation conjured images of enjoying margaritas at a beach bar with Stewart and watching the sunset. Katelyn searched the recollection for signs of Stewart's unhappiness, but all she could remember was their laughter as they discussed potential honeymoon destinations. Katelyn had wanted to honeymoon somewhere in Mexico, but Stewart convinced her a tour of the Cayman Islands would be a romantic adventure.

"And then the bastard cheated with brainless Cilla!" Katelyn slammed her laptop closed. "I need another beer."

She wandered to the casita fridge, grabbed a cold Corona, popped the tab, and took a long swig. It had been two days since Christopher had left with Jade and Sandrine. The only news since the trio's departure was that Jade didn't have any leads on the disappearance of her sister, Ezmé.

Captain Torres had returned Katelyn's laptop, camera, and passport, but his officers hadn't recovered her phone or cash. She'd had funds wired to *Citibanamex* and promptly bought herself a new iPhone. She'd added everyone's information to her new phone … except Christopher's. *What happens in Mexico, stays in Mexico,* she told herself.

Katelyn had enjoyed her quiet, productive morning, but was ready for company. She read her article one last time, then emailed it to Jessica at the *Periódico Mazatlán*. Katelyn drained the Corona bottle and decided to go in search of a late lunch in Humberto's kitchen.

She crossed the patio and strolled into the house, where María stirred something on the stove.

"Yum," Katelyn said. "That smells delicious."

"*Sopa de tortilla de pollo*." María smiled. *"Sentarse."* She motioned for Katelyn to take a seat at the nook table.

Katelyn replaced her empty Corona with a Pacifico from Humberto's fridge and sat down. The view beyond the nook window suggested another warm, beautiful day in paradise. Sipping her beer, she relished how relaxed she felt. She hadn't been so truly at peace since the debacle in Portland. No more anger over Stewart's affair. No more mourning her lost wedding nuptials. No more menacing Martínez.

She hoisted the Pacifico bottle in toast to her future, even though she had no idea what it might entail. *Probably a break from drinking,* she mused.

"*¡Disfrutar!*" María placed a bowl of steaming chicken tortilla soup in front of Katelyn, along with a plate loaded with tortilla strips, sliced avocado, and shredded *manchego* cheese.

"*Gracias,* María." Katelyn returned the maid's beaming smile, then spooned up a bite. "So good," she gushed.

"You too skinny." María patted Katelyn's shoulder. "*Comer,*" she ordered, then headed back to the sink.

Katelyn laughed and added more tortilla strips to her bowl. Spooning in another bite, she wondered what the others were doing for lunch. Stella had been excited to have a redo shopping day. She, Lucía, and Humberto had left just after breakfast, planning to return in time for dinner on the patio. Stella was picking up a thank you gift of colorful margarita glasses for Humberto and Lucía.

Katelyn slurped up the last of the soup and carried her dishes to the sink. María was off doing other tasks, so Katelyn loaded the dishwasher, her mind mulling over her to-do list. She had arranged for her and Stella to spend a week of actual vacation at Emerald Bay before they flew home to Portland, and she needed to gather her things and pack.

Dishes done, she grabbed another Pacifico and headed to the casita. It had been a bizarre trip full of enough craziness to last Katelyn a lifetime and she looked forward to much needed R&R at Emerald Bay.

Pushing the casita door open with her hip, she stepped into the small, cool abode. She checked her laptop and saw a reply from Jessica:

Katelyn ~
Your article seems spot on, but I'm disappointed the
policía haven't arrested someone. As you know, tourism

is Mazatlán's leading industry, so it would be helpful if
some maniac wasn't poisoning guests at our resorts.
Made a few grammatical corrections and changed some
of your phraseology. Let me know if you want to see
the piece again before I publish this week's paper.
Always ~ JS

Katelyn replied:

No need to see article again ... Thanks, K

She knew whatever changes Jessica made would only serve to make the article better. She drank some beer and headed for the small closet. "Might as well get the packing over with."

She grabbed her suitcase, carried it to the bed, and lifted the lid. A small, white box sat in the middle of the empty luggage with a note from Lucía. Katelyn scooped up the small slip of paper and read the message:

Katelyn ~ Lisa Reyes delivered this gift for you
after discovering Christopher had left it behind
in the cabin. Lucía

Katelyn picked up the box and lifted the lid to reveal a pink, bejeweled dragonfly pendant. She looped her finger through the silver chain and the twirling dragonfly refracted sunlight streaming through the windows. A folded notecard lay at the bottom of the box. Placing the necklace onto the bedspread, she scooped up the card.

This reminded me of your strip of pink hair, which,
by the way, is sexy as hell! C

Katelyn lifted the dragonfly again, admiring how the light changed the crystals from hot pink to fuchsia. She fingered her faulty color block and smiled. Maybe she *should* ask Humberto for Christopher's new number. Maybe she *could* spend a few days in LA. Maybe she *would* thank Christopher for his thoughtful gift in person.

CHAPTER FIFTY-SIX

Sarita stared at her image and selected a hunk of long black hair. She loathed the idea of cutting her luxurious locks, but she only had herself to blame.

"Estúpido," she told her reflection, setting the scissors onto the bathroom counter. She padded back to the kitchenette, poured herself a glass of champagne, and wandered onto the deck of her hotel suite. She toasted the Sea of Cortez, and the last two weeks slipped through her mind like a vacation slide show.

She had traveled along Mexico's west coast, heading south first until she'd reached the city of Salina Cruz, a surfer's paradise located on the Gulf of Tehuantepec. Then she'd traveled north to Puerto Peñasco, a quaint fishing village sitting on a small strip of land that joins the Baja California Peninsula with the rest of Mexico.

In each town along the way, Sarita stuck to small, boutique hotels and local restaurants, always paying in cash. If she decided to over-imbibe, she drank tequila or red wine in her hotel room. And when her desire for Dario overwhelmed her, she took long walks on the beach, or packed up and headed to the next town.

Only once had her need for release clouded her judgement. Her desire landed her in the bed of a handsome young tourist after dinner, dancing, and a bottle of *Cazadores*. Sarita had rented a small house for a couple of nights. The young man and his *amigos* decided to eat at the same restaurant that she had selected on her second night, and the group of friends asked her to join them. The next thing she knew, the young man's buddies had abandoned him in search of more scintillating entertainment.

To avoid the awkwardness of the morning after, Sarita left his hotel room before her lover woke. It had been a fabulous night, but one she knew she couldn't repeat, so she packed up and headed south again.

Winding her way south to Cabo San Lucas, Sarita had driven the whole day, blasting tunes from an oldies radio station, with the musky smell of blooming creosote bushes blowing through the car's open windows. Despite the distraction of the radio, her mind insisted on asking the same questions over and over. *Why had her parents lied to her about Jade dying at birth? Had they told her the truth about complications during delivery allegedly leaving her sterile? Did her parents arrange for Jade's adoption?*

Now she pondered whether she would simply fade into the flux of visitors in the popular tourist town but decided she couldn't take any chances.

"So now I must change my looks in case my one-night Romeo reports our encounter." She drained the flute, marched to the kitchen, and grabbed the champagne bottle. She filled the glass, took a long sip, returned to the bathroom, and picked up the scissors.

Sarita cut her hair into a shoulder length shag, and curls sprang up around her face now that the strands were lighter. Next, she added colored contact lenses to her brown eyes, lightening the shade to a warm tawny color. She fingered the light pink lipstick she'd bought to replace her signature blood red. In addition to the contacts, she'd added a pair of slightly magnified readers and another pair of plain sunglasses.

"Might as well take my new look to dinner." Sarita dressed in black capris and a tan blouse, slipped on sandals, and added the pink lipstick.

She checked the cash in her clutch and stashed the room key in a small zipper pocket.

A burnished orange sun backlit the tops of buildings as Sarita navigated the bustling streets of Cabo, still teeming with college kids on Spring Break. When she'd walked to the *farmacia* her first night in town, Sarita had noticed a quaint-looking restaurant a few blocks off the main boulevard. After a couple of wrong turns, she found *Mi Casa* and smiled at the building's old-world charm.

Stepping inside, a young woman greeted Sarita with a smile and asked, *"¿Cuántos para la cena?"*

"Uno." Sarita returned her smile, then followed the hostess toward the back of the restaurant, where she placed a menu on a table set for two.

The young woman scooped up the extra place setting. *"Disfruta de su cena."*

Sarita nodded and took her seat. Within seconds, a waiter brought chips and salsa to the table and filled a water glass.

"May I bring you a drink?" he asked.

"Sí, Patrón."

Jotting her order on a pad, he hurried off to the bar. Sarita took in her surroundings. Her table sat to the left of a stage equipped with various musical instruments and speakers. Colorful walls were adorned with vibrant paintings. Sarita thought if she closed her eyes, she might open them to find herself back in Durango, sitting across from Dario in *Esquilón*, her favorite restaurant. The memory of his lips on hers, his lips everywhere, sent a warm flush pulsing through her. God, how she missed him.

The waiter arrived with her shot, which she promptly tossed down. *"Otro."* She placed the empty glass back on his tray. He bowed and went to do her bidding.

Sarita glanced at the menu, but she knew no amount of food would satisfy the hunger burning in her loins.

CHAPTER FIFTY-SEVEN

The buzzing voices filled Christopher's ears, the noise almost deafening.

"Agent Temple." Assistant Director Ferris tapped his pen in front of Christopher.

Christopher blinked at his boss and sat up straighter. "Sir?" He noticed the room had gone quiet and all eyes were on him.

"Agent Davies asked if there have been any new developments regarding Sarita García."

Christopher was exhausted, hungry, and very tired of answering questions. "No, sir." He resisted the urge to rub his eyes. "García has not been seen since she escaped from Fiesta de Fuego."

More silence.

"I think we've covered enough for today." Ferris looked at his watch. "Let's reconvene tomorrow morning at ten."

Christopher reached for his notepad and pushed back his chair.

"Temple." Ferris stared him down. "Sit."

Christopher resumed his seat, crossed his arms, and leaned back. While he appreciated that Ferris was disciplining him privately, he still dreaded the impending reprimand.

Ferris crossed to a credenza and poured them each a splash of whiskey. He set a tumbler in front of Christopher, took his seat, and sipped from his glass.

Christopher held his boss's stare, trying to think of a plausible explanation for failing to take down a drug queen. Obviously, there was no good excuse for not completing his assignment, imploding a six-month investigation, and leaving the FBI with no recourse regarding Sarita García.

"Benson called." Ferris studied the amber liquid in his glass. "Agent Mendoza is refusing an administrative leave and demanding to be added to a joint task force in Puerto Vallarta."

Christopher nodded, then took a slug of whiskey. Jade had texted him the same information, albeit she'd used more colorful language. "Any new leads?" He wanted to hear what the DEA was sharing with the FBI.

Ferris shook his head. "We've been investigating the disappearance of females up and down the Baja peninsula." He consulted notes in a folder. "The task force in Puerto Vallarta has a directive to locate a trafficker named Raptor."

Christopher's interest piqued since Jade hadn't mentioned Raptor "And Jade thinks this guy is involved in Ezmé's disappearance?"

Ferris raised his eyebrows. "Guy?"

"Right." Christopher smiled. "Never assume."

"Or underestimate your target." Ferris held his stare. "Eladio Ortiz believes her sister may have been taken by Raptor's organization." He slid the folder marked PV TASK FORCE away and opened another one. "What happened, Temple?"

Christopher's thoughts spun in a circle as he tried to assimilate the news about Jade and Raptor. His instinct was to bolt from the room and rush to Jade's aide, but he knew Ferris would not approve a request for Christopher's assignment to the task force. In response to Ferris's question, Christopher shrugged and leaned back into his chair.

"I've got all night." Ferris shuffled through some documents. "Even arranged for a pizza delivery at six." He passed a piece of paper across the table to Christopher. "I ordered 'The Outlaw' from *&pizza*, the place you like on H Street."

Christopher narrowed his eyes at Ferris, then glanced down at the paper in front of him. He could see his name, along with Jade's, listed in an outline. He picked up the single sheet and studied the bullet points.

"You and I need to hash out these issues." Ferris tapped the same document lying in front of him.

Christopher waved the paper. "These points were addressed in my report."

Ferris leaned back again, outline in hand, and waited.

Christopher jumped to his feet. "We didn't have any hard evidence against the bankers, let alone García." He began pacing around the conference room. "Jade and I both thought Meyers would cooperate sooner than he did to help us bring in West."

He stared out the conference room window, watching streetlights flicker on now that the sun had disappeared behind the LA skyline. *Pizza will be here soon*, he thought.

"Sending Meyers back here was the right call," Christopher said, his breath fogging the glass.

"Right call, yes," Ferris agreed. "Did it occur to you more security was needed at the airport?"

Christopher's shoulders tightened. In hindsight, he knew he should have been with Jade and Sandrine instead of on a date with Katelyn. Would Ferris feel his lack of judgement warranted a disciplinary action? No one had mentioned Katelyn's name, but Christopher assumed his involvement with her, combined with his failure to capture Sarita García, had earmarked him for an internal investigation.

"Yes." He resumed his seat at the table. "But Captain Torres felt he had enough men assisting Agents Mendoza and Mortieau."

Ferris nodded but didn't say anything.

Christopher continued, "When I got the call that West was at Fiesta de Fuego, I thought it would be an easy arrest since he was drunk." He sipped some whiskey and held Ferris's questioning gaze. "I didn't call Jade for backup because she was taking care of Agent Mortieau."

Ferris nodded. "I know you were in Mazatlán longer than originally planned."

Christopher shook his head. "Still no excuse for not doing my job."

"Obviously …" Ferris tapped the papers in front of him with a knuckle. "Your actions are being questioned."

The tension in Christopher's shoulders seeped into his neck muscles. He tilted his head from side to side hoping to stave off a headache, then drilled Ferris with his eyes. "Get it over with and tell me what happens next."

"Temple …"

The headache exploded behind Christopher's eyes.

"You're a great agent," Ferris continued, "and you did as assigned blending in with the bankers, which was crucial to gaining intel on García. So, since this was your first solo assignment, I'm going to call it a learning exercise."

Christopher blinked, which did nothing to alleviate his headache. "I appreciate your support, sir, but—"

Ferris held up a hand. "Mark West didn't just steal from Sarita García." He smiled.

A knock sounded on the conference room door and Ferris called, "Come in."

The mild aroma of mozzarella cheese, grilled chicken, and Italian spices wafted into the room as a pizza delivery girl entered. She placed the pie and a paper bag at the end of the long table. Ferris stepped toward her and handed her a twenty-dollar tip.

She raised on tiptoes and kissed his cheek. "Thanks, Uncle Joe."

Ferris smiled at his niece. "Be safe out there, Callie."

Callie gave Ferris a salute and retreated from the conference room.

The pizza smelled delicious, but Christopher was only interested in knowing what else Mark West had managed to achieve. Ferris slipped slices onto paper plates and set one in front of Christopher.

Despite his mouth watering, he ignored the pizza. "What else did West accomplish?"

Ferris smiled over his full mouth, swallowed, then answered, "Someone left accounting ledgers for him in a hotel near Fiesta de Fuego."

Ortiz's face flashed in Christopher's mind and linked with the memory of the duffle bag West had carried from the hotel. Christopher and Torres never had the chance to check the bag's contents.

"And?" Impatience echoed in Christopher's tone.

Ferris chewed and chased the bite with a drink of water. "The ledgers arrived compliments of Captain Torres, marked *urgent* and addressed to you. The mail room delivered the package to my office, since you were out having your wounds tended."

Ferris smiled at Christopher who resisted the urge to yell, "Tell me!"

"The ledgers show incoming payments from the dealers García funneled her drugs to." Ferris wiped his hands with a napkin. "And more importantly, García's payments to Agustín Castro." He lifted his whiskey in a toast. "Which means we have a paper trail that leads us to *El Lobo*."

CHAPTER FIFTY-EIGHT

The *pulmonia* jerked to a stop in front of the Joyful Margarita. Katelyn and Stella climbed out, and Katelyn paid the driver.

"*Gracias, señorita.*" The driver tilted his head. "Glad you okay." He took the twenty dollar bill and reached for change.

"Oh, it's you!" Katelyn smiled at the driver who'd picked her up in the middle of the night almost two weeks ago.

He bobbed his head. "*¡Sí, sí!*"

Waving off the change, Katelyn gave him a salute. "Keep it, *señor*! You saved me that night."

He tooted his horn as he drove away.

"Friend of yours?" Stella asked.

Katelyn nodded. "He gave me a ride to Humberto's after I escaped from jail." *What a difference a few weeks can make*, Katelyn thought and was thankful her emotional roller-coaster had ended its run.

"This has been a helluva vacation, Lyn." Stella pulled open the door. "You should write a book."

"Ha, ha. I think I'll pass on going down memory lane." Katelyn followed Stella inside Lisa Reyes' festive bar.

When Stella found out she had a large, custom furniture order from one of her top clients, she had decided to leave earlier than planned. Wanting to send her bestie off in style, Katelyn contacted Lisa to arrange a small goodbye party. Lucía had helped her decorate an alcove of the restaurant earlier in the day. She sighed, wishing Christopher waited in the alcove with the others.

"Hola," Lisa greeted them. "Come, I have a table ready for you."

Following Lisa, Katelyn nudged Stella, whose eyes were glued to the huge sign above the bar listing all the different margaritas.

"Why haven't we been here before now?" Stella asked as she trailed after Katelyn.

"Surprise!" The welcoming crew shouted.

"What the …" Stella said, hand on her heart. "Ah, Katelyn, this is all you!"

"Since you're leaving early, we'd decided to make your last night special."

Stella wrapped Katelyn in a hug. "Thanks, Lyn …" Stella's voice quivered. "Despite the whole crazy cop thing and being kidnapped, it's been a fabulous vacation."

Nervous laughter erupted around the room and Lisa clapped her hands together. "I have *aperitivos* on the way. Stella, I've created a special cocktail to send you off … the *Hasta Luego Margarita* is on the house!"

Katelyn touched Lisa's arm as she passed by on her way to the kitchen. "Lisa …" Katelyn touched the pink dragonfly necklace. "I wanted to thank you for delivering this to Humberto's."

"You're welcome, *chica*." Lisa pointed at the necklace. "It's beautiful!"

Katelyn looked down at the pendant and fingered her swatch of pinkish hair. "It is …" she smiled at Lisa. "Isn't it?"

"Go enjoy your friends, I gotta check on the kitchen." Lisa marched off.

Katelyn headed back to the alcove, where the folding windows were opened onto a deck reaching out over the sand. When the tide came in, the waves raced under the deck and splashed against the building's foundation, sending sea spray up between the boards of the deck.

Mia, serving the *Hasta Luego Margaritas*, offered the last one to Katelyn and exited the alcove.

"Katelyn," Marco said. "I just updated everyone on Jade and her sister, Ezmé." He sipped from his glass. "Eladio Ortiz has been assigned to investigate Ezmé's disappearance in Puerto Vallarta."

"That's good, right?" Katelyn said. "I mean about him being there to help Jade."

Worry flashed in Marco's dark eyes. "*Sí* … Ortiz is also hunting a trafficker named Raptor."

"Ezmé may be one of his victims." Humberto added.

"Oh, God!" Katelyn's hands flew to her mouth. "Tha–that's awful."

Humberto nodded, but neither he nor Marco reported anything more, their silence raising the hair on Katelyn's neck. She wanted to ask if Christopher had rushed to Puerto Vallarta to help Jade but held her tongue. Like it or not, the partners had a connection, so it would make sense if Christopher wanted to help Jade find her sister.

"Who's hungry?" Lisa asked as she and Mia entered with large trays of appetizers, which they placed on a long table next to plates, napkins, and silverware.

Everyone gravitated toward the delicious aroma of pork nachos, *chorizo* quesadillas, and steak street tacos. Katelyn stood back as the others loaded plates. She brushed the dragonfly pendant with her fingertips, conjuring up Christopher's smiling face in her mind. She knew she should let their brief time together become a fond memory and move on—just as she had after Stewart cheated. Move on because life was too short, and she needed to find her own joy! *Sure, move on. Easy, peasy,* she told herself.

"Is this …" Lucía pointed to the necklace. "The gift from Christopher?"

Smiling, Katelyn nodded.

"Es muy bonita," Lucía said. "You must miss him."

Blinking to stem a rush of tears, Katelyn said, "I do."

Lucía produced a tissue. "I overheard Marco tell Humberto that Christopher is still emboiled in the García case."

Katelyn laughed, and Lucía looked confused. "Embroiled." Katelyn grinned as understanding dawned on her friend's face.

"Oh …" Lucía giggled. *"¡Sí, sí!"*

"What's so funny?" Stella joined the two women.

"Language issues," Katelyn replied.

"Got it. Come on you two." Stella motioned toward the others. "You're missing some awesome food. And Mia's bringing another round of margaritas for sunset."

Katelyn grabbed a plate. If she was going to enjoy anymore alcohol, she needed something in her stomach. Munching a taco, she wandered out onto the deck, amazed at a super-sized sun drifting toward the horizon.

"Pretty spectacular." Stella shoulder-bumped Katelyn. "Thanks again for the goodbye party."

"You're welcome." Katelyn bumped her back. "Thanks for rushing to my rescue, Ella."

"Anything for you, Lyn." Stella raised her glass. "Friends forever." She swept her arm to encompass the whole gang. "To an unforgettable vacation." She clinked Katelyn's glass. "To Agent Hottie. And to you calling him soon." Stella gulped the rest of her margarita.

Katelyn gave her a narrow-eyed stare, then broke into a grin. "We'll see." She finished her drink too.

"Okay, *amigos* …" Lisa entered the room bearing a tray, with Mia carrying a second platter. "This …" She held a glass up for everyone to see. "Is my famous Joyful Sunset Margarita and, of course, must be enjoyed at sunset!" Lisa and Mia handed a drink to everyone, then Lisa walked out onto the deck. She waved them outside. "Let's toast the close of another day in paradise!"

Katelyn finished her sangria and signaled the waiter for another. She looked at the time on her phone and estimated Stella should be landing in Phoenix, ending the first leg of her return flight to Portland.

They'd enjoyed a late, lovely breakfast at *La Cordelier*, complete with mimosas, before Stella caught the shuttle to the Mazatlán airport. As they left the restaurant, Stella had pointed to a poster announcing a romantic dinner to be served on the beach. The feast included appetizers and drinks an hour before sunset, followed by a steak and lobster dinner with wine or champagne.

"You should make a dinner reservation," Stella told Katelyn as they waited in the lobby. "Treat yourself."

Katelyn shook her head. "A romantic dinner for one doesn't sound very appealing."

"Really?" Stella countered. "A nice meal on the beach with a beautiful sunset sounds perfect!"

The shuttle arrived, and Stella hugged Katelyn so hard she thought her ribs might break.

"Make a reservation, Lyn." Stella held Katelyn at arm's length. "Put a little joy back into your life."

Stella grabbed her carry-on and stepped outside. A bellman took her luggage and escorted her to the shuttle. Before she disappeared into the large, sleek bus, she turned and gave Katelyn a thumbs up. Katelyn waved back as the doors closed.

That's when she had decided the pool and as many sangrias as she could drink sounded like a good idea.

"*Señorita,*" the waiter said as he set her drink on the small table next to her lounge chair. "Need anything else?"

"No, *gracias*, Jose," Katelyn said. "All good for now."

Jose nodded. *"¡Perfecto!"* Then he was off to serve the next guest.

Sipping her sangria, Katelyn descended the stairs into the massive pool. She waded to the far side, taking in the vast sea stretched out before her. Of all the places she'd been in Mazatlán, the Emerald Bay pool and infinity wall were her favorite. "Okay," she said to the ocean, "being at the cabin with Christopher was pretty fabulous."

Katelyn sipped sangria and stared across the bay to the Pacific Ocean. If she was honest with herself, her encounter with Christopher was just what she needed. Even though it was short and sweet, it helped to assuage the hurt and anger Stewart had caused. She might not be ready to rush back to Portland and dive into the dating scene, but at least she didn't feel like one of the walking wounded anymore.

A breeze blew pink strands across her face. As she pushed them back, she recalled part of Christopher's note, 'sexy as hell'. Even though the color block had been an epic failure, it had helped Katelyn remember she was fun. Always up for trying something new—ready for the next adventure.

Katelyn raised her glass in toast. "Okay, ocean … you and Stella are right." She finished the sangria. "We have a dinner date at sunset." Katelyn waded back to the pool stairs. "But first a nap."

CHAPTER FIFTY-NINE

While searching for any news about herself, Sarita came across an online article speculating her BMW had careened off the *Puente Baluarte*. The reporter stated evidence at the scene confirmed the car had belonged to her, but authorities had decided not to search the cavernous canyon below the bridge for her body.

Sarita smiled at the laptop screen and continued scrolling for other articles. She clicked on a link about missing women and the screen fill with a photo. Her mother's eyes stared at her from her daughter's beautiful face. Sarita studied the pictures of Jade and Eladio Ortiz, then looked at the accompanying snapshot of the young woman featured in the article. Ezmérelda Mendoza had gone missing, and the *policía* were asking for anyone who might have information regarding her disappearance to call a hotline. While the young woman was pretty, she looked nothing like Jade, their only commonality being their Hispanic heritage. The piece introduced Jade and Eladio, and their respective agencies, along with a photo of Lieutenant Amado Peña. The trio was part of a Puerto Vallarta-based task force investigating the disappearance of several women over the last six months.

Sarita studied her daughter's image. Besides seeing the likeness of Estrella in Jade, Sarita could also see herself. The shape of Jade's face was like her own, but Jade's mouth, set in a grim line, belonged to someone else.

The reality of who had fathered Jade hit Sarita like a punch to her gut, stealing her breath and flooding her eyes with tears.

She jumped to her feet, dashed from the balcony into her hotel room, and snatched her phone from the kitchenette counter. She thumbed the photo icon open and swiped through the photos she'd saved from Eladio's laptop until Marco Torres's image filled the phone's screen.

"Oh, my God!" Sarita stared at the adult version of the mysterious young man who'd swept her off her feet all those years ago. Tears slipped down her cheeks as the sultry summer night blew into her mind like a salty ocean breeze.

"Would you like to go for a walk on the beach?" Marco had asked, wiping sweat from his brow with a yellow bandana. "The air will be cooler by the water."

Sarita knew her parents would not approve of her being alone with a boy at night on the beach, but she wanted the excitement of the evening to continue. Dancing with Marco had been titillating, and the idea of being alone with him sent an unexpected rush of warmth coursing through her loins. Besides, she'd just celebrated turning fifteen at her *quinceañera*, which meant she was a woman now.

She nodded and extended her hand to him, letting him lead her from Joe's and down a short flight of stairs to the soft sand. The sea air cooled the sweat on her skin and lifted her dark curls off her neck. Marco led her toward the water, stopping short to kick off his Vans. He placed a hand on Sarita's waist to steady her, so she could unbuckle her sandals. A strong wave crashed over their bare feet and Sarita stumbled backward. Marco pulled her to him to keep her from falling, and then kissed her.

He lifted her chin and searched her eyes as if looking for permission to kiss her again. Sarita wound her arms around his neck and covered his lips, kissing him as if he were the oxygen she needed to breathe. Sea brine mingled with his musky scent, and Sarita ran her hands through his hair. Another wave brought the water up to their waists and they raced up the beach, hand in hand, laughing like *niños*.

The huge wave had soaked their clothes. Sarita looked down to see her sundress clinging to her body, accentuating her full breasts. She leaned into Marco, and he held her tight, kissing her forehead, eyes, then lips.

"Is there somewhere we can go …" Sarita began.

Marco brushed stray locks of hair from her face, his dark eyes filled with longing, then taking her by the hand, guided her toward the street. They walked silently for a few blocks, then came to an alley that led to a two-story white stucco building.

He took her hands in his, the streetlight above highlighting his handsome face, and once again he searched her eyes. "You are sure?"

Sarita smiled, then turned, still holding his hand, and walked toward the building.

Once inside the small apartment, Marco flipped on an overhead light and turned to look at her. Sarita could see desire in his eyes. She slipped the thin straps of her sundress off her shoulders, letting the wet garment fall to the floor.

Marco closed the distance between them and lifted her in his arms. He carried her to a bedroom and laid her onto the bed. Sarita slipped out of her panties and then reached for him. Marco shed his clothes and stretched out next to her.

Caressing her body, he whispered, *"Eres muy hermosa."*

When his hand stopped short of her promised land, Sarita moaned, *"No te detengas."*

"My first time …" He kissed her ear. "You?"

"Sí." She turned and found his lips.

"Then we will go slow." Marco moved his mouth to one breast, his hand on the other.

Sarita thought she'd go mad with anticipation, holding him to her, arching into his touch.

When he finally entered her, Sarita's body responded as if she'd made love many times before. As if she knew the ecstasy that awaited her.

The memory faded into the photo of Captain Marco Torres, and Sarita wiped her cheeks dry. She had always loved the romantic anonymity of her young lover, but now wondered how had she been in the same city with both the daughter she thought was dead and the grown boy she'd loved for one night, and not known who they were?

Sarita padded barefoot to the kitchenette and poured herself a shot of Patrón. She carried her drink out onto the balcony and looked across Cabo San Lucas Bay towards Mazatlán. A barrage of questions popped into her mind as she sipped the citrusy tequila. *What had Eladio said? "You see the resemblance also?" Had Marco known Jade was his daughter? And did Jade know Marco was her father? Had the three of them colluded to bring Sarita and her small drug empire down?*

It would be dangerous for Sarita to travel to Puerto Vallarta, but she needed answers. Starting with her daughter seemed to be the logical first move.

Sarita finished her shot, thumbed her phone alive, and pulled up flights to the beautiful beach resort city lining the horseshoe coastline of Banderas Bay.

CHAPTER SIXTY

"Go away," Katelyn mumbled into her pillow. When she realized someone was at her hotel room door, she called. "Hang on!" She scrambled off the bed and hurried to open the door.

"*Hola*, Katelyn," DeShawn said. "Did I wake you?"

Katelyn shook her head. "No, I mean yes." Katelyn ran a hand through her hair. "What's up?"

"Stella left this with me." DeShawn handed her a box wrapped with a pink ribbon. "She said I was to make you a dinner reservation if you didn't do so yourself, and then bring you this gift."

Katelyn laughed. "Of course, she did." She smiled at DeShawn. "I did make a reservation. I wasn't too late, was I?"

"No, but I upgraded you if that's okay?" DeShawn said.

"Upgraded?" Katelyn tilted her head. "Oh, that's not necessary, it'll just be me."

"Yes, but I wanted to make sure your meal was enjoyable, so I moved you a little farther down the beach." Holding up a hand to fend off any argument, DeShawn continued, "Bonus, you'll be closer to the bathrooms." They both laughed. "So, you're all set." DeShawn turned to leave and added, "Have a lovely evening."

"Thanks for everything, DeShawn." Katelyn gave a finger wave and closed the door.

She carried the box to the kitchenette, placed it on the table, and lifted the lid. The sight of the lilac-colored summer dress she'd admired a few days ago in a little boutique in the Golden Zone stole her breath. Lifting it from the box, she admired the beautiful Grecian top that flowed into a flirty skirt. She plucked a note from the heaps of tissue.

> *Lyn ~ What I love most about you is your ability to recover despite any obstacles laid in your path to happiness. Now, put on the damn dress, wear the dragonfly necklace and go find your effing Joy!*
> *Love ~ Ella*

Katelyn laughed, but also fought back tears. How she wished Stella had been able to stay and join her for a non-romantic, sunset dinner.

"Well, I can't let her down now." Katelyn held the dress to her shoulders and twirled in a circle, then laid the garment carefully on the bed.

She found her phone and texted Stella: *Thx for the dress! I'll toast you at dinner.*

The best thing about not having a dinner date, Katelyn decided as she took one last look in the mirror, was not stressing over her appearance. She'd used minimal makeup and pulled her hair up off her neck into a clip, leaving her curls cascading down her back. She didn't usually pick pastel colors for herself, but she liked the blended hues of the dress, necklace, and stripper stripe. Glancing at a sweater on the back of a chair, she decided she'd be back before it got cold.

Good call on the sweater, Katelyn thought. She passed by the main pool where swimmers still enjoyed the cool water and a cold beverage from the swim-up bar, something she and Stella had done their first night at Emerald Bay.

The entrance to *La Cordelier* came into view, and Katelyn could see a line of other guests waiting to be seated. Her dinner reservation was for six and she knew she was early, which meant she had time for a drink.

Katelyn waited at the outdoor bar behind the restaurant and ordered a flute of champagne when it was her turn. The bartender remembered her from the night she and Stella had closed down the restaurant, and indicated he'd start a bill for her. Katelyn raised her glass in thanks and headed for an empty bench.

The champagne tingled her nose and tasted crisp on her tongue. She had one more day and night of vacation, so she mentally kicked around ideas of how to spend her time. After discarding the usual activities such as shopping, sightseeing, or beach walk along the Golden Zone, Katelyn decided on another pool day at Emerald Bay. She could enjoy a massage in the spa, then dinner at the Bistro, followed by a couple of Kelly's Secrets at Kelly's bar.

"Perfect." Katelyn toasted her plan.

"Perdón," a husky voice said. "Is this seat taken?"

Katelyn smiled at the handsome Hispanic and scooched over. "No." She patted the bench. "Please."

The man sat and clinked her flute with his glass of beer. *"¡Salud!"*

"¡Salud!" Katelyn sipped her champagne.

"It is my first night." He extended his hand. "Miguel."

Katelyn shook his hand, strong and warm. "Katelyn."

"Muy hermoso aquí," Miguel said.

Katelyn nodded. "Yes, it's very beautiful here." She would normally welcome conversation with a handsome stranger, but now that she'd made up her mind to embrace her non-romantic dinner alone, she wanted to be *alone*.

"You are waiting for someone?" Miguel asked.

Katelyn toyed with the idea of lying, but instead said, "No. Dinner for one tonight."

"¿Qué?" Miguel wagged a finger. "No, no … you join me." He stood and extended his hand. "By tonight we are new, old friends. *¿Sí?"*

Tempting, Katelyn thought. "Maybe next time, Miguel."

A flash of blonde joined them, and Katelyn hoped her jaw hadn't actually fallen open.

"Miguel," the buxom female said. "Come, our table is ready."

"Ava," Miguel said to the beauty. "Please meet my new *amiga,* Katelyn."

"Mucho Gusto," Ava said with an exaggerated hair flip, which sent a sweet, floral aroma floating through the air. *"Miguel, todo el mundo está esperando."*

Katelyn was surprised Ava didn't include a foot stomp with her demand. Instead, she stalked off, flashing a glare at Miguel over her shoulder.

"My apologize for my sister." Miguel placed his hand on his heart. "It has been a long day."

Katelyn smiled at him. "Apology accepted."

Miguel chuckled. "Apology, *sí.*" He offered his hand again and Katelyn placed hers within his. He brought her hand to his lips, then gave her a slight bow. *"Hasta luego,* Katelyn."

"Enjoy your dinner." Katelyn giggled at the tongue-lashing Ava unleashed on Miguel when he joined their table. The bartender waved for Katelyn to approach, perfect timing because she needed a refill.

"Una más." Katelyn handed him the empty flute.

"Sí." He gave her a full glass. "And your table is ready." He pointed to a young man dressed in Emerald Bay's signature blue shirt, black pants and white apron.

"Gracias." Katelyn signed her bill, left a twenty as a tip, and followed the waiter.

A table sat in freshly raked sand, surrounded by unlit tiki torches. The ocean breeze ruffled a beige tablecloth. The sun had begun its descent and cast diamond-like sparkles across the waves. The waiter pulled out a chair for Katelyn, and it struck her as odd that an empty chair sat next to her. *Probably Stella hoping I would find a date for my non-romantic dinner*, Katelyn mused and thought about Miguel.

"Your server will be with you shortly." The waiter departed with a slight bow.

"Gracias," Katelyn said into the salty air.

"Is this seat taken?"

Katelyn's breath caught in her throat as she looked up at Christopher, his blue eyes twinkling with delight.

She shot to her feet, knocking over her chair. "You're here!"

"Yes—" Christopher began.

"Wait!" Katelyn held up a hand. "Was this your idea?"

"No—"

"How did you know I'd still be here?"

Christopher picked up her chair and brushed it off. "I asked Humberto."

"So, everyone is in on this surprise?" Katelyn asked.

"Maybe." He grinned at her. "Can we go back to, 'is this seat taken'?"

Katelyn nodded, but said, "No." She pointed to the extra chair. "It's not taken."

"Good." Christopher pulled her chair out for her. "You look …" he hesitated as she took her seat.

"That bad, huh?" Katelyn laughed.

Christopher turned his chair, so he faced her. "Hardly." He angled Katelyn toward him. "I just don't think there's an adjective to best describe your beauty."

A warm flush colored her cheeks. "I'm still relishing your 'sexy as hell' comment."

Christopher grinned and touched the dragonfly pendant, then leaned in and kissed her, a kiss promising so much more to come.

"Perdón." A voice interrupted Katelyn's bliss. "May I pour champagne?

"Sí. " Christopher moved his glass toward the waiter.

"I am Carlos." He filled Christopher's glass and topped off Katelyn's. "Luis and I will be serving you this evening."

And as if on cue, Luis appeared with a tray of appetizers, which he placed in the center of the table, then departed.

"Please enjoy …" Carlos pointed at each dish. "Garlic shrimp, marlin ceviche, and oyster trio."

"Gracias, Carlos, " Christopher said.

Carlos beamed and turned to follow Luis.

Surveying the delicious spread, Katelyn exclaimed, "If we eat all of this, I won't be hungry for steak and lobster."

"Well …" He fingered her strand of pink hair. "My only concern is your stamina for *dessert.*"

Grinning, she tilted her head. "I thought the next time we were starting with dessert."

Christopher captured her smile in a kiss. Releasing her lips, he picked up their flutes, handed Katelyn hers, then clinked her glass.

"To the cosmic wonder responsible for bringing you into my life." He held her gaze as they sipped champagne.

Christopher scooted his chair closer and put his arm around her shoulders. Katelyn leaned into him as the sun pierced the horizon, announcing the end of another day in paradise.

Carlos and Luis returned, lighting the tiki torches, checking the appetizer plates, refilling their glasses, and then disappearing.

"So do you want to tell me about your return to LA?" Katelyn asked.

"Maybe tomorrow at the pool." He fingered her color swatch. "The only thing that exists for the next ten days is us."

"Ten days?"

"Yes, if that works for you."

"I can think of nothing better." Katelyn snuggled closer to him.

"Except maybe dessert?" Christopher asked.

Blushing, she turned to him, her crimson cheeks darkening at the sight of a small box. "Another gift?"

He handed her a package topped with a red bow. "A little something to go with dessert."

Katelyn took the box, lifted the lid, and burst into laughter. She hooked a set of red, fur-lined handcuffs with her little finger.

"So, I can't get away in the middle of the night." Christopher conveyed his longing in a kiss.

Melting into him Katelyn savored the moment. She didn't know how or why this man had come into her life, but she welcomed him—and any challenges that came their way. Besides, she was more than ready to leave her heartbreak in the past and embrace the possibility of love again.

She freed her lips. "Do you suppose dessert is a chocolate torte?"

Christopher flashed a mischievous grin. "I already had them deliver one to your room."

ACKNOWLEDGEMENTS

Though heartfelt, my simple "thank you" seems lacking when acknowledging my team of editors: Samantha Waltz, Author/Editor, Joyce Wise, Editor, Jeanne Silaski, Color Editor. These women dedicated endless hours helping MALICE IN MAZATLÁN become a masterful piece of fiction. Their combined eye for detail, from sentence variety, to correcting my *literal* translated Spanish into natural dialogue, to *"a spray tan and a yippy dog"*, made me a better writer. I'd also like to thank my Beta Readers, Carolyn Adams, Mary Eastman, Sharon North, and Stacy Robinson, who bolstered my confidence with kind words of praise.

DISCLOSURES

My team of editors and readers, including myself, made every effort to ensure this novel is error free. But we're human, so please accept our apologies for any mistakes you may find. Should you uncover errors while enjoying MALICE IN MAZATLÁN, please feel free to email me at: author.kimilakay.com

ABOUT THE AUTHOR

Kimila Kay lives in Donald, Oregon along with her husband, Randy, her adorable Boston Terrier, Maggie, and feisty black cat, Halle.

Her professional accomplishments include three anthologized essays in the CUP OF COMFORT series. Kimila is currently a member of Northwest Independent Writers Association (NIWA), Willamette Writers, and Windtree Press.

MALICE IN MAZATLÁN is the second novel in a cross-cultural series, which includes Peril in Paradise, Book One, still to come Vanished in Vallarta, Chaos in Cabo, Lost in Loreto, and Fiasco in Peñasco.

VANISHED IN VALLARTA

MÉXICO MAYHEM – BOOK THREE

CHAPTER ONE

The ocean had claimed it's prize, turning and spinning the body creating a morbid marionette sinking farther into the dark depths of the sea. A few inquisitive fish swam close enough to surmise the form was not a threat to them before continuing their aquatic journey.

Eventually, the salty water would have it's way with the figure, raking it across sharp coral that would tear flesh from bones. An Ekman spiral would spin the body, ripping off limbs. The powerful swirling water finally eradicating any signs of being a human.

But this specimen became gassy before the ocean could have wreak it's havoc and began a slow ascent to the surface. Along the way, various members of the underwater society fed upon the corpse, enjoying their free meal, until the floating smorgasbord was claimed by a crocodile. The beast attacked swiftly and viciously, conquering his underwater battlefield. After all, the salty water of Banderas Bay belonged to this ferocious reptile. They came in hoards to snag their prize, fighting any other amphibious predator, and their own species, to see who would drag the sustenance to a din for future dining.

So would be the fate of this once vital person. A death by drowning before becoming saved in a larder for a ravenous crocodile. The immense, male claimed his prize, swimming the spoils across the top of the aqua water to his lair.

Then a surprise spring storm rolled in on strong April winds, whipping the usually calm waters of the bay into turmoil. The crocodile adjusted his bite, sinking his teeth deeper into the sluffing flesh and battled the strong waves.

But the undulating waters of Banderas Bay were no match for the massive reptile. To survive the crocodile let go of his prey and headed for the beach.

CHAPTER TWO

She slept as if she had no worries. As if she had no fear. As if she hadn't been abducted. For a moment, Novio wondered if he'd given her too much valium.

Tracing the curve of her luscious lips with his eyes, he imagined they would taste as sweet as fresh mango. He let his gaze caress her breasts, the silver sequin top she wore rising and falling with each breath. He thought about how soft her skin would feel beneath his hands. Then his mind encouraged him to follow the length of the turquoise mini skirt, and he sucked in air at the thought of exploring her barely covered *V*.

Ezmé stirred and called out for her sister, Jade, and shame from his impure thoughts burned Novio's cheeks. Despite his platonic friendship with Ezmé, he couldn't control his intense desire for her. He believed that like him, Ezmé was a virgin; and he dreamed of how beautiful their first time together would be.

He hadn't restrained Ezmé and when her eyes fluttered, he crossed to the bed. She flailed her arms as if she was fighting someone and her floundering sent a citrusy scent flowing through the air. Hoping she wouldn't be frightened and try to flee, Novio had prepared a speech. He would explain to her he'd befriended her as part of a plot to kidnap her for his boss. Raptor. An evil man who planned to hurt her until she succumbed to his demands before he sold her to someone who might do far worse. But he, Novio, would hide and protect her from Raptor.

Novio had prayed his boss would lose interest in Ezmé after he pointed out her flaws, even though Novio felt she had none. As he always did, Raptor dismissed Novio's comments, saying, "One man's perceived imperfections are another man's fantasy. Bring her to me and I will decide."

Already familiar with Raptor's demented treatment of women, Novio dreaded what the irrational human trafficker would do to Ezmé. As he struggled with his need to keep her safe, the memory of what led him to Raptor seeped into his mind.

Novio had taken his eighteen-year-old sister, Valéria, on a rare outing without their protective parents. They'd enjoyed a day of shopping, then dinner and he thought it was early enough in the evening that their parents wouldn't disapprove if they had a drink at his favorite club, *Bebe y sé Feliz*. At twenty-one, Novio was a regular at the hip bar and anxious to show his little sister how popular he was with all the *chicas*.

They had ordered a second round of drinks—beer for him, a Paloma for Valéria—when an *hombre* Novio didn't know crashed their table. Valéria laughed and flirted with the slick Hispanic, probably not much older than Novio, as he told an elaborate tale. Something about the man bothered Novio, but when the DJ played a popular song, he forgot his concerns and asked a pretty girl to dance.

When he returned to the table, Valéria and the Mexican were gone. That day four years ago was the last time Novio remembered being happy.

CHAPTER THREE

Jade Mendoza leaned against the headrest. She wanted to close her eyes, but every time she did images of her little sister, Ezmé, being tortured by a faceless monster flooded her brain.

Sandrine offered to drive, and her aggressiveness made Jade cringe. But Jade was thankful, since she was too tired to drive and think at the same time. They'd arrived last night at ten-thirty and had stayed with Juan Vega's pilot, Felipe, who had an apartment near the Puerto Vallarta airport. Jade and Sandrine had both slept briefly on the three-and-a-half-hour flight from Mazatlán, but sleep evaded them after they settled into Felipe's place.

This morning, after a breakfast of black coffee, they'd jumped into the bright yellow Kia Sol, compliments of Vega, and began their hunt for Ezmé. It amazed Jade that the kindness of Humberto Álvarez, and Juan Vega, reached across the miles.

Sandrine cut into her thoughts. "Joy hasn't been able to find anyone who's talked to Ezmé?"

"Not yet." Jade stared at the passing residential scenery: a sea of cream-colored stucco houses, dotted here and there with small *mercados*. She knew as her sister's chaperone, Joy felt responsible for Ezmé and would be as worried as Jade.

"What's your plan?" Sandrine braked for stopping traffic.

"Start at the last place she was seen," Jade said. *"Pub de Nopal."*

When Sandrine swung wide of a taxi, Jade palmed the dash.

"In English, please." Sandrine said.

"Prickly Pear Pub."

"You think they're open this early?"

"I'm not interested in what's inside," Jade said. "I want to walk the perimeter and look for cameras."

"Got it." Sandrine nodded. "You don't think the police already checked?"

Shrugging, Jade glanced at Sandrine, who held up a finger. "Right, right," Sandrine said. "We need to see everything through our own investigative lens."

"That …" Jade began, "and we don't know who we can trust."

"Me." Sandrine looked at Jade. "You can trust me."

A swell of tears burned Jade's eyes and she fingered them away.

"Has anyone told your folks your sister is missing?" Sandrine asked.

Jade couldn't control her emotions this time, and sobs shook her shoulders. Her crying fit stole her breath, and for a moment she could only gasp. Sandrine angled into a curb and slammed the car into park. Jade turned her tear-stained face to Sandrine, who was also crying.

After a few minutes, Sandrine handed Jade half of a napkin she found in the center console. "It looks clean," she said before blowing her nose.

"Let's go." Jade dried her face. "I told Joy we'd be at her hotel by noon."

"Yep." Sandrine pulled into traffic behind a city bus.

"I haven't called my parents yet." Jade gazed out her window at the vast Pacific Ocean. How was she going to tell her mom that Ezmé had been missing for over twenty-four hours? Jade knew the first twenty-four hours were crucial in the investigative process. She also knew that each passing hour that Ezmé was missing didn't bode well for her baby sister.

Sandrine whipped a U-turn, then slipped into a parking spot on the street in front of the *Pub de Nopal*. "Want to walk together or separate?"

"Together." Jade stepped from the Kia and turned in a circle as Sandrine joined her on the sidewalk.

"Bloody hell, it's already hot!" Sandrine whined, lowering her sunglasses from the top of her head.

The Prickly Pear Pub sat in the middle of the street. A tequila tasting room was to their left with an upscale restaurant at the other end of the block. They spotted an employee at *Perla del Pacífico* placing a sign for the special of the day, Shrimp Cocktails, on the sidewalk. Jade headed his way.

"Are we eating?" Sandrine asked as she caught up to Jade. "I'm hungry."

Glancing at his name tag, Jade said, *"Buenos días, Rico,"*

"Buenos días, señorita," he replied. "Would you like a table?"

Sandrine's *yes*, competed with Jade's, *"No, gracias."*

Jade cut her eyes to Sandrine, then smiled at Rico. Pointing to the uppermost corner of the building, she asked, "Does your camera work?"

Rico followed her line of sight. *"Sí ... "* He hesitated. "But you need to speak to the owner."

"The owner of the building or of the restaurant?" Jade asked.

"Same person." As he headed inside, Rico motioned for them to follow. "Come."

"Seriously," Sandrine whispered into Jade's ear. "We don't have time to eat?"

"Get the special to go," Jade said and followed Rico.

They wound their way past a bar that allowed patrons to enjoy a cocktail while taking in the view of the bustling *malecón* under an endless blue sky, with Banderas Bay serving as the perfect backdrop. A bartender was adding garnish to a couple of Bloody Mary's and smiled at Jade as she passed by. Jade looked over her shoulder and saw Sandrine speaking to a waitress, then stopped when Rico ducked into a serving station.

He rummaged through a couple of drawers, then handed Jade a business card. "Call *Señor* Costa. He can tell you about the camera."

"*Gracias*, Rico." She shook his hand and headed for the exit.

Jade found Sandrine sitting at the bar noshing on a *cóctel de camarones* and Jade sat on the stool next to her.

"I'm eating as fast as I can." Sandrine double-dipped a shrimp the size of a small lobster into cocktail sauce. The spicy scent of horseradish made Jade's nose tingle.

"You're fine." Jade signaled the bartender.

"Perfect," Sandrine added. "I'll have a Bloody Mary, too."

"We're not drinking," Jade grumbled, then flashed a flirty grin at the handsome barkeep.

"What can I get you?" he asked.

Jade held her phone up to him. "Have you seen this young woman?"

He looked at Ezmé's picture, then raised his dark eyes to Jade. "*Sí.* She has been here with friends."

"Was she here two nights ago?"

"Maybe." He shrugged. "Why?"

"She's missing." Jade thought she saw a flicker of concern cross his face.

The bartender broke eye-contact. "Sorry." He picked up a tumbler and began to polish it with a bar towel.

Jade flipped over Sandrine's lunch bill and scribbled their phone numbers on the back. She slid the slip of paper toward him and said, "This is our contact information."

He looked at her note but didn't pick it up. When he met her gaze again, Jade sensed he knew more than he was saying.

"Thanks." Jade climbed off her stool and headed for the exit as Sandrine placed a twenty dollar bill next to her water glass.

Sandrine unlocked the car doors with the key fob. "He knows something."

"Agreed." Jade reached for the door handle.

Before they could settle into the car, a blood-curdling scream filled the air. Jade looked at Sandrine as another chorus of shrieks came from the beach.

"Bloody hell!"

"Come on!" Jade called and hustled across the *malecón*.

The two agents cut their way through the gathering crowd and stopped at the three foot sea wall. On the beach below, another mob was forming.

Someone yelled, "Call an ambulance!"

A different voice said, "Dude, she's dead."

The cluster of people parted slightly, and Jade could see a young woman lying in the sand.

"Jade!" Sandrine called after her as she hurtled over the wall and dropped down onto the soft beach.

Racing toward the throng that hovered around the motionless figure, Jade felt as if she was running in quicksand. Sandrine caught up to her and tried to keep her from kneeling next to the young woman. But Jade had to know. Was this her sister? Would Jade's biggest fear be realized? Was Ezmé was dead?

"It's not her," Sandrine said. "Come on." She tugged at Jade, but she couldn't take her eyes off the girl. She had long dark hair, like Ezmé. She was about the same age. And she was dead.

Jade couldn't tell exactly what had happened, but the body was missing the right arm and the lower half of the left leg. Her death had been horrific. The putrid smell of decaying flesh drew bile up the back of Jade's throat. Rising to her feet, she swallowed the urge to vomit at the thought of Ezmé suffering the same fate.

CHAPTER FOUR

Eladio Ortiz stared at the thin file taunting him from the middle of his desk. The scant details within told him Ezmé had been adopted as a baby and raised by Arturo and Leta Mendoza in Tucson, Arizona. If his math was correct, Jade had been four when she gained a baby sister.

Eladio knew no matter how long he looked at the folder, it would not magically fill with tips, leads, or answers regarding the disappearance of Ezmérelda Mendoza. Or the disappearance of eleven other young women.

Lacing his fingers together, he cradled the back of his head. His assignment to this task force was better than being fired for letting Sarita García escape and disappear. But the lack of progress so far made him feel as if he were being punished.

Eladio closed his eyes and allowed an image of Sarita to fill his mind. Her dark eyes were probing his—as if he could explain deceiving her for sixteen months. And as always, his attention focused on her lips, painted blood red, and slightly parted as if she were about to say something. He could almost smell her Scandal perfume. Eladio knew he should open his eyes, forget Sarita's goodbye kiss, but he did not. Instead, he savored the memory almost as much as he'd enjoyed the actual moment her lips met his.

"*¿Qué pasa?*"

Eladio jerked out of his reverie and opened his eyes to see Lieutenant Amado Peña standing in the open doorway.

"¿Necesitas una siesta?" Peña looked at his phone. "It is only ten AM."

"You are early." Eladio opened the investigation file and shuffled the papers within.

"Yes." Peña plopped down into a chair in front of Eladio's desk. "Now that I have been assigned to this task force, I have no other cases."

Eladio frowned at Peña, who looked more like a cartel leader than a policeman. "What can you tell me about Valéria Carrizo?" Eladio asked.

Peña shrugged, then leaned forward. "Not much. She is FBI, *¿sí?*"

"Sí." Eladio held up the single sheet of paper, which held scant specifications on the young agent.

"And you are wondering why FBI and not *Federale*?" Peña stated.

The only useful intel on Valéria was that she'd attended Arizona State University at eighteen, then entered the academy after graduation.

"¿Qué dice?" Peña prodded.

"That she graduated from ASU with a master's in criminology and criminal justice and was top of her class at the academy, graduating with honors."

Eladio passed the paper to Peña, who studied the one-page dossier, then slid it across the desk toward Eladio. *"Impresionante."*

"I would like to know more about her." Eladio drilled Peña with a dark stare.

Peña plucked a *concha* roll from the box on Eladio's desk and smirked. "And you want me to see what I can find out."

Eladio nodded and his phone chimed. He looked at the text from Jade Mendoza.

Jade: *We'll be at your office this afternoon.*

"We do not need any more help," Peña grumbled and popped the last of the *concha* into his mouth.

"Need it or not …" Eladio set his phone down. "Jade Mendoza is the missing girl's *hermana*."

"¡Mierda!" Peña swore. "Too many people will be *complicado.*"

Before Eladio could respond, his phone vibrated with an incoming call. As he looked at the number, Peña's phone buzzed.

"Bueno," Eladio answered the call and met Peña's questioning gaze when he raised his eyes to Eladio. *"Sí."* Eladio disconnected.

"Tenemos un cuerpo en la playa." Peña stood.

Without responding, Eladio opened a drawer, retrieved his gun, and replayed the call in his mind. *"Agent Ortiz, we have a dead girl on the beach. You should come before she is moved."*

Peña, already on his way out the door, called over his shoulder, "I will drive."

CHAPTER FIVE

He hated the idea of killing one of his men. Especially a soldier who had proven himself to be loyal and skilled. But after four years of trustworthy service, Novio had, unfortunately, crossed a line. It wasn't surprising, given the young man's past, so like Raptor's. He knew Novio hadn't yet learned to hate women, but after some time in this business, he would.

Raptor lifted his protein shake and took a large drink, the taste of peanut butter dancing on his tongue. He looked out his office window at the bustling *Boulevard Calle Juárez* clogged with cars blasting their horns. Everyday citizens were on their way to, or from, someplace, most likely cursing the traffic jam slowing their progress.

Oh, how far he'd come since that day long ago when he and Belen had fled Guatemala with a small bag of clothes and all the money they'd saved. After months of careful planning, they knew it could take them up to four weeks to work their way through Mexico to Nogales. Once there, they would cross the border into Arizona. In love and filled with the dream of making it to America, the two young lovers had set off on a beautiful January morning. Belen's cousin had a spare room in his apartment they could stay in and had secured them jobs at a trendy Mexican restaurant. He and Belen couldn't wait to start their bright future together.

What they hadn't known—what they couldn't have planned for— was the nightmare that began after Belen broke her ankle. They'd hopped into a boxcar outside of Mexico City, and she'd fallen when the train jerked around a corner.

At the time, he'd been thankful for just a broken fibula. For the sympathetic doctor who'd tended to Belen and took only half their money. For the kind young man who'd offered them a ride to the border.

It had been the last time he was thankful.

"¿Patrón?" one of his men called from the open door of his office.

Raptor shifted his gaze to the man. *"Sí."*

"Un cuerpo ha aparecido en la playa cerca del malecón."

"In English," Raptor growled. How many times did he have to tell his soldiers to learn and speak English?

"Sí. Yes. A body is on the beach near the *malecón*," the man repeated. "The boardwalk."

"One of ours?"

"I do not know."

"Do we have a man at the scene?"

"Sí."

"Keep me apprised." He waved the man from his office.

Raptor doubted the dead girl was one of his because there had been no recent reports of anyone escaping. But since the *policía* had been notified, he needed to be sure. He also doubted she was Ezmérelda Mendoza, the young woman he'd put Novio in charge of grooming, and eventually, capturing. It had been two days since Novio had texted to say he had the girl and would bring her to Raptor. So far, they had not appeared.

Ezmé had captured his attention when she passed by his table at the outdoor *Café del Mar*. The fresh plumeria bloom she wore tucked into her long dark hair enveloped him in a fragrant cloud of citrus. He couldn't take his eyes off her, nor could he understand his fascination with the beautiful young woman. Was it that she reminded him of his youth? Was it her radiant smile or large innocent eyes? Or … was it because she looked so much like his beloved Belen?

Raptor might have been unable to explain his desire for Ezmé, but he knew he needed to satisfy his curiosity … and more.

VANISHED IN VALLARTA is slated for publication November 2023

www.ingramcontent.com/pod-product-compliance
Lightning Source LLC
Chambersburg PA
CBHW021725110726
47902CB00005B/1344